Praise for *Scorched*

"Tense and action-packed. It's a brave new world and I reveled in every page!"

—Sophie Jordan, *New York Times*
bestselling author of *Firelight*

"*Scorched* is fun, fast and greatly entertaining, a heart-pounding, twisty, time-travel fantasy with delicious dragon mythology!"

—Melissa de la Cruz, *New York Times*
bestselling author of the Blue Bloods series

"A smoking triptych of time traveling, dubious double-crossing and enough dragons to sate the hungriest of gamers and fantasy fiends."

—*Kirkus*

"Exciting and original."

—*School Library Journal*

"Mancusi grabs readers and drags them into this fantastic world full of time-travel paradoxes, mythical creatures and romance. The beginning of a trilogy you won't want to miss!"

—*RT Book Reviews*

"Fantastic, witty, fun...*Scorched* is an exhilarating, intriguing and adventure-filled fantasy. Mancusi leaves the reader hanging, even dangling, in all the right places..."

—*Desert News*

More Praise for Mari Mancusi

"So worth reading, with dark humor, a distinctive voice, and a protagonist clever enough to get herself out of trouble. Thank you, Mari Mancusi, for a great ride."

—Ellen Hopkins, *New York Times*
bestselling author of *Tilt*, on *Boys That Bite*

"Delightful, surprising, and engaging—you'll get bitten, and love it."
—Rachel Caine, *New York Times* bestselling author of the
Morganville Vampire series on the Blood Coven series

"Exhilarating! I couldn't put this book down!"
—Gena Showalter, *New York Times* bestselling author on *Alternity*

"Readers won't want to put down this captivating novel, in which Mancusi combines a rip-roaring, thrilling science-fiction story with an appealing cast of characters and terrific romantic suspense... Teens will devour this."

—*Booklist* on *Razor Girl*

"I absolutely LOVED *Gamer Girl*... This book demonstrates the hardships some teens go through, but it also tells us that there is always something to look forward to."

—*Fallen Angel Reviews* (Recommended Read)

"An action-packed story with appealing characters, dark humor, and a new spin...will appeal to adult fans of *Buffy the Vampire Slayer* as well as the Harry Potter series and the Twilight novels."

—*Library Journal* on *Night School*

SHATTERED

MARI MANCUSI

sourcebooks
fire

Published by Sourcebooks Fire, an imprint of Sourcebooks, Inc.
P.O. Box 4410, Naperville, Illinois 60567-4410
(630) 961-3900
Fax: (630) 961-2168
www.sourcebooks.com

Library of Congress Cataloging-in-Publication data is on file with the publisher.

Printed and bound in the United States of America.
WOZ 10 9 8 7 6 5 4 3 2 1

To my brother Michael who, growing up, shared my love for fantasy worlds and fantastical creatures. Who knew all that imaginary sword fighting in the backyard and hours of playing Dungeons and Dragons *would serve as early training for my future career? I only hope that Nina and Avalon can someday continue the tradition.*

PART 1:

CRACK

Chapter One

The monster was back.

Somehow Scarlet could always tell. As if she had a sixth sense, warning her when he was near. A hint of smoke, tickling her nostrils, a low growl echoing in her ears. An uneasiness prickling at the back of her neck as her pulse throbbed in her throat—her consciousness gearing up for the inevitable fight or flight that was sure to come.

Should she face him this time? Or was it better to run?

With the monster, it was usually better to run.

Her pace slowed. Her arm extended, effectively blocking her mother's path up the steps and into the run-down single-wide they'd shared for the last sixteen years. It wasn't much of a home. But it was theirs—at least until the monster had made it his.

"Wait," she said.

Her mother shot her a questioning glance, the glow of her lit cigarette illuminating her lined face. Scarlet sighed. Her mother never could sense the monster's presence. Even if she could, it would have made no difference. She'd still open the door. She'd still walk inside. She never ran from the monster—even when she should have.

Under the moonlight, Scarlet could just catch the smudge under her mother's left eye, black with traces of purple and yellow fading out into copper skin. The mark of the beast.

"We should go," she told her. She reached into her pocket, pulling out a handful of crunched up bills, tips from the lunch crowd. "I have enough for a motel. We can stay there tonight. Maybe he'll get bored and leave."

Her mother's eyes narrowed. Her gaze flickered from her daughter to the trailer's rusted-out front door then back again. Her thin lips, cracked from years of smoking, dipped to a frown.

"No way," she said, shaking her head vehemently. "This is *my* house. He's not going to scare us away."

Scarlet opened her mouth to protest, not sure what she'd say. That she was already scared? That if her mother had a lick of common sense she'd be scared too? It made no difference—her mother was already pushing past her, marching up the front steps and yanking open the screen door. As Scarlet watched, her feet glued to the pavement, the door slammed shut with a loud crash.

It was done.

For a moment, Scarlet wondered if she should run—far away from the trailer and the monster inside. But where could she go? And even if there was somewhere—how could she leave her mother behind? Her brother's words echoed maddeningly through her head, as they always did in moments like these.

Promise me, Scarlet. Promise me you'll look after Mom.

She forced her feet into submission, one after the other, up the front steps, her hand wrapping around the door handle and prying it open. Trying to still her ragged breath. Trying to quell the fear tripping down her spine.

I will, Mac. I promise I will.

The trailer was dark, only the flickering blue glow of the television set serving to light the cramped space. The monster had made himself at home, as he always did, sprawled out on the stained and ripped La-Z-Boy, a half-drunk bottle of whiskey propped next to an overflowing ashtray by his side. He wore no shirt and his bulbous gut hung over his filthy jeans. His eyes had a glazed look to them, a look that filled Scarlet with dread.

Her mother didn't seem to notice. She put her hands on her hips, staring him down. "What the hell are you doing here?" she demanded, her voice cracking at the edges, betraying her unease. "I thought I told you to leave last night."

The monster looked up lazily. "I did leave," he said in a slurred voice.

"And now you're just back? No apology? No nothing?"

"Mom," Scarlet tried, putting a hand on her arm as she glanced nervously at the monster. "Come on, let's go to the bedroom. We can watch our *Downton Abbey* DVDs. I'll make popcorn."

"No!" Her mother wrenched her arm away with a force that almost sent Scarlet sprawling. "I'm not leaving. Not without my apology." She turned back to the monster. "You can't just waltz back in here like nothing happened and think I'll just forgive and forget, no big deal."

Scarlet stood there helplessly as her mother attempted to meet the monster's eyes. When he dodged her gaze, Mom stepped in front of the television, arms crossed over her chest, purposely blocking his view. For a split second, Scarlet could almost see the reflection of her ancestors—the proud Zuni tribe that had once driven Spanish conquistadors from New Mexico—reflected in her mother's angry black eyes.

But it was gone as soon as it came, forcing Scarlet to face reality once again. Her mother was no fierce tribal warrior of old, ready to defend her land and property, but merely a shell of a woman who had downed too many rum and cokes at dinner. "Liquid courage," she had called it. More like liquid stupidity.

The monster sighed deeply. "Will you please get the hell out of the way?" he asked, trying to look around her. "I've got money on this game. Your fat ass is blocking the set."

Scarlet's mother's face turned purple. In one fluid movement, she turned, grabbing the television set and throwing it out the sliding glass door behind her. The *closed* sliding glass door. Scarlet gasped as the box crashed through the windowpane and smashed onto the back porch in a cloud of sparks and smoke and broken glass.

Oh crap.

For a moment, the monster just stared out the window in stunned disbelief. Then he rose to his feet and started toward her mother. She stared back at him defiantly, as if daring him to do his worst. The look on his face told Scarlet he didn't need a double dare.

"No!"

She threw herself in his path, a vain attempt to shield her mom from what was coming. The monster tried to shove her aside, but she stood her ground, throwing her full weight against him. He staggered, the alcohol and whatever else he was on slowing his reflexes enough to give her a slight advantage. She'd take it.

"Don't you touch her!"

Her hands shot out, shoving him as hard as she could. He flailed, losing his footing, and for a brief moment she thought she had him. But then his hands latched on to her arms, his ragged fingernails digging into her skin. Together they tumbled, following the trajectory of the television set through the broken glass window and onto the porch outside. Scarlet screamed as heat slashed at her arm and her ankle wrenched violently.

"Scarlet!" she could dimly hear her mother scream from back inside the trailer. "Bob? Are you okay?"

The monster was already on his feet. "Psychos!" he growled. "The two of you are goddamned psychos!" He stormed back into the house through the broken window, glass crunching loudly under his boots. A moment later, Scarlet heard the bedroom door slam, and her mother came running around the side of the trailer.

"Oh God, sweetie, are you okay?" she whispered, her eyes wide and frightened.

But Scarlet wasn't frightened anymore. She was pissed. She rose to her feet. "I'm fine. Mom, you have to call the cops. Now."

Her mother's face paled. "No," she said, shaking her head. "I can't."

"Why not? You kicked him out. He's trespassing."

"He's on the lease, Scarlet. He has every right to be here if he wants to be."

"Not if you get a restraining order."

Her mother was silent for a moment. "Do you remember what happened the last time I tried to do that?"

Unfortunately, Scarlet did. All too well.

"Don't worry. I'll talk to him."

"Mom, no!"

"Scarlet, I need you to go down to Maddie's, okay? Stay there until I call you."

"I'm not leaving you."

"Scarlet, you hanging around is only going to make things worse. I can handle him, okay? Just go to Maddie's and wait for me to call."

With that, her mother turned, heading back around the house and through the front door. Scarlet watched her go, fury warring with helplessness. Half of her wanted to storm into the trailer and face the monster head on. But the other, wiser half knew it wouldn't do any good. It would only put her mother in more danger.

And the monster always won in the end.

A heaviness sank to her stomach as she forced herself to turn, to limp through the trailer park on her sore ankle. As she made her way down the street, she could feel the cold, curious stares of her neighbors, hidden behind closed shades and closed doors. In a normal neighborhood, someone probably would have called the cops for her. Here, they all had too many secrets of their own.

She passed the trailer of her old babysitter, Maddie, which sat on the outskirts of the park. The lights were out; Maddie was likely asleep and Scarlet didn't want to wake her, didn't want to drag her into yet another mess—didn't want to see the pity she'd knew she'd find in her eyes.

Instead, she dove into the woods, dodging the thick underbrush and gnarled cedar trees until she came to a familiar clearing. Dropping to her knees, she pushed back the overhanging brush and crawled into the small cave behind the concealing foliage. She and Mac had found this secret hideout back when they were children and it had served as their official pirate base camp ever since.

Mac. She sighed deeply, lighting the candles she'd stashed in the corner. If only Mac were here now. He'd know what to do.

But he'd left her all alone.

She felt a sharp twinge and looked down at her arm, annoyed to realize it was still bleeding. Bleeding quite hard, in fact—the glass must have cut deep. A little scared, she yanked off her sweater, wrapping it around her arm to put pressure on the wound. But the blood soaked through almost instantly and her stomach roiled with nausea.

Did she need stitches? Should she go to the hospital? Of course, they couldn't afford a trip to the hospital. And even if they could, the hospital would ask questions. Questions she couldn't answer—not without putting Mom at more risk.

Anger rose inside her. Helpless, all-encompassing anger. At her mom. At herself. At the monster and her damn, traitorous arm. "Stop bleeding!" she cried furiously at the cut. "Just stop it!"

Dizziness washed over her and she wove and spun, grabbing on to the cave wall for support. This was not good. This was *so* not good. She closed her eyes, attempting to reset her sanity.

"Help me," she whispered in a voice so weak no one could possibly hear. "Please…help me."

Screech!

Her eyes shot open, a sudden sound ripping through her ears. Followed by a loud thud—something huge and heavy coming in for a crash landing just outside the cave. Scarlet froze.

What the hell was that?

Her first thought was of the monster, that he'd found her somehow—that he'd come for round two. But that was ridiculous. He was too drunk, too lazy to expend the energy to come after her. Besides, he had no idea where she was.

But…*something* was out there. She forced herself to sit perfectly still, her ears straining. Some kind of animal perhaps? Drawn to the scent of her blood? There were lots of things living in the Texas Hill Country. Coyotes, mountain lions— even some bears.

Frightened, she inched further into the shadows, until her back pressed against the cave's posterior wall, praying that whatever it was would go away. That it wouldn't find her. That it wouldn't—

The foliage rippled at the cave's entrance, parting like the Red Sea. Scarlet's eyes bulged. Her jaw dropped. An involuntary squeak escaped her lips as her eyes fell upon the dark silhouette framed by the mouth of the cave.

It wasn't a coyote. It wasn't a mountain lion. It wasn't a bear.

It was a monster. *A true monster,* her crazed mind corrected. Not the human kind she was used to dealing with—but an honest to goodness beast ripped from the pages of a Stephen King novel. Thick scales, slavering jaws, leathery wings.

"Oh God," she whispered. "Oh my God."

Whimpering, she tried to back away then remembered she was already as far back as she could go. What had once been her safe haven had been transformed into a prison cell.

Or a dining room, depending on your perspective.

The monster stepped closer. Scarlet's heart was now in her throat. "Please don't hurt me," she found herself begging. As if it could speak English. As if it could possibly understand her desperate pleas. But what else could she do?

It would kill her. Devour her. Leave nothing behind.

Leave her mother all alone.

"Oh, Mom," she whispered. "I'm so sorry."

The monster loomed above her, now only inches away, its heavy jaws creaking open with a long, loud hiss, revealing a cavern of razor teeth and a massive black tongue. Terrified, Scarlet squeezed her eyes shut, numbly mumbling what she could remember of the Lord's Prayer as she prepared for the pain of being eaten alive.

But it didn't come.

In fact, instead of pain, strange warmth seemed to wrap itself around her, as if enveloping her in a hug. At the same time, the sharp sting in her arm ebbed to a dull ache.

What was going on? Was she dead already? If so, the whole "being eaten alive" thing was certainly quicker than she'd expected. Not to mention a lot less painful.

She opened her eyes, half expecting to be floating through the air, looking down on her lifeless body like always seemed to happen on TV. But no. She was still on the ground, still in her own skin. She looked down at her arm, surprised and disturbed to find it dripping with a strange, black, oil-like substance. As she watched, dumbstruck, the oil seemed to seep into her skin, dissolving into her flesh. A moment later, it had completely disappeared, leaving no wound behind.

Not a scab. Not a scar. Just unblemished skin, as if there had never been a wound at all.

Scarlet looked up in disbelief, meeting the monster's eyes with her own. *Blue eyes*, she realized suddenly. *The monster has blue eyes.* And the source of the oil? It was dripping from a quarter-sized rip in one of the creature's scales.

"Did you...?" she whispered, desperately trying to put two and two together. She wasn't sure whether to be fascinated or horrified—or maybe a little of both. "Did you...heal me? With your blood?" It sounded insane, even as she was saying it out loud, but what other explanation could there be?

The creature didn't answer, of course, though the corners of its mouth seemed to lift, as if in a crooked smile. Then it turned, loping through the underbrush and disappearing from view.

For a moment, Scarlet just sat there, frozen, too astounded to move. Then a wild idea struck her and she sprang into action, fumbling for her phone, her fingers trembling so wildly she could barely load up the video app. It took even more effort to hit record on the screen.

She scrambled out of her hideaway as fast as she could, spotting the creature now standing at the edge of the clearing, unfurling the most beautiful wings she'd ever seen, bright and shining in the moonlight—as if covered with actual emeralds.

As Scarlet held her breath, overwhelmed by the majesty of it all, the creature lifted its snout to the skies, effortlessly rising into the air and disappearing into the night. Scarlet watched it go, unable to speak. Unable to even move. Then she found herself running toward the spot it had stood, searching for some sign she hadn't imagined everything.

But the monster was gone, leaving only trampled undergrowth behind.

Except...Scarlet looked down at her hands, still gripping the phone with white-knuckled fingers. Somehow she managed to press stop then load up the video. She was half-convinced there would be nothing on the recording, that the creature was some kind of ghost—or a magical being that couldn't be captured by human photography.

But to her surprise, the video was intact, the creature's image imprisoned on the screen. And as Scarlet watched the playback with growing awe, observing its breathtaking beauty, its impossible grace, she realized she could no longer call this a monster at all.

No. This, this was a dragon.

Chapter Two

*R*OAR!

    Trinity spun on a dime, her eyes locking on to the dragon hovering in the smoky sky above. It was huge and black with dull, soulless eyes, massive wings, and a spiky tail. A guttural hiss wound up its throat as its mouth creaked open, revealing a chasm of spiky teeth framing a molten core—aimed directly at her.

    Oh hell no.

    She dove to the side, somersaulting out of the line of fire. The street behind her exploded in flames, the tar bubbling in protest before melting into black sludge. The sudden heat drenched her body in sweat, her clothes now clinging as if she were in a wet T-shirt contest.

    Instead of a girl at the end of the world.

    Sucking in a breath, she dared to look back at the dragon. It had landed a few yards away, its fire extinguished, its jaws clamped shut. Summoning more heat for round two?

    She wasn't about to stick around to find out.

    She took off, lungs burning in protest as they vainly attempted to take in air thick with black smoke. The screams of those still able to scream rang through her head while the smell of roasting flesh tormented her nose. High above, menacing black shadows danced through the skies, all but eclipsing the sun.

There were so many. They were surrounded. They were doomed. They were all doomed.

Yet still she ran, forcing her feet to pound the pavement, one after another. She didn't know why she bothered—why any of them bothered. Some kind of inane instinct for self-preservation, perhaps? Stupid. Pointless. But she kept running anyway.

Diving into a nearby alley, she tried each and every door, desperately seeking shelter from the terror in the skies. But it was no use; they were all closed; they were all locked. And she could feel the eyes of those behind the doors and windows looking down on her without a scrap of pity.

Here in the Scorch, it was everyone for themselves.

Finally the alleyway dead-ended at a solid brick wall too high to climb. As she stared up at it, dismay washing over her, a shadow crossed her vision. Slowly, she turned around, willing herself not to stumble as she prepared to stare death in the face.

The dragon before her was ruby red. As big as a house. Observing her with eager eyes as its tail lapped lazily from side to side behind it. As they faced off, a small, sadistic smile seemed to play at the corners of the creature's mouth—as if daring her to even try to escape.

But she couldn't. There was no place to run. No place to hide.

And, in the end, even the Fire Kissed would burn.

❖ ❖ ❖

"Trinity, wake up, wake up!"

Trinity struggled, gasping for air, as rough arms shook her awake. She looked up, wild-eyed, unable to focus her gaze—still seeing the shadows of the deadly dragon wavering in her mind's eye. It took her a moment to realize it was her grandpa leaning over her now, an anxious expression on his weathered face. She collapsed back onto her bed, her long, black hair fanning out around her as she sucked in a much-needed breath.

"Another bad one, huh?" Grandpa asked sympathetically, grabbing a hand towel from the side of the bed and using it to mop her sweaty brow.

She grimaced, nodding, as she tried to steady her still-racing pulse. The pounding in her head was slowly fading, but the nightmarish visuals didn't seem as eager to leave. She glanced over at the travel alarm clock on her bedside table. Almost midnight.

She realized her grandpa was still looking at her worriedly. "Just like all the others," she confessed. "The world on fire. Dragons swooping down from the skies. People being burned alive." She shuddered, still hearing the screams echoing through her head, still smelling the revolting odor of charred flesh. "I mean, yeah, I know it's only a dream. But when I'm in the middle of it, it all feels so real."

Her mind flashed back to the locked doors, the suspicious eyes, the alleyway dead-ending—leaving her nowhere to go. The dragon staring her down, as if daring her to make a move.

"But it's *not* real," Grandpa reminded her in a firm voice. "Well, not anymore, anyway, thanks to you." He gave her a proud, grandfatherly look, as if she'd achieved a perfect score on her SATs or something.

Instead of having saved the world from a dragon apocalypse, as the case might be.

She groaned. Sometimes it was hard to believe it had only been three months since this whole thing had started. Back then she'd been a normal teenage girl, living in a dusty, West Texas town where nothing much happened. At the time, her biggest worry had been her grandfather's shaky financial situation and the risk of social services throwing her back into foster care—which, of course, were totally legit concerns.

But they were nothing compared to what she'd been forced to face since, after the fateful day her grandfather brought home the world's last dragon egg. After their lives had been turned upside down and after Trinity had learned her true destiny.

"My little Fire Kissed," Grandpa said affectionately. "The girl who saved the world."

She rolled her eyes. "Well, I did have a little help, you know."

Speaking of…she involuntarily glanced at the door, wondering if she'd woken Caleb or Connor with her screaming. The house they were currently squatting in wasn't all that large, and while Caleb usually managed to sleep like the dead, his twin, the soldier in the family, preferred to rest with one eye open. And though Connor never spoke of it aloud, she knew he had nightmares too. She heard him sometimes, thrashing in bed and moaning loudly. It wasn't surprising, she supposed. After all, while she was only conjuring up this post-dragon apocalyptic future in her own mind, it had once been his everyday reality.

Time travel, dragons, saving the world…it would give anyone bad dreams.

"Yes, well, I suppose every true heroine needs her sidekicks," Grandpa admitted grudgingly, ruffling her hair. "But the bottom line remains the same. You, my dear, changed our future. You kept the dragon out of the government's hands; you stopped the apocalypse. And now you can rest easy, knowing the world is safe."

He set down the cloth and reached over to her bedside

table, his slightly shaky hands winding up the small golden music box sitting on top of it. As he opened the lid, the tinkling sounds of Mozart began to fill the room and the little princess inside twirled merrily, as if she didn't have a care in the world. Trinity couldn't help a small smile. Grandpa knew her mother's music box always made her feel better. No matter what happened in life, no matter how chaotic things seemed, it was comforting to know that the princess would always be there for her, ready to dance away her troubles.

Oh, Mom, I hope you've found the same kind of peace.

Grandpa leaned down, pressing his papery lips to her forehead, then rose to his feet, giving her a small smile before heading back to his own bedroom, closing the door behind him. She watched him go then shifted her gaze to the ceiling, his words echoing through her mind as the music slowed with the clockwork.

You can rest easy, knowing the world is safe.

She shook her head. At the moment, things felt anything but safe. They were still on the run, still fugitives from the law, still considered dangerous terrorists by Homeland Security—and most importantly, still harboring a hungry, hungry dragon that was getting bigger and hungrier every day.

It was really no wonder she couldn't sleep.

Giving up, she slipped out of bed, sliding her feet into a pair of worn slippers before padding out of the barren space currently serving as her bedroom. There had been so many bedrooms over the last three months she didn't even bother to decorate anymore. None could compete, anyway, with her real bedroom back in Old Oak Grove, its walls plastered with posters from her favorite video game, *Fields of Fantasy*.

Unfortunately, video games were another thing of the past, with real life eclipsing any possible excitement virtual reality could hold.

As she tiptoed down the stairs, by habit she reached out for the light switch, only to be reminded there was no electricity in their latest squat—a small, Hill Country ranch house, a hundred or so miles from her hometown. Though she missed having electricity as much as any sixteen-year-old would, she knew she really couldn't complain. This was, by far, the best place they'd come across to hide in during their time on the run. Unlike some of the past places, here everyone had their own bedrooms and Emberlyn was cozy and comfortable, sleeping in the adjacent barn.

Emberlyn. Emmy. She sighed deeply. What were they going to do about Emmy?

She thought back to the day of the dragon's hatching. When the future still seemed promising and bright. The Dracken had promised to help her, to usher in a new race of dragons that would bring about a future filled with prosperity and health. Dragons had the power to heal people, they said, to sniff out natural resources, to divine water in the desert. They were going to save mankind.

It was only later that she learned that the Dracken hadn't come back from the future to save the world but to destroy it in some kind of sick Noah's Ark 2.0, using dragon fire instead of a flood. They'd barely escaped with their lives—and now she was stuck with a dragon and no idea what to do with her.

Not that she didn't love the little—or not so little—dragon with all her heart. She was Emmy's Fire Kissed. Her guardian and protector. Bonded together and sharing a common life force. Though Emmy had only been in her life for three short months, Trinity couldn't imagine a world without her.

If only she would stop growing!

It had been easy to pledge to take care of a dragon the size of a small Chihuahua. But now Emmy was more like a fat Labrador, going on Great Dane. Connor and Caleb spoke of dragons as big as houses back in their time. How on earth were they going to hide her when she grew to full height?

Not to mention feed her. Thank goodness Grandpa was an experienced hunter and was able to provide daily deer to fill her stomach, supplemented by whatever road kill Caleb or Connor could collect. But the herds were thinning, and several days this week, they'd all come home empty-handed. Which meant soon they'd be forced to move again, to find another abandoned house or farm or ranch to hide the world's last dragon in.

She shook her head. Rest easy? Yeah, right.

She reached into the kitchen cabinets after lighting the lantern, pulling out a box of cereal. No refrigeration meant no milk, but it was better than nothing. And maybe the carbs would at least make her—

"Ow!"

She jerked as, out of nowhere, a throbbing pain snaked up her arm.

What the hell?

It came again. A fierce sting, nearly taking her breath away. Hands shaking, she managed to yank up her sleeve, forcing herself to look down, a bit terrified as to what she'd find. Texas had its share of creepy crawlies, and being on the run meant no ER visit if a lonely scorpion or spider had decided to use her for target practice.

But there was no bite. Her skin was smooth, unmarred, cool to the touch.

And yet, it hurt like a mother…

She stepped nearer the light to make sure, her confusion mixing with fear. But while her arm still pulsed in pain, the skin remained unmarked. She pressed down gently with two fingers, her mind racing with possibilities. What would make her—

Could it be Emmy?

She startled at the thought. It was one of the strange side effects of being bonded to a dragon. If Emmy suffered some kind of injury, she would feel it herself. That was the theory, anyway. But since it was more than a little difficult to harm a dragon using present-day technology, she hadn't had a chance to experience this phantom pain for herself.

Had something happened to Emmy?

Stomach churning, she reached out to the dragon with her mind. Another benefit to being bonded: they could talk to one another without speaking—if they were in the same vicinity. In fact, there had been plenty of nights over the last few months when they'd both stayed up late, chatting from house to barn. Until her giggles got too loud and Grandpa had come in to scold her. Dragon sleepovers—so much awesome.

But now…

Are you there, Emmy? she probed. *Are you okay?*

She frowned, glancing down at her arm again. The pain had subsided a bit, from a piercing throb to a general ache. But still…

Emmy? she tried again. *Can you hear me?*

The resounding silence sent a cold chill clawing up her spine. "She's probably sound asleep," she tried to assure herself.

"A deep sleep. That's all." But even as she said the words, she was already halfway out the door, heading toward the barn. Just in case.

It was a warm night with a full moon, the stars painting a sprawling portrait across the big Texas sky. It was beautiful—majestic—breathtaking even, and on another night Trinity might have taken time to stop and look up and appreciate it properly. But now her eyes were locked on to the barn doors as her quick steps ate up the distance between the buildings, her chest tightening.

She's fine. She's going to be fine. Maybe a little grumpy at being woken up in the middle of the night—but otherwise totally fine.

She reached the barn. Forcing her breath to steady, she pulled open the double doors and stepped inside. Her nose wrinkled at the smell of decaying flesh permeating the air. Emmy was a lot of wonderful things, but a neat eater was not one of them. And while Trin was constantly offering to muck out the place or open some windows to air things out, Emmy always refused. Like most dragons, she preferred dark, closed-in spaces, and this suited her just fine. She had even created her own little makeshift burrow at the back of the barn to cuddle up in.

But now that burrow was empty. There was only a pile of crushed hay, littered with bones, confirming Trinity's worst fears. She swallowed hard. Where was she? Had something happened? Had someone found her? Had they taken her away? She raced around the barn, nausea threatening to consume her as she desperately searched for something dragon shaped, all the while calling out her name.

Emmy? Where are you? Please answer—you're scaring me!

But there was no answer. Her dragon was gone.

Chapter Three

"I'm going to kill you, you overgrown gecko."

Caleb Jacks stopped for a moment to catch his breath, scanning the treetops above. Searching for something—anything—remotely dragon-like. But the branches only swayed gently in the night breeze, as if mocking his desperation.

"I'm serious!" he cried out. "I'm going to go Saint George on your ass if you don't get out here this second."

But his words were met with silence.

And so he pressed on, racing through the forest, stumbling over rocks and roots, the wind stinging his eyes as branches whipped at his face. As he swung his dim flashlight about, every shadow, every flash of movement seemed to take on a dragon shape. But each time he got close, he found only an oddly formed rock or a gnarled stump or a panicked deer caught in a midnight graze.

How had this happened? He'd only turned his back on her for a quick second to check the basketball score on his phone. He'd become curiously addicted to early twenty-first-century sports while whittling away time at their last squat, which still had electricity and cable TV. Now that they'd moved on, his only link to civilization and sports scores was through the disposable cell phone Trinity insisted he carry. And he had been desperate to know the score of the all-important game going into overtime.

So he'd looked down, taken his eyes off the dragon—only for a second. And when he'd looked up again, she was gone.

"Hey, Hot Wings! Get back here and stop playing games!"

Where had she gone? In all the times he'd snuck her out for a nighttime fly, she'd never left his sight before. Was she just growing braver as she grew older—more confident of her surroundings? Or had something called to her, drawing her away?

Either way, he had to get her back. Get her home safe and sound before anyone noticed she was gone. Before Trinity noticed. The Fire Kissed would kill him if she knew he'd taken her dragon out without permission. And if something were to happen to Emmy...well, Caleb didn't even want to think about what that meant for him.

For the entire world, for that matter.

Maybe she got bored and headed home, he told himself, reluctantly giving up the search. Maybe he'd get back to the farmhouse and find her curled up in her burrow, snoring loudly, fast asleep. *Yes, that was probably it*, he tried to reassure himself as he lumbered out of the forest, attempting to still his racing pulse as he went. She got tired. She went back. They could laugh about it in the morning.

Oh please let us be able to laugh about it in the morning.

As he trudged over the rolling fields on his way back to the farmhouse, he found himself glancing up into the moonlit sky with uneasy eyes. It still felt strange to cross an unprotected stretch of land aboveground like this. In his world, it would have been a death sentence, with deadly creatures ready to swoop down and flambé you alive at a moment's notice.

But his world—two hundred years from now—no longer existed, he reminded himself. They'd come back in time. They'd altered the future. There was no longer any reason to fear.

At least that's what he liked to tell himself. But in his heart, he knew there was still plenty to be scared about. The new time line they'd created was nothing more than an elastic band that could snap back into place at a moment's notice. One mistake. One misstep.

One missing dragon, falling into the wrong hands...

He shook his head. She was in the barn. She had to be.

"Caleb!"

He looked up, guilt stabbing him in the gut as his eyes fell upon a dark shadow tearing across the field, black curls streaming out behind her in waves. His heart lodged in his throat. Oh no. She was awake. And from her frantic pace, he could make a pretty good guess that Emmy was not in the barn after all.

Half of him wanted to run, to turn around and flee the scene. To not have to explain to her what had happened. To not have to take responsibility for what he'd done. He imagined the horror draining the blood from her face, followed by furious disappointment welling up in her eyes. She would kill him. She would flecking kill him.

But there was no place to go.

He planted his feet on the ground, forcing back his fear. She reached him a moment later, her ebony eyes piercing him with concern.

"Have you seen Emmy?" she asked, her voice breathless and scared. "She's not in the barn and we've been looking everywhere. Is she with you?" She glanced behind him, scanning the darkened landscape, wringing her hands together anxiously.

"Um…" He squirmed, shuffling from foot to foot, a thousand lies fighting to escape his lips. She didn't know he took Emmy out. He could tell her he had no idea, that he was just out on a midnight stroll. He hadn't seen the dragon at all. She might believe that. Then again, she might not.

"Look, Trin, I—"

A loud screeching interrupted his words. He looked up, his eyes locking on a dark shadow dive-bombing them at top speed.

"Look out!"

On instinct, he threw himself against Trinity, a vain attempt to protect her from the terror descending from the skies. But he lost his balance and they tumbled to the ground in a tangle of limbs. His heart was beating so loud in his ears that it took him a moment to realize she was laughing.

Oh, right.

He rolled off her, his face burning with embarrassment, just in time for none other than Emmy herself to come in for an exuberant landing, charging toward her mistress and covering her face with rough kisses. Caleb groaned, slapping his hand over his face. *And…here be dragons. Right on schedule.*

Trinity squealed in protest, trying to give Emmy a disapproving look, which was proving difficult since she'd clearly caught a bad case of the giggles. Emmy took advantage, continuing to slurp her guardian's face with unabashed glee, as if she hadn't seen her for a week.

"Okay, okay! I get it!" Trin protested, still laughing. "You're happy to see me! Geez. You don't have to knock me over about it."

Caleb rose to his feet, watching awkwardly, suddenly feeling like an interloper at their joyous reunion. Working with the Dracken, he'd witnessed a lot of dragon/guardian bonds but never one as strong as Trinity and Emmy's. He had to admit sometimes it made him envious. To have someone who cared about you that much—to have someone look at you with such adoration in their eyes…

Disentangling herself from her dragon, Trinity scrambled to her feet, finally managing that disapproving glare she'd been fighting for. But Emmy was ready for it, giving her guardian a sweet, overly innocent look back, as if to say, *who me?*

But Trinity wasn't playing that game. "Don't even think about it," she admonished, wagging her finger at the dragon. "You had me worried sick. Why would you just take off like that? You know you're not supposed to leave the barn." Then a thought seemed to come to her. "How did you get out, anyway?"

Caleb bit his lower lip. *Don't tell her it was me. Don't tell her it was me,* he begged the creature silently. But, of course, unlike his brother and Trin herself, who had the very convenient superpower of bending people's wills using only their minds, Caleb could only pray the dragon would take pity on him.

Instead, Emmy turned to give him a very distinct look, selling him down the river with a single toss of her head. He couldn't hear what she was saying, but from the look on Trinity's face, he was pretty sure the dragon wasn't disavowing all knowledge of his participation in her little midnight field trip.

He sighed. No good deed and all that.

Sure enough, a moment later Trinity's eyes leveled on him. "What the hell, Caleb?" she demanded.

He gave her his best guileless look. "What?" he asked, holding up his hands in feigned innocence, though he was pretty sure it would do no good.

"Gee, I don't know. Big green dragon? Flying around the Texas Hill Country without a care in the world? Instead of, oh, being locked up in the barn where she belongs?" She shot him a pointed glare, as if daring him to argue. "Any of this ringing any bells?"

Caleb shuffled his feet, wondering which explanation would piss her off the least. "Maybe she was sleep flying?" he tried, grasping at straws. "You know, I've heard of dragons who do that. Kind of like sleepwalking except…" He trailed off, catching her expression. Yeah, he probably wouldn't have bought that one either.

"Oh come on, princess," he cajoled, switching tactics. "Don't be mad. You know how she hates being cooped up in that stinky barn all the time. She's a dragon. She needs to get her fly on every once in a while."

Trinity crossed her arms over her chest, her eyes flashing fire. "Yeah, well, what if someone saw her? What if they captured her? Or reported her to the government?"

He stiffened, offended by her implication. Even though he'd been petrified of the very same thing only a few minutes before. "It's pitch black. Like one a.m. In the middle of nowhere, Texas. Trust me, we've never even seen another—"

He clamped his mouth shut. Crap. He hadn't meant to insinuate—

"You've done this before!" she exclaimed, a growing realization dawning on her face. "This isn't the first time you two have snuck out while I've been asleep."

It wasn't. In fact, he'd been taking Emmy out to fly almost the entire time they'd been on the run. Something, he told himself, she should be thanking him for. There was no way Emmy would be half as docile as she was if she'd been cooped up in a dark barn all this time. And no one wanted a restless dragon on their hands. It usually ended in something—or more likely some*one*—getting burned.

And not in the figurative sense either.

"Trust me, Trin, it's no big deal," he tried again. "We're always careful. We stay below the tree line. She never leaves my sight."

The lies rolled off his tongue, leaving a bitter taste in his mouth. Where had she gone tonight? Why had she taken off like that? He glanced over at the dragon, narrowing his eyes, trying to demand answers. But Emmy refused to meet his gaze.

Thanks a lot, Sulfur Breath. See if I do you any favors again.

Trinity turned to the dragon. "And you! You've been going behind my back this whole time?" Caleb could hear her anger was now laced with hurt. "You didn't even think to tell me?" So much for the happy family reunion. At least he wasn't to take the entire blame.

"There you are!" interrupted an all-too-familiar voice, cutting through the night air. Caleb's shoulders slumped. Oh great. This was getting better and better.

He turned to see his brother, Connor, the great and glorious Dragon Hunter, fast on approach. His twin had obviously been roused from sleep to help find the missing dragon. He was still wearing plaid flannel pajama pants and evidently hadn't even had the time to throw on a shirt. Caleb rolled his eyes. His twin never missed an opportunity to "accidentally" show off his perfect washboard abs—especially if Trinity happened to be nearby.

Connor looked from Trinity to Caleb and back again, his eyes filled with trademark suspicion. "What's going on?" he demanded.

"Nothing," Trin blurted out before Caleb could speak. "We found Emmy. Everything's okay."

Caleb raised an eyebrow, surprised to hear her cover for him. But maybe he shouldn't have been. After all, she was always trying to serve as peacemaker between him and his twin.

Not that it really ever worked. Even though the two of them were supposed to be fighting on the same side for the first time in their lives, they still could never manage to agree on anything. Not to mention Connor was always on Caleb's case about one thing or another. Whatever Caleb tried to do, it was always wrong or not good enough for his hero brother. Half the time he didn't know why he bothered trying.

He watched as his twin turned to observe Emmy, who looked back at him with cagy eyes. He stifled a laugh. He secretly enjoyed the fact that Hot Wings still didn't completely trust Connor, and for good reason too. Once upon a time—not long ago in fact—it had been Connor's mission to slaughter the poor dragon before she could even hatch from her shell, in an attempt to send her race hurtling back into extinction. And while time and Trinity had managed to soften the hunter's opinion on the reptile species as a whole and grudgingly allow it to continue its existence on the planet, Connor would never become an Emmy super fan. And vice versa.

"How did she get out of the barn in the first place?" Connor asked, giving him a suspicious look. "I locked it from the outside before I went to bed." His eyes roved over the dragon. "And what's wrong with her arm?" he added.

"What?" Trinity cried, following his gaze. Her eyes widened and Caleb caught her looking down at her own arm before returning to Emmy. She dropped to her knees before the dragon. It was then that Caleb saw it—a black crust dried over her one soft scale. Dragon blood.

Uh-oh.

"Emmy, what happened?" Trinity demanded, reaching for the dragon's paw. Emmy snorted, batting Trinity's hand away with her snout before backing out of reach, giving her mistress an accusatory look. Still annoyed at being yelled at, he supposed. Trinity gave the dragon an unhappy look then turned back to the boys.

"What did she say?" Caleb asked worriedly.

"She says she doesn't know what happened," Trinity replied, not sounding like she believed it for a second. And for good reason. Dragon scales were tough—they could withstand bullets even—so it wasn't like she could have just caught one on a branch or something and had it tear away. She locked her gaze on him. "Do you?"

He squirmed, not sure what to say. He'd just told her Emmy never left his sight. To admit he didn't know what had happened to her would mean admitting the dragon had taken off on him. Which would mean admitting he'd made a foolish decision to take her out in the first place. He wasn't about to go there—not in front of his brother anyway. The last thing he needed was to give Connor more ammunition to use against him.

He already had plenty.

"So it was you who let her out, wasn't it?" Connor concluded, storming toward him with marked aggression. "Caleb, we've talked about this. A hundred times in fact. Emmy cannot leave the barn! Ever!"

"No, *you* talked about it," Caleb blurted back, allowing his anger at his brother's self-righteousness to drown out his rising guilt. After all, Connor didn't give a crap about Emmy. The only reason he wanted her alive was because killing her meant Trinity dying too. And the oh so noble knight in shining dragon scale couldn't stomach the idea of murdering his very own damsel in distress. "I told you it was a stupid idea from the beginning!"

He glanced over at Emmy, praying she'd back him up on this. "I mean just look at her!" he added. "She's a dragon—an intelligent, magical creature—not some pet you can just coop up inside and expect to piss in a litter box."

Out of the corner of his eye, he could see Trinity wince and he regretted being so crass. But he was on a roll now, and the words kept tumbling from his lips.

"What was the point of rescuing her anyway, if you're going to just let her rot away in a barn for the rest of her life? Seriously, she would have been better off with the Dracken. At least they knew how to treat her with the respect she deserves."

Trinity gave him a horrified look. "That's not fair," she protested.

"No, none of this is fair," he volleyed back, unable to stop himself now. "Not to poor Emmy anyway. You say you care about her? Well, maybe you should start showing it."

And with that, he stormed off, leaving them behind, heading back to the house with hurried steps. He could feel Trinity reaching out to him with her mind, desperate to continue the conversation, but he quickly slammed down the walls, shutting her out of his head. He didn't want to hear her excuses. He'd tried to do something good—something noble even—to aid the dragon that everyone was supposedly so gung ho to save. And as usual, all he got was grief for his troubles.

He stomped into the farmhouse and up the stairs to his bedroom, slamming the door behind him. Gut-wrenching fury tore at him as he paced the floor, over and over until he became half-convinced he'd wear a hole right through it. A few minutes later, he heard voices outside and stole an involuntary look out the window, immediately wishing he hadn't. Connor and Trinity stood outside the barn—evidently having locked Emmy back inside—and were whispering to one another in urgent voices he couldn't quite make out. He scowled, standing there, powerless to turn away.

She always took Connor's side. Always listened to him. Always took his advice. They were supposed to be a team. They were supposed to be working together. But no matter how hard Caleb tried, somehow he always ended up the odd man out.

He watched Trinity step toward Connor, her expression grim, her eyes drowning in sorrow. Caleb frowned, feeling sick to his stomach at the naked pain he saw radiating from her pale face. He'd meant to lash out at his brother, but *she* had been the one hit by his shrapnel.

Which wasn't fair. Despite Connor's dubious intentions when it came to dragon saving, Caleb had never doubted for a moment Trinity's love and dedication to little Emmy. After all, she'd sacrificed her entire life to keep the dragon safe. And for him to imply that she was worse than the Dracken was nothing more than cruel.

Regret threatened to smother him. It was all he could do not to race down the stairs and out the door, grab her and pull her into his arms—apologize for hurting her, for putting her dragon in danger. Promise to never worry her again.

Instead, he stood by the window, frozen in place. Instead, it was his brother who opened his arms, inviting Trinity into an embrace, giving her all the comfort she needed and then some. As he was always more than willing to do.

Caleb squeezed his hands into fists, the anger inside threatening to boil over. If only Trinity knew how close Connor had come to killing her in his misguided attempt to save the human race from dragons. Would she still so willingly fall into his arms? Sometimes it was all Caleb could do to hold back the words—the story of how he'd saved her life from his brother's bloody crusade.

But that would only complicate things further and hurt Trinity more than he could bear. Besides, Connor was strong. Smart. A soldier. They needed him if they had any hope of making this all turn out okay. So Caleb forced himself to keep his brother's secret, day after painful day—knowing Trinity would never feel for him what he felt for her.

His fingers reached involuntarily to his mouth. It had been months since they'd shared a kiss, deep in the otherworld known as the Nether, and yet at times, he could still feel the ghost of her lips against his own. A feeling he both wanted to exorcise and keep forever.

He forced himself away from the window, too sickened to watch his brother comfort her now. Glancing at his unmade bed, he wondered if he should just crawl under the covers and try to sleep. But he knew he would only toss and turn. And any sleep would include restless, unhappy dreams about her.

There was only one thing to get him through the night. Reaching into his nightstand, he pulled a small sapphire from his dwindling stash, palming it into his trembling hands. For a moment, he stared down at it, considering the idea that he could put it away, resist the pull of the Nether, and try to get a normal night's sleep. Wake in the morning like a normal person, rested and refreshed.

He laughed bitterly, giving up on the pretense. Closing his fingers around the gem, he shut his eyes. "Hang on, Fred," he whispered to his dragon. "I'm on my way."

Chapter Four

"Come on, Trin. Don't let him get to you."

Trinity looked up at Connor. His eyes were stern but sympathetic. She gave him a weak smile.

"I know," she said. "But I can't help it. I mean he has a point, right? All I want to do is what's best for her."

"Which is exactly what you're doing," he reminded her firmly. "Look, my brother may have a kind heart and good intentions, but he's always been reckless. He doesn't think things through. Taking her out is dangerous. What if she'd been seen? And we still don't know what really happened with that broken scale."

Trinity thought back to the scale, her brow furrowing. "Do you think she's telling the truth when she says she doesn't remember? I mean, I felt it myself when it happened—on my own arm, thanks to our little bond. If the pain felt anything like that for her, there's no way she wouldn't notice."

"I don't know," Connor replied doubtfully. "I'm just glad it wasn't serious. It's not like we can just take her to the vet if something worse happens. Which is, again, why she needs to stay in the barn, where it's safe."

"I know," Trin said with a moan. "I do. I just wish she didn't hate it so much in there."

"Yeah, well it beats being dead, right?"

Connor's tone was deceptively light, but there was a thread of bitterness underneath, making Trinity's skin prickle. As she glanced up at the former hunter, she wondered, not for the first time, if he was having second thoughts about abandoning his original mission. After all, in a matter of months, the guy had gone from being a celebrated Dragon Hunter to a glorified babysitter, responsible for the care and feeding of a creature whose progeny had murdered his father and decimated his world. That couldn't be easy.

"Look, Trin," Connor added, catching her expression. "You're right. Emmy probably would be happier if she was given more freedom—just like the rest of us. I mean, I don't imagine you love spending your days holed up in some abandoned farmhouse either. Away from your home, your friends. We're all making sacrifices here. Emmy doesn't get a pass."

She sighed. As always, he made perfect sense. As much as it pained her to see Emmy so miserable, there was too much risk involved in letting her loose. The Dracken for one thing. While Darius—and maybe his co-leader Mara—were still in prison, that didn't mean others had given up the search for Emmy. The Potentials, for example, the group of kids the Dracken had gathered from around the world to help raise the new crop of dragons. They would still believe that Emmy had the power to save their home countries from poverty and war, and that Trinity had stolen her away from them. They weren't going to just give up and go home.

"And that's not even counting the rest of the world," Connor reminded her, evidently reading her thoughts—or maybe just the look on her face. "Imagine what would happen if people learned there was a fire-breathing beast on the loose in Texas."

She cringed. "It'd be open season on dragons," she admitted. "If the government didn't swoop in and take her away first."

"And then we'd be right back where we started," Connor concluded. "Emmy would be cloned and those violent hybrid dragons would be let loose on the world. The apocalypse, all over again. Everything we've worked so hard to prevent would have been for nothing."

And her nightmares would finally come true.

She nodded slowly, frustration building up inside of her, threatening to explode. "I hate this!" she blurted, squeezing her hands into fists. "I'm supposed to be her guardian, not her jailer!" She turned to Connor, looking up at him with anguished eyes. "What are we doing?" she demanded. "Running from place to place, barely surviving. We have no plan. No way to make any of this turn out okay." She raked a hand through her tangled hair. "Maybe it would have been better to let her die in her egg." Her voice broke. "At least that way it would be over. She wouldn't have to suffer like this!"

She started to turn, but Connor grabbed her, tugging her into his arms. "You don't mean that," he scolded in a fierce voice. "I know you don't mean that. You're just upset. And you're scared. We all are."

Trinity swallowed hard, her whole body trembling with emotion. "I can't even tell you...When I walked into the barn. When I saw she was gone." She closed her eyes, shuddering. "If I had lost her...after all I promised..."

"You're not going to lose her," Connor interrupted. "Not

now, not ever. Remember, she chose you—out of everyone else—to be her guardian. The one to keep her safe. And you've already proven yourself more than worthy of that choice. You saved her from the government agents. You saved her from the Dracken. Hell..." He gave her bashful grin. "You even saved her from me. And that's saying something. I'm usually damn good at my job."

She chuckled despite herself and Connor pulled her closer. With her ear flush to his chest, she could hear his heartbeat, strong and steady, just like the dragon hunter himself. Suddenly she felt bad for having doubted his intentions. After all, he'd sacrificed everything he believed in, abandoned his quest for revenge against the species that had destroyed his world. And it had all been for her.

Connor pulled away from the hug, his hands finding her face and his eyes holding hers with a piercing gaze. Her breath hitched. Sometimes she forgot how blue those eyes of his were. Like the summer sky on a cloudless day. Eyes that could give a person hope—something that admittedly was in very short supply.

"You're doing the right thing," he told her. "Not the easy thing. But the right thing. Emmy may not understand it now, but she'll appreciate it later. I truly believe if we stay strong and keep out of sight until we figure out what to do, we'll find a way to make this all turn out okay. For Emmy...and the rest of the world."

He trailed off, staring at her with an intensity that made her shiver. Then he gave her a goofy smile. "You may be her Fire Kissed," he teased, "but we're all on Team Dragon here."

She couldn't help but laugh at this and the tension broke

between them. Grandpa had made that joke about a month ago, after skimming through one of her teen romance novels, and it had stuck ever since. It sounded so cheesy, but she kind of liked the sentiment all the same. She wasn't alone. They were all in this together.

"Can you unlock the door?" she asked, gesturing to the padlock. When Connor gave her a questioning look, she shrugged. "She's part of the team too, right? I don't want her to feel all alone." She paused then added, "You can lock up behind me and come get me in the morning."

Connor did what she asked, though he didn't look too thrilled about it. But she gave him her best reassuring smile then stepped inside, closing the door behind her. She waited to hear the click of the padlock then felt her way to the back of the barn. It was pitch-dark, but she could hear Emmy's soft breaths, guiding her steps. Kneeling down, she reached out until her hands connected with the dragon's satiny soft scales. When Emmy opened her eyes, they glowed like blue diamonds in the darkness.

You're back, the dragon observed, her normally sweet voice sounding a little cold. *Did you forget something?*

"No," Trinity replied. "I just wanted to talk to you." She reached out to stroke the ridges on Emmy's snout. Usually it was the dragon's favorite spot to be scratched. But this time she only jerked her head away, small puffs of smoke billowing from her nose.

"You're mad at me, aren't you?" Trinity observed sadly, reaching over to pull the LED lantern out from under a bench and flick on the switch. She wondered how much of the conversation Emmy had caught between her and Connor outside the barn. Sometimes it was hard to remember how self-aware the dragon had become over the last couple of months. While in some ways she was still very pet-like, in other ways she had become very human.

With very human emotions.

No, you're *mad at* me, *remember?* Emmy corrected in a sulky voice. *Because I left the barn without your permission.* Her mimic of Trinity's voice was dead-on, and Trin felt her face flush.

"I'm not mad," she protested. "I was just scared. When I saw you weren't in the barn...I thought something bad had happened to you, Ems. And when I found out Caleb has been sneaking you out all this time and you've been keeping it from me? What am I supposed to think about that?"

And there it was, she realized with a start. It wasn't that Caleb had been sneaking Emmy out that had been bothering her—not really. It was that Emmy hadn't told her he was doing it. They were supposed to be bonded—as close as two souls could be. And yet the dragon had been keeping secrets from her. Were there other secrets as well?

Her eyes fell to Emmy's broken scale and her heart panged.

Don't you trust me?

The dragon's question was stark and simple, spoken without judgment or rebuke. But it felt like a knife to the gut all the same. Trust had never come easy to Trinity, not after all the times the people in her life had disappointed her. And Emmy knew that—better than anyone. For her to throw it back in Trin's face now felt intentional.

"Of course I trust you," she said, her voice cracking at the edges. "I trust you more than anyone else in the world. It's other people I don't trust, Ems. If they were to see you. If they were to find out you were here..."

What, they might take me away? Emmy questioned, raising a scaly eyelid.

When Trin nodded, the dragon huffed. *I'd like to see them try. I am a dragon, after all. I'm not afraid of a few humans.*

She looked so offended that Trinity had to laugh. "Yes, yes, you're a great and terrible Smaug," she couldn't help but tease. "But we're hoping to keep the peace here, remember? That's sort of the whole point of doing this."

She stopped short, realizing Emmy didn't look amused. In fact she looked kind of angry. "I'm sorry," Trin said. "I was just being stupid."

The dragon bristled. *Do you think the idea of me protecting you is stupid?*

"No, Emmy. Of course not. I'm just saying—"

I thought I was here to help people. Why can't I do that? There are people out there, Trinity. People who are hurt. People who are dying. I could help them. I know I could. I could make things better, instead of just rotting away uselessly in a barn.

"Oh, Emmy." Trinity's heart wrenched. "I want you to be able to do all of that too. But it's not that simple. There are people out there who want to use you—and not for helping people either. If you show yourself, they'll take you away."

A low growl rumbled in Emmy's throat. *I repeat: I would like to see them try.*

Trinity closed her eyes, frustrated beyond belief. She had come in here to apologize to her dragon. But it seemed everything she tried to say was only making things worse.

"Look, Emmy, you've got to understand—"

Will you please put on my show? the dragon suddenly

interrupted, effectively declaring the conversation over. *I want to watch my show now.*

Trinity stared at her for a moment then shook her head. "Sure," she said, giving up. "Let me get the player."

Reaching under the wooden bench where the lantern had been stored, she pulled out the portable DVD player she'd bought the dragon a month ago. It was the kind that you could charge in the car, which allowed for watching without electricity. "What do you want me to put in?"

Merlin, Emmy declared, not surprisingly. She'd fallen in love with the Arthurian BBC show from the first episode, declaring that the dragon Kilgharrah was rather hot—no pun intended.

"Sure," she said with forced brightness, trying to take the high road. "Let me cue it up." She worked the remote then turned to the dragon. "Did you want me to text Connor for popcorn or something?"

No, thank you, Emmy said in a clipped voice. *But you can ask him to let you out of the barn if you like. So you can go back and sleep in your own bed.*

"Oh. Okay," Trin replied, trying to speak past the lump that had solidified in her throat. "Sure. If that's what you want."

She rose to her feet, the hurt settling into her stomach like lead as she walked toward the door. She turned to the dragon, giving her one last look. "I'm sorry, Emmy," she said. "I know it sucks. But it's for the best. It really is. For your own safety and the safety of the entire world…no one can know you exist."

Chapter Five

Ten million views. Ten million views in the last ten hours. Scarlet stared at the thirteen-inch computer monitor in Vista High's tiny school library, scarcely able to believe her eyes. Ten million, six hundred thousand, three hundred and twenty-three—no, make that twenty-four—views of her dragon video since she'd uploaded it—a mere ten hours before. She couldn't believe it; people from all over the country—all over the world—all logging in and watching her little home movie.

And commenting too. While some professed amazement that such a creature had been caught on tape—smack dab in the middle of Texas, no less—others were a bit more... skeptical...to say the least, posting the wildest conspiracy theories on how she had managed to doctor the footage before uploading. From comments insisting the dragon was nothing more than a tiny insect up against a studio green screen to those who suggested an entirely computer-generated beast, ripped from the popular *Fields of Fantasy* video game, the theories went on and on. Some of the accusations were so complicated, in fact, she was pretty sure that even a master CGI expert at LucasArts would find them difficult to replicate.

"Whatcha looking at?"

Startled, Scarlet jumped at the voice. Her hands flew to the keyboard, guiltily alt-tabbing out of Internet Explorer and back to the Civil War essay she was supposed to be working on for her American history class, until she realized it was only Rebekah.

Her best friend leaned over the chair, tossing a lock of bright blue hair over her shoulder as she eyed the computer screen with mock suspicion. "Did I catch you looking at porn again, young lady?" she scolded. "How many times do I have to tell you? There's no sex in study hall."

Scarlet snorted. "It was YouTube, thank you very much."

Her friend tapped a finger to her chin. "YouTube, huh?" she repeated. "Funny, I was quite certain that was on the prohibited website list at Vista Memorial High."

"Not if you're using it for research."

"Right. Research." Rebekah gave her a knowing look. "So what you're saying is if I were to, say, hit alt-tab on your computer right this very second, I'll be taken to some kind of Civil War reenactment relative to your history assignment? As opposed to, say….a Two Sad Boys concert video or other such non-educational drivel?"

Scarlet rolled her eyes. "Um, sure. As long as you don't require any proof whatsoever of that statement—then yes. Yes, you would."

Rebekah pounced on the keyboard. Scarlet tried to stop her, grabbing it back, giggling. As they wrestled over the keys, the librarian at the other end of the room gave them a nasty look, forcing Scarlet to reluctantly surrender.

Rebekah let out a triumphant cheer, followed by an overly

dramatic alt-tab—just to rub it in. "Now, let's see what you're really trying to—"

She stopped short, her eyes lighting up as she stared at the screen. "Oh, dude, I saw this this morning!" she crowed, hitting play on the video to start it up again. "This thing is amazing. I mean, I'm sure it's totally doctored and stuff. But it's so freaking cool. Watch this—here's where the dragon spreads its wings and..." She trailed off, catching Scarlet's face. "What?"

Scarlet debated on whether or not to come clean to her friend. "I've seen it," she admitted at last.

"And what, you're not totally blown away? This amazing, once-in-a-lifetime video is just Tuesday to your sad and world-weary teenage heart?"

"No. It's cool," Scarlet corrected. "It's really cool. It's just..."

"You think it's fake."

She shook her head. "Actually, I know it's real."

"And you became a professional video authenticator when?"

Scarlet decided to go for it. "When the video in question came from my own cell phone."

"What are you talking about? This video was clearly uploaded by..." Rebekah scanned the screen for a user name. "Scarlet-with-the-lead pipe-in-the-library." She frowned. "Oh."

Scarlet gave her a sweet look. "You were saying?"

"Back up a minute," her friend demanded. "Start from the beginning. And don't you dare leave anything out."

And so Scarlet did, though she conveniently forgot to mention the whole "how she ended up in the woods in the first place" part, of course. Rebekah was a good friend. But she lived on the proverbial right side of the tracks, and the only family issues she had to deal with was Daddy having the nerve to deny her a new car for her super sweet sixteen and her brother refusing to let her drive his old beater. In other words, she wouldn't understand.

Besides, how could she explain the rest? The whole dragon thing was about as unbelievable as you could get in the first place. Then you add supernatural healing through some kind of weird dragon blood transfusion to the mix? She was pretty sure Rebekah would be speed-dialing the men in white coats before she could even finish her tale.

She glanced involuntarily down at her arm. At the smooth, unbroken skin. In fact, if anything, it actually looked better now than before she'd cut herself on the broken glass. She felt better too. After getting Mom's call that it was safe to come home around two a.m., she'd expected to be exhausted when her alarm went off the next morning. Instead, she felt great. Completely awesome, in fact. As if she were highly caffeinated but without all the jitters.

Coincidental? Or did the dragon blood have something to do with that too?

She realized Rebekah was still staring at her.

"What?" she asked, feeling a little sheepish.

"You saw a dragon," her friend stated. "A real-life dragon."

"Yes."

"And you put it on YouTube."

"As you do."

"And now that shiz has gone viral?"

Scarlet's eyes fell to the counter. Ten million, six hundred thousand, five hundred and thirty-three views. "See for yourself."

Rebekah squealed. Literally squealed. "Dude! Do you know what this means?" she cried, jumping up and down. The librarian shot her another look, her finger to her mouth in an overly exaggerated *shush* gesture. Rebekah dropped her voice to a stage whisper. "We're going to be freaking rich!"

Scarlet raised an eyebrow. "Rich? What do you mean rich?"

"Um, hello? Have you been living under a social media rock, Scarlet-in-the-conservatory?" Rebekah put her hands on her hips indignantly. "Do you know how much money you can make selling the rights to viral videos these days? I mean, two-day-old babies are scoring complete college tuitions from their parents uploading their pathetic adventures in pukeland. And this is a hundred times cooler. A thousand!" She reached down to hit play on the video again. "Is this the entire clip? Is there something else you cut out that maybe we can sell to the networks? Like, as an exclusive or something?"

Scarlet shook her head. "This is all I've got. The dragon was only there for a minute. Then it flew away."

"Right." Disappointment flashed across her friend's face for a second then she quickly recovered as she watched the dragon spread its wings again. "Well, do you think we could find it again? We could get more video and then auction it off to the highest bidder."

Scarlet hesitated, gnawing at her lower lip. "I'm not sure that's a good idea," she said at last. After all, the dragon had saved her life. She didn't deserve to be exploited. Exposed. "I mean, let sleeping dragons lie and all that." She started to close the window.

"Let sleeping dragons pay for my new car, more like!" Rebekah interjected. "Come on, Scarlet-in-the-billiard-room.

We could be talking thousands of dollars here. Maybe even millions. Are you so rich that you don't need a payday like that?"

Scarlet's hand froze on the mouse.

"Millions?" she repeated hesitantly.

Her mind flashed to the night before: her mother walking back into the trailer to face the monster. Putting her life at risk yet again because they had no place else to go. Her lousy tips could only get them a night or two in a crappy motel.

But if they had real money...If they had *millions*...

"I'm serious," Rebekah affirmed. "My dad knows this viral video agent guy. His whole job is, like, to get people paid for their cool videos. And let's face it, it doesn't get much cooler than this."

Scarlet stared at the screen as the video looped, her stomach now swimming with nausea. She watched as the dragon spread its wings, pushing hard against the ground with all four paws then shooting up into the sky.

Promise me, Scarlet. Promise me you'll look after Mom.

Ten million, six hundred thousand, six hundred and twelve views...

I will, Mac. I promise I will.

"Okay," she said. "Tell your parents you want to go to the game on Friday. We'll go find us a dragon."

PART 2:

SPLINTER

Chapter Six

"Hey, Mom, I'm home!"

Fifteen-year-old Connor stepped inside the limestone cave apartment, coughing to clear his lungs as the mechanical door slid shut behind him, sealing the unit off from the smog-choked tunnels outside. Even the nicest neighborhoods these days were having issues with clean air, despite the Council's best efforts.

He waved a hand as he kicked off his boots, trying to dissipate any lingering smoke into the apartment's ventilation unit. His mother was constantly working to keep the place dirt free—a nearly impossible task when you lived a quarter mile underground. But she never complained. To even have an apartment at all—never mind a real two-bedroom with four walls and a true door—in this day and age was, to most, an unattainable dream.

"Connor! You're home!"

He looked up to see his mother come out from the bedroom, wearing a thin floral housedress, her hair tied up in a kerchief. She looked frailer than he'd remembered. As if she'd lost weight. And her skin was so pale it was nearly translucent. When she threw her arms around him in a hug, he was half-afraid he'd break her like a china doll.

"How was it?" she asked, her watery eyes gleaming with excitement. "Did you slay a dragon this time?"

"Better," he pronounced with as much bravado as he could muster, leading her over to the plastic sofa and sitting her down beside him. "We found an entire clutch of eggs, way up at the top of the mountain. We had to use these things—these bouncers—to get us up the steep parts. The other team had lured the mother away with their Hunter songs, leaving the eggs totally unprotected. We gathered them all up and blasted them with our gun-blades." He mimicked locking and loading his weapon. "Adios, dragon spawn! Die, die, die!" he crowed.

And then they had screamed. Horrible, blood-curdling screams as the babies boiled alive in their eggs.

But no one wanted to hear that part.

His mother laughed, as he knew she would, rubbing his head with her hand, like she used to when he was little. "My son the Dragon Hunter," she pronounced, looking at him with affection. "If only your dad could see you now."

Connor winced at the mention of his father. His death had been the reason he had enrolled in the Academy and become a Dragon Hunter in the first place. It was his opportunity to avenge his father's death and destroy the creatures that had destroyed his world.

Turned out he was good at it too, having inherited his father's gift to sing the dragons close before gutting them with his gun-blade. They called him a natural, and he had risen high and fast. They called him a hero. He even had fan pages on the transweb, designed by giggly girls from the very best stratas.

He grimaced. If only they knew what a dirty, nasty job it really was. Not half as glamorous as people made it out to be. They saw him as a celebrity. When in reality he was nothing more than a glorified exterminator.

But he was doing what he had to, to keep his father's memory alive and, more importantly, to keep bread on the table. And the last thing he wanted was for his mother to know how much the job weighed on him. She would try to get him to quit, insisting she didn't need the fancy apartment or refrigerator full of food. But even she couldn't argue the necessity of her meds. Dragon Hunter families got first dibs on supply—a reason in and of itself to stay in service.

"How are you feeling?" he asked, peering at her with concerned eyes. It was hard to believe it had been only six months since she'd been diagnosed with bone cancer, due to a vitamin D deficiency developed from a sunless existence below ground. Even with the medicine, she'd fallen so far so fast.

Just one more reason to hate the dragons.

She gave him a wan smile. "Oh, I'm getting along fine," she insisted, but her eyes betrayed her words.

"Sit," he told her, rising from his own seat. "I'll make you some tea."

"That's okay, sweetheart. I think we're out."

Connor frowned, walking over to the small kitchenette and pulling open the refrigerator door. "There's nothing in here!" he cried, turning back to his mother. She stared down at her lap. "I send you money for groceries every week. Why is your refrigerator empty?"

His mother sighed. "I was going to go shopping yesterday, but I felt a little nauseated," she confessed. "And then this morning…" She trailed off, looking guilty.

Connor was at her side in an instant, dropping to his knees. "What, Mother? What happened this morning?" he demanded, pretty much guessing her answer well before she voiced it.

"I got a call from the judge," she replied. "Caleb got himself arrested again last night. Some kind of breaking and entering." She shrugged her bony shoulders. "I used the money to bail him out."

Connor stared at her in fury. "That money was for *you*, Mom. Not him."

"Oh, sweetie, I'm fine," she protested, waving a hand at him. "Remember when I used to cook for you guys on the Surface Lands—back when you were kids? Your father always said I made the best stone soup known to man."

Connor jerked to his feet, squeezing his hands into fists, trying to keep his temper in check in front of her. "I'll be back," he told her as he stuffed his feet back into his boots. "Just stay here. I'll be back soon."

"Where are you going?" his mother asked, her voice anxious.

"I'm going to have a little talk with my brother."

Chapter Seven

When Caleb failed to show up to breakfast the next morning, Trinity barely gave his absence a second thought. It wasn't unusual for him to sleep until noon. And now that she was aware of his nightly adventures in dragon flying, she finally understood why he'd been so exhausted all this time.

She was exhausted too; once Connor had let her out of the barn, she'd gone upstairs to her bedroom to try to get some sleep. Instead, she'd lain awake, rehashing the conversation with Emmy over and over again until she wanted to throw up. A few times she tried to open the connection between them—to apologize for the fight—but Emmy had either fallen asleep or intentionally shut her down. It wasn't until the sun started peeking over the horizon that she finally fell into a restless slumber, only to be woken up an hour later by Grandpa calling her to breakfast.

When lunch came and went and Caleb still hadn't emerged from his bedroom, she decided to go check on him. She was dying to talk to him—not only to apologize for the night before, but also to get his advice on Emmy. Since Caleb was the only other person in their group who had ever worked with dragons, he usually served as expert when Emmy got into one of her moods.

"Caleb? Are you there?" She quietly pushed open his bedroom door, not wanting to startle him. She needn't have worried; he was still thoroughly passed out on the bed, his eyes rolled to the back of his head. To the casual observer, he might have looked dead, or at least locked in a deep coma. But Trinity knew better.

He was back in the Nether. Again.

She sighed, mixed emotions swirling through her as she looked down at him. Part of her wanted to shake him into consciousness—all the while screaming at him for being so irresponsible. For checking out on her when she needed him once again. Lately these trips were getting all too frequent and each one was lasting far too long.

Of course, anytime she asked him about it, he got all defensive. She got to see Emmy every day. This was the only way he could spend time with his beloved dragon Fred.

Trinity got that, she did. But at the same time, she knew all too well the consequences of spending too much time in the Nether. Not only could it rot you and your brain from the inside out like it had her mom, but, according to Connor, it could also have an addictive quality. The more you went, the more you wanted to go. The reality of the Nether fusing to your brain cells, making the fantasy world seem more solid—and more desirable—than real life. There were people in his time, Connor told her—*Netherheads* they called them—who would sell everything they owned—and maybe some things they didn't—just for one more trip.

She glanced over at Caleb's nightstand. She wanted to respect his privacy, give him his space, but she needed to know how bad this was getting. So she pulled open the drawer and started counting the Nether gems he had stashed inside. Last week he'd had thirteen. Now...

Only two.

Ugh. Heart racing, she leaned over the bed, prying open Caleb's fingers and plucking the sapphire he'd grasped in his hand. Sometimes she could jerk him back from the Nether by simply disrupting the energy flow between him and the gem. But this time Caleb only grunted, shifting positions but refusing to regain consciousness.

She'd have to go in after him.

Dropping the gem back into his hands, she closed her own hand around his, trying not to wince at the clammy coldness of his skin as she attempted to prepare herself for entry. She didn't like going to the Nether. Sure, it was kind of cool at first—a place beyond time and space, existing in the collective unconsciousness of dragons. The Nether could be anything you wanted it to be. You could do anything you wanted to do while in its embrace. It could be a true paradise.

It could also be a true prison, digging its claws into your consciousness, ripping away your sense of reality—your desire to live a real life. Visit too often and the Nether would rob you of your health and send your brain into atrophy. And while it became easier and easier to enter, it became harder and harder to leave.

She closed her eyes and gripped Caleb's hand and thought of her mother...who never did.

◆ ◆ ◆

A gust of wind whipped at Trinity's face, prompting her to open her eyes. She looked around. The bed was gone. The farmhouse was gone. In fact, the whole state of Texas was gone.

In its place was a broken world, an arid desert stretching out as far as the eye could see. The soil below was parched and cracked, with dead trees raising their gnarled claws toward the sky. In the distance, a blood-red sun bruised the horizon in a motley of purples and pinks.

She cringed. Caleb was evidently not in a good state of mind.

She scanned the emptiness, a feeling of dread encroaching as she searched for a sign of her friend. At first she came up empty. No sign of life in this nightmare world. Then, shielding her eyes with her hand, she looked up to the sky, finally locking onto a small black shadow far in the distance.

There you are.

She waved her arms wildly in the direction of the shadow, jumping up and down in an effort to get either dragon or rider's attention. At first neither seemed to acknowledge her efforts, and she wondered if they really couldn't see her or were ignoring her on purpose.

She kept jumping and waving anyway. She'd come all this way—to this ugly, dead place—she wasn't about to leave until she'd had her say.

At last her efforts were rewarded, with a great, teal dragon as large as a one-story house coming in for a graceful landing a few yards away, the ground groaning under her weight. Caleb was straddled across the creature's massive back, wearing black leather riding pants and a loose white T-shirt, his eyes shielded by dark sunglasses and his mouth twisted in a frown.

"Fred!" Trinity greeted the dragon, keeping her tone light and breezy. At least one of them would be happy to see her. "Good to see you again, girl! And may I say you're looking extremely shine-a-licious today," she added with a grin. "Are you using a new shampoo to get those scales so sparkly? You simply must tell me your secret!"

Fred bounded over to her with typical Fred-like exuberance, inadvertently taking her rider along for the ride, as Trinity knew she would. After greeting Trin with a huge slurp on her face, the dragon started sniffing her pockets with a determined air. Trin couldn't help but laugh as she attempted to shove the enormous snout away. Emmy might be a TV addict, but Fred was addicted only to TV dinners.

"Hang on, girl, I've got you covered."

She closed her eyes, conjuring up a large leg of lamb in her mind—extra bloody, just as she knew Fred preferred. A moment later, the leg manifested in midair—yet another neat trick of the Nether—then dropped before the dragon with a loud plop. Fred proceeded to attack it with gusto, slurping and chomping happily, the bones crunching under her rock-hard molars. Trinity watched, amused and only a little nauseated. She only wished it were this easy to feed Emmy in real life.

"Oh, Sparknado," Caleb lamented with an exaggerated sigh, sliding down the dragon's wing and landing on the ground with a thump. "After all I do for you. And still you'd sell me out for nothing more than a stinky soup bone." He slapped the dragon's neck affectionately, shaking his head.

As he approached Trinity, she couldn't help but notice how pale and worn he looked—even here in the Nether, where you were supposed to be able to look any way you wanted to with a simple manifest. She frowned. He was using too much spark, coming here day after day, and it was clearly draining him.

"Nice place," she remarked wryly. "Come here often?"

He looked around, as if noticing the dreary backdrop for the first time, then shrugged. "Sorry, Princess. If I'd known you were stopping by for tea, I would have conjured up Buckingham Palace in your honor."

Trinity rolled her eyes. "Can we talk?" she asked, her voice sounding more plaintive then she'd meant it to.

"It's a free Nether."

She sighed. Of course he wasn't going to make things easy for her. And maybe she deserved for it to be hard. She shuffled from foot to foot. "Look," she attempted, "I'm sorry about last night, okay? I probably overreacted. It's just…when I went out to the barn and I couldn't find Emmy…"

Guilt flashed across his face before he could hide it. "You thought the worst."

"You could have told me you were taking her—"

"If I had, would you have let me go?"

She grimaced. "Honestly?" she admitted. "Probably not."

"*Definitely* not," he corrected. "And believe me, I get it. I do. You're trying to keep her safe. Out of sight, out of harm. I totally understand." He paused then muttered, more to himself than her, "I understand more than you can ever know."

Trinity caught his eyes involuntarily flickering to his dragon, and her heart panged at the anguish she saw ghosting his face. In her self-righteous indignation, she'd conveniently forgotten what had happened to Caleb's own beloved Fred in real life. The reason he had to come here to spend time with her now.

"Caleb…" she tried.

He waved her off. "It doesn't matter. The point is, danger-ous or not, it has to be done. Keeping dragons locked up long term is asking for trouble. Sweet as Emmy is, if she doesn't get to fly around once in a while, she's going to start getting restless. And then she'll start growing wild. Dangerous."

Trinity sighed, thinking back to their conversation in the barn. Emmy had been so frustrated. So angry. And that was after spending the night flying free. What would she have been like if Caleb hadn't been letting her stretch her wings on a regular basis?

"She has to understand it's for her own good."

"She's a teenager, Trin," Caleb replied bluntly. "Or the dragon equivalent of a teenager anyway, seeing as they mature much faster than we do. But the idea is the same." He gave her a hard smile. "Imagine a thirteen-year-old who can breathe fire. Do you want to be the one to tell her she's grounded and can't go to the mall?"

Trinity grimaced. "Point taken."

His smile faded. "Keep her locked up and, at best, she'll start to resent you. At worst…" He shrugged. "She may turn against you. Find another to bond with instead."

Trinity stared at him, startled. "What?" she cried out before she could stop herself. "She wouldn't do that. I'm her Fire Kissed. We're bonded."

We're destined…

"Only because she chose you to be," Caleb pointed out. "And she can un-choose you just as easily."

Trinity bit her lower lip, wanting to argue. Wanting to insist that Caleb didn't know what he was talking about. That Emmy was like her sister, her daughter, her best friend—that the dragon would never even think to leave her side. But how did she know that for sure? She thought back to Emmy's secret nights with Caleb. Her mysterious broken scale.

Emmy had asked Trin if she trusted her. But did Emmy trust Trin?

Slumping to a nearby boulder, she scrubbed her face with her hands. *I'm doing the best I can, Em. You know that, right?*

She felt Caleb's pitying stare. "I'm sorry," he said suddenly, his voice softening. "Trust me, I'm not trying to freak you out." He dropped to his knees and took her hands in his. His touch was warm, gentle, and against her better judgment, she found herself meeting his eyes with her own. For one fleeting moment, she wished she could just hide out here in this world forever and leave all the struggles of real life behind.

But that, of course, was impossible. Caleb might be able to justify checking out, but she couldn't. The world needed her. And so did Emmy.

"Look, Trin," Caleb continued. "I'm only trying to get you to face reality. We can't go on like this, despite what my illustrious brother might think. We have to do something. We can't keep running away."

"You're one to talk about running away," she couldn't help but mutter.

"Excuse me?" Caleb's eyes grew hard. He dropped her hands.

She sighed then made a sweeping gesture over the bleak world around them. "How many times have you come here in the last few months?" she asked. "It seems like every time I turn around, you're back in the Nether."

"That's a bit of an exaggeration, don't you think?"

"Is it?" She raised an eyebrow. "You had thirteen gems last week. How many do you have left?"

His face flushed. "I don't know. Plenty, I'm sure. I didn't count them."

"Well I did," she said, "before I came here to find you. You have two left. That means in the last week you've come here eleven times."

A shadow of horror crossed Caleb's face, as if he himself hadn't realized how much he'd been using. And maybe, she thought uneasily, he hadn't.

"You shouldn't be going through my stuff," he growled, as if that were the real issue here. "And besides, what do you care how often I come?" He scrambled to his feet, turning away so she couldn't see his face. "This is between me and Fred. It has nothing to do with you. I come here for her. She needs me."

He gave the teal dragon a heartbreaking look, and Trin winced at the anguish she recognized on his face. She tried to imagine what it would be like if Emmy was the one who had died. Would she herself be finding reasons to come here every day?

Still…

"Look, I'm sorry. I love Fred too," she said. "She's a great dragon. Super smart and super sweet. But she's also dead, Caleb. And there's nothing you can do to change that fact." She sighed, hating the harsh hurt she was piling on with her reality check. But it had to be done. "Emmy, on the other hand, is still alive. *She's* the one who needs our attention now."

Caleb scowled, the sand swirling around his legs as if swept up in a storm. Behind him, lightning slashed across the sky, mirroring his mood. "She doesn't need me. She's got you and my brother. I'm just the a-hole who put her life in danger, remember?"

Trinity shook her head. "Caleb, I already apologized for—"

"Look, you and my brother obviously have everything worked out perfectly between you. Emmy doesn't need me screwing things up all the time. Hell, it'd probably be better for everyone if I just stayed in here with Fred forever."

"That's not true," she cried, her heart breaking at the hurt she could hear hidden beneath his anger. "We *do* need you."

But he had already turned from her, storming across the arid plain, leaving her and his dragon behind. She watched him go for a moment, her stomach lurching with nausea mixed with fear. He wouldn't really stay here, would he? In this horrible, lonely place?

Her mind flashed to the last time she'd seen her mother—of her sunken cheeks, her ghostly pallor, her glazed-over eyes. The Nether had stolen away the woman's very soul and, in the end, death had been the only possible means of escape.

Trinity hadn't been able to save her mother. But Caleb...

Somehow, she found her feet, sprinting after him, reaching him and jerking him around by his arm. His gaze caught hers, trapping her where she stood, and for a moment they just looked at one another as her knees threatened to buckle out from under her.

"*I* need you," she corrected in a hoarse whisper. It was the only thing to say.

He stared at her for a moment, anger and hurt warring on his face, as if he wanted desperately to believe her but just couldn't. Despair washed over her and she found herself moving toward him. Wanting to show him what she couldn't speak.

But before her lips could brush against his, he pushed her away, with a gentleness that belied the tortured look on his face. "Don't," he said in a strangled voice. "Please don't, Trin. It'll only make it harder." He stared down at the ground. "And it's so damn hard already."

Trin's heart broke. "Caleb—"

He shook his head vehemently. "Look, I'll be there for you, okay?" he cried. "You know I will. I dedicated my life to you long ago and nothing has changed. Whatever you want, whatever you need from me, I'll do it. I'll always do it." He gave her an anguished look. "Just please don't ask me to walk away from my dragon. That's the one thing I can never do." He paused, turning away. "Even for you."

Chapter Eight

There it is," Scarlet whispered as she crouched down behind a rusty tractor, a few feet from the darkened farmhouse. Her gaze traveled to the adjacent barn and she closed her eyes to listen. While her ears could pick up nothing beyond the typical cicada and cricket chorus soundtracking the Texas night, her mind caught something else entirely. She opened her eyes, beckoning for Rebekah to catch up. "It's in there," she told her friend, pointing to the barn. "I'm sure of it."

Rebekah joined her behind the tractor, peering around its rear wheel and leveling her eyes on the darkened farmhouse and barn. Then she turned back to Scarlet. "How do you know?" she asked, her voice filled with skepticism. "It's so dark I can barely see my hand in front of my face, never mind a fire-breathing beast hiding out in a barn."

Scarlet shrugged, not sure how to explain. Truthfully, she had no idea *how* she knew—just that she did, without a shadow of a doubt. Almost as if she'd been gifted with some kind of crazy dragon-homing device directly implanted into her brain. Had the dragon's blood connected her to the creature in some weird psychic way, letting her know where it was at all times? That was, of course, how these things always seemed to play out in the fantasy novels she'd read, where poor peasant girls of no consequence bonded with dragons and became heroes of the realm.

But this wasn't a fantasy. It was real life. And how this was all happening was a complete mystery. But it didn't matter, she told herself. The important thing was they were there. They'd get in, they'd get their video, and they'd get back to the football game before anyone knew they were gone.

"Why would a dragon be hiding out at the Old McCormick place anyway?" Rebekah added, looking doubtfully at the neglected yard, strangled by weeds. "You'd think a creature of myth and legend would choose someplace a little more...I don't know...glamorous?"

"Maybe the Four Seasons was booked for the weekend," Scarlet suggested wryly.

"Or they just couldn't afford the fire insurance premiums?"

Scarlet giggled, gesturing for Rebekah to follow her as she left the tractor and crept toward the barn, careful to keep her footsteps light and not make too much noise. The last thing they needed was to scare away the dragon before they could film it.

Just one shot. One really good shot, Scarlet told herself. *That's all we need.*

She still admittedly felt a little guilty about the whole thing. Like she was some evil paparazzi, stalking the poor dragon in order to exploit it for cash. But she made Rebekah promise they'd remove the identifying geotags and not tell anyone where they filmed the footage. This way, the dragon couldn't be tracked down by anyone else who might have a more nefarious purpose in mind.

No dragons will be harmed in the making of this video, she reminded herself. *And no mothers will be either...ever again...if all goes to plan.*

She imagined her mother's face when she presented her with the check. It didn't have to be the millions that Rebekah had bragged about—just a few grand for a security deposit and a U-Haul rental. Enough to pack their bags and drive out to New Mexico, to get a place on the reservation near Grandmother and start a new life, just the two of them. Leaving the monster behind for good. He was too lazy, too unorganized, and, of course, too broke to follow them that far. And she was pretty sure out of sight meant out of mind.

Somehow she managed to reach the barn without tripping over any rusty farm equipment. Rebekah joined her a moment later, flicking on her cell phone and shining it at the front doors. The dim light revealed a large, imposing padlock, securing the doors in place. Damn. Scarlet felt a sinking feeling in her stomach. It was locked from the outside. Which meant there was probably no dragon squatting on the inside. Had she been wrong?

"Maybe someone locked it inside the barn?" Rebekah suggested, a little too kindly, as if trying to spare Scarlet's feelings.

"Yeah, maybe," she muttered, walking around the barn with her own cell phone shining, standing on her tiptoes to try to look in the windows. Unfortunately, it appeared as if they'd all been blocked out from the inside with dark blankets. She sighed, returning to Rebekah, disappointment dropping like lead in her stomach.

"I don't know," she said, shrugging. "Maybe my sixth sense was just a side effect of today's Salisbury steak special..."

Rebekah gave her an exaggerated shocked look. "Are you

saying you're already thwarted, Scarlet-in-the-library-with-the-revolver?" She clucked in mock disappointment.

"I take it you're not?"

"Come on. No way is some pesky padlock going to keep me from fame, fortune, and a Ford Fiesta. Watch and learn, grasshopper."

Scarlet watched, eyebrows raised, as her friend pulled out a portable handsaw from her backpack, likely swiped from her father's toolbox. "Will that break the lock?" she asked, a shred of hope rising within her.

"Well, it's no sonic screwdriver, but it should do the job," Rebekah replied with a grin. She grabbed the lock and began sawing.

"Remind me to text you next time I get locked out of the house," Scarlet said with grudging admiration.

But as her friend worked at the lock, her apprehension grew. What if she was wrong about all of this? What if they went through all this trouble to break and enter only to find nothing more than a rusty toolbox and a few dusty saddles inside?

Then we'll be right back where we started from, she told herself. *Nothing lost, nothing gained.*

But if she was right…

Promise me, Scarlet, promise me you'll look after Mom.

She squared her jaw. The dragon would be there. She had to be.

"Ta-da!" Rebekah proclaimed a moment later as the lock cracked open. "It's show time!"

"Shhh…" Scarlet hissed, slapping her on the arm. "Can we at least vaguely attempt to be stealthy here?" There were no lights coming from the farmhouse, but still. You never knew who might be in earshot. And then there was the dragon itself, if it was indeed in the barn.

"Sorry," Rebekah whispered. "I just got excited. Who knew a life of crime could be so exhilarating?"

Scarlet didn't dignify her with an answer. Instead, she reached out, wrapping her hand around the door handle and slowly pulling it open. The rusty hinges groaned in protest, and for a moment the door refused to budge. But with Rebekah's help, they finally managed to pry it open enough to slip through.

"Ew!" Rebekah whispered as she stuck her head in—then quickly back out. "It's like the freaking bog of eternal stench in there!" She pinched her wrinkled nose. "Someone seriously needs to change drago's litter box." She reached into her bag for her dad's video camera. Pulling off the lens cap, she turned it on and switched it to night vision. The view screen illuminated an otherworldly green color as the inside of the barn came into focus.

"Okay," she whispered. "I'm rolling. Here be dragons— take one." She slipped into the barn, panning the camera from left to right. Scarlet followed, her misgivings increasing by the second. It was so dark all she could focus on was the glow coming from the camera, a green circle bobbing in midair. She squinted at it, trying to see what—

A pair of round eyes blinked back at her.

"Oh my God! Oh my freaking God!" Rebekah shrieked, dropping the camera to the ground.

"Shhh!" Scarlet hissed. "What are you—"

She felt her friend push past her, diving for the door.

"Get back here!" she cried, dashing after her. "What about your Ford Fiesta?"

But Rebekah was already halfway to the tractor. By the time Scarlet got there, her friend was on her bike and ready to go. From the glow of her cell phone, Scarlet could see her face had turned pure white.

"Forget it. It was a crazy idea," Rebekah declared. "I'm going back to the game."

"You left your dad's video camera in the barn."

"He can buy a new one. Did you see that thing, Scarlet? Did you see it?"

"Yes, I saw it. That was kind of the whole point of coming here, remember?"

"I thought you were joking," Rebekah cried, sounding close to tears. "I thought we were just messing around. That it was going to turn out to be a mutated goat or something. But that thing…It's real. It's…" She shook her head angrily. "Get on your bike and let's go."

Scarlet surprised herself by shaking her head. "No."

"Are you insane?"

"We came here to get that video. I'm not leaving until I get it." After all, it was just a new car for Rebekah. But Scarlet's whole future depended on these particular fifteen seconds of fame.

"Fine. But if you're not back in twenty minutes, I'm going to call the cops."

Scarlet let out a frustrated breath. "You won't need to. I'll be in and out. No big deal."

Rebekah gave her one more disparaging look then pedaled her bike off down the road. Scarlet watched her go, sighing, then turned back to the barn. She was on her own.

"Okay, dragon," she muttered. "Hope you're ready for your close-up."

Slowly she made her way back to the barn. The door was still cracked and she wondered, for a moment, why the creature hadn't tried to follow them outside. With careful steps, she slipped through the doors and found the camera on the ground, still rolling and glowing green. Picking it up, she scanned the barn again, her hands shaking so hard she wasn't sure even steady cam could compensate.

"Hey, dragon," she whispered hoarsely. "Are you in here? I'm not going to hurt you. I just need a little video, okay? It's for a good cause, I swear."

As if in answer, the dragon stepped out from the shadows. Now that her eyes had adjusted a bit, Scarlet could make out her silhouette. It was small. Well, small for a dragon, anyway. The night before in the woods, she'd been so freaked out, she'd pictured the creature to be larger than life. But in reality, it wasn't much bigger than her neighbor's Golden Retriever. Was that normal for real-life dragons? Or was she just a baby?

She trained the video camera on the creature. "That's it," she whispered. "Good girl. That's a good girl."

Good girl? What does she think I am, some kind of dog?

Scarlet squeaked, nearly dropping the camera. She staggered backward, her eyes bugging from her head as she stared at the dragon.

"Oh my God, you can talk?" she cried.

The dragon looked just as startled. It backed up slowly, looking at Scarlet with wary eyes.

You can hear me?

The voice whispered across her consciousness like a gentle

breeze, though the creature's mouth never moved. It was high-pitched, young, definitely female—and definitely belonging to the dragon standing in front of her. Even though that was, of course, totally, utterly impossible. But then, so was everything else about this whole scenario.

An excitement swelled in Scarlet's stomach. A dragon—a talking dragon. This was getting cooler and cooler by the second.

"I can hear you just fine," she said, feeling a little silly talking out loud to the creature. But it seemed rude not to answer her, and she had no idea how to do the whole mental telepathy thing.

The dragon gaped at her for a moment, looking as astounded as Scarlet felt.

How is that possible? she asked at last. *Humans can never understand anything I try to tell them. Well, besides my Fire Kissed, of course, but she's different.* The dragon paused, peering at her with suspicious eyes. *Are you sure you're human?*

"Uh, yeah, last I checked," Scarlet stammered, still overwhelmed by the fact that she was actually conversing with a creature of myth and legend in a rundown Texas barn. If only Rebekah were still here—though it sounded like it was quite possible that her friend would not be able to hear the dragon, even if she were.

But Scarlet could hear her just fine. Much like she'd been able to sense her presence in the barn without knowing why.

"Maybe it has something to do with your blood?" she added, a thought striking her. "That's how I was able to track you down. I mean, that's my theory anyway."

The dragon cocked her head in question. *My blood?*

"Yeah, you know," Scarlet said with growing confidence. "Remember last night in the woods? You healed my arm with your blood. And ever since then, I've been able to feel you somehow. Like, where you are." She considered this for a moment. "Maybe it's like when people give vampires their blood; they become psychically connected for all eternity." She couldn't help a small smile at this. Imagine being psychically connection with a dragon! How cool would that be?

The dragon raised a scaly eyelid.

Are you a vampire?

"Well, no, of course not," Scarlet admitted lamely, feeling her cheeks heat. She wasn't sure if that had been a sincere question or if the dragon was teasing her. (A dragon…teasing her!) "Vampires don't really exist, obviously. I mean, I don't think they do. Of course up until yesterday I didn't think dragons existed either, so really, what do I know?"

She was rambling. Babbling like a fool. To a dragon!

Dragons don't really exist either, the creature informed her. Scarlet watched as she nudged something under a nearby bench with her nose. A moment later, a weak beam of light shone through the barn. Some kind of battery powered lantern? *Well, not anymore anyway. As far as I know, I'm the last one. The rest died out millions of years ago.*

She said this matter-of-factly, but Scarlet thought she caught a flicker of sadness in her eyes and was reminded suddenly of a movie she saw as a kid. A fantasy cartoon about the world's last unicorn. The unicorn had been lonely, desperate to find others of her kind. She wondered if this dragon was lonely too.

"What are you doing in here anyway?" she found herself asking, looking around the barn now that she had some light. It was packed with rusty farm equipment and old saddles, and there were definitely bones of unidentified animals mixed within the hay. She wondered if she should be scared—this dragon was clearly not a salad eater—but then decided if she'd wanted a midnight snack, she would have already gotten started. "Did someone capture you last night after you healed me?" She frowned, suddenly angry at the idea of someone trapping the dragon in a place like this. A beautiful, exotic creature like her should not be locked up in a cage.

But to her surprise, the dragon shook her head. *This is where I live.*

"What?" Scarlet cried before she could stop herself. "You live here? In the Old McCormick barn? Since when?"

A few weeks? A month? I'm not entirely sure.

Scarlet, who couldn't imagine spending ten more minutes in this dark and smelly place, shuddered. "Then why were you locked in?" she asked, trying to put the puzzle pieces together. "I mean, if this is your home and all."

The dragon's face fell, and for a moment she didn't answer. Then she sighed. *She says it's for my own good.*

"She?" Scarlet questioned. Another puzzle piece. "Who's she?"

My Fire Kissed. She's human, like you. She lives in the main house with the boys.

"And leaves you locked up in the barn?" Scarlet finished, feeling offended on the dragon's behalf.

The boy used to take me out to fly, the dragon told her, looking up at her with heartbreakingly sad blue eyes. *That's how I found you in the cave. But then she found out. And she was angry with me. She says from now on I can't leave the barn.*

"Ever?" Scarlet asked, incredulous. "But that's horrible!"

She shot a glance at the house, her mouth twisting into a frown. She had half a mind to speed dial PETA or at least the Vista Animal Control. There had to be some kind of animal cruelty law against keeping an exotic beast captive in a barn twenty-four/seven—like when people smuggled in tigers from China and kept them in their apartments.

"Maybe I should have a word with Miss Fire Kissed," she determined, rising to her feet. But the dragon leapt into her path, her eyes wide with alarm.

You can't! she cried. *She'll be furious if she finds you here. And the boys might try to hurt you.* The dragon stared dejectedly at the ground. *I like you. You're the only one I can talk to besides her. I don't want you to get hurt.*

Scarlet clenched her fists in frustration. "I know, but..."

Besides, she's not here, the dragon added sadly. *She went to the game. With the hunter.*

"What?" Scarlet stared at the creature. "She's not even here? She's at the freaking football game?"

Fury flowed through her like hot lava. It was too much. This girl—who had been gifted the most amazing gift ever—a freaking magical talking dragon of all things—had actually chosen to take off and hook up rather than stay home and devote her life to the care and feeding of this beautiful, majestic gift she'd been given? What the hell was wrong with her?

"So what's this chick's plan then? Is she going to just keep you here forever? Until you die of old age?" Scarlet demanded. "Is that what you want?"

The dragon hung her head. *It's what she wants that matters.*

"Who cares what she wants? She can't even be bothered to stay home with you!"

You don't understand. The dragon's voice was anguished now. *She's my Fire Kissed. She knows what's best for me.*

Okay, that did it. Scarlet didn't know what a fire kissed was exactly. But she did know the conversation was getting far too familiar. After all, how many times had she had it with her mother over the years of living with the monster?

It's for my own good.

It's what he wants.

You don't want to make him angry.

No matter what horrible thing the monster decided to do, her mother always found a way to excuse it—and position herself permanently under his thumb.

Just like this poor, sweet dragon. This beautiful, regal creature who should be soaring through the skies, wild and free. Instead she was cooped up in a dark, smelly barn, her wings all but clipped, making excuses for a girl who obviously cared more about possessing her than keeping her happy.

It was time for some tough love.

"Look, I'm sure this girl—your Fire Kissed—is cool and all. She's probably really nice. But you can't just let her order you around. I mean, like you said, you're a dragon, not a dog. You may share a bond, but that doesn't make you her slave. You should be able to make your own decisions."

A glimmer of light seemed to flash in the dragon's eyes. *Do you really think so?*

"I know so," Scarlet confirmed, now on a roll. "Like when you found me and saved my life. Which was amazing and awesome by the way—thank you very much. But what if you hadn't? What if you had listened to this girl and stayed home instead? Then I'd be dead. Would that be better? If I had died?"

The dragon looked horrified. *No, of course not.*

"Look, I understand you feel grateful for all she's done for you. But that doesn't mean you have to always obey without question. You need to stand up to her. Tell her what you want, what you need. Insist on the respect you deserve." She grinned. "Like, hey you—I'm a dragon! Hear me roar!"

She raised her fist in solidarity, starting to really get into the argument now. For a moment she imagined herself as some kind of dragon activist, fighting for reptilian rights. Of course, if this was the last one of her kind, it might not be much of a career.

Still, if she could save one dragon...

You're right, the dragon said suddenly. *You're absolutely right. We're supposed to be a team. I should be able to have a say.*

Scarlet nodded eagerly, excited the dragon was actually listening to her. Unlike, say, her mother who would always blow off her protests and tell her she didn't understand before making more excuses about why she needed to stay. Maybe Scarlet would never be able to help her mother—but maybe, just maybe she could help this dragon.

"Yeah! You tell her!" she crowed. "You tell her who's the big, bad..." She trailed off. "Wait, where are you going?"

The dragon turned to look back at her from the barn's entrance. *To go find Trinity, of course.*

"Um..." Scarlet shifted from foot to foot. "You're just going to leave the barn? Right now?"

Yes. Why not now? The door is open. Who knows when I will get another chance?

Scarlet's heart beat wildly in her chest. Suddenly this seemed very, very wrong. She followed the dragon outside. "Do you really think this is a good idea?"

It was your idea, the dragon reminded her pointedly.

Oh right. Scarlet bit her lower lip, her thoughts whirling madly. She'd been so eager to prove her point, so wrapped up in the similarities of the dragon's situation and her mother's that she hadn't stopped to realize the creature would take her literally.

Had she just inadvertently set a fire-breathing beast on her hometown?

But she's not violent, she reminded herself. *She's gentle. Sweet. She saved my life. She's not going to go hurt anyone. She just wants to be free. And she totally has the right to be free.*

Still, as she watched the creature spread her wings and push off on her back feet, leaping into the air, she worried. And she continued to worry as the dragon disappeared into the night sky. Had she just made a huge mistake?

Well, there was nothing she could do about it now. Shaking her head, she headed back into the barn, grabbing the video camera and pulling out the memory card, crushing it under her heel. Now that she knew the dragon on a personal level, there was no way she'd be able to exploit her online. She'd have to find another way to raise the money for her and her mother.

"Hey! Who are you? What are you doing in there?"

As she stepped out of the barn, her eyes fell upon a guy around her own age, running out of the farmhouse, brandishing some kind of strange-looking gun. Crap. Scarlet staggered backward, her gaze darting around the yard, looking for somewhere to run.

But the guy had already reached her. Grabbing her by the neck of her shirt, he yanked her toward him, gun to the back of her head as his blue eyes pierced hers with frightening intensity. "Who are you?" he demanded. "And what were you doing with Emmy?"

Emmy? The dragon's name was Emmy?

"Emmy had to run a little errand," she told the boy, trying to will her voice to stay casual. "I'm sure she'll be right back when she's done."

The guy stared at her, an incredulous look on his face. "You let her out of the barn?" He looked up into the sky, his eyes wide and frightened. "Why would you let her out of the barn?" He slapped a hand over his face. "Oh man. Trinity is never going to believe this is not my fault."

Scarlet's heart beat wildly in her chest, the feeling that she'd just made a huge mistake raging back with a vengeance. "I was just…" she stammered. "I just wanted to help her."

"Well, you didn't help her," the boy sputtered. "You put her in danger. Not only her," he added, "but the entire world."

Chapter Nine

ook! There she is! There's Caitlin!"

Trinity couldn't help a small squeal of delight as she spotted her best friend, clad in a short blue skirt and matching tank top, enthusiastically waving a pair of blue-and-white pompons as she ran onto the field with the other cheerleaders. It was all Trin could do not to dive off the bleachers and tackle the girl with the biggest bear hug ever known to friendkind. She hadn't realized how much she'd missed her until she saw her face again.

"Remember what you promised," Connor scolded, giving her a warning look. Which didn't seem as fierce as it might have had he not been wearing a ridiculous fake mustache, plaid flannel shirt, and trucker hat. She knew her own disguise was probably equally silly: a blond shag wig to hide her trademark black curls and huge Hollywood sunglasses to conceal her dark eyes. In fact, she'd pretty much had to promise her firstborn child to get Grandpa to even consider letting her come to the game in the first place after Connor had presented her with the tickets last week; he thought it was far too dangerous. But the Dragon Hunter convinced the elder man that the opportunity for her to see her old high school team, The Mighty Oaks, take on the Vista Vultures in spring football was too important to pass up. And he would ensure her safety personally.

She realized Connor was still glaring at her. "I know, I know," she grumped. "I'm not stupid, you know. Just excited." She glanced out over the field at the players running to the line of scrimmage. The night was warm, with a slight breeze and the smell of barbecue from a nearby food trailer permeating the air. It was funny—back in the day she didn't really even like high school football and would usually turn down Caitlin's never-ending invites to attend one of the games. But now, the normalcy of it all was a little slice of Heaven.

Connor's expression softened. "I know," he assured her. "And I'm glad we got to come." He grinned. "Go Mighty Oaks!" he added, grabbing her hand in his and raising it into the air.

The gesture was meant to be friendly—school spirit and all that. But the electric sparks that jolted through her made it feel otherwise, and her mind flashed guiltily to Caleb's face as he'd pulled away from her in the Nether earlier that week. For one paranoid second, she imagined him watching her now from across the field, his eyes filled with hurt.

It'll only make it harder. And it's so damn hard already.

And it was. It was so damn hard. Both boys had given her so much—sacrificing everything they had, everything they were—to keep her and Emmy safe. One a knight in shining armor. The other her wayward rogue. It was crazy how two boys who looked completely identical on the outside could be so different on the inside, and even crazier how each of their differences excited her in a different way. If this were one of her teenage romance novels, she'd probably be having torrid affairs with both of them as she tried desperately to make up her mind.

But that was out of the question. Especially now, with the two brothers already at one another's throats, the tension between them taut as piano wires and ready to snap at the slightest provocation. She had to stay strong, keep them both at an arm's length. Love them both—but be with neither. Unlike her favorite heroines, she couldn't afford to be Team Connor or Team Caleb.

In her story, it was Team Dragon or the end of the world.

Not that the whole dragon partnership was going all that well either. Emmy was still pissed at her, and Trinity had all but decided to skip the game entirely to stay home with her and try to make amends. But Connor wouldn't hear of it. She'd been looking forward to this night for days. Emmy would have to understand. And if it made her feel better, they could swing by the Wal-Mart on the way so she could buy Emmy the last season of *Merlin* as a peace offering, which seemed like a great idea. She hugged the bag to her chest now, imagining the excitement on the dragon's face when she presented her with her gift. Emmy would have to forgive her and then they could spend the rest of the night curled up bingeing on their favorite show.

But first, the game. She leaned forward as the Mighty Oaks' quarterback let the ball fly, straight into the arms of running back Mike Brukowski, who went tearing down the field, the ball gripped firmly under his arm. As he passed the group of cheerleaders, Trin noticed Mike nod his head at Caitlin, and Caitlin wave back with a shy smile. Trinity's eyebrows rose. Her friend had had a crush on Mike since he transferred sophomore year. Had they finally hooked up?

Unexpectedly, tears misted her eyes. Once upon a time, she

would have known that. She'd be the first to know that. Hell, she wouldn't have put it past Caitlin not to text her a selfie mid–first kiss—unable to wait to share the news. They'd been so close. They'd shared everything. Now her best friend was a complete stranger with a life that Trin knew nothing about.

And vice versa.

It had only been three months, and yet so much had changed. She had changed—irreparably and forever—and she'd never have the luxury of this kind of normalcy ever again. Sometimes she wished she could take the blue pill like in *The Matrix* and go back to how things used to be. When she was a normal girl with normal worries of tests and teachers and boys who either liked you or didn't. A girl who didn't have the fate of the world falling through her fingers.

You're being selfish, she scolded herself. *The world needs you. Everyone out there on the field, in the stands—they need you. Even if they don't know it.*

"You okay?" Connor asked. He looked at her, his blue eyes rimmed with concern. Had he read her mind—overheard her troubled thoughts? No, he was far too polite to pry into her consciousness uninvited—it was probably written all over her face. "Do we need to go?"

"No." She shook her head. No matter how painful this was, there was no way she was going to walk away now. This might be her last chance to embrace her old life—and she was going to hold on to it with both hands for as long as it lasted.

The game turned out to be pretty exciting—with the two teams evenly matched and the score bouncing back and forth in each school's favor so many times that Trin lost count. They were tied and going into overtime when Connor returned with two mustard-covered hot dogs and an obscenely large Diet Coke. Trin's mouth watered as she took a bite of her dog, rejoicing in the salty goodness. It'd been quite a while since they'd eaten much of anything beyond Top Ramen.

"Hot dogs, football, a warm spring night—I've got to admit, sometimes your world ain't half-bad," Connor remarked with his mouth full as he polished off his own dog.

She couldn't help a small grin. "Thanks for forcing me to come," she said. "It's really nice to be out and—"

"OH MY GOD!"

A voice, followed by a scream, suddenly cut through the night air, silencing the steady hum of voices around the stadium. As everyone looked around, trying to identify the source of the cry, Trinity glanced over at Connor in alarm. "What was that?"

He shook his head, his expression tense. "I don't—"

Panicked voices rang out, drowning the rest of his words. Trinity watched in confusion as everyone started scrambling to their feet at once, the hum of the stadium now rising to an unsteady roar. An icy fear tripped down her back as she climbed onto her seat to get a better look. Connor joined her a moment later and together they craned their necks and stood on tiptoe trying to figure out what the heck was going on.

Then she saw it. Saw exactly what was going on.

Or, more precisely, *who*.

No.

No, no, no!

The world went silent, like a movie gone into special-effects mode, the scene playing out in slow motion before her eyes. People running, people screaming. Eyes bulging, mouths gaping.

A small green dragon, standing at the fifty-yard line, innocently flapping her wings while scanning the crowd.

See, Trinity? I'm perfectly fine! No big deal!

Emmy, no!

Trinity turned to Connor. "How did she get out?" she demanded, the panic rising inside her, threatening to consume. "Do you think...Caleb...?" But even as she said his name, she doubted he would have been that stupid. And he didn't have a key to the new padlock either. But what other explanation could there be?

Connor didn't answer. He didn't have to, she supposed, seeing as the how made no difference. It didn't matter how she'd gotten out—just that she had.

And the dragon was officially out of the bag.

Maybe if there had been only one person to see her. Or maybe even just two or three, then she and Connor might have been able to do something. To use their psychic gifts to convince people their eyes were playing tricks on them. But there was no way to convince an entire stadium full of people that they hadn't seen a real-life medieval monster come in for a landing in the middle of the local high school football field.

Go home, Emmy! she pushed to the dragon. *You need to go home now!*

But the dragon didn't answer.

"I'll get the van," Connor told her. "You get Emmy."

She dove from her seat, taking the steps two at a time, dodging the crowds the best she could. As she made her way toward the dragon, the wig flew from her head and her sunglasses were trampled, but she no longer cared. No one would notice her now. Not when there was a freaking dragon to focus on.

Finally she made it to the field where she found Emmy surrounded by a curious crowd, all eyes glued on her. The dragon seemed to be eating up the attention too, prancing around like a circus clown, tossing her head and flipping her tail and doing little barrel rolls to the delight of her attentive audience. It would have been totally cute if the implications weren't so terrifying.

"Get out of my way!" Trinity cried, trying to fight her way through. "Emmy, stop that! Now!"

They like me! Emmy cried. *They really like me!* She was beaming from ear to ear.

"Emmy, please! You don't know what you're doing!" Trinity cried with a sob.

"Trinity? Oh my God, Trinity, is that you?"

A familiar voice broke through the cacophony. Trinity turned, suddenly finding herself face-to-face with none other than Caitlin herself. Her friend stared at her in disbelief—as if she were seeing a ghost. "What are you doing here?" she cried. "Where have you been?"

Trinity opened her mouth, but before she could speak, Emmy's cry ripped through the air.

She whirled around, her eyes widening in horror. In the moments she'd been distracted, the once-friendly crowd had turned on the dragon. She couldn't tell what had happened exactly, only that a small boy was on the ground, screaming bloody murder, and several people were on their knees trying to come to his aid. Had Emmy accidentally hit him with her tail while spinning around? Or maybe stomped on his foot? The dragon's coordination was iffy at best, especially when she was excited.

Whatever had happened, fascination had now split into fear and fury. And calls of "Get it!" and "Take it down!" now rang through the air. One of the players had grabbed the chain used to mark first down length and was waving it in Emmy's direction like a lasso, trying to loop it around her neck. Another had thrown a large blanket over her back, which had tangled in Emmy's wings and prevented her from taking off. Emmy snorted and struggled and Trin could see the terrified whites in her eyes, the foam at her mouth.

"Trinity?" Caitlin said again. "Please talk to me! Everyone's saying all these things. They think you're a terrorist. They think you did all this stuff against the government. I told them you wouldn't. That there was no way you'd be mixed up in any of this but—"

Emmy let out a horrifying cry—drowning out all other noise. Trinity's gaze darted from the dragon to her best friend, feeling as if she were being torn in two.

"I'm sorry, Caitlin," she stammered. "I—I'm sorry. I love you. But I—can't."

She turned her back on her best friend, diving into the crowd, kicking and pushing her way through in a desperate attempt to reach her dragon. From behind her, she could still hear Caitlin's protests and pleading, but she pushed them out of her mind. Caitlin was part of the past she left behind, as much as it broke her heart to think it. She had to concentrate now on the future.

Caitlin loved her. But Emmy needed her.

She burst from the crowd just as Mike Brukowski looped the chain around Emmy's neck. He was trying to drag her forward, like a dog on a leash, as the crowd cheered him on. Almost everyone had their phones held up, taking pictures and video with unabashed excitement as Emmy writhed and yanked against the chain, screeching mournfully.

"No!" Trin cried. "Stop it! Leave her alone!"

But they didn't stop. And Trin knew what would come next. Emmy would only be trying to protect herself—but that wouldn't matter in the end. The flames would burst from her mouth. Someone would be in the way. That someone would die. And things would suddenly get a lot, lot worse.

She dove at Mike, slamming her fist into his face as hard as she could. He screamed, caught off guard and knocked off balance by the force of the blow, falling to the ground and thankfully letting go of the chain.

But Trin's relief was short-lived as Emmy realized she now had the advantage. The chain that had once held her down had now become her weapon and she whipped it at the crowd, sending them sprawling backward. The metal slapped against another child, knocking him over, and he screamed in agony.

"Emmy, stop! It's okay! Please stop!" Trin begged, tears running down her cheeks. "Please, please stop!"

But Emmy couldn't hear her now. And the flames were rumbling in her throat. Her jaws started to creak open…

Trinity dove for the dragon—knowing even as she did it that it might be too late. That Emmy, in her panic, wouldn't recognize her and would aim her deadly breath on Trin herself. But she had to take the risk. There was no other way.

She reached the dragon, grabbing the blanket and throwing it to the ground. Then she jumped onto the beast's back, wrapping her arms around Emmy's neck. She squeezed her as tightly as she could then gave the command.

"Fly, Emmy!" she screamed. "Fly now!"

And so the dragon did.

Chapter Ten

If you were to close your eyes and imagine someone riding on the back of a dragon, you might conjure up images that could be described as "majestic" and "beautiful" and "regal." Maybe even "graceful" and "elegant" might come to mind. Sadly this was not the case for Trinity as she desperately tried to hang on to Emmy's neck as the dragon took flight.

Emmy might have grown a lot since she'd hatched the size of a baby bird—but she still wasn't near the size of something ride-able, like, say, a horse. She had no space between her wings and neck for Trin to wrap her legs around, and so she was forced to kick them out behind her and let them dangle in thin air, her belly chafing painfully against the dragon's back as together they tumbled through the skies.

The phrase "flying by the seat of your pants" might have come to mind, if anything had been able to come to Trinity's mind beyond the fact that she was quite possibly about to die.

"Don't look down, don't look down, don't look down," she chanted to herself as her arm muscles burned in protest. She'd been afraid of heights pretty much as long as she could remember, and though she trusted the young dragon with her life in a purely esoteric sense, it wouldn't be Emmy's fault if she were to, say, not be able to hold on.

As they tore through the skies, the implications of what had happened hit her hard and fast. Their cover had been blown wide open. There would be no hiding now. They'd have to find a way to slip out of town, maybe out of the state. Find another squat to hole up in before the authorities descended.

If she survived this flight at all.

And even then…She thought back to all the cameras flashing, the video rolling. Emmy swinging the chain and knocking out that poor little boy. By the end of the night, they would be the top news story on every channel. On the front page of every paper. Blowing up Facebook, Instagram. Dragons trending on Twitter.

I thought they liked me! Emmy's voice suddenly burst through her thoughts, sounding confused and upset and scared. *Why did they try to hurt me?*

Trinity closed her eyes. This was not the time to say I told you so. "I'm sorry, Emmy. People are weird sometimes. Especially about stuff they don't understand."

But I didn't do anything wrong. I was just…dancing. So the little ones would laugh.

"I know, Em. I know…" Trin squeezed her neck, feeling the tears slip down her cheeks. "It doesn't make sense. But now you know. And from now on we can't—"

Whizz!

What was that? Horrified, she dared look down at the crowd below, her eyes falling upon the distinct outline of a rifle, pointed in their direction. Were they actually shooting at them? There were strict laws against packing heat on school grounds, but that didn't mean everyone followed them. And each one of them probably felt more than justified in their God-given right to shoot down the creature that had invaded their Friday night lights.

Not that their bullets would do much good. Emmy's scales were stronger than titanium and only special bullets—made in the future—could pierce her single soft scale to have a prayer of bringing her down. That was one of the reasons it was so easy for dragons to take over the world the first time around. They were practically immune to traditional weaponry.

Trinity, on the other hand, was not. And with her and Emmy's life force intertwined, a bullet meant for the dragon that ended up hitting her instead could do them both in.

Another shot rang out. Trinity jerked as blood burst from her arm. She screamed, losing her grip on Emmy's neck as white-hot pain cannonballed through her entire body. For a moment she thought she would let go altogether, that she would tumble off the dragon and fall screaming to her death below. But somehow she managed to hold on, gritting her teeth and pulling herself back into a semi-stable position. But the trail of blood streaming in the wind told her she wouldn't last long.

"Emmy! You have to land. Now!" she told the dragon. "I can't hold on!"

The dragon turned her head to regard her mistress once again, her blue eyes now locking onto Trinity's arm. She gave a loud, angry snarl then changed direction, picking up speed and heading for a copse of trees up ahead. Trinity squeezed her eyes shut, trying to focus on anything but the pain piercing her skin. But visions of tumbling to her death from hundreds of feet up honestly didn't serve to make her feel much better.

She won't let me fall. She won't let me fall.

Emmy dove down, trading altitude for the protection of the trees, and Trin felt the branches scrape her face and claw at her arms and legs as they dropped into the forest. One particularly gnarly limb slapped hard against her wounded arm, and for a moment she almost lost her balance completely. But somehow she managed to keep a fragile grip on the dragon until Emmy came in for a semi-graceful landing in the middle of a small clearing.

Trin rolled off, crashing down onto the ground with a loud oomph. A rock dug into her back and her ankle jarred. But the pain barely registered, she was so happy to be on solid ground again.

"Emmy..." she tried, wanting to express her gratitude. She tried to turn her head to acknowledge the dragon. But it felt so heavy. So, so heavy.

And a moment later, she fell into blackness.

Chapter Eleven

Scarlet walked her bike down the side of the road on her way back to the football stadium, confusion and concern weighing her every step. From time to time, she glanced up into the sky—half hoping to see the emerald green dragon, Emmy, swimming among the glittering stars. But save for a few bats diving for mosquitos, the sky remained empty.

As if the whole night's adventure had been nothing more than a dream.

Or a nightmare as the case might be. The boy had been so furious at her—she was half-convinced he'd shoot her with his strange-looking gun and end things then and there. Instead, he'd taken off, running through the fields, screaming after the dragon, leaving Scarlet behind to wonder what it was she'd just done. She'd tried to ask the boy questions—like why had they locked the dragon in Mrs. McCormick's old barn in the first place—but he'd only given her a disgusted look before turning away.

And so there had been nothing left to do but to gather her things and head back to Vista Memorial High, where her mother was supposed to pick her up after the football game. If she hurried, maybe she could even catch the end of the game, she told herself, desperate to cling to a shred of normalcy in a night gone wild. The Vultures were playing their biggest rivals, the Mighty Oaks, and it was bound to be an exciting game.

It wasn't until she got closer to the stadium and found it strangled by police cars, fire trucks, and ambulances that she realized just how exciting it must have been.

"What the…?" she whispered, picking up her pace, the flashing lights of the emergency vehicles lighting her way as the sirens wailed in her ears. Had something happened? Had there been a school shooting or some kind of bomb threat? She'd seen plenty of those on the news in the last couple of years—but nothing like that had ever happened in Vista.

As she drew closer, she started to recognize people she knew. It was a small town and everyone would have come out to support the home team. But no one was tailgating now. Instead, fellow students huddled in close circles, girls sobbing, boys curling their hands into fists, while full-grown men and women staggered past, looking dazed and shell-shocked under the parking lot lights. Reporters were arriving too, leaping from their news vans to lay siege on the emergency teams, waving their microphone flags and demanding answers. What could have happened? Scarlet's pulse kicked up in growing alarm.

She stopped a girl heading in the opposite direction. Her hair was mussed and black mascara ran down her cheeks. "What's going on?" she asked. "Why's everyone freaking out?"

"Didn't you see?" the girl cried in an incredulous voice, wobbling on pencil-thin legs that didn't seem strong enough to support her thin frame.

Scarlet shook her head. "See what?"

But the girl just shrugged helplessly, as if the *what* in question were too scary to even speak aloud. She muttered a few half-intelligible excuses then bolted in the other direction. Scarlet watched her go, terror rising inside of her. This had to be a coincidence, right? It couldn't be related to the dragon. Emmy was such a tiny thing—no bigger than a large dog. Surely she couldn't have caused this amount of chaos in the short time she'd been free.

Could she?

You put her in danger. Not only her but the rest of the world.

"Scarlet! Is that you?"

She whirled around in time to see Rebekah running toward her. Her friend's face was stark white and stained with tears. She threw her arms around Scarlet, almost knocking her backward with the force of the hug, and squeezed her so tight Scarlet was half-convinced she'd pass out from asphyxiation before her friend released her.

"You're okay!" Rebekah was babbling into her ear. "I thought…Oh God, I thought…"

Scarlet struggled to free herself from her friend's death grip. "You thought what?" she demanded. "What the heck is going on here, Bek?"

Rebekah stared at her, an incredulous look on her face. "The dragon, of course!" she cried, her voice choked with tears. "The one from the barn. It swooped down out of nowhere and started attacking people for no reason!"

"What?" Scarlet whispered hoarsely. "But that's impossible." She thought back to Emmy. Sweet, gentle Emmy. Why would she do something like that? It made no sense.

"Don't you see?" Rebekah wailed. "This is all my fault! I opened the barn. I set it free. All these people—all of…this… It's because of me!"

No, Scarlet wanted to say. *I did. In fact, I all but talked the dragon into it.* But she found she couldn't speak the words out loud. It would only make things worse.

"It was a nightmare," Rebekah continued in a hollow voice. "Everyone screaming and running—trying to get away. Mrs. Hutchinson from the post office fell and got trampled. They had to take her away in the ambulance. And Tommy…" She squeezed her eyes shut, as if unable to continue.

Scarlet stared at her, a feeling of cold, black dread washing over her. "Tommy?" she prodded, trying to speak past her fear. "You mean your cousin Tommy?" Tommy was eight and Rebekah's pride and joy.

"They took him away in an ambulance," her friend said flatly. "The dragon…" She squeezed her eyes shut. "Oh, Scarlet, I think I killed my own cousin."

Scarlet shrank back, her knees buckling, the guilt and panic threatening to swallow her whole. She wanted to tell Rebekah it wasn't her fault. That it was she who had been the complete idiot, thinking it was a good idea to set a real-life dragon loose on the town.

But at the same time, her brain couldn't reconcile the cause and effect. Emmy wasn't a monster. She was sure of it. Only a few nights ago, she'd saved Scarlet's life for no reason. Why would she go and attack a stadium full of people a few days later? It didn't make any sense. There had to be more to the story. Some logical explanation why such a mild-mannered creature would suddenly go on a killing spree.

Not that this would matter to Tommy…

"Rebekah, what are you still doing here? I thought I told you to go home!"

The two girls turned as a man's voice broke through the night air. Scarlet recognized Rebekah's father on approach, his steps slow and his face grave. Her friend ran to him, throwing herself into his arms, clinging to him desperately as sobs shook her body.

"Dad!" she cried. "Oh, Dad, I was so scared!"

Don't tell him about the barn, Scarlet thought as she watched them worriedly. *Now is not the time for confessions.* Suddenly she was glad she'd destroyed the video evidence. When she got home, she'd delete the YouTube upload as well.

Rebekah's father stroked his daughter's hair, soothing her with low whispers. Scarlet stood to the side, shuffling from foot to foot, suddenly feeling awkward and out of place. Not to mention consumed by guilt. She wanted to run, to hide, to find a quiet place to try to sort out all that had happened. But at the same time, she felt glued to the spot. She wondered if she should call her mother. Had she seen the whole thing on the news by now? If so, she'd probably be freaking out.

Suddenly she spotted none other than the monster himself, ambling toward them, his bar buddies in tow. She bit her lower lip. The last thing she wanted was to deal with him, but at this point she was desperate to get home.

Making up her mind, she waved him over. "Can I get a ride with you?" she asked. "I don't want Mom to have to come out here now."

He gave her a suspicious glare. She wondered if he even remembered what had happened between them earlier in the week or if his drunken state of mind had made him block the whole thing out. When she'd woken the next morning, she'd found the broken sliding glass door taped up with cardboard, but no one had said a word about how it had gotten that way. She'd decided it was best not to bring it up.

"Sorry, I'm not going home right now," he told her. Even from where she stood, she could smell the stench of whiskey on his breath. He gestured to his friends. "Me and the boys have got some business to take care of." He patted the revolver strapped to his side and laughed harshly. "We're gonna go bag us a beast."

Rebekah's father looked over at them, his mouth dipping to a frown. "I think you might want to leave that to the professionals, boys," he said carefully, gently prying his still-clinging daughter off of him. "Sheriff Thomas said the government's sending out some Homeland Security agents to figure things out. They should be here within the hour. And word is, whatever it is, they want it alive."

The men exchanged amused looks. Scarlet's mom's boyfriend slowly shook his head. "The thing is...Bud...I've never really been the type of man who's content to sit around, picking his own ass, waiting for a bunch of Washington boys to show up and play cowboy," he drawled. "Sorry, that just ain't me."

His boys broke out in laughter at this, sending a chill down Scarlet's spine. She prayed Emmy had gotten far away from here by now. Out of the reach of the rednecks. No matter what had happened in the stadium, the dragon didn't deserve to be hunted down by these drunken louts.

One of the monster's buddies—Robert, she thought he

was called—spit a wad of tobacco onto the ground. "This is Vista," he declared. "We take care of our own in Vista."

"And we certainly ain't gonna leave it alive," insisted a third man. He was younger, goateed. Maybe one of the sons. His grimy T-shirt read "Drinks well with others." "That thing practically killed a kid right there on the field. What if it decided to come after your little girl here next?" He shot a lecherous sneer at Rebekah.

Rebekah's father scowled, stepping protectively in front of his daughter. "I just think—"

"Awh, don't you get your panties in a twist, Rearden," her mom's boyfriend interrupted, slapping him hard on the shoulder. "We'll have this beast bagged and tagged and mounted above the fireplace before those government boys even know what hit 'em." He reached for his pistol, locking and loading with a toothy grin. "Kapow! *Adios, muchachos!*"

His friends cheered at this, raising their own firearms in mad salute. High-fives and fist bumps were exchanged, followed by a silver flask. As they all took hardy swigs, Scarlet could only hope that the alcohol would screw with their aim.

She stared down at the ground, guilt stabbing at her gut. Poor Emmy. This was all her fault. She thought she was doing something good—getting the dragon to stand up for herself—but instead, just as the boy at the barn had predicted, she'd inadvertently put the dragon's life in danger. If only there was some way to warn her. Or to help her escape.

But then her eyes fell upon her mother's boyfriend and a feeling of hopelessness overwhelmed her. She couldn't even protect her mother from this monster. And he claimed to love her mother.

Emmy was truly screwed.

"Well, I can't stop you," Rebekah's father tried, giving it one last effort. "And I wish you the best of luck. Though for all we know, it's long gone by now. Flown the coop. You have no idea where to even start to look, do you?"

"I do."

Startled, Scarlet whirled around, her horrified eyes leveling on Rebekah. Her friend stepped out from behind her father, squaring her shoulders and taking a step toward the mob.

"Rebekah, no…" Scarlet whispered.

"The old McCormick place," Rebekah stated flatly. "That's where it lives." She squeezed her hands into fists. "Now go kill it dead."

Chapter Twelve

E mmy? Where are you, you overgrown barbecue grill?"
Caleb ran down the field, scanning the night sky, déjà
vu hitting him hard and fast. This was perfect. Just perfect.
He'd managed to lose the dragon again. And this time it wasn't
even his fault. Emmy had been safe and sound, locked up in
the barn when Connor and Trinity had left to go to the game,
and Caleb had more than learned his lesson about taking her
out for a walk. So when Grandpa had asked if it was okay for
him to go out hunting, Caleb figured, why not? Emmy was
on official lockdown, with no chance of getting out. Unless,
of course someone intentionally broke into the barn to let
her out. But who could have predicted something like that?
They'd been there three months and no one had ever come
within a mile of the farm since day one.

You might not have predicted it, but you could have stopped it, a
voice inside his head nagged. *If you hadn't gone to the Nether again.*

He scowled, pushing the voice away. What else was he supposed to have done to pass the time, all alone in a dark house
while everyone else was off having fun?

He thought back to Trinity's shining eyes—her excited
face when Connor had presented her with the tickets. Okay,

sure, he'd gotten Caleb a ticket too. And Grandpa had even offered to stay home and watch Emmy so the three of them could have a night out together. But Caleb found he couldn't stomach the idea of spending hours sitting on the bleachers next to Trinity—so close he could smell her baby powder scent…and yet, at the same time, so many miles away.

He imagined sitting there, feeling like a third wheel as she and his brother laughed and teased one another and made inside jokes he didn't understand. It was a torture he wouldn't wish on his worst enemy, and in the end, he'd decided it was better to stay home.

To palm that gem.

To escape into the Nether one more time.

"Damn you, stupid dragon," he swore. He knew he was going to get blamed for this. Once more, he'd look like the bad guy and his brother would somehow prove the hero. His only chance was to find Emmy and drag her back to the barn before anyone got home and realized she was gone.

"Caleb!"

He froze, his eyes falling on the van, fast on approach, Connor's head sticking out the open window. His shoulders slumped. So much for getting her back unnoticed. And as his brother got closer, Caleb caught the frantic look on his face. He already knew, he realized. Even better.

"It wasn't my fault!" he blurted out as Connor pulled up a few feet away. "Some girl broke into the barn and—"

But his brother only waved him off. "We've got bigger problems," he interrupted. "Emmy just decided to perform her own halftime show in the middle of Vista stadium. In front of half the town, nonetheless."

"What?" Caleb stared at him, fear sliding down his back. "Where's Trin?" He tried to look into the van, praying to see her inside. But the passenger seat was empty. It was then that he noticed the flashing lights in the distance. Police, fire, ambulance. This was not good.

"I don't know," Connor admitted, and Caleb could hear a thread of hysteria wind through his brother's normally placid tone. "She jumped on Emmy's back and took off flying." He cringed. "She could be…anywhere."

The concern in his voice was palpable and Caleb could clearly hear what his brother was leaving unsaid. Emmy wasn't old enough, wasn't large enough, to safely take on a rider. If Trinity couldn't hold on while the dragon was air bound…

"It's worse than that," Connor interjected, evidently reading his thoughts. "They opened fire. I think…maybe…" He trailed off, his face now ashen under the van's headlights.

Caleb's heart wrenched violently. "No!" he cried, grabbing Connor by the shoulders and shaking him hard. "She's fine. We'd know it if she wasn't. *I'd* know."

The words shot from his mouth like a cannonball, as if somehow he could make them true by sheer force of will. But he would know, wouldn't he? They'd spent so much time together. They'd shared so much over the last few months. He'd kissed her. He'd loved her. He'd know if something had happened to her.

Wouldn't he?

This is your fault, the voice inside of him nagged once again. *If you'd stood guard like you were supposed to—if you hadn't run away to the Nether, Emmy would be safe and sound. Trinity would be safe and sound, having fun, enjoying being normal for the first time in months.*

But no. You were too weak. Too selfish. And now you probably killed the both of them.

"She's fine. She's fine. She has to be!" he repeated, his voice sounding strangled and choked. He could feel his brother staring at him with pitying eyes, but he refused to acknowledge him. Refused to acknowledge any possibility other than the idea that Trinity was absolutely one hundred percent fine.

"Um, hey? Excuse me?"

The sudden female voice made the two brothers whirl around. Caleb's eyes widened as they fell upon none other than the very same girl from the farmhouse. The one who had broken into the barn and freed Emmy and started this whole mess in the first place.

"You!" Caleb cried, hot anger spilling over him like lava from a volcano. "Do you know what you've done?" He stalked toward her, grabbing her and shoving her hard against the van. She cried out in a mixture of surprise and pain. But Caleb ignored her, pinning her to the vehicle, his nails digging into her soft shoulders. It was all he could do not to strangle her on the spot. To hurt her like she'd hurt Emmy.

Like she might have hurt Trin.

"Stop it! Caleb, let her go!"

Caleb felt himself being jerked away, shoved roughly aside. He hit the ground with a loud oomph and pain shot up his arm. He looked up to see his brother approaching the girl, giving her a careful once-over and asking if she was okay. Furious, he scrambled back to his feet.

"It was her!" he cried, pointing a shaking hand in the girl's direction. "She was the one. She broke into the barn and let Emmy out."

Connor gave him a steely look then turned back to the girl, speaking in a measured tone that made Caleb want to kick his twin's self-righteous ass. Didn't he get that she was the enemy? The one who had sparked this inferno?

"Is this true?" Connor asked. "Did you set Emmy free?"

The girl nodded, tears streaming down her cheeks. She glanced fearfully at Caleb then back at Connor, swallowing hard. "I thought I was helping her," she choked out. "She looked so sad, all alone in a dark barn. I only wanted to help her."

"Congratulations," Caleb growled, glaring at her. "You did a bang-up job at that."

Connor shot him a look. "You're not helping, Caleb."

The girl hung her head. "I didn't know," she protested. "Believe me, I had no idea."

"Look," Connor said, clearing his throat. "I think it would be best for you to just go home, okay? Just forget any of this happened."

The girl surprised Caleb by shaking her head vehemently. "No," she said. "You don't understand. There's this group of men—my mom's boyfriend and some of his bar buddies. They're drunk and armed and looking for the dragon. I've got to find her—before it's too late."

Caleb stared at the girl, feeling his knees buckle out from under him. And here he thought things couldn't have gotten any worse. Now, even if Trin had somehow managed to survive her dragon ride, she and Emmy could still be mowed down by a bunch of drunken rednecks.

"That's just great," he spit out, forcing his anger to swallow his fear. "But thanks to your little prank, we have no idea where she is."

The girl bit her lower lip, a gesture that oddly reminded Caleb of Trin. "That's not actually true," she said quietly.

"What do you mean?" Connor demanded, finding his voice. Suddenly he was the one standing too close, towering over her small, trembling frame. She looked up at him with frightened eyes.

"A few days ago," she managed to squeak out. "I was… hurt. The dragon found me. She healed my arm. And ever since that, I…" She trailed off with a helpless shrug. "Man, I sound completely crazysauce, don't I?"

But Caleb found himself shaking his head, the events of the last few days finally pulling together in his mind. So that's where the dragon had disappeared to. Why she'd returned with a broken scale.

Damn you, Emmy. After all Trinity's done for you…

He approached the girl, forcing a tight smile to his lips. "Actually, that makes perfect sense," he said. "Now how about you take us to the dragon?"

Chapter Thirteen

Hang on, Trinity. We're on our way.

Connor watched as his brother put the van in park and yanked out the keys while the girl, Scarlet, was already scrambling out the back door. They'd need to walk from here on out, she'd told them. The dragon was hiding deep in the woods, inaccessible from any roads.

Popping open his own door, he slid out of the van and onto the soft dirt below, his eyes never leaving their guide, who was now diving into the woods, her long, straight brown hair streaming out behind her as she ran. He shook his head. Stupid girl. What had she been thinking, breaking into a barn, setting a wild animal free? It was idiotic at best. At most, suicidal.

Then again, he thought, was it any different than what Trin herself had done the first time around, when Emmy was locked up in a government lab, being experimented on and cloned? She and her Dracken pals had also come to the same daft conclusion that setting a fire-breathing beast and her brood free was the right and proper thing to do.

It wasn't really their fault, he knew. Dragons had an uncanny ability to make humans feel sorry for them, to present themselves as vulnerable and weak—appealing to peoples' protective, nurturing instincts and convincing them they were doing the right thing by helping them. Not unlike how dogs had neatly wrapped humanity around their own fuzzy paws with their big brown eyes and wagging tails. Dogs—and dragons—made people feel needed, wanted, loved, and accepted. Feelings they didn't always get enough of from their fellow man.

And so people willingly deluded themselves that these survival instincts, honed by years of evolution, were actually true emotions. True love. And they'd do whatever it took—even putting their own lives in jeopardy—to keep these creatures from harm.

But if the tables were turned, would a dragon do the same thing for a human? Would he sacrifice himself and his own happiness for the sake of mankind? That spirit of self-sacrifice was, after all, the one thing that separated man from beast. And no matter how smart or magical dragons appeared, they were still, at the end of the day, only animals.

He thought back to the stadium. Of Trinity diving into the mob, throwing herself on Emmy's back, taking off into the skies. Of the locals, pulling out their guns and opening fire. Had she been hit? Had she been killed? As much as Connor wanted to believe his brother's angry assertion that they would know, somehow, if she were gone, Connor was also a realist. And Caleb hadn't seen her—barely holding on as Emmy desperately clawed her way to higher altitudes. It would be tough enough for someone to ride a dragon as small as Emmy to begin with, without having to dodge bullets to boot. All they'd have to do was graze her leg or arm to throw her off balance. Send her careening to her death, the dragon soon following her into oblivion.

And then it'd all be over, his father's voice pointed out. *Mission accomplished, despite all your screw-ups.*

He gritted his teeth, pushing the ugly thoughts from his mind. Sure, it would be nice to have this all be over. To have no more reason to hide, to live in fear. No more possibility of a dragon apocalypse looming on the horizon. But not at the cost of Trinity's life.

Just like the dragon, his father taunted. *Luring you in. Convincing you to protect her. Going against all you've been taught, all common sense.*

"Shut up!" he muttered. But the thought had already seeded itself, poisoning his mind, refusing to leave as they crashed through the woods. Would his tenderness toward Trin, his protective instinct, ultimately bring about the end of the world? Was she an innocent girl who deserved to live—or a disease, worming inside of him, eating away his good intentions? Causing him to turn his back on everything he believed in? Endangering everyone he loved?

He should want her dead. It would be best if they were both dead.

And yet somehow, all he could hope for—all he could pray for—as they ran through the forest, was that she would be alive, unhurt, safe. That she would look up at him with those big dark eyes of hers then smile and tell him everything was okay.

He groaned. Seriously, the Academy should revoke his Dragon Hunter degree.

"Over here!" Scarlet cried out, interrupting his reverie. He followed her and his brother into a clearing surrounded by thick, gnarled cedar trees and littered with rocks and weeds. Scarlet was standing in the center, hands on her knees, obviously winded from her sprint through the woods.

"In there," she told them, pointing to an overhang draped by foliage. "There's a cave. Emmy's hiding in there."

Connor narrowed his eyes as his soldier's instincts kicked in. He glanced at the girl, realizing suddenly how little they knew about her. What if this was some kind of trap? What if Homeland Security agents were even now waiting in the bushes, ready to ambush them when the girl gave the word? His hand automatically felt for the pistol he kept strapped under his shirt. Then he looked to his brother. Caleb shrugged, also looking a little uneasy.

There was only one thing to do. Closing his eyes, he listened to the girl herself. Taking in her thoughts, directly from her own head.

I'm sorry, Emmy. I thought I was helping. I'm really, really sorry.

Okay. He let out a breath. At least she sounded sincere in her regret. And he felt no presence of anyone else in the vicinity. So, ignoring the now encroaching headache—the lovely parting gift he got from using his powers—Connor dropped to his knees, brushing away the overgrowth and peering into what did appear to be some kind of small cave. There was a flickering of light…Then…

ROAR!

Connor stumbled, losing his balance and falling onto his back like a turtle upended. Rocks and roots dug into his skin, but he ignored them, reaching under his shirt and whipping out his gun. Pointing it at the entrance, ready to—

"Don't shoot!" cried a voice from inside. A very familiar voice.

His jaw dropped. "Trinity?" he stammered in barely more than a whisper. "Is that you?"

"Connor?"

She was alive. She was *ALIVE*.

Connor tossed the gun aside and dove through the brush, crawling on his hands and knees as fast as he could, desperate to reach her. Desperate to see her with his own eyes. To know the voice wasn't some hopeful hallucination. That she was really there. That she was really okay.

And then there she was. Right there in front of him, her face illuminated by candlelight. Filthy and frightened and yet—oh God—so beautiful. Beautiful and very much alive.

He threw his arms around her, squeezing her so tightly he was half-afraid he'd break her bones. In an instant, all the poisonous thoughts of how she'd be better off dead evaporated, and all he could focus on was her.

The world could all go to hell, as long as he had her in his arms.

"Oh, Trin. Oh, Trinity."

He could feel heavy eyes boring into his backside, and he reluctantly pulled away from their embrace. Emmy was sitting there, next to Trin, watching him suspiciously. He gave the dragon a rueful smile, his grudging thank you for keeping her safe and not letting her fall. Even if it had been only to ensure the beast's own survival, rather than some showcase of true affection.

"Trinity!"

He turned to see Caleb and Scarlet crawling into the cave behind him. His brother looked as relieved as Connor felt and gave Trin an awkward hug of his own. Connor watched curiously as they avoided each other's eyes, and he wondered, not for the first time, if something had gone down between them. Then he pushed the jealous thought from his mind. It didn't matter now. All that mattered was she was safe.

He turned back to Scarlet to thank her for leading them here, surprised to realize she'd gone straight to Emmy. He watched as she gave the dragon a tentative pat on the snout. "I'm sorry," he heard her whisper. "I think I gave you some bad advice."

Connor watched as the dragon sniffed the girl for a moment then rewarded her with a large slurp to the face. Evidently all had been forgiven. Scarlet looked taken aback for a moment then she started laughing out loud, throwing her arms around the dragon as if they were best friends.

"Oh, Emmy! I'm just so glad you're okay."

Connor stole an uneasy glance over at Trin, who was watching the scene play out with a small, puzzled frown. Not surprising. He'd never seen Emmy show much affection or interest to anyone but her Fire Kissed before. Who was this girl anyway? And what kind of bond did she and the dragon share?

"So what happened?" he asked Trin, attempting to relieve the tension in the air. He gave her a once-over. She didn't appear hurt; maybe the bullet had missed her after all.

Trin shrugged, reluctantly dragging her eyes away from the stranger talking to her dragon. "I don't really know," she admitted. "Last I remember I'd been shot. I was falling off Emmy's back as she came in for a landing. She must have dragged me in here after I passed out. When I woke up, I was completely healed."

"She probably healed you with her blood," Scarlet broke in suddenly. "Her blood has magical healing properties, you know."

Connor could see Trinity bristle. "Yeah, I know that," she said in a tight voice. "She and I have been together for a while now, thanks." She started to turn back to Connor.

But Scarlet wasn't finished. "Yeah, she told me," she said. "She also told me you went off on a date and left her stuck in the barn?" She gave Trinity a disgusted look. "No offense but that's really not cool. Poor Emmy deserves better than that." She turned to the dragon, scratching her snout. "Don't you, Emmy?"

Connor watched as Trinity's face turned a disturbing shade of purple. "Who the hell is this?" she demanded, turning back to him. "And why is she here?"

"She's the one who let Emmy out of the barn in the first place," Caleb interjected. "The one who started this whole mess."

"She also helped us find you," Connor broke in. His brother had such a knack for making every situation worse. At Trinity's questioning look, he went on to explain the impromptu blood transfusion that Emmy had evidently performed before. "And now the two of them seem to share some kind of link. She can hear Emmy talk and she can pinpoint her location too."

"What?" Trinity stared at Emmy, the hurt and confusion on her face making Connor's heart squeeze. Stupid dragon. "So that must be how…" She gave the dragon an accusing look. "You told me you didn't know how you broke your scale."

Emmy shuffled from foot to foot, looking appropriately guilty. Trinity watched her for a moment then sighed and shook her head, looking as if she was doing everything she could to hold back tears.

"Look," Connor said, trying to regain control of the situation. "We can settle all of this later. Right now we have more pressing concerns. Our position has obviously been compromised. The military is likely on their way."

"It's time to say *hasta la vista* to Vista, baby," Caleb piped in helpfully.

"What about Grandpa?" Trinity asked, peering through the cave's mouth to the forest outside, as if hoping the older man would suddenly materialize. "Is he with you?"

"He was still out hunting when I left the house," Caleb informed her in an apologetic voice. "I tried to call him on that cell you gave him, but shockingly, he didn't answer."

Connor sighed. Trin's grandpa was a stubborn old duff. And his mistrust of technology was legendary. Not to mention extremely inconvenient in times like this.

"Right," Trinity replied. She glanced at her watch. "Well, he's got to be back by now. One of us needs to go retrieve him so we can get the hell out of Dodge."

Connor opened his mouth to volunteer, but before he could speak, Scarlet piped in again. "You mean the old McCormick place?" she asked. When they all looked at her, puzzled, she added, "The farmhouse where you were stashing the dragon?"

"Yeah," Caleb replied with a scowl. "You know, the place where you decided to start this whole mess to begin with?"

She flinched at the jab, and Connor saw her face pale. "What is it?" he demanded.

"It's just…" She cringed and looked away.

"What?" Trinity cried now, her voice shrill and anxious.

Scarlet hung her head. "My mom's boyfriend and his buddies. That's where they were headed, last I heard. They're drunk and angry and…" She trailed off with a sigh. "If your grandfather somehow got in their way…"

"Why didn't you say anything before?" Caleb demanded, his eyes flashing with fury as he glared at her. As if he needed another excuse to be pissed at this poor girl.

"I…I didn't know there were more of you," Scarlet cried, backing away. "I was only thinking of her." She glanced over at Emmy, who seemed to have stepped closer to her, taking on an almost protective stance.

"We have to go get him," Trinity announced. "Now."

She made a move toward the exit, but Emmy was too quick, stepping to the right and effectively blocking Trin's path, her reptilian mouth set in a firm line, her nostrils flaring. As if to say, *Just try it.*

"Come on, Emmy," Connor tried, though he knew it would probably do no good. "Nothing's going to happen to her, I promise. I'll guard her with my life."

But Emmy didn't even spare him a glance, her eyes locked determinately on Trin. Connor muttered a curse. They were wasting time. "Don't be stupid, Emmy," he tried again. "If there's trouble, we'll need her gift to—"

"I'll stay with you, Emmy."

Connor watched in disbelief as Scarlet crawled up to the dragon again, reaching out and stroking her nose tentatively. For a moment, Emmy did nothing, then, slowly, she dropped her gaze from Trin and turned to Scarlet instead.

"I know you're scared," Scarlet whispered. "And you don't

want to be left alone in the woods. But let them go. I'll stay with you until they come back, okay?"

Connor could almost feel the frustration radiating from Trinity as she watched the scene play out in a mixture of dismay and disbelief. Even more so when Emmy curled her head into the girl's lap and started grunting contentedly as Scarlet scratched behind her ear.

He knew what Trin was thinking—they'd been so close, had shared everything over the past few months. And yet somehow she'd managed to misread the dragon now. Emmy hadn't been afraid of Trin getting hurt. She'd been afraid of being left behind.

"Emmy," Trin tried, her voice cracking dangerously. But it didn't matter. The dragon didn't even look in her direction, only snuggling closer to her newfound friend. Trin's face crumbled, and Connor's heart ached at the naked pain broadcasting from her eyes.

"Come on," he said gently, taking her hand in his. "We need to go. We have to go get your grandfather."

"I'll stay here with Emmy too," Caleb added, glaring at the girl with eyes filled with suspicion. "Make sure this chick doesn't try anything funny." He looked at Scarlet with such indignation that, in any other situation, Connor would have laughed.

But there was not much to laugh about now. Trinity sighed deeply then nodded her head. "Okay," she said at last. "You're right. We need to go." She turned back to the dragon, giving her one last beseeching look. "We'll be back, Emmy, okay?"

Connor couldn't hear the dragon's answer. But the sad look on Trin's face told him all he needed to know.

Chapter Fourteen

After Trinity and Connor had taken off into the woods, Scarlet had stayed in the cave with Emmy while Caleb stood watch outside. The dragon was clearly exhausted from the whole ordeal, not to mention weak from her second blood transfusion in less than a week. With Scarlet softly stroking her scales, it didn't take long for her to close her eyes and fall into a troubled sleep.

Not wanting to disturb her further, Scarlet carefully made her way back outside. There she found Caleb, sitting on a nearby log, digging something out of his boot. She watched as he tossed the object from hand to hand. It was small, round, red. Some kind of jewel?

"What's that?" she asked curiously.

Caleb's face turned bright red. He stuffed the object into his pocket. When he pulled his hand back out, she noticed his fingers were shaking.

"None of your business," he retorted, his voice sounding a little hoarse. For some reason, he suddenly reminded her of her brother, Mac. He'd had secrets too. Secrets that he claimed were "none of her business."

Except they actually were.

"She's asleep," she announced, deciding not to press him. He wasn't her brother, after all. Just a stranger who blamed her for everything that had gone down. And for good reason too.

Caleb's troubled face twisted into a smirk. "Well, aren't you the great dragon whisperer," he muttered.

She drew in a breath. "Look, I think we got off on the wrong foot. Can we start over?"

"Depends on what you want to start with."

"How about an apology?"

She gave him a rueful look. "I'm really sorry. I had no idea."

Caleb held up a hand. "Cheer up, Buttercup. They're just going to blame me for the whole thing anyway. Like they always do."

"What?" Confused, she cocked her head. "Why would they blame you? You weren't even there."

He nodded grimly. "Exactly."

They fell silent for a moment, giving Scarlet a chance to study him closely for the first time. Now that he wasn't actively yelling at her, she realized he was actually pretty cute, with a long, lean frame and shaggy brown hair that fell into his eyes. His eyes were strange too. So piercing blue they seemed to glow in the dark. It was funny, she thought. He looked exactly like his brother. And yet somehow, at the same time, they both seemed entirely different.

"So are you the good twin or the bad twin?" she asked curiously.

He raised an eyebrow. "Excuse me?"

"You know, between you and your brother. There's always a good twin and a bad twin, right? Are you the bad one?"

"Bad to the bone, baby," he said with a snort. But he

didn't sound too proud of the fact. If anything, he sounded pretty regretful.

"Well, that's a relief then," she declared. When she felt his questioning look, she shrugged. "I mean, you can never really trust the good twin, right? They're always too…perfect. Like, there's got to be something going on beneath that goodie-two-shoes surface of theirs. For all we know, they could be bottling up a mountain's worth of depravity."

Caleb rolled his eyes, but she could see a hint of a smile playing at the corner of his mouth. "Why are you still here again?" he asked, his tone a little more kind this time.

"What do you mean?"

"I mean, you're not a part of this whole mess. You could just go home. Go to sleep in your own bed and pretend the whole thing's been nothing more than some bad dream." He shook his head. "Do you know much I would love to do that if I could?"

"Yeah, well, you obviously haven't been to my house," she mumbled.

He looked up sharply. "What?"

"Nothing," she said quickly. "In any case, I can't leave. I need to make sure Emmy's okay. It's my fault everyone's out there, looking for her. If I hadn't broken into the barn in the first place…"

She trailed off, feeling unhinged. This was all her fault. And if something happened to that beautiful dragon, she would never be able to forgive herself. She glanced over at the cave, a small sob escaping her.

Caleb rose to his feet. He put an awkward arm around her shoulder, as if not used to the idea of trying to comfort someone. She supposed it was more the kind of task in the "good twin" handbook.

"Hey," he said gruffly. "It's not your fault. Well, not entirely. The whole thing was a perfect storm of good intentions and bad moves by all of us. Even Emmy herself. You may have opened the door, but she walked out."

Scarlet found herself leaning into him, resting her forehead against his solid chest. "But I told her to," she whispered hoarsely. "I mean, I was only trying to help. I thought…"

She trailed off, thinking not of Emmy this time but of her mother. Her pale face, covered in bruises. The broken glass door. Yet another instance where she'd tried to do some good but had only made things worse for everyone. An overwhelming feeling of helplessness washed over her.

"Look, I get why you did it, okay?"

She pulled away, surprised. Caleb met her eyes with his own glowing ones, staring at her so hard that she felt as if he was searching through her brain.

"You…do?"

He nodded grimly, releasing her and turning away, walking toward a nearby tree and leaning up against it, staring down at his feet. "I used to let her out too. Pretty much every night. I felt bad for her, you know? Cooped up in that icky barn, all day and all night, with nothing to do but watch videos? What kind of life is that for a dragon?" He shook his head. "I figured it was no big deal. I could keep an eye on her, make sure she didn't stray too far. And it was fine when she was younger. But now she's going into puberty and she's developed a real mind of her own…" He grinned ruefully.

"Yeah, I noticed," Scarlet said with a small smile.

"Anyway, a few nights ago, I lost her. I guess that's when she was off healing you. But Trinity discovered she was gone and realized what I'd been doing. She was…not happy, to say the least."

Scarlet bristled as she thought of Trinity. "Yeah, well, she's one to talk."

"No, no," Caleb protested. "She means well. Really. She's just scared. She's been given this overwhelming task of taking care of the world's last dragon. And she's trying to do whatever it takes to keep her safe. Which isn't easy, as you saw tonight. We had a pretty decent setup at the old farmhouse. It's going to be tough to find somewhere that nice again."

"So you're going to keep running then? When are you going to stop?"

Caleb gave her a wry look. "You'd have to ask the good twin about that. He runs the show. I'm just the comic relief." He winked at her and she had to laugh.

"Seriously, how did you end up with the world's last dragon?"

His smile faded. "It's a really long story. And, to be honest, the less you know, the better. After we're gone, you can go back home and forget you ever met us."

His words sent a small ache through Scarlet's bones. She hadn't realized, up until that moment, that some part of her had been secretly hoping they'd invite her along for the ride. But that was ridiculous. Caleb might have understood why she did what she'd done, but Trinity was clearly not a fan of her work. And she and the good twin were definitely running the rodeo here.

Besides, she couldn't leave her mother alone. Especially not tonight. Once the monster realized the dragon was out of his rifle's reach, he'd head down to the pub to drown his sorrows. By the time he stumbled home, he'd be frustrated, wasted, and ready to take it out on his regular punching bag.

She could feel Caleb watching her again, his eyes filled with what looked like concern.

"What?" she asked, a little unnerved.

He shook his head. "Nothing. It's none of my business."

She was about to ask him what he meant by that. After all, he couldn't have heard what she was thinking. But at that moment, there was a rustling at the cave's entrance. They both turned to see the dragon emerging.

"Emmy!" Scarlet cried, rushing toward her. "Are you okay? Do you need something?"

But the dragon didn't answer—simply spread her wings and pointed her nose to the sky. Scarlet's heart leapt to her throat.

"Stop! Where are you going?" she cried. But it was no use. The dragon was already gone. She turned to Caleb. His pale face mirrored her own.

"Can you tell where she's going?" he asked in a strained voice.

Scarlet drew in a breath, closing her eyes, trying to focus. Then she opened them again. "Yes," she said.

"Then come on," Caleb replied, grabbing her arm. "Let's go."

Chapter Fifteen

Trinity's lungs burned as she raced after Connor back to where they'd parked the van, a thousand panicked thoughts invading her brain. *It'll be okay. It'll be okay,* she chanted over and over again in her head. *You're worrying over nothing. It'll totally be okay.*

But try as she might, all she could seem to focus on were the innumerable scenarios where it would *not* be okay, each more frightening than the next. A gang of redneck thugs, beating Grandpa senseless. Government soldiers, arresting him and taking him away.

No, she scolded herself as the van came into view. *They're only there for the dragon. They won't care about him. He'll be fine. They'll leave him alone.*

Connor tossed her the keys and she jumped into the driver's seat. She revved the motor, and they pulled out onto the main road, heading toward the farmhouse. She glanced over at her passenger, who was staring straight ahead, out the window, his face tense and his shoulders squared. He was worried too, she realized, the thought not making her feel any better.

He caught her looking at him and quickly masked his

concern. "I'm sure he's fine," he told her. "He's a tough old geezer. He's not going to get himself caught."

She forced herself to nod and turn back to the road, flicking on her high beams to better see into the darkness. There were no streetlights in this section of town, and the bumpy vacant road seemed straight out of a horror flick. She half expected some inbred cannibal to leap in front of the van, brandishing a chain saw.

But the road remained thankfully chain-saw-massacre free, and soon the entrance to the ranch came into view. But when her headlights flashed onto the old wire gate, she realized it had been bashed open, possibly rammed by a large truck.

"They're here," she whispered.

Connor gestured for her to stop the van. He hopped out of the vehicle and went over to examine the gate. Then he beckoned for her to join him.

"We'll walk from here," he told her. "Just in case."

She nodded, not wanting to think about what he meant by that. Suddenly, chain-saw-wielding cannibals seemed the least of her worries. Biting down on her lower lip, she instinctively grabbed onto Connor's wrist as he started down the dark, dirt driveway that led to the farmhouse and barn. Connor, having lived most of his life underground, had far better night vision than she did, something that would come in handy right about now.

As they walked down the long dirt road, the crickets chirped merrily, oblivious to the tension in the air, but otherwise the night was as silent as the grave. In any other situation, Trin realized, it would feel strangely intimate: being alone together like this, in the dark of night, walking hand in hand under a blazing portrait of stars. In another world, it could have been a romantic post-game stroll. In another world, Connor would pull her toward him, tracing her cheek with his gentle fingers. He would whisper something about how beautiful she looked in the moonlight then press his lips against hers.

But this wasn't another world. And they weren't on some starry-eyed midnight stroll. They were on a rescue mission. And all their lives were in danger.

Connor suddenly jerked to the side, pulling her along with him, ducking behind an abandoned tractor about fifty yards from the house. She dropped down, watching him scope out the scene with a determined look on his face. His soldier's face. Sometimes it was hard to remember that the same sweet boy who had bought her a hot dog at the game tonight while cheering on her team could so easily transform into a cold-hearted killer. She was glad he was on her side. Glad that he cared about her grandpa as much as she did.

"Can you feel him?" he asked, shooting her a sideways glance before returning to his surveillance. "Is he here?"

Trin pursed her lips, trying to still her whirling thoughts and concentrate on using her gift as a sort of psychic homing device to scan the area for Grandpa. She closed her eyes, searching for a sign of his spark.

"He's here," she affirmed, opening her eyes again. "At least I think so. I can't pinpoint him exactly, but I feel like he's near. Though…" She frowned worriedly. "He doesn't seem to be moving."

"He could be sleeping," Connor replied in a clipped tone, as if unwilling to let her voice any other possibility.

"Yeah." She forced a nod, trying to push down the

encroaching dread rising within her. "He gets tired after a long hunt. He probably went to bed."

Connor pulled his gun from its holster and gave her a succinct salute. "On the count of three, I want you to run to the house. I'll cover you. Once you're inside, I'll follow."

"Okay," she agreed, hoping he couldn't hear the fear in her voice. "Count me down."

On three, she took off, running across the yard as fast as her feet would take her, forcing her eyes to focus on her destination rather than all the dark shadows looming. Her ears strained, listening for gunshots, though deep down she knew by the time she'd be able to hear them, it would be too late.

But thankfully the air remained gunshot free, and a moment later she was able to reach the relative safety of the house. She collapsed onto the couch, gasping for breath. Then she scrambled back to her feet just as Connor entered behind her, still brandishing his gun.

He gave her a small smile. "You've been working out."

"Gotta keep my girlish figure." She scanned the empty room. "Maybe Scarlet was wrong," she suggested. Then she remembered the gate. "Or maybe they were already here and took off when they couldn't find a dragon? I didn't see any trucks parked outside."

"True…" But Connor didn't seem convinced. He cased the room, eyes darting to every corner. Trinity felt a chill trip down her spine.

"Grandpa?" she cried out, heading into the kitchen. She pulled a flashlight from the wall and flicked it on. "Are you here?"

But there was no answer. There was, however, a knapsack

on the counter, Grandpa's hunting bag, still packed with provisions. She frowned. He'd definitely returned from his hunt. So where was he now? Déjà vu gripped her as she remembered the last time she'd been in a house, looking for her missing grandfather. How innocent she'd been back then. How naïve.

"I'm going to go check the barn," Connor said, peering out the window. "He might be cleaning his kills out there. You wait here, just in case."

"I should go with you," she protested. But he shook his head.

"Go upstairs and gather up whatever you think we can carry out of here. After this, we're not coming back."

His words sent an ache straight down to her toes. Not that she'd been attached to this house any more than any of the others they'd crashed at over the past three months. And yet the idea that they'd once again be forced to go, to leave everything they knew behind…

"Okay," she relented. "But hurry. In case the men come back."

Connor nodded then pulled his gun from the waistband of his jeans and made his way out the front door. Trinity watched him exit and then headed to the stairs, taking them two at a time. There was only one thing in the house that she really needed, she thought. One thing she couldn't live without.

Bursting into her bedroom, her eyes locked on the treasure in question—her mother's music box—still sitting on the nightstand by her bed. She let out a sigh of relief, not sure why she'd been so worried. After all, it was only a treasure in her eyes.

She approached the box, pulling it into her hands, holding it against her chest. Had it really only been this morning that she'd woken and wound it up and let the princess twirl? After all that had happened tonight, it felt like a lifetime ago.

And soon it would feel like another life entirely. By morning, they'd be far, far away from here. Maybe at their destination. Maybe not even halfway there. Even the thought of traveling again filled her with exhaustion. And the idea that it would just keep happening—that they'd never find a place to stop for good. Never find a place that was totally safe...

She sighed. These were not thoughts to dwell on now. She glanced out her bedroom window, hoping to see Connor and her grandpa exiting the barn. Instead, her eyes caught a flash of light turning into the yard. She froze. Car headlights.

Panic rioting within her, she dropped to the floor, still clutching the music box under her arm. Peering out the window, she watched as the pickup truck with a dented front grill came to a halt outside the barn. Two men hopped down from the truck bed and two others got out of the cab. They were talking loudly and, to Trinity's horror, heading straight for the barn.

Connor! Get out of there! she tried to send.

But they were already making their way through the front door and she knew there was no back way out. What would they do when they found him inside? Of course, they wouldn't know he was involved, she told herself. Maybe he could bluff his way out. Connor was good at that kind of thing, and he also had his gift of persuasion if all else failed.

But they were drunk, Scarlet had said. Angry, looking for a fight. And he was the only one there.

She scrambled to her feet, out of the bedroom, and down the stairs, slipping and almost losing it in her haste to get outside. Grabbing on to the handrail, she somehow managed to keep her balance and dove for the front door. She wrapped her hand around the handle and pulled it open...

...only to find herself face-to-face with a grizzled, unshaven man in a cowboy hat and plaid shirt.

The man's gaze leveled on her, his eyes sharpening in recognition. "You!" he cried. "You're the one who—"

Trinity dove to the side, dodging him and running down the driveway as fast as her legs could carry her. Behind her, she could hear him swear loudly, and a quick glance told her he wasn't going to be content to let her escape. She picked up the pace as best she could, hating that she was basically abandoning Connor to get away. But what else could she do?

Don't be stupid, she could almost hear him say. *Save yourself and Emmy if you can.*

She almost made it all the way to the van. But before she could open the door, rough arms grabbed her, yanking her backward. She screamed, fighting him with all she had, but it did no good. He might be drunk and a little unsteady on his feet, but he was big, outweighing her by at least a hundred pounds. And as he dragged her, kicking and screaming back to the barn, it was all she could do to keep her grip on the music box.

"Let me go! Connor! CONNOR!" she cried.

What's going on? Are you okay?

She startled as Emmy's voice rose in her consciousness. Her panic must have been so high that the dragon had felt it from where she was in the woods.

I'm fine, she tried to push at Emmy. *Just stay with Caleb. Do not come here under any circumstances.*

The man tossed her through the open barn doors and she landed painfully in a pile of dirty hay mixed with old bones. "Look what I found," the man said with a barking laugh as he stepped in after her.

She looked up, scanning the room until she found Connor. He was standing against the wall, his gun trained on the three rednecks...who had their own guns pointing at him. A real standoff, like you'd see in the Westerns her grandpa always liked to watch.

Somehow she managed to scramble to her feet, brushing the hay from her jeans. She could feel the men's eyes fall on her curiously.

"You!" the one in the middle cried, repositioning his weapon from Connor to her. He had greasy, slicked-back, blond hair and a beautiful example of meth mouth. "I saw you at the stadium. You...you rode that...thing." He spit out the word *thing* as if expelling poison. Trinity felt her hackles rise despite herself.

"Her name is Emmy," she growled. "And yes, I rode her. So what?"

"Trin..." Connor said in a low warning voice. *Don't piss them off.*

She knew he was right. But she'd also had her share of dealing with guys like this from her years spent in foster care. She knew that showing too much fear could be worse than not showing enough.

"Where is it?" the man demanded after spitting out a wad of tobacco. "What did you do with it?"

She stole a glance at Connor, who stood beside her looking cool and casual on the outside. On the inside, however, she could feel him working overtime, using his gift in an attempt to bend the men's wills, wrestling them under his mental control. It was tough—even for those strong with the gift like Connor—to take on multiple minds at the same time,

133

and they were clearly outnumbered. But she knew it was the only chance they had to get out of this mess. And maybe she could help.

"None of your business." She clutched the music box so tightly her knuckles turned white. Forcing her mind to focus, she pushed the man's mind as hard as she could.

Don't shoot us. Walk away. Walk out of the barn and never come back.

"Oh it's our business all right," the man growled, resisting her attempt. He stalked over to her, grabbing her by the arm. She cried out in pain as his filthy, ragged nails dug into her skin.

Let me go. Walk away. Get out of here and never look back.

Pain stabbed at her skull, the side effect of using her gift. But she gritted her teeth and kept pushing anyway. After all, a headache was nothing compared to a bullet in the brain.

"You have five seconds," the man added, pressing the gun against her head. The metal was cold and hard against her skin, and she could smell the reek of whiskey on his breath. It was all she could do not to cry out in fear.

"Five…four…"

You don't want to shoot me. You don't want to—

"Three…two…" The gun jabbed into her temple painfully, and this time she did cry out. She glanced desperately at Connor, who shot her a helpless look back. He was trying—she could tell. But it wasn't working. Sometimes it didn't. And if it didn't—

Please don't…Please don't…

"No!"

A voice from the rafters suddenly rang through the air,

followed by the crack of a rifle's recoil. A moment later, her assailant's chest exploded, hot blood splattering her face. He stared at her, a split second of terror freeze-framed on his face, followed by recognition, before he stumbled into her, nearly knocking her down as he slumped to the ground.

For a moment, she couldn't move. In fact, none of them did. They stood frozen in place—everything seeming to happen in slow motion as their minds worked overtime to comprehend what had just happened. It was then Trinity caught a snow-white head poking up from the barn's loft. A soft gasp escaped her.

"Grandpa!" she cried.

The barn burst into chaos, gunshots ringing out from all directions. The rednecks dove for cover as Grandpa rained shots down from above and Connor let his own lasers fly. Trinity, the only one unarmed, ducked behind a wheelbarrow so as not to be caught in the crossfire.

But her safety was short-lived. The mustached guy found her and grabbed her by the back of the arms, pinning her against his chest like a human shield and dragging her into the middle of the barn. "Hold your fire!" he screamed. "Or she dies."

The gunshots ceased instantly. She saw Connor peek up from the horse stall he'd been hiding behind, his face grave but appearing uninjured. The other three men were on the ground, writhing, their gushing wounds staining the barn's floor crimson, their entrails hanging out like spaghetti. It was all Trin could do not to vomit at the scene.

"Just let her go, man," Connor said, taking a cautious step forward. "And we'll let you walk away."

It was then that she realized her captor was trembling like crazy. "Look, man," he stammered, "I didn't want to do this. My uncle…he made me come. I didn't mean…"

"You didn't do anything," Connor said in a gentle voice. "We're all okay. Just walk out the door and pretend you never saw us."

Walk away, walk away. You never saw us. Walk away.

The effort to push now was almost unbearable—like knives stabbing into her brain. But somehow she forced herself to keep at it, and soon she could feel his hard swallow against her back. "Okay," he agreed, loosening his grip. "I'm going to give her back to you. Don't shoot me."

"We won't. Just let her go. And it will all be over."

Let her go, let her go, let her go. Trin could hear both Connor and her grandfather chanting now. She glanced up to see her guardian leaning over the top of the loft. He gave her a small smile. She smiled back weakly, praying this was going to work.

Let her go. Walk away. You never saw us.

Suddenly, the man shoved her forward. She fell to her knees, hitting the ground hard and yelping in pain. But just as she was about to turn around, the barn erupted into flames.

"No!" she heard Connor cry. "Emmy, no!"

Emmy! Oh God. She should have known the dragon wouldn't have been content to stay away when she realized something was wrong. And now she was here, dive bombing into the barn, fire blazing from her mouth. Trin's former captor screamed, throwing himself into the hay to try to stop, drop, and roll, as they'd all been taught in school. But dragonfire wasn't so easy to put out, and the hay went up instantly, the flames ripping through the wooden barn. Trin's ears caught the cracking of wood and the smoke choked her lungs.

"Emmy! No!" she cried. "Stop!"

"Trin! Get out! Now!" she heard Connor command. His voice sounded a thousand miles away.

She stumbled to her feet, her legs still wobbly from the effort of using her gift. She looked around the burning inferno that had once been a barn. It was old, she realized with dismay, and half-decayed, and they hadn't had rain for weeks. Her eyes lifted to the loft above. The fire was climbing the walls at an alarming speed. "Grandpa!" she cried. Was he still up there?

She felt Connor grab her hand, trying to drag her away, but she shook him off. Throwing the music box to the ground, she dove for the ladder, taking the rungs two at a time, her hands and feet struggling for purchase on the rotted wood.

"Trinity!" she could hear Connor cry from below. "Get down here!"

She ignored him, swinging up into the loft, now filled with smoke and fire. Her eyes fell on her grandpa, lying on a bale of hay, his back pinned by a collapsed support beam.

"Grandpa!" She dropped to her knees. "Grandpa, are you okay?" She attempted to push the heavy beam off of him. But it was no use.

"Connor! Get up here!" she screamed.

"I can't!" he yelled back. "The ladder's gone."

She glanced down. Sure enough, the ladder had caught fire and was no longer climbable. She tried again to move the support beam. But Grandpa reached out and locked a white hand on her arm. His eyes, watery from the smoke, focused on her.

"You need to go," he told her in a hoarse voice. "Leave me and go. Now!"

"No!" she cried. "I'm not—!"

A crashing sound interrupted her words as part of the ceiling came hurtling down only a few feet away. Trin yelped in pain as a charred piece of wood hit her in the back.

"Emmy!" she screamed. "Help me!"

The dragon appeared, seemingly out of nowhere. At Trin's instruction, she clamped her claws down on the support beam, lifting it off of Grandpa. Trin was about to let out a sigh of relief until she saw what it had been covering up.

"Grandpa," she whispered. "Oh no, Grandpa."

He'd been shot, the bullet having gone straight through from stomach to back, leaving a gaping wound behind. And there was blood. So much blood he was practically bathing in it. He gave her an apologetic look. "I'm sorry, sweetie," he said.

"Emmy!" she shrieked. Then she turned back to him. "Just relax. It's going to be okay. Emmy can heal you with her blood. Just like she healed me from my gunshot wound." She turned around. "Emmy! Heal him. Quick!"

But the dragon only looked at her, shuffling from foot to foot.

"Come on, Emmy! What are you waiting for?"

I can't heal him, she said at last.

"What? What are you talking about?" Trinity's voice was screeching with hysteria now. "Of course you can heal him. You healed me, didn't you?"

Emmy nodded, looking tortured. *I healed you. And before that I healed…Scarlet. The healing blood comes from a single scale. It… takes a while to regenerate.*

Trinity stared at her, incredulous. "What?" she whispered. "You mean it's gone?" She glanced helplessly at Grandpa then back at the dragon. "But it can't be gone!"

The barn shook and another fiery support beam came crashing down. From below, she could hear Connor crying out her name desperately.

"Trinity," her grandpa interrupted in a hoarse voice. "You need to get out of here. Now!"

"No." She shook her head, sobs tearing from her throat. "I'm not leaving without you. Emmy's going to fix you. Please, Emmy!" she cried. "You have to try."

But Emmy only shook her head. *I can't. I have nothing left.*

Fury rose within Trinity now, crashing over her helplessness. "How could you?" she screeched, rising to her feet, storming over to the dragon. "How could you waste your blood on some stupid stranger? And now…now you can't even save your own family!"

Emmy took a step back, looking wild and horrified. She whined and smoke puffed from her nostrils.

"Without him, you wouldn't even be here! You'd be stuck in your egg in a block of ice! Everything you are is because of him! And this is how you repay him?"

"Trinity, stop it!" Grandpa cried. "There's no time for this nonsense. You need to get out of here. The fate of the world depends on your survival."

"I don't give a crap about the fate of the world!" Trinity cried. "I only care about you." She collapsed on top of her grandfather, holding him tight. She could feel him reaching out and placing a shaking hand over hers.

"I love you, baby. But you must go on. You must face your destiny. If you can't do it for yourself, then do it for me." He turned to the dragon. "Emmy, get her out of here. Now!"

Emmy turned to her, a bound and determined expression

on her reptilian face. Trinity shook her head vehemently, realizing what the dragon planned to do.

"Get the hell away from me! Don't you even try to—"

The dragon's talons dug into her back, lifting her into the air and flying her through the barn. She screamed and thrashed, kicking uselessly at thin air, but of course it did no good. No sooner had they flown down from the loft than the ceiling collapsed behind them with a shuddering crash.

"Grandpa!"

But there was no answer. And, she realized, as Emmy flew her out of the barn and across the field to safety, there never would be. Ever again.

PART 3:

FRACTURE

Chapter Sixteen

Strata-D—Year 188 Post-Scorch

Connor stepped out of the apartment, the mechanical door sliding silently shut behind him. He sidled onto his motorbike, kicking it into gear. A moment later, he was zooming down the narrow, rock-lined tunnel toward the outskirts of town, his bike's headlight the only illumination in the cave darkness. After a few turns he ended up at his destination—the South Side Elevator. He parked his bike and walked over to the operator, handing him a couple of coppers and asking him to take him down to Strata-D

"But that's Shanty Town," the operator protested, looking at Connor's fancy Academy uniform doubtfully.

"I know," Connor said, gritting his teeth. "Just take me." He handed the man a few extra coppers, and soon they were descending into the bowels of the earth.

Strata-D—better known as Shanty Town—was not a recognized part of the Underground and therefore outside the official jurisdiction of the Council. Which made it a great place to go if you were looking to buy or sell something illegal—or rip someone off who was.

Connor was pretty sure he'd find his brother there, looking to do all of the above.

He stepped off the elevator, wrinkling his nose as the overwhelming stench of urine and feces assaulted his nose. The placc was overbuilt, floor to ceiling, with battered tin outbuildings lit by rusty lanterns, offering booze and girls and other black market treasures for just a few coppers. Outside vendors lazily catcalled punters, inviting them to step inside, "Just for a minute!" promising the time of their lives.

Their eyes greedily fell on Connor as he passed, and they stepped up their cries, blocking his path to offer rusted watches, hallucinogenic drugs, and necklaces of fake dragon teeth. He pushed past them, wishing he'd changed clothes before coming down, as he headed toward the town square, peering into each open-air bar for a sign of his brother.

Finally he reached the center of town, decorated with ropes of multicolored Christmas lights strung across metal sculptures shaped to look like trees. He stopped in front of one of them, realizing he'd been followed by half the town, the ragtag group of people swirling around him with awe in their eyes.

"How goes the dragon slaying?" asked one woman with a gaggle of kids clinging to her threadbare skirts.

"Are we winning the war?" added a stooped man who looked old enough to practically remember the Scorch itself.

"What about the Dracken? What are you doing to stop the Dracken?" asked a teen boy whose face was half-covered in scarred-over burns.

"Everything is going great," Connor assured them, as he'd been taught to say by the Academy. Too much truth was trouble, as his teachers would say. "We're gaining ground every day."

"Well, thank God and the Great and Powerful Council for that," sneered a voice in the back. The crowd parted and Connor watched his brother, dressed in little more than filthy rags, saunter down the path, dragging a nasty-looking mutt behind him. Dogs were technically illegal down in the Underground—the Council claimed they required too much food that could be better allocated for human consumption—but many in Shanty Town kept them for protection.

"Caleb," Connor greeted in a tight voice. "It's been a while." He took in his brother's sunken eyes and scowling mouth, not sure if he wanted to hug him or strangle him to death. Caleb should have been living at home, with his mother, enjoying all the luxuries Connor's salary could provide. Instead, he preferred to hang out here.

"Well, I'd hardly expect a great Dragon Hunter like yourself to bother with something as silly as family," Caleb replied, his voice thick with sarcasm. "You're way too busy saving the world!"

Connor shifted from foot to foot, feeling suffocated by the sudden wire-tight tension in the stale, underground air. Caleb had never gotten over the fact that the Council had chosen Connor, not him, to join the Academy and become a Hunter after their father's death. Caleb was the firstborn by seven minutes. Caleb, by right, was the one who was supposed to shoulder their father's legacy. But it had been ten-year-old Connor who had single-handedly slain the dragon that had murdered their father. And when Connor went before the Council, dragging a severed dragon's head behind him, Caleb had been all but forgotten. And while this was not Connor's fault in any way—he'd only done what he'd had to do—Caleb had never forgiven him.

"I've come to talk to you," Connor told him. He glanced at the crowd, who was currently watching the exchange with excited eyes, probably hoping for a good fight between the twins. "Alone."

"Fine. Follow me."

Caleb turned and stalked through the crowd, dragging his dog behind him. Connor had to run to catch up. A few minutes later, he found himself sitting on a rickety metal stool in front of a makeshift tin-roofed bar at the end of a narrow alleyway. Caleb ordered a shot of whiskey from the greasy-haired, one-eyed bartender—there was no drinking age down in Shanty Town—handing him a single copper coin in payment. The man turned questioningly to Connor, but he waved him off. The Academy advocated abstinence in anything that might hinder your reflexes. You never knew when they were going to call you into service.

"So what do you want?" Caleb demanded after downing his shot. He slammed it down on the grimy bar and ordered a second.

Connor watched the bartender pour the drink, the liquor splashing onto the bar. "I was just at Mom's. She told me you ended up in jail again last night."

Caleb cursed. "Mom should mind her own business."

"It *is* her business when she spends her grocery money bailing you out."

"I didn't ask her to do that."

Connor raked a hand through his hair, frustrated. From

below, Caleb's dog growled softly, a warning against the sudden movement around his master. "Caleb, if you keep this up, they'll throw you in the mines."

His brother shrugged. "So what? Half my friends are already there anyway."

"But you should be home, taking care of Mom. She needs you."

"She doesn't need me. She has you, the golden son, to take care of all her needs."

He was impossible. Simply impossible. "What do you want, Caleb? Do you want money?" Connor demanded, reaching into his pocket for his purse. "Your own apartment?" He dumped the leather bag's contents onto the bar. From the corner of his eye, he saw the bartender eyeing the pile hungrily.

"What are you, crazy?" Caleb cried, scooping up the thirty pieces of silver—Connor's entire takeaway pay from his last mission. "That's a good way to get yourself killed down here!" He shoved the coins back in the purse and presented it to his twin. Connor shook his head.

"It's yours. Use it to get out of here. You're my brother. You don't have to live like this."

Caleb's face twisted. He dropped the bag unceremoniously back onto the bar "I *like* living like this. And I don't want your money. You can't just buy me, like you do everyone else, Connor. It won't work."

Connor let out a frustrated grunt. "Caleb, don't shut me out like this," he pleaded. "We're brothers. Twins." He closed his eyes and tried to find their former link. But his brother had long since severed it.

"Don't you get it?" Caleb asked, a look of disgust clear on his face. "I want nothing to do with you. And I never will. So get the hell out of here and go be the hero you're destined to be." He scowled. "And let me be the loser I am."

Connor rose from his seat, defeated. Leaving the purse on the table, he turned and trudged back down the alley toward the elevator. Before turning the corner, he found himself taking one last look back at the bar and his brother, just in time to see Caleb grabbing his purse and tossing its contents into the air. As silver coins rained down on the grime-caked street, beggar children appeared out of nowhere, scurrying for the money with excited squeals. Caleb looked up, catching Connor's stare of disbelief, and smiled smugly.

Connor shook his head and turned the corner, arriving at the elevator and instructing the operator to take him up to Strata-A. It was hard to believe how much easier it was to fight fire-breathing dragons than deal with his own twin.

Chapter Seventeen

Scarlet kicked at a piece of blackened wood as she made her way through the ruins of the old McCormick place. The fire, with help from the night wind, had leveled the compound before the fire department could even arrive—leaving a charred skeleton of what had once been the main house behind it. The barn—where the fire had originated—was completely gone, only a scorched shadow left to mark where it once had stood.

Scarlet sighed, feeling exhausted. All she wanted to do was go home and sleep for a week. But between the after-funeral gathering her mother was hosting for Bob and his fallen friends and the TV news crews camped out nearby, there would be little chance of getting any actual rest.

She considered going back to the trailer, to help her mother entertain her guests. By now the place would be overflowing with casseroles and condolences from neighbors and friends. But how could she bring herself to stand there, pretending to mourn, accepting the saccharine sweet sympathy the ladies from church would be doling out in droves?

"So sorry for your loss," they'd say.

When in reality, she had only won.

The monster was gone. Her mother was free. Her grand-mother had flown in to attend the funeral, carrying return tickets for both of them to join her on the reservation in New Mexico—to start a new life. It was everything Scarlet had ever dreamed of and more. She had won the freaking lottery in just one night. And things would never be the same again.

She should have been ecstatic. She should have been danc-ing in the streets. Instead, her legs felt like lead, her heart weighed down by guilt—her mind consumed with thoughts of Emmy. Where was she? Was she okay? Had she escaped the government agents that had swarmed into town with their mammoth tanks and heavy artillery? Sure, Scarlet's life was about to become much better. But at what price to the dragon who had made it so?

The news reporters were calling the incident an act of terrorism. The president himself had called Emmy a violent fiend. But Scarlet knew better. She knew the sweet, gentle creature who had healed her in the woods would never do something to purposely cause any harm. Emmy had been scared, trapped, forced to defend herself. And if she'd wanted to, she could have done much worse. Everyone who had been hurt had already been released from the hospital. Rebekah's cousin had suffered nothing worse than a broken nose. The only Vista casualties were four ignorant rednecks who'd seen fit to take the law into their own drunken hands. They deserved what they had gotten and more.

But try to say that to anyone in town. Emmy had no fan club here in Vista.

When she and Caleb had finally arrived at the barn on foot, they'd found Connor and Trinity covered in ash and reeking of smoke, Trinity practically comatose with grief. And when Scarlet had learned that the girl's grandfather had been killed in the fire, it felt as if she'd been the one to personally light the match. If only she hadn't uploaded the video. If only she hadn't gone back to the barn. Her desperate attempt to make life better for her own family had ultimately destroyed another's.

And Emmy...The dragon wouldn't speak to her. Wouldn't speak to anyone actually. She'd curled up in a ball in the back of the van, staring listlessly at the wall. Scarlet had tried to comfort her, stroking her nose and whispering in her ear. But the dragon refused to acknowledge any of it. Finally, Scarlet gave up and left her alone.

"Take care of yourself, Emmy," she whispered as Caleb slammed the van doors shut. But the dragon didn't answer. Caleb turned to her, giving her a regretful look.

"She's just upset," he told her. "Don't take it personally."

"She blames me."

"Actually, I think she blames herself." He peered at her with those blue eyes of his. "You gonna be okay? I hate just leaving you here like this. Can we give you a lift back to your house at least?"

She shook her head. "I have my bike. I'll be fine."

They fell silent, looking at one another. Then Connor poked his head out the back window. "You do remember we're running for our lives, right, Caleb?"

"I'll be right there." He sighed, giving Scarlet a rueful grin. "Good twin calls, I must obey." Then he reached out and gave her an awkward hug. His breath was warm across her bare shoulders. "Good luck, Buttercup."

"You too, Bad Seed."

And that was it. Caleb climbed into the van, and a moment later the vehicle roared to life, taking off down the dirt road at way too fast a speed.

Leaving her all alone.

That had only been three days ago, but it already felt like a lifetime. She knew in her heart she'd probably never see Emmy again. Yet at times she could still seem to feel the dragon somehow—if she closed her eyes and searched deep within herself. It was as if she could hear Emmy's heartbeat in her ear, feel the warmth of her breath on her face. The bond between them still felt so strong—even with the physical distance increasing. She tried to tell herself that it was enough to know Emmy was still alive and still okay. But instead, all she felt was an all-encompassing loneliness that threatened to drown her a little more each day.

She shook her head. This wasn't helping. Being here, thinking about it all. She needed to go back to town. Go to a movie. See if Rebekah wanted to hit the mall. Her friend had been texting her all day, but Scarlet hadn't had the heart to reply. It all seemed so pointless now. Living a shell of a life in this nowhere town when she knew there was something so much bigger—so much more magical—just out of reach. It was like Harry Potter being expelled from Hogwarts and being forced back under the stairs.

But just as she was about to turn and leave, a shadow crossed her path. She looked up, steeling herself for yet another nosy reporter, desperate for some kind of story angle that hadn't already been covered half to death on the nightly news. Instead, her eyes fell upon a girl around her own age with olive skin and large brown eyes. She was accompanied by half a dozen other kids, all seemingly of different nationalities. Which was unusual, to say the least. In Vista, Texas, you were pretty much either white or Latino or some combination of the two. Even Scarlet herself, with her Native American heritage, usually stuck out like a sore thumb here.

"You," the girl said in an overly authoritative voice. "Have you seen the dragon?"

Scarlet rolled her eyes, her curiosity deflating. She should have known. In addition to the media, the tourists and gawkers had been pouring into town daily. Flying in from all over the country and, by the looks of these kids, all over the world. Descending upon the town, hoping to get a glimpse of the mythological beast they'd seen on the news. It was unbearably annoying, though admittedly not bad for tips. This morning the diner had been standing room only for her entire shift.

"They've set up an information booth down at Town Hall," she said, trying to sidestep the visitors. "They can tell you everything you need to know."

The girl narrowed her eyes. "Can they tell me where she went?"

Scarlet stopped short. There had been a lot of talk about Emmy on the news and around town. In fact, people would pretty much talk about nothing else. But this was the first time she'd heard the dragon referred to as a *she* rather than an *it*.

"Sorry, she's long gone," she said with a shrug. "No one knows where she went."

Except for me, she thought, as she started to head back to the place she'd stashed her bike. *And it's not like I'd tell you.*

"Why not?"

"What?" Reluctantly Scarlet turned around. She found the

girl staring at her with eyes so intense they sent a shiver down her spine.

"Why won't you tell us where Emmy went?" the girl repeated pointedly.

Scarlet's mouth dropped. "How...how do you know her name?" she stammered. And maybe a better question: how had she known what she had been thinking? "Are you friends with Trinity?" Her heart started beating fast in her chest.

The girl glanced at her companions. "Yes," she said. "And Caleb and Connor too. We were part of the same group. We got separated three months ago when the government raided our compound."

A boy stepped forward. Tall, blond, good-looking. "We've been out here, searching for months, trying to find them again," he added in an Australian accent. "When we saw the news about the football stadium, we came straight away."

Scarlet stared at him, speechless, trying to sort out what he was saying. Trinity, Connor, and Caleb hadn't mentioned being a part of a larger group. But then, there hadn't been much time for details. And it did seem strange it was just the four of them with the grandfather, hiding out like they were without any sort of plan.

Another girl stepped out of the group. She was Asian, petite, and wearing blue braids in her hair. She looked at Scarlet with desperate eyes. "Please," she urged. "If you know something, you must tell us. We have to find them and Emmy before it's too late."

Scarlet narrowed her eyes suspiciously. "Too late for what?"

"A vaccine," interjected the first girl quickly, before the blue braids girl could answer. "It was created by our leaders and meant to help Emmy adjust to the current atmosphere. Dragons are particularly susceptible to all the toxins in our air—seeing as they were never meant to live in our time period. If Emmy doesn't get this vaccine soon, her immune system will fail. She'll grow sick and she'll die."

"Is this for real?" Scarlet stammered. But even as she asked the question, she could see the answer, written clearly on their faces. They were for real all right. And dead serious too. Could Emmy's life actually be in danger?

"I'm sorry," the first girl interjected. "I know this is a lot to take in, and unfortunately we don't have a lot of time." She gave Scarlet a pleading stare. "Look. I can tell you care about Emmy—and that means we're on the same team here. All we want to do is find her and bring her back to the people who can keep her safe. You don't want anything bad to happen to her, do you?"

Scarlet didn't know what to say. Of course she didn't want anything bad to happen to Emmy. But how could she be sure of who to trust? She scanned the group, her mind working overtime. They seemed sincere. But at the same time, there was something strange about them—the way they were looking at her, with a communal focused gaze, intense as a laser beam. As if they were trying to bore holes into her brain.

This was way too weird.

"Look, I—"

The girl in front suddenly grabbed her hands, squeezing them tightly. Scarlet staggered as a jolt of something hard and heavy slammed through her consciousness. For a moment she felt frighteningly cold. Then she felt as if she were being burned alive.

And then…

Her mind flashed with a vision. Of Emmy, bony and sallow skinned, lying in a corner, weeping. There were open sores on her flanks and her blue eyes were dimmed to gray.

Emmy needs you, Scarlet. Please don't let her down.

The girl let go of her hands. Scarlet conceded a step, her mind a tumble of confusion and fear. She looked up, meeting the girl's eyes with her own. "I can help you," she heard herself saying, though she had no idea where the words had come from. "I can lead you to Emmy."

The other kids broke out into sighs of relief. A few of them grinned at one another and a couple others exchanged hugs. The girl who had grabbed her hands gave her a grateful smile.

"Thank you," she said fervently. "My name is Rashida. And these are the Potentials. We're glad to have you on board."

Chapter Eighteen

"Come on, Trin. You have to eat something," Connor begged, holding out a slice of feta-and-pineapple-topped pizza in her direction, looking at her with pleading eyes. Trinity stared at it dully for a moment then turned back toward the blank motel room wall across from her. From behind, she could hear Connor's frustrated sigh, followed by the sound of the pizza slice being tossed back into its cardboard box.

"Leave her alone," his brother's voice interjected. "She just lost her grandpa."

"I know that, Caleb," Connor ground out. "But starving herself isn't going to bring him back. And she needs to keep up her strength if we're going to get through the days ahead."

Trinity bit her lower lip as they continued to argue as if she weren't in the room. In a way, she supposed she wasn't. Her body might be present, but her mind was far off in a distant world of hurt and pain and guilt she couldn't seem to escape.

It had been Connor's suggestion to come here—a no-tell motel in southeast Colorado, a full day's drive from the farmhouse where it had all gone down. He said it would give them a chance to regroup, to wash the ashes from their clothes—to figure out what they were going to do next. They had enough money left over from what Caleb stole from the Dracken to rent two rooms for two weeks. By then, hopefully they'd have a plan.

Instead, all they'd done was stare at the television set for the past week, flipping through the national news stations and watching the shaky home videos taken at the football stadium. Emmy's grand debut had become an international sensation, and everyone was trying to guess what she could be. Some pundits claimed she was some kind of secret genetic experiment gone bad, escaped from a government lab. Others claimed it was a mechanical hoax created by some publicist to help an upcoming Hollywood blockbuster go viral. There were theories of terrorism, of course, and even a few religious sects proclaiming it a sign of the coming apocalypse—the devil in the form of a dragon.

The president himself had flown to Texas to visit the victims of what FOX News had oh so cleverly dubbed "The Touchdown of Terror." After a few PR shots of Mr. President walking the football stadium and the burned out barn, he took to the podium and, as the cameras rolled, vowed to find this menace and keep America safe—by any means necessary.

At this, Caleb had rolled his eyes. "You people are a sensitive lot, aren't you?" he sneered. "In my time, we'd pray for a single day with as few casualties as this."

Trinity snuck a glance over at the menace in question, who was currently curled up in a corner of the room, staring at the TV, her cracked black tongue lolling from her mouth. She hadn't eaten all week and had refused almost all water. She had even rejected the idea of Trin going out and buying a DVD player so she could watch the last season of *Merlin*. Worse, she hadn't spoken a word since they left Vista.

Trinity felt a lone tear slip down her cheek. All she wanted was to go over to Emmy, to wrap her arms around her and pull her close. To bury her face in her satiny soft scales and cry until she had no tears left to shed, absorbing the dragon's strength as her own. But she knew if she did, Emmy would only stiffen and pull away.

And it would be all her fault.

Her mind flashed back to the barn, regret threatening to smother her. She'd been crazed, out of her mind with fear when she'd said those horrible things. When she'd all but accused Emmy of killing her grandfather with her own four paws. At the time, she'd felt so helpless. Forced to stand by and watch the life force of her very last family slip through her fingers like so much sand. Grandpa had sacrificed everything for her when she needed him the most. But when he needed her? She was powerless to save him. Because she couldn't control her own dragon. And the gift of life that should have been reserved for him had been wasted on another.

That stupid Scarlet. It had been all Trinity could do not to strangle the girl when she and Caleb had showed up during the aftermath. When she had dared look at Trinity with pitying eyes. Who did she think she was? How dare she interfere like she had? She acted like she was part of Team Dragon. Like she had some kind of claim on Emmy.

I'm *her Fire Kissed,* Trinity had wanted to scream. *You're no one. Just someone my dragon took pity on. You are nothing to her!*

But looking at Emmy now, she was no longer sure. And Caleb's words in the Nether came raging back to her once again.

She can un-choose you just as easily.

Find another to bond with instead.

And the worst part was, Trin wasn't sure she didn't deserve that.

Her ears caught a familiar sound, and she whirled around to see Caleb had opened her mother's music box and wound it up. She'd originally thought it had been lost in the fire, but it turned out Connor had picked it up and chucked it outside the barn while she was busy trying to rescue Grandpa. Now, the princess twirled and Mozart tinkled and twanged merrily, a bizarre soundtrack to the bleak scene.

She knew Caleb meant the gesture to be soothing—it had been the only thing that could lull her to sleep some nights over the last three months. But now all the music could conjure up was the nightmare at the farmhouse. If she hadn't run upstairs to get the box—if she hadn't separated from Connor and let him go into the barn alone. If Emmy had just stayed behind like she told her to…

If…if…if…IF!

"This stupid thing!" she screeched, her voice approaching glass-shattering decibels. She grabbed it off the nightstand, staring down at its golden shell, the beautiful princess, with vitriol boiling her blood.

"Trin…"

She chucked it against the wall as hard as she could. It bounced then fell harmlessly back onto the bed. Fury consuming her, she grabbed it again, slamming it against the headboard—over and over and over again—trying to destroy the thing that had inadvertently destroyed her life. From the corner of her eye, she could see the boys looking at her with white, startled faces and her ears picked up Emmy's worried whine. But she couldn't stop. Not until it had been completely annihilated.

On a fifth swing, there was a tinkling of glass and a crunch of metal. The box shattered, its pieces raining down onto the bed below. The little princess lay sprawled out onto the pillow, looking up at her owner helplessly, her once-strong legs now twisted and broken. Tears rained down Trinity's cheeks as she realized what she'd done.

"No," she rasped, looking down at the ruin of her only worldly possession. "I didn't mean…"

Desperately she grasped at the broken pieces of wood and metal, trying to put them back together somehow. It was all she had left of her family. She had to fix it. She *had* to.

"It's gone, Trin," Connor said gently, grabbing her shaking hands and clasping them in his own. "I'm sorry, but it's gone."

It's gone. Never had such simple words held so much weight. Her mother was gone. Her grandpa was gone. Soon Emmy would probably be gone too.

An overwhelming hopelessness washed over her like a tidal wave, and she leaned over the side of the bed to retch. But with nothing in her stomach, all she could manage were choking dry heaves.

"I can't do this anymore!" she sobbed, still hanging off the bed. "I just can't…"

Strong arms wrapped around her, pulling her back onto the bed. Connor tugged her into an embrace, locking her against his solid chest. A moment later Caleb joined him, laying his cheek against her back, stroking her neck with gentle fingers.

"You're not going to give up," he whispered. "I won't let you."

"We've come this far," Connor added. "We're going to keep going."

"We're Team Dragon," Caleb finished. "And we are strong."

She drew in a shaky breath, trying to still the raging panic inside of her and concentrate on the two brothers' touch. To appreciate the moment of peace between them as they worked together to comfort her. For once there was no bickering, no fighting, no bitter rivalry. Just a family coming together. Her new family. Totally different, totally dysfunctional. But hers all the same.

A sudden crash interrupted them. Trin looked up to see Emmy, tripping over a trash can in her haste to get to the adjoining hotel room, where Connor and Caleb slept. The dragon squawked furiously at the trash can, kicking it onto its side then turning to fly out of the room. Trinity bit her lower lip then turned to the boys.

"I'll be back," she told them.

She rose from the bed, walking into the other room and shutting the door behind her. Emmy was at the back, staring intently at the blank wall, while fluttering her wings with marked frustration.

"Are you okay?" Trinity asked quietly.

She didn't expect a response. She'd tried this—many times before over the last week—and had been greeted with nothing but silence. But this time...

You should leave me here. I've been nothing but trouble for you since the beginning. You should have never let me hatch from my egg. I can only bring you misery.

Trinity's heart wrenched at the pain she heard in the dragon's voice. Pain she had caused through her own selfishness.

"That's not true," she managed to say past the huge lump in her throat. "You've brought me great happiness. That day you hatched from the egg? That was the happiest day of my life."

But Emmy only shook her head, refusing to look at her. *You've sacrificed everything for me. Your home, your family. And I've given you nothing in return. Nothing but pain and death.*

"Emmy…"

Why am I even here? What purpose does my life serve? I thought I was supposed to save people. That's all I was trying to do. She hung her head. *I didn't realize some lives were worth more than others.*

She said this simply, as if it were a fact she'd learned in school. But it sent an arrow of guilt straight into Trinity's heart. Her hateful words from the barn came rushing back to her, and she wanted to throw up as the reflection of her own ugliness came into sharp focus.

"That's not true," she said slowly. "All lives are precious."

But you said…

Trinity closed her eyes and took a deep breath. "I know what I said. But I was wrong to say it. You saw someone who needed your help and you acted. That's not a bad thing. In fact, it's pretty amazing." She gave the dragon a rueful smile. "You have a big, beautiful heart, Emmy. And you should never, ever feel guilty about going and aiding someone who needs your help—no matter who it is."

Even Scarlet?

"Even Scarlet," Trinity declared. "Though I doubt we'll be seeing much more of her anytime soon." That troubling ship, at least, had sailed.

Emmy gave a long sigh then looked up at Trinity with mournful eyes. *I'm so sorry,* she said.

"Me too," Trin told the dragon. She paused then patted her lap. "Dragon cuddle?" she asked hopefully.

Emmy grinned, hopping up into her lap as she used to

do when she was little. She didn't really fit anymore, but Trin wasn't about to complain. She laid her head on the dragon's soft scales and absorbed her strength, her heart feeling as if it would burst from her chest. Emmy grunted contentedly and for a moment, all seemed right with the world again.

She wasn't sure how long they stayed like that, but eventually, Emmy slid down from her lap. The dragon gave Trin a shy smile then pushed back through into the adjoining room and over to her previously untouched food dish, nudging the beef bone with her snout then taking a tentative first bite. The satisfying sound of crunching bone that soon followed made Trin's heart soar.

"Well, all right!" Caleb declared. "Hungry dragon is hungry again. The universe has been restored."

Trin chuckled at that. Actually chuckled. If you had told her five minutes before she'd ever laugh at anything ever again, she wouldn't have believed it. But now she had hope again. If they stuck together, maybe it would turn out all right. Grandpa was gone and nothing would bring him back, but his dying wish was that she carry on. And she was determined not to let him down.

She rose from the bed and wandered back into the room with the boys.

"What about the music box?" she asked with a sigh, looking down at the shards of glass and wood on the bed.

"That, I think is irreparably damaged," Caleb admitted with a small snort, picking up a broken princess leg and turning it over in his hands. Trinity sighed.

"I can't believe I did that," she groaned, gathering the pieces together while trying to do the same with her composure. "That was all I had left of my..." She trailed off.

"What?" Connor asked, exchanging a look with his brother.

Trinity frowned, reaching into the rubble and pulling out a small, folded up piece of parchment. "What's this?"

The two boys shrugged. "Was it in the music box?" Caleb asked.

"I guess so?" she replied doubtfully. She didn't understand how it was possible—she'd opened that box a hundred times over the last three months, winding it up to watch the princess dance while thinking about her mother.

"It's probably just winding instructions," she murmured as she unwrapped the paper, her fingers trembling so hard she could barely hold on to the edges. "Or maybe a receipt from the store it was bought it from." But even as she said the words, she didn't believe them. Whatever it was—it was something important. She didn't know how she knew that, but she did.

"Your father gave me this," her mother had said. *"He told me that when you were old enough I should give it to you."*

Trinity assumed she'd meant the music box. But could it have been something else entirely? As she unwrapped it, she felt something fall into her lap. She reached down, feeling a piece of cold metal against her fingers.

"What is that?" Connor asked curiously.

She pulled it up, more confused than ever. "Some kind of pendant," she exclaimed, examining it closely. "Like a snake, chasing its tail."

"That's called an Ouroboros," Caleb pronounced after taking a closer look. "And it's not a snake. It's a dragon."

Trinity turned the pendant over in her hand, feeling a weird buzzing prickling at her skin. It was almost as if the pendant were alive somehow, pulsating in her hand. But that was crazy, right? She opened her mouth to speak, to let the boys know what she was feeling. But the buzzing got louder and louder, and a moment later she found herself succumbing to blackness.

Chapter Nineteen

Trinity opened her eyes. She was lying flat on her back, staring up at the ceiling, strange plastic monkeys weaving and bobbing above her head while a cheerful lullaby tinkled in her ears. She tried to move, but her arms appeared to be pinned to her chest and her legs felt floppy, as if all her muscles had atrophied. Panic rose as she tried to lift her head, to figure out where she was and what had happened. But she couldn't. She was trapped. And her mouth opened in a scream.

"Are you okay, sweetie?"

A woman leaned over her. A young woman in her early twenties, with black eyes filled with affection. It took Trinity a moment to realize it was none other than her mother. Well, her mother as she'd appeared in photographs from sixteen years ago, anyway. Right after Trinity had been born.

And suddenly she realized what must be happening. Connor and Caleb had shown her how to use gems to channel memories from the Nether. The Ouroboros must have been infused with this particular memory—of her as a baby—triggering at her touch and taking her back with it.

Was this why her mother had been so insistent on her taking the music box while she was in the Nether? Had she meant to impart something important to her daughter that she hadn't dared say aloud in case the Dracken were listening?

"Hush, my dear Trinity," her mother murmured, stroking her forehead with gentle fingers. "Your father will be home any minute now."

Trinity stared up at her mother, wanting desperately to have the ability to speak. Her father? But her father was dead. He'd died before she'd been born. At least that's what her mother had always told her. But when she tried to ask the question now, it came out only as frustrated gurgling.

Her mother reached for a bottle. But before she could place it in Trinity's mouth, there was a loud clattering at the door. Her mom rose with a smile. Then she turned back to Trin. "See?" she cooed. "I told you he would be back."

From her vantage point in the cradle, Trinity could just make out the outline of the front door, which, a moment later, swung open. A handsome man with styled hair not unlike the tenth Doctor burst into the room, his eyes wide and his face pale. Trinity's mother's excited smile fell from her lips.

"Is something wrong, Cameron?" she asked, crossing the room with quick steps. She reached for him, but he backed away at the last minute, forcing her to hug the air.

"No time to explain," he sputtered, his eyes darting around the room. "I'm endangering everything by even being here—he said I shouldn't come. But I had to see you one last time."

Her mother stared at him, her face awash with confusion. "What are you talking about?" she demanded. "Is this some kind of joke?"

"I wish it were," the man—Trin's father!—replied, shaking

his head. "But I'm afraid it's very real. And very dangerous too. I need you to grab your things—whatever you can pack into the car—and leave tonight. Take Trinity and go to your father's place and don't come back here again."

"You want me to pack up and go to Texas?" her mother cried. "Tonight?"

"Yes," he replied, as if the request wasn't the least bit insane. "Go there and stay there and when they call you to tell you I'm dead, do not let them know—under any circumstances—that you saw me here tonight."

"Cam, stop it! You're scaring me!" she cried, her voice cracking at the edges. "Why would they tell me you're dead?"

He drew in a long breath, biting his lower lip, just as Trinity always did when she was unsure of what to say. Then he stepped forward, taking her mother's face in his hands and meeting her eyes. "I was meant to die tonight," he said, his tone ultra serious. "There was a fire at my lab. Just a freak accident, but I was supposed to be trapped under some lab equipment and die. But he saved me. He said he needs my help and I'm the only one he can trust. But no one can know I'm still alive."

"He? He who? Who the hell are you talking about?"

"His name is Virgil Hauer. He's a scientist from the future and he's come to save us all. But Em, I'm telling you now, they can't find out about any of this. If they learn that he's here and I'm alive, they'll come after both of us. And we won't be able to make the preparations for what's to come."

"The future?" her mother screeched. "Cam, you're talking crazy. We need to get you to a doctor and—"

He glanced at the door, as if he half expected someone

to burst through at any moment. Then he crossed the room to Trinity's cradle. He looked down on his daughter, his eyes hollow and wild and sad. "You're such a little thing," he said in a hoarse whisper. "Can the fate of the world really lie in your tiny hands?"

But Trinity couldn't answer. She just stared up at the father she never knew, too powerless to even lift her head. She watched, helplessly, as he leaned down, his mouth to her ear.

And he whispered…an address?

"Cam, I'm going to call 911 okay? We'll get you to the hospital. They'll give you something that will help."

"No!" he cried, whirling around to face her. "Don't call anyone! Didn't you hear anything I just said? You can't tell anyone you saw me here tonight! I'm supposed to be dead. If anyone finds out I'm still alive, the entire time line could spiral out of control, sending mankind down a devastating track." He raked a hand through his wild hair. "Do you understand what I'm saying?"

"No," she whimpered, taking a hesitant step backward. "I don't understand any of this. Are you really leaving? When will I see you again?"

His face softened. He stepped toward her, taking her trembling hands in his own. "I don't know," he admitted. "Maybe never. But at least you'll know I'm alive, right? That I'm out there, trying to save the world." He reached out, brushing a lock of hair from her eyes. "I'm so sorry, sweetheart. I love you so much. All I wanted in life was to make you and our beautiful daughter happy. But that was never meant to be." He leaned forward to kiss her.

She shoved him away, her face a mask of rage. "You

bastard! What, did you meet someone else? That girl from your lab? Are you running away with her or something? God, at least have the decency to tell me the truth, not this sci-fi/fantasy bull. I mean, do you think I'm an idiot?" She gave him a deadly glare. "If you walk out that door now, you'd better never even think about coming back."

"I won't," he said simply. "Not because I won't want to—I'll want to more than anything—but I won't be able to." He gave her a tortured look. "I don't want to hurt you. Trust me, the only thing that makes any of this bearable is knowing that you and Trinity will be safe. Virgil promised me that. He said they know better than to screw with the time line before the Reckoning is scheduled to take place. They need Trinity for what they're planning and they won't risk hurting her beforehand."

"Need her for what? Cam, she's just a baby!"

He reached into his pocket and pulled out a small object. From her vantage point, Trinity couldn't see what it was exactly, but she had a pretty good idea all the same. "You need to give this to her," he told her mom. "On Christmas Eve when she's fourteen years old. That'll give her two years to prepare for the Reckoning. And once she has the egg, the pendant will lead her to me. By then, Virgil promises we'll be ready. Everything will be in place."

"In place for what?" her mother whispered, her voice cracking.

He gave her a sad look. "I'm sorry, but it's best if you don't know. And anyway, I've got to go. Virgil's waiting for me and we have a lot to do." He grabbed her and kissed her hard on the mouth. At first she resisted, trying to fight him, but then gave up, surrendering into his arms, sobs shaking her entire body.

"I love you, Emberlyn," he murmured. "And I will always love you."

And with that, he tore away from the hug, stalking toward the door, not looking back as he stepped through, out of their lives forever.

Chapter Twenty

Trinity opened her eyes to find Connor and Caleb staring at her intently. The pendant slipped from her fingers and onto the bed. For a moment she couldn't speak, as if she were still that infant girl lying in her cradle. Helpless, powerless, scared.

"Oh, Mom…" she whispered.

All her life, she'd blamed her mother for being weak, for letting the voices take control and steal her away from the daughter who needed her. But now, realizing what she'd had to go through, she couldn't blame her for wanting to retreat from reality. She'd lost her husband, lost her home, was forced to become a single mom, never knowing what had really happened to the man she loved. And yet somehow, she'd managed to cling to life until she was able to keep the promise she'd made to her daughter's father—even if she could have had no idea whether he was telling her the truth.

Do you think I don't know? I've always known. Your father knew. And I was going to tell you.

No wonder that Christmas Eve had been so important to her mother. It was supposed to be the day that Trinity learned her true destiny. Her mother had obviously planned to give her the pendant and tell her the story of her father that night, so she'd be prepared for when she first encountered the egg two years later. Instead, the Dracken had showed up—taking her mom away before she could tell the tale. Leaving Trinity to face her future clueless and alone.

It was still hard to wrap her head around: that her father had known about the Reckoning. That someone had come back from the future to tell him—to warn him about what his baby daughter would be forced to do. That alone was incredible. But what did it mean for her now? Was her dad still out there somewhere? Hanging out with the time traveler who had seen fit to save his life? He said they would be making preparations. Could it be possible they had a plan for Emmy?

"Trin," Connor said gently. "Where were you just now?"

And so she told them, not leaving anything out, her heart swelling with pain as she spoke of the anguish she'd seen on her mother's face. The desperation in her father's eyes. They'd loved one another so strongly. And yet destiny had ripped them apart.

"Virgil Hauer?" Caleb exclaimed when she had finished. "Are you sure he said Virgil Hauer?"

"Yeah," she replied, puzzled. "Why? Who's Virgil Hauer?"

"Only the Dracken's chief scientist," Caleb informed her excitedly. "Or he was, anyway, back in our time. Virgil was a quantum physicist, specializing in time travel. In fact, he was the one who originally perfected the system that sent all of us back. He used to work for the Council until he got angry at how they were dealing with the dragon problem. He broke away from them to come work for the Dracken." He shook his head in amazement. "I didn't know him too well. He was pretty high up on the food chain and well, as you know, I wasn't much more than a glorified errand boy. But everyone looked up to him."

"I don't understand," Trinity interrupted, narrowing her eyes. "If he went back in time with the Dracken, how could he have met up with my dad? This was years before you guys made the trip. I was only a baby."

"That's just it," Caleb replied. "He didn't go. He disappeared three days before the trip was supposed to take place. He even trashed his own lab beforehand, destroying all the equipment he'd built for the journey. In fact, for about a day and a half, the Dracken weren't sure if they'd have to abort the entire mission because of the damage he'd done." His face twisted, remembering. "Everyone was so mad. I was mad," he added. "At the time I thought, here was this duffhead scientist, screwing up our chances to save the world." He paused. "But now..."

"Now you're thinking he might have gotten wind of the Dracken's true mission?" Trinity concluded, a feeling of excitement welling up inside of her. "Like maybe he realized the Dracken were planning to use dragons to burn down the world and he wanted to stop them?"

And he needed my dad's help to do it, she thought to herself. Her dad had mentioned his lab being burned to the ground. If he had a lab, he must be some kind of scientist himself. A genius scientist who could help them out of the mess they were in.

If only she'd gotten the message in time. Before Grandpa...

"It would make sense," Caleb agreed. "He knew the quantum physics of time travel better than anyone. He could have easily reprogrammed the machine to go back years earlier—before the Dracken were scheduled to arrive. He could have looked up your dear old dad and warned him about what was going to happen."

"He not only warned him. He saved his life," Trinity reminded him. "But then what? Where have they been all these years? Are they still out there hiding somewhere? Why haven't they tried to make contact?"

"Maybe they have," Caleb said. "You were supposed to get the pendant two years ago, remember? Maybe they expected you to bring the egg to them as soon as it arrived at the museum. They might not have realized anything was wrong until you failed to show up the day after the Reckoning." He shrugged. "And let's face it, since then, you've been pretty tough to track down."

"Good point," Trinity replied, reaching for the pendant and turning it over in her hands. The metal felt warm, pulsating against her fingers. "My father," she breathed. "Still alive. Waiting for me." She looked up. Surprised. "And I know where he is!" she cried, astonished. With shaking fingers, she reached over to the nightstand, jerking the drawer open. Grabbing the pen and paper inside, she scribbled down what she now remembered her father whispering in her ear. As a baby, it wouldn't have made any sense. But going back to the memory now...

"Cerrillos Road?" Caleb read. "Fauna, New Mexico? How did you...?"

"I don't know." Trinity shrugged. "It just...came to me. Weird, right?"

"Not really. Your father—or maybe Virgil—must have

embedded a memory into the Ouroboros," Caleb said. "It would be the safest way to store it, without writing it down for anyone to find."

"So then we can find him!" Trinity exclaimed, the unfamiliar feeling of hope now rising in her chest. "We could totally go and find him!" Her heart started pounding wildly. They could find him. He could help them. Everything could be okay and—

"No," Connor suddenly injected. He'd been so quiet Trinity had almost forgotten he was in the room. "No way."

She shot him a surprised look. "What do you mean, no way? Why not?"

"Simple. We have no way of knowing if this is some kind of trap," he replied, squaring his shoulders, channeling his inner soldier once again. "This guy was Dracken, remember?"

"He left the Dracken," Caleb argued. "He sabotaged their mission."

"Or so it seemed to you at the time," Connor corrected. "But you yourself knew nothing of the Dracken's true purpose back then. How do you know this wasn't all part of the plan? Make it look like he defected and then have him go back in time early to set things up. Save Trinity's dad's life so they could use him to convince Trinity to believe his story. What would Trinity have been asked to do, had she gotten the Ouroboros when she was supposed to, two years before the Reckoning? Bring the egg directly to this guy, Virgil? So he could turn it over to his buddies at Dracken HQ?" He shrugged. "Maybe that's why they ended up having to send you to go collect her instead. Because they realized they screwed up, picked off the mom too early, before she could tell Trinity what she was supposed to do."

"That's one hell of a lot of conjecture," Caleb remarked, raising an eyebrow.

"But it's possible, right? It would make sense. More sense, in my opinion, than saving Trinity's dad because he needs him for some science project he's working on. I mean, this guy Virgil's a genius from the future, right? Why would he need help from some twenty-first century duff?" He glanced over at Trinity. "No offense."

"Plenty of reasons," Caleb broke in before she could reply, his voice rising in annoyance. "He's a stranger in a strange land. Maybe he needed this twenty-first-century duff to show him the ropes. Gather materials, find them a place to hide out, drive a car. Or maybe Trin's dad is a genius scientist in his own right. Maybe he was working on some technology similar to Virgil's. And Virgil knew he could trust him because he'd want to protect his daughter. And with the Dracken assuming he died as he was supposed to, he could work under the radar and put a plan in motion."

"Maybe," Connor said, not sounding like he thought any of this was likely. "But we don't know for sure. There are too many unknowns, too many contingencies, and right now we can't afford unnecessary risk. Especially after what just happened." He frowned. "You saw the TV. The whole world is out looking for Emmy. If she's spotted…"

"So what's your plan then, oh mighty dragon hunter?" Caleb retorted, scrambling to his feet, his hands on his hips. "Just hang out here and wait for them to track us down? What are we going to feed Emmy in the meantime? How are we going to exercise her?" He shot a glance at the adjoining room, where Emmy was still busy eating. "You've seen how depressed she's been since we got here. What's she going to be like in a week? A month? A year? What about when she starts going wild with hunger? She's not going to be cool with being cooped up here, watching BBC shows on the television, I can tell you that right now."

"Caleb," his brother said in a warning tone.

"But hey, maybe that's what you're secretly hoping for," Caleb plowed on, glaring back at his brother. "In fact I bet it'd be pretty convenient for you to just sit around and wait for someone to come and take out Emmy or Trinity for you. Mission accomplished without getting your hands dirty. That'd be pretty sweet, huh?"

Connor rose, stalking over to his brother and grabbing him by the collar. With exaggerated force, he shoved him against the wall, causing a framed print of a desert cactus to crash onto the floor. Emmy poked her head into the room, whining nervously as she glanced from brother to brother.

"You listen to me," Connor growled, his face only inches away from Caleb's. "If I wanted Emmy dead, she would be flecking dead, rotting out in the Texas sun with vultures picking at her bones." His eyes glowed in fury as he stared his brother down. "But no. I've done everything in my power to keep her safe. It was *your* recklessness that got us in this mess to begin with. And I'll be damned if I'm going to let you continue to put our lives in danger with your impulsive schemes." He shoved Caleb against the wall again before releasing him, stalking to the other side of the room.

Caleb glared at him, hatred burning in storm-tossed eyes. "You're going to keep them safe, huh?" he spit out. "Funny, I remember you making a similar promise to Trinity's grandpa. But that didn't work out so well for him, now did it?"

Connor lunged at him, his fist connecting with Caleb's face so fast that Trinity couldn't track the movement. But she heard the cracking sound as the blood fountained from Caleb's nose.

"Connor!" Trinity cried, horrified. She looked from brother to brother, now locked in a standoff, each glaring at the other with so much fury that if looks could kill, Trin was sure they'd both be messy puddles on the floor.

Caleb brushed the blood from his nose with his sleeve and took a threatening step toward his brother. Without thinking, Trinity threw herself between them.

"Stop it!" she screamed, her voice cracking. "Both of you! Just stop it! You're brothers! You're supposed to be on the same team. On my team," she added, choking on the words. "Please. I need both of you."

"And what if you can't have that?" Caleb asked in a tight voice, staring down at her with angry eyes. "What if you had to make a choice between us? Who would you choose?"

Trinity looked from one brother to the other, words failing as the lump in her throat threatened to throttle her. "That's not fair," she choked out at last. "That's so not fair."

"Yeah, well, welcome to my world," Caleb spit out, glaring down at her, trapping her in a furious gaze. Then he turned his head, swinging around and heading for the door. It slammed shut behind him, leaving Connor and Trinity all alone.

Chapter Twenty-One

D id you want room service or something?" Connor asked, looking down at Trinity with concern in his eyes. "Or I could order some Chinese delivery. What is it you like—extra duck sauce?"

She sighed, forcing herself to shake her head. The simple gesture seemed to take all her remaining strength. "I'm not hungry."

Connor gave her a rueful look then climbed onto the bed beside her, lifting her head and laying it in his lap, stroking her hair with gentle hands. As he worked through the tangled curls, she half wondered if she should be objecting to this display of uninvited intimacy, but somehow she couldn't seem to muster the strength to argue or pull away. Instead, she found herself closing her eyes, surrendering to his touch, allowing him to soothe her frayed nerves with his magic fingers. Connor always knew the right thing to do, the right thing to say to make her feel better.

Caleb on the other hand…

"Should I go after him?" Connor asked, catching her glancing at the door again. It had been about a half hour since Caleb had taken off on them. Without his cell phone or his room key. She kept expecting a knock on the door, but it didn't come.

"No," she said with a shake of her head. "I'm done chasing him down, begging him to come back every time he storms off. He's got to learn—he can't say things like that and then expect everything to just be okay." She forced her eyes away from the door. "Just let him do his thing. He'll be back once he calms down. He always is."

Connor sighed. "I worry about him," he said. "He's going to the Nether way too much. He looks like death warmed over and his mind is beyond fragile. We need to be careful about sharing too much of the plan with him, as long as he's palming."

"He keeps saying he's just doing it to see Fred," Trinity said. "But I think there's more to it than that." She frowned. "Do you think we should stage an intervention or something?" she added. "You know, like they do on TV?"

"Do you think he'd listen to words of wisdom from the guy who just kicked his ass?"

Trinity made a face. "Good point."

Connor groaned, raking a hand through his hair. "I'm sorry, Trin," he said for what felt like the thousandth time since Caleb had left. "I don't know what I was thinking."

"Probably about the horrible things he was saying to you," she reminded him. "He knows Grandpa's death wasn't your fault. He was just trying to hurt you."

"Are you sure about that?" he said slowly. He paused, the silence stretching out so long between them that she wondered if he actually wanted an answer. Instead, he spoke again. "It wasn't nice of him to say. But that doesn't make what he said untrue. Which is probably why it made me so mad."

"What are you talking about?"

He scrunched up his face. "I promised you I'd protect him. I said I wouldn't let anything happen to him. And then…" She could hear his hard swallow. "And then I did."

She looked up, catching the naked pain on his face, and guilt gnawed at her stomach. She'd been so selfish, so lost in her own grief that she'd barely acknowledged the fact that he would be suffering too. He loved her grandpa. The two of them had first bonded while trying to rescue her from the Dracken, and since then the older man had become almost a father figure to him. And, of course, he would blame himself for it all. He was Connor Jacks, after all, legendary Dragon Hunter. Able to leap tall buildings in a single bound and save everyone he loved without breaking a sweat.

Except that wasn't actually true.

"Connor, it wasn't—"

He waved her off, refusing her attempts to alleviate his guilt and pain. "I promised you I'd keep him safe. I'd keep all of you safe. And I failed. I've failed over and over again—no matter what I set out to do."

"Connor, stop," she commanded, sitting up from his lap. "It's not in your job description to keep all of us safe. We're a team. We all make our own decisions. Grandpa made his."

A small smile tugged at Connor's mouth despite his best efforts. "I guess he did," he said. "And he saved both our lives by doing it. Seriously, that guy was the toughest old bastard I ever met."

Trin giggled. "He was," she agreed, the tears splashing down her cheeks. "And he loved you too—he appreciated all that you did for him. I mean, just think—because of you, he was able to live long enough to see a dragon. Do you know how much that meant to him? To see his life's work literally come to life?" She smiled through her tears. "All of his life people laughed at him. They called him a fool. And because of you, he was able to die knowing they were wrong. That's something," she insisted staunchly. "In fact, that's a lot."

They fell silent for a moment, each lost in their own memories. Finally Trin dared to speak. "Connor?"

"Yeah?" His voice was quiet, hesitant, as if he were afraid of what she was going to ask. Which wasn't surprising, she supposed, considering she was a little scared too.

"Do you have a plan?" she blurted out. "Do you have any idea what we should do next?"

She held her breath, waiting for the confident Connor she knew to assure her that he had things all under control. That he knew what they should do. That it all would turn out okay.

"Truthfully?" he asked after a pause.

"Of course."

She could see his fingers tighten into fists, his knuckles whitening over the bone. He sighed. "I haven't a damn clue."

Her heart went out to him, aching at the vulnerability she saw etched across his face. She knew how hard it must be for him to admit something like this out loud. After all, he was the soldier. The one always in control of every situation. And now? He was as broken as the rest of them.

"You know what?" she whispered. "That's okay. It's really okay, Connor. You don't always have to be the superhero in this story. Maybe give someone else a turn for a change." She gave him a half smile. "Seriously, I bet I could totally rock a lasso of truth if I had half the chance."

He didn't smile back, just stared at her, his blue eyes flickering with something she couldn't quite define but that sent her heart fluttering all the same.

"You want to go find your father, don't you?" he said at last.

She found herself nodding. "How can I not?" she asked. "I mean, this is the first lead we've had since we escaped from the mall. How can we just ignore it? If he's really out there, waiting for us…with a plan…"

Connor's fingers wrapped around her hand, squeezing it tightly. "I know how much you want it all to be true," he said, looking at her with earnest eyes. "And believe me, if someone sent me a message about my dad still being alive? I'd move heaven and earth to find him. But we don't know the whole story behind this Virgil guy your father's supposedly working for. And we have no idea what his true intentions might be."

Trinity pulled her hand away. "It's not that I don't see your point," she said. "But at the same time, at least we'd be doing something. It'd be a risk, sure. But we could be cautious. We could take steps to protect ourselves. At least we'd be going forward instead of running in place." She squeezed her eyes shut then opened them again. "I'm sick of hiding. I'm sick of running away. I promised to take care of Emmy and I haven't had any way to keep that promise up until now. If there's even the slightest possibility of my dad and Virgil being able to help her? Well, how can I just let that go without finding out for sure?"

Connor was silent for a moment. Then, to her relief, he gave a small nod—a simple gesture but it made her heart soar. She knew he didn't think it was a good idea. But he was willing to take a chance. For her. For Emmy. For all of them.

"But Trin, listen to me. From here on out, we have to be more careful. We can't take any more risks. No more leaving Emmy alone—even for a second. One of us needs to have an eye on her at all times. Our situation is even more precarious now than it's ever been. And if she gets out and causes more trouble…hurts any more people…" He trailed off, leaving the unsaid words dangling in the air.

"She won't," Trinity promised, excitement welling up inside of her. "I swear she won't. I'll keep an eye on her twenty-four/ seven. She'll never leave my sight. She won't have the chance to even swat a fly."

Connor gave a small smile at that. Then he shook his head. "I don't know how you do it," he said quietly. "I mean, I trained for this. I chose this life. But you—" He pressed his lips together. "You shouldn't have to be involved in any of this. You should be that carefree girl I saw in the football stands, laughing and eating a hot dog and cheering on her team. You should be worried about school and what you're going to wear to the dance." He lay down on the bed, staring up at the ceiling. "How did you get yourself mixed up in this mess, with two idiots from the future who have no idea how to help you?"

She looked down on him with aching eyes. He looked so sad, so lost, like a little boy, not a fierce soldier. Her heart swelled. It was so strange to see him like this. And maybe a little scary. But it was also honest.

She gave him a rueful smile. "I'm just lucky I guess."

He looked up at her. "No," he said. "We're the lucky ones."

They stared at one another. Their faces inches away. Trinity could feel Connor's hot breath against her skin and knew he wanted to kiss her. The look on his face was undeniable. But he was also holding back. This was her decision to make, not his. He would not touch her unless she made it clear she wanted him to. The power and control that gave her made her head spin.

Until she realized she had no power. Or control.

She lowered her head and their lips met. Clumsily at first, noses knocking into one another, then coming together, Connor's mouth brushing against hers with impossible, velvety warmth. Her breath hitched as he gently rolled her over, lowering her onto the bed and climbing on top of her as he continued to cover her face and neck with slow, drugging kisses.

She closed her eyes, trying at first to catalog all the sensations his touch sent coursing through her, then gave up and surrendered to them all. His hands, his mouth, his hard planes, melting into her soft curves. She found herself reaching up under his shirt so she could run her fingers up and down his smooth, muscled chest. His buttons started to come undone.

She knew she should feel guilty at what they were doing. This was not the time. This was definitely not the place. But at the same time, she found she couldn't stop. Because, she realized, she needed this. Needed this one pure moment of selfishness to block out the grief and pain she'd bottled up inside. One moment of not being the girl who would save the world—but just the girl who would love a boy.

It'll only make things harder…and they're so hard already.

Ugh. She glanced involuntarily to the door, the spell broken, reality smacking her upside the head as guilt gnawed at her insides. "Connor," she said weakly, as he trailed kisses down her neck, his mouth nibbling at her collarbone. God, he felt so good. "Connor, you have to stop."

He did. Of course he did. Connor always would. He would never even think of taking what she wasn't ready to give. And while half of her wanted desperately for him to ignore her protests, to keep kissing her as if he couldn't hear a word she said, the other half was grateful for his self-control.

That didn't mean it was easy for him. He rolled onto his back again, staring up at the ceiling, his face flushed and his breathing heavy. It took all of her willpower not to climb on top of him and resume where they left off. Kiss every inch of him until there was no place left unexplored. But she swallowed hard and somehow resisted the temptation.

Connor groaned. He reached up to button his shirt. "Sorry," he said. "I don't know what I was...I shouldn't have..." He sighed. "I just..."

He trailed off. But that was okay. She knew exactly what he meant.

She leaned over and indulged herself in one last kiss, this time to his forehead.

"I think we both 'just' in this case," she assured him.

He chuckled softly, gazing into her eyes with unabashed adoration. And suddenly everything inside of her wanted it to start all over again. Thankfully, before she was able to give in to temptation, she caught movement at the adjoining room's door. Mischievous eyes peeking in from the other room.

She felt her face heat. *I thought you were going to watch TV*, she reminded Emmy.

The dragon's eyes danced. *This is suddenly far more entertaining.*

But Connor was already pulling himself up off of the bed. "Go ahead, Emmy," he told the dragon. "She's all yours. I've got to get some sleep. Or at least take a cold shower." And with that, he headed to the other room, pulling the connecting door closed behind them. Trinity watched him go, waves of longing crashing over her. Then she shook herself and turned back to the dragon. Emmy had hopped up onto the adjoining bed and was watching her curiously.

"What?" she asked, her face still feeling hot.

You were kissing him. Like Arthur kisses Guinevere on my show.

"Yeah," Trin said. She stared down at her lap. "I guess I was."

The dragon's eyes lit up. *Does that mean you love him? That you will marry him and become his queen and live happily ever after?*

Trinity groaned. "Did anyone ever tell you that you watch way too much TV?"

The dragon just grinned.

Okay, okay, maybe I like him a little, she admitted, going into silent talking mode to ensure Connor wouldn't pick up anything from the next room. *But it doesn't matter. I have no time for happily-ever-afters in my life, thank you very much.*

She said it as a joke, but it came out sadder than she'd meant it to. She closed her eyes, thinking of her grandfather in the barn. His shaky hand grabbing her arm. His watery eyes locking onto hers.

You must go on.

You must face your destiny.

If you can't do it for yourself, then do it for me.

She opened her eyes. Emmy was gazing at her with a worried expression on her face. *You've already given up so much for me,* the dragon said sadly. *I just hope that someday I can do the same for you.* She paused then added, *Perhaps I can start now.*

She hopped off the bed, exaggeratingly stretching her neck out and yawning loudly. Then she wandered into the next room. A moment later, Connor poked his head in.

"Um, I have a dragon in my bed?" he said in an uncomfortable voice. "She just waltzed right in here and jumped up and refuses to leave."

Trinity laughed. *Oh, Emmy.* She smiled at Connor. "I think that's her not-so-subtle hint that you and I should hang out and watch TV." Okay, so the dragon probably hoped for more, but that was as far as it could go. And Trin was okay with that. "Will you order some Chinese food?"

Connor grinned. "Extra duck sauce?"

"You know it."

Chapter Twenty-Two

Who would you chose? Who would you chose?

Caleb raked a hand through his hair as he stormed down the street, cursing himself out as he went. What had possessed him to go and say something like that to her? Trinity had just lost her grandfather, her very last family. She was confused, frightened, out of her mind with grief. And what had he done? Tried to force her to make a choice between him and his brother. Then stormed off and left her alone with him. Probably making that choice really, really easy in the process.

His hand reached for his nose, wondering if his brother had broken it. Wondering if he cared if he had. He should have never gone and baited Connor in the first place. His brother had been right to hit him after what he'd implied. It was no one's fault Trin's grandfather was killed. Unless it was Caleb's for not guarding Emmy better in the first place.

But he'd been so frustrated. To have this glimmer of hope, sparkling just out of reach—the first hope they'd had in what felt like an eternity—only to have Connor shoot it down altogether.

He should have taken a breath. Listened to his brother's argument then presented his own, listing concrete reasons why going to find Virgil and Trin's dad would be a good and logical idea. He could have told them about all the peace campaigns Virgil had held back in the day, the essays he'd penned on finding a better world. He could have told them about Virgil's dragon, Solaris, slain during a battle over an outer territory the Council had abandoned. Virgil had loved Solaris with all his heart, as much as Caleb loved Fred. But he'd been willing to risk her life to go out there and help those who couldn't help themselves.

All those arguments could have brought Connor—or at least Trin—over to his side. Instead, he'd alienated them both even further, lashing out at the girl he loved and storming from the room like a bratty child. What was wrong with him these days? Sure, he'd always been a bit hotheaded, but this uncontrollable rage was on another level entirely, his fuse feeling shorter and shorter with each passing day.

All that time spent in the Nether, a voice inside him taunted. *It's rotting you from the inside out.*

And suddenly he realized what he had to do. To prove to both of them that he wasn't the weak link they believed him to be. That he was as strong as Connor was—that Trinity could rely on him as a full member of the team.

He'd begged her not to ask him to leave Fred behind. And, to her credit, she hadn't—not once. But in the end, that was exactly what he needed to do.

He reached into his pocket, hands trembling, his breath coming in short gasps as he pulled out his final gem. His one and only connection to his beloved dragon.

"You can do this," he muttered to himself. "You can do this for her."

Mind made up, he switched paths, heading down a dark alleyway toward the dumpster that squatted near the back. He paused in front of it, his heart racing as he pinched the gem between his two fingers. Just one flick of his wrist and it would all be over. He would finally be free.

"Come on," he urged himself. "You can do this."

But his hand refused to move. And instead of walking confidently away, mission accomplished, he found himself sinking to his knees.

"Fred," he whispered. "Oh, Fred."

He closed his eyes, the tall dragon looming in his imagination now. Bounding around him, big and goofy and hungry. Batting her eyelashes at him. Begging for just one last treat. It made him smile and it made him weep. Once upon a time, Fred had been the only one he'd had in the entire world. The only one who cared if he lived or died.

The vision twisted then. The happy, hungry Fred disappearing into thin air. And in her place a dragon who was hardly recognizable. Grotesquely thin, with scales that were dull and cracked and eyes that had lost their luster. Standing in the middle of nothingness, shivering, whimpering, and completely alone.

She looked up at Caleb with big eyes filled with pain and confusion. *I waited for you,* she seemed to say. *I waited for you, but you never came. Did I do something wrong? Did I beg too much? Did I snore too loud? Was I not worthy to be your dragon? Is that why you threw me away without even saying good-bye?*

Caleb's eyes flew open and his stomach wrenched. It was all he could do not to throw up then and there. But he forced himself to swallow hard and concentrate on the gem, still in his hand.

"I'll just say good-bye," he found himself stammering. "Just a quick good-bye. She deserves that at least. To know why I have to leave—that it's nothing to do with her. That she's amazing. The best dragon a guy could have."

Just one more time. What could it hurt, just one more time?

Chapter Twenty-Three

"Do you feel them? Are they close?"

Scarlet closed her eyes, trying to pull up another image of Emmy in her mind as Rashida and the other Potentials had taught her. She'd led them this far, to some cute little touristy town in southeast Colorado, but she hadn't been able to narrow it down to more than just this generalized area. So the rest of the Potentials had set up camp in an abandoned housing development on the outskirts of town earlier that day, and now she and Rashida were combing the streets for some sign of Emmy.

"I don't know," she confessed, scrubbing her face with her hands. She was exhausted and a little sick from the long trip they'd taken in the fume-filled school bus stolen from a junkyard. Now, even the prospect of seeing Emmy again was starting to pale with the worry of how far away from home she really was. The only real place she'd ever traveled to before now was to see her grandmother on the reservation. And that didn't really count.

Why had she agreed to come along? What had possessed her to join up with this strange team of so-called Potentials and their quest for the missing dragon? To walk away from her mother, her friends, her school, and her job—without telling anyone where she was going?

All her life, Scarlet had been the responsible one. The one who picked up the pieces when those she loved fell apart. She wasn't the type of girl who just ran away. So why had she done it now?

She tried to tell herself it was out of concern for Emmy. She'd already screwed up so badly—this was a chance to make good, to get her the vaccine she needed. But as the day wore on, even that noble idea had started to feel…itchy. Like it wasn't quite right. More troubling: every time she tried to think back to the moment when she'd agreed to join the group, her head began to hurt and she couldn't quite focus on the memory. As if it were dancing in the back of her brain, just out of reach.

Had they messed with her mind somehow? Tricked her into thinking it was all her idea? That was impossible, of course. But try as she might, she couldn't push the idea away, and as the sun began to set over the horizon, her troubling thoughts only multiplied.

Suddenly her mind prickled, as if fairies were dancing across the neurons. She stopped in her tracks and cocked her head, trying to understand the strange sensation. Then, without warning, a windy trail of golden sparks seemed to roll out before her, glittering temptingly.

"What the hell…?" she murmured.

Rashida caught her expression. "Do you feel something?" she asked. Then she closed her own eyes, breathing in deep. A moment later she opened them. "I think it might be Caleb," she exclaimed. "He's giving off some crazy energy signals and he's not that far away either."

Caleb. Scarlet's heart involuntarily skipped a beat. She had to admit, she'd been hoping he would be the one they found first. He may have been the bad twin, but he'd also been the most understanding. And his good-bye hug had been warm.

"Come on," Rashida said excitedly. "If Caleb's nearby, that means Emmy is too!"

They picked up their pace, down the snowy streets, avoiding puddles best they could as they followed the sparkling trail. Soon the cute, touristy wine bars and sporting goods stores started to fade away, replaced by the seedier establishments Scarlet was more used to. Pawnshops, cash advance places, shooting ranges, and liquor stores with bulletproof glass. She could feel the suspicious stares of the men and women loitering outside, but she kept her head down and her eyes averted best she could.

At last the path dead-ended in a dark alleyway, seemingly empty save for an overflowing dumpster propped up in the far corner. Scarlet frowned, scanning the scene. A dead end? What would Caleb be doing down here?

She glanced over at Rashida. Before the girl could speak, there was a noise—a bottle skittering across the pavement. Had they been followed? On instinct, they dove into the shadows.

A moment later, two twenty-something-year-old men wearing matching Carhartt jackets and jeans stalked into the alleyway and headed toward the dumpster. Even in the darkness, Scarlet could see their crooked grins and their eager eyes.

Were they planning to go dumpster diving? Mac would do that sometimes back in the day, when they'd come home to find Mom passed out on the couch and nothing but beer in the fridge. *You wouldn't believe the food people throw away*, he'd tell her. *We'll feast like kings and queens.*

Oh, Mac. If only you were here now...

"Well, well, what do we have here?" one of the men suddenly exclaimed, jolting Scarlet back to present. She watched as he and his friend abandoned the dumpster and leaned over a large lump beside it. A human-shaped lump, Scarlet realized with growing unease. Some guy was lying there, motionless, his head slumped forward, his hands clasped together on his lap.

Was that Caleb? What was he was doing out here all alone and passed out? Was he hurt? Was he...dead? A surge of panic shot through her.

Rashida frowned, catching Scarlet's eyes with her own. *We can't let them hurt him. He's our only link to the dragon.*

They'll probably just rob him, Scarlet sent back silently, as they'd taught her to do. Since she'd joined up with the group, they'd been trying to teach her how to use her newfound gifts—psychic powers she'd evidently inherited from Emmy's little blood transfusion. *We should just wait here till they leave.*

Rashida nodded. *Yeah,* she agreed. *Then we can—*

"Hey! Isn't this that guy?" the first man cried.

His friend looked up from rummaging through Caleb's pockets. "What guy?" he asked, sounding impatient.

"Yeah, this is totally him. The AWOL soldier guy from a few months ago. I saw it on the news. The government's been looking everywhere for him."

The second man snorted. "What the hell's he doing here then?" He started to dig back into Caleb's pockets. But his friend swatted him away.

"Dude, there's probably a reward out for him," he said excitedly.

That got the second guy's attention. He straightened up. "You think so?"

"They're looking for him, aren't they?" The man grinned. "I bet there's a big reward for this guy. We just gotta drag him down to the police station and collect."

Oh no. Scarlet stifled a gasp. They couldn't let these guys just take him away. The police would arrest him. Lock him up, probably throw away the key.

What should we do? she sent back to Rashida worriedly.

The Potential flashed her a look. *Follow my lead.*

Before Scarlet could reply, Rashida stepped out of the shadows, clearing her throat as she whipped a knife from her pocket. The two would-be bounty hunters jumped— obviously startled—and whirled around to face her. Their eyes glittered maddeningly under the streetlights, and Scarlet cataloged them quickly from the safety of her hiding spot. Small but wiry. One sporting an ugly scar on his cheek. The other with arms sleeved in tattoos.

Just Mom's type, she thought, a little bitterly.

"Get away from him," Rashida commanded now that she had their attention. Her voice was authoritative and fierce, sending a chill down Scarlet's spine. She sounded very strong. Still, she hoped her new friend understood how dangerous these monsters could be.

"And what are you going to do if we don't, sweetheart?" the scarred man asked, grinning widely and revealing a few missing teeth.

She shrugged. "Probably gut you to start. Then, if I'm feeling extra generous, I'll feed you your entrails, so you won't die hungry."

They exchanged glances, then tattoo guy broke out in a barking laugh. "Yeah, well, as pleasant as that sounds, we're a bit busy right now. So why don't you go run and play and leave us to our business? Before you get hurt."

"I think you're mistaken," Scarlet said, stepping to Rashida's right. "We'll be giving the hurt, not getting."

"Oh yeah?" The man snorted. "This I have to see."

He'd barely finished speaking when Rashida lunged at him, slashing out with her blade, slicing into his shoulder without hesitation. For a moment the man just stared at her, as if shocked into paralysis as the bright red blood soaked through his jacket.

"You little whore!" he whispered.

He sprang into action, using his full body weight to slam her into the wall. Scarlet watched in horror as the back of her new friend's head smacked into brick, and for a moment she was afraid he'd knocked her out right then and there. But somehow Rashida managed to stay conscious, kneeing him in the groin instead. As he stumbled backward, clutching his privates, Scarlet had to resist the urge to cheer.

Score one for the little girls.

The man turned to his friend. "Stop standing there!" he screamed to him. "And cut these bitches!"

Tattoo guy didn't need a second invitation. He dove at Scarlet, surprising her with his sudden move, his nails digging into her arms, drawing blood. She fought wildly, kicking and hitting, wishing she had a weapon like Rashida.

For a few fleeting moments, she was able to hold her own, clawing an ugly gash down the side of the man's face and ripping open his shirt. But eventually he proved too strong, knocking her to the ground and climbing on top of her, pinning her down with his body's weight. He leered at her, his face dripping with blood.

"Now, now, little kitty. It's time for you to be declawed."

She screamed, desperately trying to wriggle out of his grasp as his hands clamped down on her throat, crushing her larynx and cutting off her air supply. In an instant, she couldn't breathe; she couldn't move. She couldn't even plead for her life. And any attempts to pry his hands off of her were proving fruitless. Out of the corner of her eye, she could see that the scarred man also had Rashida, back up against the wall, having evidently stolen away her knife. There would be no help from her.

The monsters had them. And they were not going to let them go.

I'm sorry, Caleb. I tried…

Suddenly an inhuman screech tore through the air. Scarlet looked up, eyes bulging, heart panging with sudden hope.

It couldn't be.

Could it?

At first she thought she must have been hallucinating. The lack of oxygen making her brain play tricks on her. But then her captor let out a very real scream and blood splashed down onto her face as his hands fell from her throat. For a moment she was blinded. Then her vision cleared. The man who had had her by the throat was now levitating three feet above her…

…locked in the talons of a dragon.

"Emmy!" Scarlet managed to croak, relief flooding her like a tidal wave. "You came."

The dragon tossed the man aside, as if he were a bag of feed. He hit the brick wall with a horrifying thump, his body sliding down the side and collapsing in a bloody heap. He didn't get up.

"Oh my God!" the second man cried, staring from his buddy to the dragon and back again, Rashida all but forgotten. "It's…it's…that thing!"

"Her name is Emmy," Scarlet declared, forcing herself to her feet. She moved next to the dragon, placing a protective hand on the back of her neck. "And, spoiler alert, she's about to flambé your ass."

Emmy snorted, puffs of black smoke steaming from her nostrils, as if to prove Scarlet's point. She took a menacing step forward, raising her head to meet her enemy's eyes. Scarlet watched with a mixture of excitement and fear. Gone was the gentle creature from the barn. The one who had licked her face and saved her life. The dragon before her now was a wild and deadly beast—hungry for prey. She was very glad to be on the same team.

"Don't even think about it," she growled, as the man took a tentative step toward his fallen friend. "Trust me, it won't end well."

Thankfully the guy seemed to come to the same conclusion. He took one last look at his buddy then took off, bolting down the street as fast as his legs could take him. The two girls watched him go, Scarlet still marveling at what had just happened. She'd been so sure they were dead, that this would be the last evening of their lives.

Instead she'd been saved a second time. From a second monster.

Rashida frowned, glancing over at her. She looked worried. "He's gonna go tell people," she said in a low voice. "We've got to get Emmy out of here before he comes back. Otherwise there could be trouble." She reached into her pocket and pulled out her cell phone. "I'll text the others and have them bring the bus." She turned to Emmy. "Just hang on a second, okay? Don't go anywhere. Help is on the way."

But the dragon already was turning away, her nose pointed to the sky. Concern flooded Scarlet. "Where are you going?" she asked.

Emmy gave her an apologetic look. *I must get back to Trinity. She will worry if I'm gone.*

Right. Of course. "Okay, but just wait a second." Scarlet turned to Rashida. "She's gotta go. Quick, give her the vaccine before she takes off."

"What?" Rashida asked, sounding genuinely puzzled.

Scarlet frowned, impatiently. "The vaccine! Give her the vaccine before we lose her again." She reached out to pet Emmy. "Hang on. We've got something important to give you." She turned to look expectantly at the Potential.

"Oh. Right. The vaccine." Rashida's face flushed. "I...I... don't...have it on me."

Scarlet stared at her, incredulous. "You don't have it on you? Why wouldn't you have it on you?"

I'm sorry, Scarlet. I must go now.

Emmy started flapping her wings, kicking snow into the air. Rashida's eyes grew wide with fear. "Wait!" she cried. "Don't leave! We can help you! Scarlet—tell her we can help her!"

Scarlet stared at her, a cold chill tripping down her spine. Then she turned to the dragon. *Go!* She told her silently. *Go now.*

Emmy took flight, pushing off her back feet and soaring into the sky. Scarlet watched her go, her heart squeezing as the dragon disappeared behind a rooftop.

Stay safe, she begged her.

"Damn it!" Rashida swore, squeezing her hands into fists. "She was right here in front of us! We totally had her!"

Scarlet was silent for a moment, staring up into the once-again empty sky. "There's no vaccine, is there?" she said quietly. "You made that up to get me to help you find her."

Rashida sighed. She walked over to Caleb. "Can you help me over here?" she asked, grabbing his shoulders and shaking him violently. "Wake up, Caleb!" she cried. "You stupid idiot. We've got to get out of here."

Against her better judgment, Scarlet joined her. She poked Caleb hard. "You need to get up," she told him. "It's not safe here."

Finally Caleb shifted, his face turning upward. His eyes fluttered open, at first unfocused then locking onto hers. She'd almost forgotten what crazy eyes he had—a kaleidoscope of blues and greens, swirling around in a storm of color.

"Where…?" he started, looking around the alley, his face awash with confusion. Then he turned back to her, his eyes lighting up as they focused on her face. "Buttercup!" he exclaimed. "What are you doing here?"

"Evidently I'm saving your ass, Bad Seed," she replied with a wry smile. "Are you okay?"

Her eyes roved over him. He didn't look okay. In fact, he looked like hell. His face was pale, his eyes glassy, his skin covered in goose bumps. She swallowed, déjà vu hitting her hard and fast.

Another alley, another dumpster, another life.

"She's fine," Rashida interrupted briskly, taking his arm and trying to yank him upright. "She's helping us rescue

Emmy from your little girlfriend. Now come on! Get on your feet you lousy Netherhead, or I'll leave you in the gutter where you belong."

Caleb rose to his feet, his legs shaking. He could barely stand, Scarlet realized with growing dread. "I'm not going anywhere with you," he announced. Then he turned to Scarlet. "Buttercup—"

Before he could finish, he stumbled, his legs giving out from under him as he fell, his eyes rolling to the back of his head, losing consciousness again as he hit the ground with a thump. Scarlet cried out in horror, dropping to her knees before him, while Rashida swore under her breath. "God, he's even more pathetic than I remembered him," she muttered.

Fury surged through Scarlet. She rose back to her feet, hands on her hips. "Rashida, what's going on here?" she demanded. "What do you mean you're rescuing Emmy? And what about the vaccine?"

Rashida sighed. "Look," she said, "the truth is, Trinity infiltrated our headquarters. She pretended to be one of us and then she turned Caleb against us. She used him to break the dragon out so she could have her to herself. We've been trying to track them down and rescue Emmy ever since." She gave Scarlet a rueful look. "I'm sorry I didn't tell you. But I was afraid Trinity had brainwashed you as well. And we'd gotten so close. I couldn't afford for you to walk away and refuse to help."

Scarlet scowled. "So you lied to me."

"Only about the vaccine. And about being friends with Trinity," Rashida protested. "The rest is true. Emmy's in trouble. We're trying to help her. And if we don't save her soon, the world as we know it could be in grave danger."

Scarlet opened her mouth to speak, but a roar of an engine drowned out her words. The other Potentials had arrived, pouring out of the van, surrounding her with excited faces.

"Where's the dragon?" one of them finally asked.

Hopefully far, far from here, Scarlet thought mournfully. *With enough sense to stay away from you.*

Chapter Twenty-Four

Trinity shifted, feeling drowsy and warm as the sun flittered through the windows, teasing her eyelids awake. For a moment she had no idea where she was. Only that she felt overwhelmingly cozy and comfortable. She'd slept through the night for the first time in what felt like forever, without a single nightmare to wake her.

She burrowed into the pillow, hoping to chase a few more minutes of blissful slumber before getting back to the reality she didn't want to face. But then something solid shifted at her back, a weight falling gently over her side. Her eyes flew open and she turned her head, only to find Connor snuggled up against her, his arm draped solidly across her waist.

Now she was wide awake, her heart beating wildly in her chest as she wondered what she should do. How had this happened? Last thing she remembered was finishing up their Chinese food and discovering that really terrible *Fields of Fantasy* movie was playing on HBO. They must have fallen asleep in the middle of the movie.

Slowly, as not to wake him, Trinity slipped out from under Connor's arm and sat up in bed. The loss of connection sent an unexpected ache through her, and she glanced down at his sexy, rumpled figure, a rueful look on her face. How easy it would be to crawl back into bed. To let him hold her and cuddle her and keep the nightmares at bay. To absorb his strength, warm skin to warm skin. And remember his promise that she would never be alone.

But that couldn't happen. *This* couldn't happen—ever again. There was too much going on right now for her to be sidetracked by romance. Her body may have betrayed her, but her mind was set. And she wouldn't put herself in that position—that oh so comfortable position—ever again.

Connor would understand this, she told herself. Even if Caleb refused to.

Caleb. She bit her lower lip, looking around the room again, now noticing his obvious absence. When he'd stormed out the night before, she'd assumed he'd be back eventually, tail tucked between his legs and his mouth full of apologies— just like every time before. But the other bed was still made. And a quick peek into the adjoining room told her he hadn't returned at all. Which was probably for the best, she realized, feeling a stab of guilt. If he had seen her and Connor, locked in each other's arms…

Her eyes caught the television set, which had been left on all night. The station had cut to a breaking news piece and the video showed blue and white and red emergency lights flashing against the backdrop of some random brick alleyway. Police tape had been stretched across the crime scene and EMTs were wheeling some poor schlub on a stretcher into a waiting ambulance. She gave a tight smile. At least they'd finally stopped talking about Emmy for five seconds and moved on to other tragedies going on in the world.

But before she could reach for the remote to turn off the set, her eyes caught the scrolling text at the bottom of the screen

Another touchdown of terror?

A gasp escaped her. She flicked off the TV then ran to the other room to turn on the other one, grabbing the remote to turn up the volume. The reporter was holding the microphone out to a terrified looking man sporting a long scar down his cheek.

"It killed him!" he cried. "He wasn't doing nothing. Just minding his own business. And this…thing…swooped down and dug its claws into him and threw him against the wall!" He made a swinging gesture with his arms, to illustrate his point. "Killed him dead. Right there in front of me. And then this girl? She was, like, petting the creature like it was some frigging St. Bernard, saying I was next." He shook his head, droplets of spittle flying from his mouth. "I barely escaped with my life."

Trinity glanced over at Emmy, who was still sleeping at the foot of the bed, snoring contentedly. Was this some kind of prank? A copycat crime?

She turned back to the TV. The program had cut to the reporter, now standing live in the alleyway where it had all gone down. "The military is on their way and authorities have instituted a lockdown on the city. Everyone is asked to stay indoors until the search for this creature is complete. If you do catch sight of it, please call 911. Do not approach it under any circumstances." She stared straight into the camera, a severe look on her overly made up face. "This is Daisy Solomon reporting live from San Angels."

Wait. What? Trinity dropped the remote onto the bed. San Angels? That's where they were now. But Emmy was here. How could she have…?

Panicked, she turned to the sliding glass door leading out to the balcony. The *open* sliding glass door, she realized in dismay. Connor must have opened it in his attempt to cool off the night before and had forgotten to close it when Emmy made her sudden appearance. It was the kind of mistake the Hunter never would have made. But he'd been distracted. *She'd* distracted him.

And Emmy had taken advantage.

She looked over at the dragon who was still lying curled up on the bed, the tears welling in her eyes.

"What did you do?" she whispered.

Emmy lifted her head sleepily, looking at Trinity with genuine confusion. It was then that she saw the blood crusted on the creature's claws, confirming her worst fears.

"What has who done?"

She looked up guiltily, realizing Connor had walked into the room and was staring at her. Terror churned in her stomach as her mind whirled with lies. She couldn't let him know what Emmy had done. Not after she'd promised nothing else would happen under her watch. What would he say if he found out another person had been killed? More importantly—what would he decide to do about it?

If she gets into any more trouble…hurts any more people…

Oh, Emmy, what have you done?

She grabbed the remote and turned off the TV, struggling to retain her composure. "Sorry, what did you say?" she asked in a stumbling voice, as if she hadn't heard him.

"I said…Wait, Trinity? Are you okay?" he asked, peering at her intently. "You look like you've seen a ghost."

"Um, yeah. I'm…fine. I'm just…" Oh God, oh God. "I just have to use the bathroom, okay?"

"Oh. Right. Sorry to barge in on you." He headed back into the other room and shut the door. Trinity turned back to Emmy.

"Talk. Now," she hissed. "And I don't want to hear you say you don't remember."

Emmy turned away, unable to meet her eyes. *You don't understand,* she began.

"You're damn right about that."

The dragon gave her a hurt look. *She was crying for help. She was scared. These men…they were hurting her. What was I supposed to do? You told me I should save people if I could.*

Oh God. Trinity didn't even know what to say as her words from the day before were thrown back in her face. "I didn't mean by murdering someone else!" she cried.

He was hurting Scarlet. I couldn't let him hurt Scarlet, Emmy said stubbornly.

Trinity froze. She stared at the dragon incredulously. "Wait, what? What do you mean Scarlet? Is Scarlet here?" Her heart started pounding in her chest. Had the girl followed them all the way to San Angels? "What would Scarlet be doing here?"

I don't know. But I think she's in trouble, Emmy confessed. *She was with that girl. That bad girl who tried to kill you back at the mall.*

It was all Trinity could do not to fall over backward at this point. "Rashida? Are you sure it was Rashida?" This was getting worse and worse.

The dragon nodded reluctantly. *She wanted me to come with*

her. She said she could help me. But I remembered what you said. And I came straight back here.

"Thank God." Trinity scrubbed her face with her hands. Still, this was not good. This was so not good. The Potentials were here. The military was on its way. They had to get out of here and fast.

A knock came to the door. "Trinity? Everything okay in there?"

She drew in a shaky breath, not sure what to say. Half of her wanted to tell Connor to pack his things—that they needed to get out of town, to not pass go, to not collect two hundred dollars. But then Connor would want to know why. Especially with Caleb still missing. After all, she wasn't exactly known for leaving people behind.

You have to tell him, a voice inside of her nagged. *He can't help you if he doesn't know what's going on.*

But what about Emmy? If Connor found out the dragon had gotten out again—and killed someone this time—there was no way on earth he was going to agree to stick with the plan to go find her father. He'd want to get far away then hunker down. Wait for the heat to cool, no matter how long it would take. And in the meantime, Emmy's future would be put on hold all over again. And who knew how long her dad and Virgil would even wait for her? They were already three months behind schedule. What if they gave up and disbanded? What if Emmy's one possible ticket to salvation expired because Trin listened to someone else instead of her dragon?

No. She couldn't do that. She *wouldn't* do that.

"Caleb's still missing," she blurted out, her mind grappling for a plan as she pulled open the door to face him. "Can you go see if you can find him? He's probably just zonked out in the Nether somewhere. I'm sure he didn't go far."

Connor sighed, not looking happy about the idea. But he reached for his shoes all the same, just as she knew he would. Connor was nothing if not dependable. She watched him, her heart aching as she remembered the feeling of his warm arms, spooning her against him. It already seemed like a lifetime ago.

"Look, Trin," he said, shifting from foot to foot. "I'll apologize, okay? I'll tell him it was my fault. That you had nothing to do with any of it."

Her heart broke as she realized that he was misinterpreting her real upset. Thinking she was worried about the fight he and his brother had had. And she was, of course she was. But that wasn't the half of it. And if only he knew what she was truly stressing about, he might not be so sympathetic.

"This thing between my brother and me," he continued. "It's been going on a long time. And it's not fair for us to keep putting you in the middle. From now on, I'm not going to let that happen. We're going to act like a real team. I promise." He gave her a shy grin. "Team Dragon forever."

His earnest eyes were like a punch to the gut. He had sacrificed everything for her and the dragon. Put his trust in her assurances that she had it all under control. Even after all that had happened—he still stood by her side. Even as she lied to his face.

"Connor..." she started, before she could stop herself.

"Yeah?"

She shook her head. "Nothing," she said quickly. Too quickly. "Just...if you find him?"

"*When* I find him."

"Right." Her mouth twisted. "Tell him…tell him I'm sorry."

He gave her a heartbreaking look. "Trin, you didn't do anything wrong. To either of us. You have to know that. None of this is your fault."

"Yeah," she said, turning from him, unable to bear the sight of his regretful eyes. "Sure. I'll see you soon, okay?"

She could feel his gaze upon her, but she refused to turn around. Finally he sighed, and she could hear him turning, heading toward the door. Only when it closed behind him with a loud crash did she dare turn back to where he'd just stood, staring into the now empty room.

You didn't do anything wrong. To either of us.

"Not yet anyway," she said with a sigh then turned to her dragon.

Chapter Twenty-Five

"Come on, Caleb. Where are you?"

Connor raked a hand through his hair as he exited yet another bar without having found his twin. He'd already traversed the entire town at least twice and been in almost every restaurant or shop he had come across that had been open for business. Which, oddly enough, few had been. In fact, the whole town seemed eerily quiet, as if everyone were sleeping in.

He'd texted Trinity a couple of times to make sure Caleb hadn't gone back to the motel, but each time she assured him that she hadn't seen him and he hadn't called. Connor didn't want to admit it, but he was beginning to worry about his twin.

He's like a bad copper, he reminded himself. *He's bound to show up.*

But as the morning surrendered to the afternoon, Connor's apprehension began to grow. Where was he? Had he left town? Caleb had taken off many times during their arguments, but he'd never gone far. Not to mention the van was still parked out in front of the motel and their money was all in the safe, meaning he would have had very few options, even if he did want to take off on them.

At last Connor decided he would grab some food at the local pub and bring it back to Trinity. They could eat and then regroup. Maybe look at a map and figure out where he hadn't checked yet.

So he headed into the pub and sidled up to the bar. After ordering two burgers—and then changing that order to four to accommodate Emmy—he settled on a stool and waited. The bartender wandered over, filling up a pint glass and pushing it in his direction.

"What's this for?" Connor asked.

"Your bravery." The bartender grinned, filling up another glass and holding it out to toast. "And for being my one customer for the day!"

"Is it some kind of holiday?" Connor asked, glancing at the door. "The whole town is dead."

The bartender raised an eyebrow. "Didn't you hear?" he asked, sounding a little incredulous.

An uneasy feeling wormed through Connor, though he wasn't sure why. "Hear what?" he asked.

The bartender reached for the remote and pointed it at the television above them. He pressed a button and the volume rose through the empty bar.

"The victim was identified as twenty-three-year-old Travis White, a drifter who has had his share of run-ins with the police."

"I don't get it," Connor said, looking back at the bartender. "Some homeless guy died?"

The bartender's face lit up. "Died? Dude, he was ripped apart limb from limb. My buddy Dave works over at the coroner's office. He texted me a few pics. You want to see?"

"Um, I guess?" Connor said doubtfully, really confused now.

The bartender pulled out his phone. "They're trying to decide if it's the same one as down in Texas," he said as he scrolled through his texts. "The police aren't saying. But I think it is. I mean, how many dragons can there be in the southwest—"

Connor dropped his beer. It smashed onto the bar floor, glass shards exploding in all directions. "Dragon?" he whispered.

"Yeah, you know, like what happened at that stadium in Vista. Man, you need to start watching the news," the bartender scolded, grabbing a rag and handing it to a stunned Connor. "You mind wiping that up? Anyway, the military is on their way. They're the ones who told everyone to stay inside. But I said to my wife, I got a business to run and—"

"I've...got to go," Connor blurted, on his feet. He reached into his wallet and threw a wad of cash on the counter, not bothering to count it.

"Hey, wait! Don't you want your burgers?"

But Connor was already outside the pub, racing down the street as fast as his legs could carry him. Reaching the motel in record time, he dashed up the stairs then down the hall until he came to their rooms. He pulled the card key from his pants' pocket, his hands shaking so badly he could barely shove it into the reader. Once the green light finally flashed, he burst into the room.

"Trinity! They've found us. We've got to..."

He trailed off, scanning the empty space.

Trinity wasn't there.

Nor was Emmy.

He ran into the other room, just to make sure, his heart slamming against his rib cage. Had the military already come?

Had they found them and taken them away? Fear wrenched in his stomach so hard he nearly doubled over in pain.

"No," he whispered. "No, no, no!"

Forcing himself to close his eyes, he sucked in a much-needed breath as he attempted to regain his soldier's sanity. When he opened his eyes again, he took another look around the room, more slowly this time, taking in all the details.

Like the fact that Emmy's bed was no longer by the radiator. And Trinity's suitcase was no longer under the bed.

He ran to the safe, spinning the dial with shaky hands. He had to do it twice, but it finally popped open. As he stared into the velvet-lined box, he felt all his worst fears coming true. The van keys were gone. So was much of the money. In its place was a page of motel stationery, scribbled on in Trinity's handwriting. Somehow Connor managed to pluck the letter from the box and stagger over to the bed, plopping down on the mattress to start reading.

Dear Connor and Caleb,

This is by far the hardest letter I have ever had to write. Even putting pen to paper feels like ripping out my heart from my chest with my bare hands. But I've been too selfish for too long. I hope you can understand.

Emmy chose me to be her Fire Kissed. To put her first and keep her safe from harm. But it seems I haven't been very good lately, keeping up my end of the bargain. I've been distracted, dealing with the drama and the fights and the tangled loyalties of our little group, and I haven't done what I promised to do. We call ourselves Team Dragon, but half the time the dragon is the last teammate we consider when weighing our options.

I love you both. Never doubt that for a second. You gave up your entire worlds to come to Emmy's aid, and I will never forget that. But now it's time for me to do the same thing.

Please don't try to follow me or contact me—it will only make things harder. I hope we will be able to meet again someday. But I truly have no idea whether that will be possible.

Love always,
Trinity

Connor's hands fumbled with the note as numbness spread over his entire body. His knees buckled and he fell back onto the bed. Unable to move, unable to even think. On instinct, he reached out with his gift again, searching for some sign of her, desperate to regain the connection—to beg her to come back. For a fleeting moment, he thought he could feel her, but a second later, the sensation was gone.

And so was Trinity. Maybe forever. Anger rose up inside of him, warring with his fear. He wanted to blame Caleb—for his childishness, his recklessness. But he knew in his heart he was just as much to blame. What he'd gone and done. What he'd promised never to do.

He thought back to her soft lips, hungry against his mouth. Her head, heavy against his chest as his fingers tangled in her hair. He should have never allowed any of that to happen. He'd promised her he'd stay strong. Instead, he'd been weak. Allowed his vulnerability to show. Gave into temptation. And it had cost him.

It had cost him everything.

He lay back on the bed, staring listlessly up at the ceiling, his heart feeling as if it would tear in two. It took every ounce of strength in his body not to run after her, to search the streets until he wore holes through his boots and bloodied his feet—refusing to give up until she was back in his arms where he could protect her and keep her safe. Instead, he forced himself to stay put, to respect her wishes, and let her strike out on her own path.

He tried to imagine her now behind the wheel of the beaten-up old van, a determined look on her face. A small smile tugged at his lips at the image.

That was his Trinity. Stubborn till the end.

"Take good care of her, Emmy," he whispered, though he knew there was no way for the dragon to hear him. "I hope you know how lucky you are to have her as your Fire Kissed."

PART 4:

FISSURE

Chapter Twenty-Six

*H*ot damn, will you look at that?"

Sixteen-year-old Caleb peered out the glass windows of the elevator in the direction Digger was pointing, his eyes sweeping the barren, burned-out city ruins below. They'd broken through the surface of the world a few moments before and were now shooting up into the air, sliding along a thick vertical track in a three-sided glass tube. The code he'd pickpocketed from that Netherhead down in Shanty Town the day before had worked like a dream—activating the secret private elevator, conveniently mapped out in the guy's wallet. And Caleb and his buddies were now on their way up to a real, honest-to-goodness sky house.

"You really think one of the Dracken lives up here?" asked Burr, one of Caleb's drinking buddies from Shanty Town. He hadn't had much time to gather a crew, seeing as the code would probably change the second Mr. Rich Guy realized he'd been ripped off during his black market journey of self-indulgence. And it was a degenerate lot to say the least.

"Who *else* would live above ground?" Digger asked

disdainfully. He flexed his meaty arms and cracked his knuckles. He'd just gotten out of ten years at a forced labor camp mining operation. And would be asking for ten more if caught on this job. But the spoils from pulling off such a heist—in a real sky house—were well worth the risk.

"I used to," Caleb admitted, looking down at the rusted iron ruins below. He could almost see him and his brother, chasing each other through the rubble, pretending to be Hunter and Dragon. "My family and I lived up here when I was a kid."

It seemed a million years ago. When he was just a normal boy with a family who loved him and the possibility of a real future. Until, of course, that fateful day when his brother ruined everything, vaporizing Caleb's entire universe with one clumsy fall. It was Connor's fault that their father was killed—and yet somehow his brother walked away from the murder scene a hero. And from then on, no one remembered Caleb even existed.

"Man, that must have sucked dragon eggs," Gunn, the youngest of the crew, remarked, spitting the black tar he'd been chewing onto the elevator's glass floor. "I'd be freaking out if I were up here, worrying about dragons every day." He turned to Caleb. "Of course, I don't have a big time Dragon Hunter in my family like *some* people."

Caleb scowled. Seriously, was there nowhere he could go to escape his brother's legacy?

Thankfully, at that moment, the elevator creaked to a halt and its door silently slid open, revealing the interior of a large circular room, covered in windows, providing a 360-degree view of the ruins below them. Caleb gave a low whistle and motioned for his crew to follow him out.

"Okay, now be careful," he instructed. "I told Penny to keep the owner busy at her place for the next few hours. But we don't know if he set up any alarms or traps. Grab whatever you can—the smaller it is, the easier it'll be to hock later. And meet back here in ten minutes."

The crew nodded their greasy heads then dashed around the large room, peeking in chests and pulling back curtains. The home was dripping in rich reds and golds and stocked with real wood furniture—something not even the richest Council members could afford down below. Caleb couldn't help but marvel how each piece had been carved with intricate designs and painted with vibrant colors. The floors were made of marble and great tapestries hung on the walls, depicting beautiful golden dragons with mouths blazing crimson fire. It was so opulent it nearly took his breath away.

But the real awe of the room came from the sun outside, peeking in through the many windows and gracing the entire place with warm rays of light. He imagined himself sprawling out on the sofa by the wall, napping peacefully under the sun's gentle caress.

But there would be no sleep. It was time to steal. So as his crew busied themselves by pilfering everything not nailed to the floor, Caleb decided to climb the sweeping staircase in the center of the room to see what else he could discover.

At the top of the stairs, he found a large bedroom, complete with a huge, carved wooden canopy bed, draped with thick velvet curtains. He pressed a hand down on the bed's surface, trying to imagine what it would be like to sleep there. The Dracken probably had no trouble getting girls to come home with them.

Off the bedroom, he discovered an even greater find—a library, filled floor to ceiling with hardcover books with real paper pages. Caleb pulled one out at random, putting his nose to the book to breathe in the comforting musty smell. He shook his head, completely awed by the whole thing. What would it be like to read from these kinds of ancient tomes, instead of just downloading stories to a reader? He found himself turning to page one, dying to read real print just once in his life.

But he got no further than the first sentence when a sudden scream caused him to drop the book. Racing from the library, he ran through the bedroom and down the stairs, almost tripping over Gunn's body, lying bleeding on the white shag rug. Horrified, Caleb looked around the room, trying to determine what had happened to his friend. Before he could figure anything out, another piercing scream rang out through the air.

Screw this. Caleb dashed for the elevator, only to find the door sliding shut in his face. Digger shrugged helplessly then gave a small wave as he cowardly shot back down to the earth below, leaving Caleb trapped in the sky house with whatever was killing the others.

"Get back here, you bastard!"

He bashed his fist against the door, but it did no good. He'd have to wait for the elevator to reach the bottom and pray Digger would at least have the heart to send it back up to him once he got out.

If he managed to stay alive that long.

Suddenly he felt a hot blast of air at the back of his neck. He froze, his breath stolen from his lungs. Slowly, he forced himself to turn around, with no idea what he'd find—or if he'd even live long enough to find anything at all. His eyes rose slowly, coming face-to-face with...

A dragon. An actual dragon...*inside* the house.

The creature stared back at him with big eyes and blood-stained teeth. She had teal scales that sparkled from the light outside and was about the size of one of the meat cows back home. His eyes bulged from his head. She was both impossibly beautiful and totally terrifying all at the same time, and he realized, vaguely, that he should try to back away. To get out of the line of fire. But the glass elevator shaft effectively blocked his path, and there was nowhere else to go. He was trapped.

About to become dragon lunch.

Squeezing his eyes shut, his hands uselessly covered his face in a vain attempt to ward the creature off. He thought wildly of his mother and his brother and wondered if either of them would even notice he was gone. They'd probably never know exactly what happened to him. They might not even care. In fact, there was no one in the entire world that would be all that broken up about Caleb Jacks's death. Except, he supposed, Caleb Jacks himself. And he wasn't even a hundred percent sure about that.

You don't know if you want to live? How sad.

Huh? He pulled his hands away, jerking his head from left to right, trying to determine where the sudden voice was coming from. But there was no one there.

No one? The voice repeated, amused. *But I'm right here in front of you.*

Caleb's mouth dropped open. The dragon's lips hadn't moved. But he'd heard her, as clear as if she were speaking aloud.

"How did you...how do you do that?" he asked in a quaking voice.

The dragon's mouth curled, almost as if she were smiling. Then she stepped closer and sniffed his face. Caleb tried not to wince as the dragon's breath tickled his nose, praying the creature wouldn't decide to take a test bite. Then, to his surprise, he felt a wet roughness on his cheek.

Had the mighty dragon that had just taken out his crew actually licked him?

"I think she likes you."

A new voice came from the direction of the staircase. Caleb watched as a good-looking guy, dressed in a fine linen suit, drifted down the stairs with ultimate grace.

"Back off, Trinity," he commanded. "Caleb's had enough of you for the moment, I think."

Trinity? Caleb gawked. This deadly beast's name was Trinity? Like that legendary girl from his history texts?

Trinity the dragon—if that indeed was her name—huffed twin puffs of smoke from her nostrils, as if annoyed by the man's command, but obediently took a few steps backward, curling her long, scaly tail inward and looking expectantly at the Dracken.

Caleb staggered, barely able to comprehend what was happening here. He'd heard rumors of the Dracken, of course, that they could somehow make dragons bow to their will. But to see it happen in real life? Mind-blowing, to say the least.

"How did you...?" he stammered. "I mean..." He realized dimly that he might never be able to form a complete sentence again.

"Tame a dragon?" the man finished in a kindly voice. "Why, it's easy, if you have the gift."

"It…is?"

"Caleb, thank you for coming. My name is Darius. We've been expecting you. Sit down." The man ushered him over to the sofa by the window and gestured for him to be seated. Caleb forced himself to follow, not taking his eyes off of the dragon for a moment. She was still watching him closely, her mouth open and her tongue lolling out in a friendly looking pant. At the moment, she actually looked less mean than his dog back home.

"Don't worry, she won't bite," the man teased. Caleb shot an involuntary look at the bloody corpses of his comrades nearby, his stomach lurching. "Oh right," Darius chuckled. "What I meant was, she won't bite *you*."

Caleb sank to the couch, his heart beating a mile a minute. He folded his hands to keep them from shaking. "Are you going to kill me?" he blurted out, unable to help himself.

Darius laughed softly. "Absolutely not," he replied. "After all, you have a precious gift. It would be a great waste to kill you."

"A gift?" Caleb raised an eyebrow skeptically. "I think maybe you're mistaking me for my brother, Connor. He's the Dragon Hunter, not me."

Darius frowned. "Personally, I don't consider the ability to destroy life much of a gift, Caleb," he replied. "Do you?"

Caleb looked over at him, surprised. Darius was perhaps the first person he'd ever met who didn't think his brother walked on water.

"Your brother's gift is to destroy. Yours is to bring life. And if you agree to work with us, we can bring a lot of life to a lot of people. We may even be able to bring your father back from the grave someday." He paused, then added, "But I think we'll start with something a lot more simple."

Caleb squinted at him, his brain whirling. Was this guy for real? What kind of gift could he possibly have? Him, the brother no one wanted. "What do you have in mind?"

"Your mother suffers from bone cancer, yes?"

Caleb nodded reluctantly, wondering how this man knew so much about him and his family. He suddenly realized stealing the elevator code probably wasn't the lucky accident he'd assumed it to be.

"Well, for starters, we can cure her of that."

"*You can?*" Caleb cried, against his better judgment. Could they really do that? She'd been so sick for so long—it seemed impossible. But then, so was a big-ass dragon licking his face…

He imagined waltzing into the hospital, past the doctors, his mother's cure clasped in his hands. *Him*—the so-called useless son—finally doing something worthwhile. Something his brother—even with all his superpowers—hadn't been able do.

Darius smiled. "With your gift, we can do all that and a lot more as well,"

"This gift…" Caleb forced his thoughts back to the present. "You keep talking about a gift. What gift do I have that's so valuable to you?"

"Why, isn't it obvious?" Darius asked kindly. "You were born a guardian."

Chapter Twenty-Seven

H ang on, Em, I think we're almost there."

After pulling up to the stoplight just outside of Fauna, New Mexico, Trinity stole a glance into the back of the van. Before he died, Grandpa had made the vehicle "Emmy proof" by adding a flame-resistant coating of paint to the walls and blacking out the windows to deter any potential spies. He'd even added a little nest of blankets for the dragon to sleep on, creating a cozy cave. But while Emmy normally enjoyed her plush accommodations, today she couldn't seem to relax, pacing from wall to wall, puffs of smoke twining from her nose.

"Are you okay?" Trinity called back to her.

I'm just excited, Emmy replied. *Do you really think your father can help me? Do you think he has a plan?*

She gave the dragon a small shrug before turning back to the road. "I wish I could say for sure," she said. "But I honestly have no idea. I mean, the whole thing seems absolutely crazy, right? But then everything about this has been crazy from the start. And if there's any chance that he can help? Well, we gotta find out for sure." She gripped the steering wheel with both hands. "Don't worry. I promised to protect you, Emmy. And I'm going to keep that promise, no matter what. No more distractions—no more boys—from now on, it's all about you."

She wondered if Connor had returned with his brother yet. If they'd found her note. She felt like such a coward, just taking off like that, without even saying good-bye. Not to mention stealing some of their remaining cash and her grandpa's van. After all they'd done for her...

But she'd had no choice. They would have tried to convince her to stay. To say that they'd change—that things would be different from there on out. That they'd work together this time, no more drama, no more fights, no more putting Emmy last. And maybe, for a time, that would be true. But then they'd find themselves at another standstill. And Emmy would be the one to suffer.

As she pulled out from the light, Emmy padded up to the front seat, effectively claiming shotgun. Trinity wondered if she should insist the dragon return to the back of the vehicle. After all, if someone were to peer inside, they might catch a glimpse of something they weren't supposed to see. But in the end, she allowed it. She was feeling a little lonely now that she was on her solo mission, and Emmy's company definitely helped.

As she turned a corner at the next light, a large shopping center loomed in front of her, a lone behemoth in an otherwise undeveloped desert. She stared at it for a moment, puzzled, wondering if she'd made a mistake. But no, a quick glance at her phone's GPS told her this was the address she'd gotten from the Ouroboros.

She'd expected a secret laboratory. Or a hidden bunker

deep in the desert maybe. Something. Anything. Except for this.

A Wal-Mart Supercenter?

A little unnerved, she pulled into the busy parking lot. She let the engine idle for a moment as she watched a harried-looking mom herd three children into the store, while a man in a mustache and cowboy hat exited with arms filled with purchases. A few teens hung outside, leaning against the store's exterior wall, playing handheld video games, while another kid in a trademark blue smock corralled shopping carts into a long train.

Trin sighed, suddenly envying the normalcy of the scene. She tried to tell herself these carefree Wal-Mart shoppers had hopes and fears and stresses and worries just like everyone else—just like her—but in her heart she knew it wasn't the same.

She glanced over at Emmy who was watching her curiously. "What do you think?" she asked. "Why would Dad send us here?"

Emmy peeked her head up to look out the window. *Because he wanted you to buy me something shiny?* she suggested, batting her eyes at Trin.

Trinity snorted. "Yeah, I'm sure that was it," she said with a laugh. "Forget the fate of the world and concentrate on some retail therapy."

You did say it was all about me, Emmy reminded her slyly.

Trinity groaned. "I'll see what I can do, okay? You stay here. I'll be back in a minute."

Can't I come with you?

Trinity sighed, noting the pleading look on the dragon's

face. "You know I'd want nothing more," she assured her gently. "But it's too dangerous. You do remember what happened at the football stadium, right?"

Emmy gave her a regretful look. *I was hoping you'd forgotten.*

"Trust me, I will never forget that little adventure," Trin said with a laugh. Then seeing Emmy's hurt expression, she softened. "Look, I'll keep the link open between us, okay? You'll be able to hear everything that's going on the whole time. And if I need help, you'll be the first dragon I call."

Emmy nodded, seeming appeased by this. She leapt into the back of the van and curled up in her pile of blankets. Relieved, Trinity popped open the door and stepped out of the van, locking it behind her. She looked around for a moment, making sure no one was watching her. But everyone seemed to be going about their business, not giving her a second glance. Finally satisfied, she headed into the store.

"Okay, Dad," she murmured. "Ready or not, here I come."

Once inside, she grabbed a cart and began going down the main aisle, feeling a little stupid, not sure who—or what—she should be looking for. Her father would have aged sixteen years since the vision she'd seen—would she even recognize him now if she saw him? She studied the faces of each person she passed, but none looked even remotely like dear old Dad.

Anything? Emmy asked impatiently from the van.

Trinity shook her head before remembering the dragon couldn't see her. *No,* she sent instead. *I mean, I don't think so. But it's a big store and a lot of people—it's going to take a while to cover it all.*

She tried to sound optimistic, not wanting Emmy to think they'd made a mistake coming here, but as she walked down aisle after aisle with no sign of her father, a sinking feeling began to settle in her stomach. Was she crazy to have even come? What had she expected to find? Her dad popping out from aisle thirteen with a rollback special on a can of dragon-disaster removal? Heck, even if he had originally planned to meet her here, he would have expected her to show up months ago. How long would he have staked out the superstore before giving up or accidentally alerting the security detail?

Did you find him yet? Emmy broke in again. *Does he have a plan to save me?*

Trinity sighed. This was useless. *I'm coming back to the van,* she told the dragon. *Just let me grab some supplies while I'm here. At least then it won't have been a total waste of time.*

She stopped in the grocery section to pick out a rack of ribs for Emmy then, remembering the dragon's request, headed to the jewelry counter, choosing the most glittery costume jewelry necklace she could find. She smiled a little as she tossed it into the cart, imagining the look on Emmy's face when she pulled it from the bag. She'd been through a lot, poor thing. It was the least Trin could do. And maybe it would soften the blow a little that her big plan had been a big fail.

She had just finished paying when Emmy's voice invaded her consciousness again.

Better get out here, Trin. We've got company.

What? Heart in her throat, she grabbed the bag and ran out of the store without bothering to take her receipt. When she stepped outside, she almost dropped her purchases. Her van was now surrounded by what looked like the same teens she'd seen hanging out by the wall as she'd entered. But now they had put their video games away and were concentrating on....

...taking photos?

"What are you doing?" she demanded, running up to them, heart pounding in her chest. "Leave my van alone."

The three teens turned to her. One by one their mouths fell open in shock. One of them actually dropped his iPhone, and it fell to the pavement with a loud clatter.

"It's her," the girl wearing black-rimmed glasses and a "timey-whimey" *Doctor Who* T-shirt said in an awed whisper. "You were right. It's totally her."

The boy who had dropped his phone fumbled to pick it up so he could resume taking photos—this time of Trinity herself.

"Stop that!" she cried, horrified. "Give that to me." She lunged for the phone, but the boy dodged her nimbly. "What do you think you're doing?"

Did they recognize her? She'd been on the news quite a bit. But still...

"Cut it out, Nate," the third boy commanded in a voice that made Trinity guess he was the leader. He was Asian, sporting a blue streak through his bleached blond hair. She watched as he took a step toward her, and she half wondered if she should try to make a break for it. But where would she go? Not to mention she couldn't just leave Emmy in the van. Her heart pounded in her chest as she waited for his next move.

To her surprise, he held out his hand. "My name's Luke," he said in a casual voice. "I'm sorry about Nate and Natasha here. They're just a little starstruck."

Trinity stared at him. "Starstruck?" she repeated doubtfully.

"Yeah, you know," he said with a small laugh. "It's not every day we get honest to goodness celebrities here in Fauna."

Trinity realized he was still holding out his hand. Not wanting to be rude, she reached out, giving it a tentative shake. "Um, I don't know who you think I am," she stammered. "But I'm not—"

"Trinity Foxx, dragon rider?"

She dropped his hand like a hot potato. It took everything inside of her not to bolt in the other direction.

Luke grinned. His teeth were a little crooked, making him look slightly mischievous. "Oh, we know all about you, Trinity Foxx," he assured her. "We've been following you from the very beginning. Ever since the government tried to steal the dragon egg from your grandpa's museum. You may have heard of us. Free-Emmy-dot-com?" He looked at her expectantly.

She gaped at him. "Free-Emmy-dot-com?"

"Well, I guess you probably haven't had a lot of time to surf the web these days," Luke said, looking slightly disappointed. "Anyway, we're currently the number one visited Emmy fan site in the world. We get over two hundred thousand unique visitors every day," he added proudly.

For a moment, Trinity found herself speechless, trying to process all he just said. "Okay, back up a second," she blurted out at last, holding up her hands. "You made a fan site for my dragon?"

"No, we made *the* fan site," Nate interjected.

"There are dozens of websites about Emmy," Luke explained patiently. "Possibly hundreds if you count Tumblrs and Facebook fan pages. But none are as comprehensive as ours. We only post photos and videos after a careful authentication process. People come to us when they want to know the truth."

"Oh my God! I cannot believe you're really here!" Natasha burst out with a shriek. She bounced up and down, clapping her hands together. "I mean, we figured you were probably beating it down to Mexico by now, after that whole thing went down in San Angels. We've got a ton of stringers, waiting at the borders, hoping to catch a glimpse of the van." She beamed. "But instead you've come here! To our hometown!"

Nate leapt forward, waving his phone in Trinity's face. She took a hesitant step backward. "Can we interview you?" he begged. "Just a few questions."

"You don't know how much it would mean to your fans," Natasha added with a pleading look. "To get an exclusive shout-out from Trinity Foxx herself."

Fans? She had fans? "Um," Trinity stammered, looking from one of the teens to the other. Of all the things she expected to happen, this was definitely not one of them. "I don't know if that's a good idea," she said. "I'm kind of on the run, you know."

"Right. Of course," Luke interjected, waving Nate and his phone away. "You don't want anyone to know where you are. Totally understandable. The last thing we need is for the government to locate you and come to take Emmy away. Who knows what would happen to her if she fell into their hands." He grimaced.

"They'd probably dissect her," Natasha said with a scowl. "Study her like a science experiment in one of their secret labs."

"Or maybe they'd clone her and make her into a weapon," added Nate a little too eagerly. "Send her off to fight in the war. Like in that book where they use dragons to fight Napoleon. That was so cool."

"Cool in a book, but not real life," Luke broke in, giving Nate a reprimanding look. "Don't worry," he assured Trinity. "We're on your side. Anything you need, we can hook you up."

"Um, thanks. But I really don't think I need—"

"Hey, Luke," Nate interjected, nodding his head to the left. "Don't look now but the lamestream media is about to crash our party."

Trinity followed his gesture, letting out a dismayed gasp as she recognized a brightly colored CBS news van pulling into the Wal-Mart parking lot, followed by NBC and FOX.

Luke glared at Nate. "Did you forget to mask the geocode when you uploaded the van shot again?"

Nate looked offended. "No way, dude," he said. "I'm a professional. But um…" He glanced down at his phone. "Maybe they recognized the Wal-Mart in the background?"

"Good work, genius," Luke retorted, smacking him upside the head. He gave Trinity an apologetic look. "We need to get you out of here. Fast. Or you're going to end up on the evening news." He turned to Natasha. "Get the truck! Quick!"

Trinity glanced over at the news vans, slowly cruising the parking lot, apprehension coursing through her. "I'll just drive away before they see me," she told Luke, making for her vehicle.

"Not a good idea," Luke said shaking his head. "They know what your van looks like. Everyone does. If you pull out of the parking lot now, they'll totally see you. And they *will* chase you down."

"You're kind of, like, the story of the century, you know," Natasha added a little apologetically.

Trinity glanced at the live trucks with growing dismay. "Then what I am supposed to do?" she asked. "I can't just leave Emmy here."

"Of course not," Luke replied. "But don't worry. We'll just load her up in our truck and sneak both of you out. We can come back for the van later."

Trinity frowned. "So you expect me to just go with you?" she asked. "I don't even know you."

"And you won't have a chance to get to know us if you don't come with us now," Luke pointed out. "Because the cops will come, and you will be locked up, and they will throw away the key."

"You're not only the story of the century," added Nate. "You're, like, America's most wanted, yo." He posed in exaggerated, fake gangster style.

Trinity bit her lower lip. As much as she'd like to deny it, she knew they were right. And though it was risky to trust these strangers, it would be even riskier to stay behind and get caught. Making up her mind, she dashed to the back of the van, unlocking and opening up the door. A moment later she found herself face-to-face with Emmy, who was blinking uneasily in the sudden bright sunshine.

We've got trouble, Em. We're going to have to switch vehicles, okay?
Emmy looked at her in alarm. *We're going to leave the van?*

It was the last thing Trinity wanted to do. The van was the last connection she had to her grandpa. His rust bucket pride and joy. If they left it behind now, there was no telling what would happen to it—along with everything she owned inside.

But then she caught sight of the news trucks, turning into their row. "We have no choice," she told the dragon. "We're running out of time."

For a moment Emmy stared back at her doubtfully. But finally she nodded her head. Trin let out a breath of relief as the dragon flapped her wings and half flew, half jumped into the cab of the pickup that had pulled up behind the van. Once she was inside, Trin slammed the door behind her.

"Okay," she said, turning to Luke and his friends, who she realized were gawking at her with astonished faces. She gave them a puzzled look. "What?"

"I can't believe it!" Nate whispered. "It was her. It was really her."

Oh. Right. Of course. Emmy had become so familiar to Trin at this point, sometimes she forgot how exotic she actually was.

"I've seen the dragon with my own two eyes." Natasha made a mock swoon. "I could totally die now and I wouldn't even care."

"Or, you know, you could stay alive and get us the hell out of here," Trinity suggested wryly. "Anytime now would be great, in fact."

"Right. Let's do it!" Luke cried, dashing to the passenger side and popping open the door. Trinity hoisted herself up and dove into the backseat, with Natasha and Nate piling in behind her. Luke ran around to the driver's seat.

"Free Emmy!" he crowed as he dove in and turned the key in the ignition.

"Dot com!" chorused his two friends, high-fiving one another as he stepped on the gas and they pulled away.

Trinity glanced back at Emmy, who was peering at her with marked skepticism.

I don't know either, Ems, she said with a sigh. *But it beats being caught, right?*

The truck pulled away seconds before the news vans pulled up. Trinity craned her neck to watch as reporters and cameramen spilled out of the vehicles, surrounding the van, cameras rolling. A moment later, they were followed by a few police cars. Thankfully none of them seemed to notice the lone truck rolling out of the parking lot and onto the street.

Her heart ached in her chest as they pulled out of sight. *Oh, Grandpa.*

"You okay?" Natasha asked, catching her look.

"Yeah," she said, shaking herself. "And thank you. I appreciate the rescue."

"Of course," Luke said. "We appreciate the chance to help." He glanced over at her with a small grin, brushing his bleached blond hair from his black eyes. "After all, that's what the Order of the Dracken is for!"

Chapter Twenty-Eight

Trinity's heart lurched. She looked from Luke to Nate and Natasha, then back to Luke again.

"Excuse me?" she managed to stammer.

Had they really just said what she thought they'd said? There was no way. Absolutely no way.

Except, what if there was?

"I...thought you said your website was Free Emmy."

"Our website, yeah," Luke agreed. "But we already sorta had a group name. You see, we originally all got together because of this video game we play. It's called *Fields of Fantasy* and—"

"She knows *Fields of Fantasy*, you tool," Nate interrupted. "Remember? We looked up her character?" He gave Trinity a slightly accusing look. "We tried to friend you like five different times."

"I...haven't been able to play lately," Trinity sputtered, her mind whirring with the implications of what the boys were saying. "I've been a bit...busy."

"Of course you have!" Natasha agreed comfortingly, giving her brother a dirty look. "After all, who has time for video game dragons when you have the real thing?" She giggled, peering into the back of the truck where Emmy was pacing nervously.

"Anyway, yeah, so you remember the Dracken Heights dungeon that they put into the ex pack, right?" Luke continued. "The dragon one? That was the first dungeon we rocked as a group. When we formed our guild, it seemed like a natural name." He grinned at his gamer buddies.

Trinity somehow managed a weak smile, even though on the inside she felt like throwing up. She thought of all the movies she'd seen about time travel over the years. The ones where despite everything you tried to do, things ended up exactly the same in the end. The ripples you made in the pond weren't enough to stop the huge-ass tsunami on approach.

According to Caleb and Connor, she'd gone and founded the Order of the Dracken the first time around, after discovering the abuse Emmy was suffering under the hands of the government. But since the government never took Emmy this time, there had been no reason for the Dracken to ever be formed.

And yet, here it was. Here *they* were. A group who had formed for the sole purpose to "free Emmy" just like before. Could something like that possibly be a coincidence? Or was the time line trying to smooth itself back out? If only Connor or Caleb were here, they might be able to explain the significance—or hopefully insignificance of something like this. But she was alone.

She realized Natasha was staring at her worriedly. "Sorry," she said. "It's been a long day."

It was funny; when she thought of the Dracken now, she pictured Darius and Mara and their strange dragon-worshiping friends from the future. But the original Dracken hadn't been a bunch of cult crazies looking to purge the world by fire. Just a couple of kids who wanted save the dragons.

Kids like Luke, Nate, and Natasha.

She didn't know whether that was a comforting thought—or a more worrying one.

In any case, there was nothing she could do now, and at least she knew she was in no immediate danger. So she forced herself to settle into her seat and not look longingly back at the Wal-Mart as it disappeared in the distance. She harbored no hopes of returning to her van; by evening, she was positive it would be impounded by local police or Homeland Security. All she had left now were literally the clothes on her back... and her dragon in the back of the truck.

They headed down a main road, lined with strip malls for a few miles, then drove into a neighborhood of modest, flat-roofed adobe houses, shaded by a decent number of trees. Luke pulled up to a small bungalow, enclosed by a chain-link fence. Parking in the driveway, he ushered everyone out then headed toward the garage's side door. Trinity went around to the back of the truck and opened it. Emmy blinked at her, still looking a little worried, but she obligingly hopped down and padded into the garage.

Trinity stepped inside behind her, not sure what to expect. What she wasn't expecting was the garage to have been converted into the ultimate geek cave. Vintage *Star Wars* posters hung over threadbare couches, while rickety computer desks were piled high with cables and mice and monitors and other equipment. And the *pièce de résistance*, at the center of the room was a huge projector screen TV.

"Welcome to the Dracken Lair," Nate pronounced, coming in behind her. "Where all the magic happens."

"Yeah, you wish you could get some magic to happen," Natasha scoffed, following them inside. She turned to Trinity. "The only kind of fcmales he ever manages to score are pixelated."

"Oh yes, but you've got *all* the dudes knocking down your door," Nate shot back. "What with your sexy mastery of Tolkien Elvish and all."

"What's that?" Trinity interrupted, her eyes locking onto a bulletin board across the room covered with newspaper clippings and computer printouts. She stepped closer, startled to see a collage of photos of herself thumbtacked to the board. From last year's high school yearbook picture to an action shot from an old track meet, to a shot of her standing in front of the museum for the debut of Grandpa's unfortunate *Chupacabra Corpse* exhibit that she'd actually managed to get some press to come out for. (She'd later had to issue an apology when the corpse in question turned out to be nothing more than the remains of a mangy coyote.)

In addition to photos, there were newspaper articles, with headlines blazing about Emmy's touchdown of terror. Some of these articles came from legitimate old-school newspapers like the *New York Times* and the *Wall Street Journal*. Others looked a little more conspiracy theory–esque.

But it was the photos tacked under the headline "Emmy?" that really intrigued her. Some had obviously been taken at the football field the day Emmy made her grand debut. Others seemed to be screenshots of Emmy taken in some kind of woods. Still others were completely unrecognizable and didn't look anything like the dragon. Blurry shadows rising above trees, glowing eyes in a dark cave…

"What are these?" she asked curiously.

Luke peered over her shoulder. "Eh," he said. "Most likely fakes. We've been getting a lot of those lately, as our hits have gone up. In fact, there have been close to a thousand Emmy sightings reported since the whole football game thing." He laughed. "Our girl makes more appearances than a dead Elvis these days."

"It's our job to investigate each and every sighting," Natasha chimed in. "They need to be verified before we put them up on our site. After all, we have a reputation to uphold," she added a little proudly.

"Right," Trin said, swallowing hard. "A reputation."

"Check it!" Nate cried from the other side of the room. He'd sidled up to one of the computers and had pulled up MSNBC and FOX News, running both streaming videos from different browser windows. Trinity watched with sinking dread as video of the van she'd recently abandoned popped up simultaneously on both screens.

"According to police, this van is registered to Charles Foxx, the man who is wanted by Homeland Security in connection with an alleged terrorist plot," the announcer was saying. "Police have evacuated the parking lot until the bomb squad can make a sweep."

A photo of her grandfather popped up on the screen, making Trinity's heart ache all over again. It was hard to believe it'd been only a little over a week since the barn fire in Vista. It seemed like both yesterday…and a lifetime ago. Would it ever stop hurting her heart to see his face? She wondered if he was looking down on her now from somewhere. Keeping watch over her and Emmy. She smiled a little at the idea of her guardian becoming her guardian angel.

The reporter had finished talking, and the station rolled the video, beginning with a rather unattractive junior high photo of Trinity when she was still in her braces. (Seriously, that was the best they could dig up?) The photo was followed by a grainy video of the Vista football field, replaying someone's home video of her jumping on Emmy's back and flying through the skies. Trinity still couldn't believe she'd actually gone and done that. It looked ten times as dangerous from this third person perspective as it had felt at the time. And it had felt pretty damn dangerous then too.

But I didn't let you fall, Emmy reminded her. She could feel the dragon nudge her leg and she looked down. She smiled at her.

"That's very true," she said, scratching her snout. "You did good."

She looked back up to see the three kids staring at her in amazement.

"What?" she asked, a little confused.

"You just answered her, didn't you?" Natasha said in an awed whisper. "She talked to you with her mind and you answered her!" She let out an excited whoop. "Oh my God, it's just like Eragon and Saphira! Or one of those Anne McCaffrey books. Trinity, you're like Lessa! A twenty-first century Lessa and Ramoth! Or maybe Laurence and Temeraire—"

"And now you see why *she* doesn't get many dates," Nate concluded smugly, giving his sister an affectionate look.

Trinity laughed uneasily then turned her attention back to the computer monitor. The reporter had come back on camera.

"Authorities are asking the people of Fauna to stay indoors and use extreme caution," she was saying. "The creature is considered extremely dangerous. If you do have any information, please call 911."

"Yeah, I don't think we're going to be doing that," scoffed Natasha, pointing a remote control at the monitor. The volume muted. Natasha gave Trinity a comforting look. "Don't worry," she said. "You're safe with us."

"How can you be sure?" Trinity asked doubtfully, glancing at the closed garage door. After all, what if someone had seen them leave the parking lot and had followed them here? Were they, even now, only moments away from being surrounded by a SWAT team? Once again she wished desperately for Connor or Caleb. Why had she thought it was a good idea to leave them behind? She turned to her new friends. "Do you have any guns?" she asked hopefully

"Please. We don't need no stinking guns," Luke scoffed. "We have computers."

She raised an eyebrow. "Computers that shoot laser beams from their webcams?"

"Better." Luke gestured to Nate. "Can you pull up that video we got the other day of Emmy at the Grand Canyon?"

"I thought we weren't going to run that one," Nate said, jabbing at the keyboard anyway. "We couldn't determine origin."

"Change of plans," Luke said briskly. "The Feds are probably watching us. The media definitely is. I mean, you posted that shot of the van and they were on the scene in like ten minutes. I think it's time to feed them another bread crumb."

Nate grinned at that, obviously getting the idea. Trin watched as he pulled up a video of a dark shadow crossing the sky. "This is so obviously CGI'ed," he said with a snort. "Not that any of the lamestream media will be able to tell."

"Wait," Trinity interrupted. "I'm confused. What are you doing?"

Luke turned to her. "Come on now, don't you remember?" he said with a sly wink. "You ditched your van yesterday in some random Wal-Mart parking lot in good old Fauna, New Mexico. You were feeling the heat closing in—and decided you needed a new ride. Then you took off with your dragon, never looking back. Last we know, our little touchdown of terror was miles and miles away from here, taking in the sights of the great and glorious GC."

"That's what the Google says anyway," Nate proclaimed, pressing a few buttons and publishing the video to their site. "And we all know the Google never lies."

Huh. Trinity watched as the video looped on their site. That actually was a pretty smart idea. Maybe she should have been posting a little faux travelogue of her own from the start of this whole thing.

"Can I see your website?" she asked, overwhelmed by curiosity at this point. She couldn't believe there even was a website about Emmy—no, hundreds of websites, they'd said. All devoted to her dragon.

You're a superstar, she teased Emmy, this time remembering to speak through their bond.

Nate offered up his chair, and a moment later she was staring at the FreeEmmy.com blog page, which began with a fantastically stylized illustration of her and her dragon—done up

250

as if they were manga superheroes or something. Below that was a list of blog entries full of alleged sightings, background information on her, and some pretty good fan art of Emmy. The sidebar listed a whole bunch of links to similar sites.

"You guys did all this?" she asked, more than a little amazed. She noted the number of comments on each posting—in the hundreds—and gave a low whistle.

Luke nodded, plopping down on a chair beside her, his cheeks flushed with pride. "Pretty cool, huh?" he asked. "We used to do an alien conspiracy website until it got shut down by the NSA when they decided we'd gotten too close to the truth."

"Wait, I thought you said we forgot to pay our web hosting bill?" Natasha objected. Luke's face reddened.

"Yeah, well, whatever. Aliens are lame, anyway."

"And dragons are so hot right now!" Nate quipped. "Especially after that video."

"What video?" Trinity cocked her head in question. "You mean the football stadium thing?"

"No, no!" Luke shook his head. "This was before that. Look." He loaded up the archives and selected one of the entries. A shaky cam, nighttime video, obviously taken by a cell phone, of Emmy walking through the woods then taking flight. It was only about thirty seconds long, but it was definitely her. Probably on one of the nights Caleb had taken her out. Trin's eyes narrowed as she caught the uploader's screen name.

Scarlet. Of course. She must have taken it the night Emmy found her and healed her. The night that had started it all.

Trin frowned, stealing an involuntary glance over at Emmy,

wondering yet again what the deal was between her dragon and this girl. Did Emmy just feel bad for her? Was Scarlet just especially needy? Or did they really have a true connection between them? She felt an involuntary stirring of jealousy. Scarlet had traveled all the way from Vista to San Angels to find Emmy. How soon before she showed up in Fauna? And what would happen once she did?

"This video got like ten million hits in its first twelve hours," Nate explained. "It pretty much broke the interwebs."

"Though of course we already knew all about Emmy," Luke bragged. "Months before any of this happened I'd found this forum where a museum owner—your grandpa— was bragging about a dragon egg he'd had shipped from Antarctica. I'd tried to contact him to find out more but by then the museum had burned down and he was on the run from the law." He grinned widely. "That's when I knew this had to be something big."

"And how did you know I call her Emmy?" Trinity asked, looking up for a moment.

"You shouted her name at the football stadium," Luke explained. "One of the videos we watched caught it."

Trinity continued to scroll through the blog, amazed at how they'd managed to put so many of the pieces together. Not everything was completely right and obviously they didn't know the big time-travel piece of the puzzle, but it was impressive Internet research all the same. They even had a link to her museum's old Facebook page. She clicked over to find a big goofy advertisement for Foxx's Fantastical Fossils and her heart panged.

"That's your grandfather, right?" Natasha asked gently.

Trinity stared at the photo. Her grandfather was dressed in a Tyrannosaurus rex costume and was holding a sign that read "Fossils rock!" He looked ridiculous and heartbreakingly beautiful all at the same time. "Yeah," she said quietly. "That's him. He…died in the fire."

"And so…now you're all alone? We heard these rumors that you were with two guys. Two twin guys?" Luke shook his head. "I don't know. We don't always get everything right."

"No guys," Trinity said, clicking the back button and returning to their website. "It's me and Emmy against the world."

She caught Emmy's curious look out of the corner of her eye but brushed her off. *They don't need to know about them,* she told the dragon. *It'd be too hard to explain anyway.*

"So," Luke said after she closed the web page. "Can I ask you something?"

"Um, sure."

"What were you doing there, out in the open like that? In the middle of a freaking Wal-Mart parking lot of all places? I mean, I know you had no idea just how famous you've become. But you had to know there was some chance you might get recognized, right? Why take the risk?"

Trinity hedged for a moment, wondering how much she should tell them. Then she decided to go for it. "I was looking for my father," she admitted at last. "I believe he's the one person who can help me and Emmy." She found herself reaching into her pocket, fingering the Ouroboros, turning it over in her hand. Why had it led her to the Wal-Mart? That was still question number one. "I was told I might find him there. But…I don't know. Maybe I got bad information."

"What's his name?" Luke asked. "Maybe we've heard of him."

"And if not, we can always look him up," Nate added. "I'm an expert at tracking people down online."

"Well, I guess his name is Cam," Trinity said, remembering what her mother had called him in her vision. "Cameron, maybe?" She shrugged. "I have my mother's maiden name. So I have no idea what his last name would be." She sighed. "Not very helpful, huh?"

"Wait a second," Nate interrupted, his eyes wide. He turned to his friends. "Do you think she's talking about Mr. Law?"

"Who's Mr. Law?" Trinity asked, her heart pounding wildly in her chest. "Does he live in Fauna? He would be a scientist. Maybe working in a lab or a hospital…"

She trailed off, not liking the way they were exchanging glances with one another. "What?" she demanded.

"Well, it's probably not the same guy," Luke hedged.

"But there is a guy named Cameron Law," added Natasha. "He works at the Wal-Mart where we found you."

"No," Trinity said shaking her head. "That couldn't be him. My dad's a big-time scientist. He wouldn't be working in a…" She trailed off as Nate handed her an iPad Mini, with the Wal-Mart website pulled up. Specifically the Employee of the Month page.

"Is that him?" he asked, pointing to the December winner.

Trinity stared down at the photo, scarcely able to breathe. The man had lost some of his hair and his face was thinner and more lined. But the resemblance to the man in her vision was unmistakable.

It was her father. The Wal-Mart employee of the month was her dear old dad.

Numbly, she handed the iPad back to Nate, closing her eyes

and trying to control the sudden tidal wave of emotions flowing over her. The man she'd pinned all her hopes on, the one her mother believed could save her and the dragon. He wasn't some genius scientist after all. He worked at the local Wal-Mart.

"Hey!" Luke cried, putting a hand on her shoulder. "What's wrong?"

It was too much. She let the tears flow out of her, splashing onto the keyboard. Until that very moment, she hadn't realized how much she was depending on this all working out. For there to be some sort of daddy-fueled rescue magic just around the corner, ready to provide a pretty little happily ever after for her and Emmy.

"I'm sorry," she babbled, feeling old and exhausted and scared. "I just…I thought…" She couldn't continue. "He was supposed to be my only hope!" she blurted out at last.

"And why can't he be?" Natasha demanded, looking a little offended. "My mother was a Wal-Mart checker for years while going to nursing school. And she's smarter than anyone I've ever met."

"And who knows, maybe it's just a cover," added Luke. "Maybe he has a secret lab underground or something and he's using his Wal-Mart discount to get cheap supplies to help fight crime."

"Yeah, you know, even Superman worked for a newspaper," added Nate, pulling off his black-rimmed glasses. "All superheroes need day jobs to serve as their cover."

Trinity couldn't help but smile at this. "I suppose you could be right," she relented, though she still wasn't entirely sure.

"We're totally right," Luke declared. "We'll track him down tomorrow and you'll see for yourself."

Chapter Twenty-Nine

A re you going to stand there admiring yourself all night, or do you think you'll get some sleep at some point?"

Trinity watched with amusement as Emmy tossed her head at the cracked mirror in the corner and bared her teeth. She'd been preening at her reflection ever since Trinity had presented her with her necklace earlier that evening.

"Guess it's safe to say I did good?" she teased, fluffing up her pillow before lying down on the couch in the geek cave garage. Luke had gone home about an hour ago, and Nate and Natasha had retreated to their bedrooms after heating up some microwave lasagna for her and plying her with blankets. Their mom worked the overnight shift as a nurse, they'd told her, so there would be no one to walk in on her and her dragon during the night. And they promised to be back first thing in the morning, armed with breakfast and a plan to track down dear old Dad.

Emmy turned to her, her face practically glowing. *Red is a good color on me, don't you think?* She craned her neck to give Trinity a better look. She had to admit, it did add a nice little flair, a glittery ruby nestled amongst a sea of emerald scales.

"Yes, yes, you look gorgeous," she assured her with a smile.

"Utterly gorgeous. Now come to bed. It'll still be there in the morning, I promise."

Emmy snorted, twin puffs of smoke bursting from her nostrils. *Of course it will still be there*, she declared indignantly, though her eyes were dancing. *No one would dare steal treasure from a dragon.*

Trinity smiled, a feeling of warmth wrapping around her. She liked seeing Emmy so happy. If only she'd known all it would take was a piece of junk jewelry, she would have rummaged one up months ago.

Emmy took one last look at herself in the mirror—vain dragon!—then headed over to the second couch, hopping up and turning around three times before settling into the cushions.

"Comfy?" Trin asked with amusement.

The dragon nodded. *Are you?*

"Yeah, not bad," she said, shifting to lie on her back. She stared up at the dark ceiling, feeling a strange mixture of happiness and longing. This was good, she told herself. This was right. But...

You miss them.

She looked over to find Emmy peering at her from the other couch with sad eyes. She gave her a rueful smile. "Yeah," she admitted. "I know it's stupid but—"

It's not stupid, Emmy admonished. *You like them. And they like you. The Hunter likes you so much he lets you kiss him. And he cuddled with you all night long.*

Trinity groaned as her mind betrayed her with a sudden flood of memories. Connor's warm lips whispering across her face. The weight of his body melting into her own.

And the other one. He's very nice as well. I know you don't like that he took me out flying. But he really was very careful. And he always did it for you. Everything he does is for you.

Trin closed her eyes, seeing Caleb's haunted, hollow face. His shaky hands. His pale skin. His anguished voice crashing across her consciousness. Telling her it was so hard already.

Her heart panged. Had Connor found him? Was he okay? Was she a terrible person for leaving them both behind?

"Okay, I miss them," she admitted. "But I don't want you to think I regret leaving them behind. It had to be done. Your well-being is way more important than my love life."

Emmy gave her a sad look. *What makes my happiness any more important than yours?*

"Are you kidding me? I'm just, like, one inconsequential girl," she reminded her. "You're, like, the savior of the world."

Well, I couldn't save anything without you.

Trinity sighed, reality creeping in uncomfortably around the edges of the conversation. She didn't want to go there, not now. But at the same time, she could no longer ignore the elephant in the room.

"Oh, I don't know. I'm sure you and Scarlet could manage to get along somehow if I were gone," she said, trying to sound casual. But even she could hear the hurt in her voice. She'd been forcing it down ever since she'd discovered Scarlet had followed them to San Angels—and that Emmy had once again seen fit to risk everything to save her.

Emmy looked at her sharply. *What do you mean by that?*

"Come on, Emmy," Trinity drew in a breath. "Do you think I don't get it? Scarlet's my backup, right? That's why you started bonding with her in the first place. You felt I wasn't living up to my end of the Fire Kissed bargain and you wanted to make sure you weren't left stranded. And now you've been stringing her along, leading her from town to town, just in case."

Emmy looked at her, horrified. *Scarlet was hurt. She needed me. That was the only reason I…Do you really think I would try to replace you?*

Trinity hung her head. This was coming out all wrong and she was sounding like a paranoid fool. But still! She swallowed hard.

"I just want you to know that I would understand if you were," she said at last. "I mean, let's face it, I haven't been a very good Fire Kissed to you. And if you ever decided that you made a mistake by choosing me…" She broke off, unable to continue. Not wanting it to be true.

Emmy stood, hopping off the couch and padding across the room. When she reached Trinity, she lowered her head until their faces were only inches away. Even in the darkness of the room, Trin could see her blue eyes glowing strong.

Dragons do not make mistakes.

She was so vehement—her tone so sure, so fierce—it sent chills to Trinity's toes. She wrapped her hands around Emmy's neck and squeezed her tight, feeling as if her heart would burst. For a moment, neither of them moved and neither of them spoke.

"I'm sorry," Trin said at last, finally finding her voice again. "I didn't mean to doubt you. Or myself. I just…I want to do what's best for you, you know? That's all I want. And I'm so afraid that if I do the wrong thing—or I make the wrong move—I'll lose you forever."

Emmy pulled away, meeting her eyes with her own. *Silly Fire Kissed,* she said with a smile. *You can't get rid of me that easily.*

Chapter Thirty

"Any sign of the cops?"

Trinity peered out the truck's passenger side window, scanning the nearly empty Wal-Mart parking lot the next morning. It was dawn—too early for all but the most dedicated of shoppers. Only a few RVs intruded on the emptiness, parked at the perimeters, but they were quiet and dark, their inhabitants likely still asleep.

Her van was gone. Not a big surprise, but it still made her heart sink a little. In addition to the memories of her grandfather, the van had come to symbolize a certain amount of freedom—she could go anywhere she needed to go with that van. Do anything she needed to do. Now she was back to being dependent on the kindness of strangers.

Her eyes fell on the store itself. Could her father really work here? And if so, why? Had he just needed a steady job to pay the bills, while waiting for her and Emmy to arrive? Sixteen years was a long time, she told herself; he'd probably need to have some kind of income, a low-profile job where they didn't do a big background check, seeing as he was supposed to be dead and all.

That said, it was more than a little disconcerting to watch

all the dreams she'd had of a sterile laboratory, filled with futuristic technology that could help save her and Emmy, fade into a bright yellow bouncy ball of a big box store.

Her new friends, on the other hand, seemed more optimistic. Lucas had come to pick her and Nate and Natasha up bright and early, happily skipping out on school to help her with what they had jokingly been calling their *Operation: Find Daddy* quest. As if the whole adventure was some kind of video game come to life. Once upon a time, the gamer girl in her might have laughed at that. But things had been too real for too long at this point.

"No cops," she said, reluctantly pulling her head back into the truck. "Looks okay."

If he can't help us, he can't help us, she told herself. *No big deal.*

Except that it was a big deal. A huge deal, in fact. She hadn't quite realized, she supposed, just how much she'd been secretly counting on this miracle until it had started to fizzle. What would she and Emmy do if her dad couldn't help them? Where would they go? The Dracken kids seemed cool, but they were just kids themselves, and eventually their mom might catch on to the extra girl and extra large reptile squatting in their garage. The money she'd taken from Connor and Caleb wouldn't last long, and her criminal status assured her she could never apply for a real job. Hell, she didn't even have her own transportation anymore.

She sighed, missing Connor and Caleb and her grandpa more than ever. The life of running from the law and hiding out together seemed almost blissful compared to her dark, unknown future.

She gritted her teeth, shoving the worried thoughts to the

back of her mind. There was no use borrowing trouble, as Grandpa used to say. Her dad had promised to help her. She had to hang on to that promise with both hands and have a little faith.

As Luke drove the truck up to the front of the store, Trinity pulled down the visor mirror and checked her reflection. Natasha had done her best, but she had gotten a bit... *enthusiastic* with the makeup. Looking now, Trin could barely recognize herself, which she supposed was a good thing. She pushed up the mirror then looked back at the store, her heart pounding in her chest.

"Maybe this was a bad idea," she blurted out.

"What are you talking about?" Lucas cried. "Your dad said he could help you. How could that be bad?"

"You're not scared are you?" Nate blustered. "I mean, how can *you*, of all people, be scared? You're Trinity Foxx, for Captain Kirk's sake! You ride freaking dragons for a living."

"That's a bit of an overstatement, actually..."

Natasha gave her a disappointed look. "Do *not* make me have to stop fan-girling you," she scolded. "I spent way too much time on my *Trinity is a rock star* Tumblr theme to have you fall apart now."

Trinity sighed. "Okay," she relented. She supposed that was one kind of motivation. She popped open her door and dropped down to the sidewalk. As she closed the door behind her, she felt Emmy perk up from inside the truck.

Be careful, the dragon warned. *Call me if you need me.*

I will, she assured her. *Don't worry.*

She didn't love leaving Emmy alone in the back of the truck, but what was the alternative? Walk into Wal-Mart with a dragon on a leash, hoping people mistook her for a labradoodle?

She walked inside, the glass doors sliding silently shut behind her. She stood still for a moment, not sure where to even begin in the overwhelmingly large store. Her dad could work in any department—or in an inaccessible back room. He might even have the day off—or he could have called in sick. And what if someone recognized her as she walked around the—

"Welcome to Wal-Mart!"

The voice made her nearly jump out of her skin. She whirled around, a small cry of relief escaping her as she realized it was only the store's greeter, standing behind her. He was an older man, dressed in a blue vest covered in multicolored buttons, and he beamed back at her with a guileless grin on his face. He was balding on the top and appeared as though he hadn't made friends with a razor in at least a week. She swallowed hard, trying to steady her racing pulse. Not her father.

"Sorry," she said, feeling her face flush. "You scared me."

"Definitely didn't mean to." The man smiled amicably, running a hand through his thinning gray hair. "Just wanted to welcome you to our humble store. Can I offer you a button?" He looked at her hopefully.

Trinity cocked her head. "Excuse me?"

He reached into his pocket then extended his hand toward her. Clasped in his fingers was a yellow, smiley-face button. She stared down at it, horribly confused. Then she managed to shake her head.

"Oh. No, that's okay. I don't really need—"

A flicker of shadow crossed the man's face. "Oh I think

you do," he said. "I think you've been looking for this button for a very long time." He paused, his eyes leveling on her, the smile fading from his lips.

Take it, Trinity. It's from your father.

Trinity gulped as the words tripped across her mind, clearly from the man in front of her, though he never moved his lips. "How did you—"

He shoved the button into her hand then turned so abruptly it left her reeling. The doors behind her had opened, she realized. A mother and three kids were walking into the store.

"Welcome to Wal-Mart!" the man greeted in the same cheerful voice. But he didn't, Trinity realized, force a button on them. And he didn't call them by name.

Somehow she managed to get her feet to cooperate, walking through the store, her legs feeling as if they were made of lead as she clutched the button in her hands. She made her way to the bathroom, selecting the handicapped stall and closing the door behind her. Only then did she allow herself to look down at the button.

At first glance, it seemed like every other button. Bright yellow smiley on the front, metallic pin on the back. But then she noticed a small scrap of something caught in between. Digging her fingers into the sides, she managed to pry it apart with some effort.

A small piece of folded paper fluttered from the button. Trin gasped, scrambling to grab it before it fell into the toilet. She could barely breathe as she pulled open the paper, staring down at the scrawling text.

SHATTERED

Meet me at the back of the store at midnight tonight.
Tell no one.
P.S. Bring Emberlyn.

Chapter Thirty-One

H ow's he doing?"

Scarlet looked up as Rashida entered the bedroom just after nine p.m. The Potential glanced over at Caleb, who was still passed out on the bed, same as he'd been for the last two days. Rashida had insisted he needed to be tied up, just in case, though Scarlet really didn't see the point. He was too weak, too out of it, to try to escape, even if he wanted to.

The Potentials had taken turns watching over him while Scarlet had refused to give up her perch by his side, save for a few brief breaks for sleep. Now that she was aware they'd lied to her about the whole vaccine thing, she wasn't about to leave them alone with Caleb for too long, just in case.

Rashida had tried to talk to her during her shift, insisting again that their motives hadn't been malicious. That Trinity was a vicious dragon thief who had infiltrated their headquarters, seduced Caleb, and taken off with the dragon. That the fate of the world rested on them being able to get Emmy back where she belonged. And Scarlet had to admit she could hear the conviction in the girl's voice; she really seemed to believe everything she said.

But if all that were true, why not just tell Scarlet that from the beginning, instead of feeding her a lie?

Rashida had sworn it was only out of desperation—she couldn't have been sure Scarlet hadn't been bewitched by Trinity too. But deep down, Scarlet was sure there had to be more to the story. She said nothing, however, not wanting to lose their fragile trust until she was sure she and Caleb could make an escape if needed.

And so she'd sat there until the sun peeked over the horizon, watching Caleb toss and turn in a restless sleep, dabbing his damp forehead with a towel every time it got too sweaty. Truth be told, it was an all too familiar routine for her. How many times had she done the same for her brother over those last few months? Not that he ever appreciated her efforts. She wondered if Caleb would, if he could tell somehow that she was there—that she hadn't left his side.

He moaned and writhed, and her heart wrenched at the pain she saw etched on his face. Scarlet wished, for the thousandth time, there was something she could do to relieve it. That had always been the worst part for her. The helplessness she felt when watching those she cared about suffer—even if the cause of their suffering had come from their own doing.

"No real change," Trevor, the Australian kid who'd taken the last watch, reported to Rashida. "He hasn't woken up since we got back."

Rashida frowned. "Man, that's crazy," she said. "He must be a true Netherhead for the hangover to affect him this bad."

There was that word again. "What is this Nether thing anyway? Some kind of drug?" Scarlet couldn't help but ask. She had to admit, Caleb certainly looked like he was on drugs, with his pale skin and bruised eyelids. She wondered, not for the first time, if he should be taken to the emergency room. But perhaps that would bring up too many unanswerable questions.

"Not exactly," Rashida said, turning to her. "From what I understand, it's more like a kind of place. Another dimension or something—where all the dead dragons live. People travel there with their minds by channeling their energy through special gems."

Scarlet stared at her. She'd heard of some weird drugs in her day. But one that took you away to some kind of dragon heaven? That was a new one. She waited for Rashida to say she was joking, but her expression remained ultra serious.

"It's hard to wrap your head around, right?" Trevor asked with a laugh. "But I've done it myself, so I know it's real. It's pretty spectacular if you want to know the truth."

"Yeah, until you end up like him," Rashida broke in, gesturing to Caleb with a derisive snort. "Though I suppose in this case, it's for the best. Keeps him quiet until the boss shows up."

Scarlet cocked her head. "Boss?" she repeated doubtfully, her pulse kicking up in concern. "What boss?"

Rashida and Trevor exchanged looks. "Her name is Mara," Rashida said at last. "She's one of the Dracken I told you about. We've been trying desperately to reach her—ever since we got separated back at the mall. And this is the first time I was able to get through. She evidently was in jail—but now she's out and reunited with some of the others. When I told her we had Caleb, she got really excited and said they'd come right away."

"Wow," Scarlet said slowly. "That's…really great."

"It's more than great. It's out of this world fantastic," Trevor corrected, his eyes shining his enthusiasm. "We won't have to be on our own anymore, scraping to find a place to stay or something to eat…" He trailed off, catching Rashida's expression. "No offense, love," he added. "You've done great by us. But you have to admit, being back with our fearless leaders sounds pretty damn good right about now."

Again, doubt prickled at the edges of Scarlet's mind though she wasn't sure why. Maybe because it all sounded too good to be true—or that the facts weren't adding up the way they should. Like, for example, if the Dracken had gathered all these kids from around the world to raise dragons, why had they abandoned them when the plan went sour? And why were they only showing up now, when the kids finally had something they wanted? Scarlet knew there had to be more to the story. Something they weren't saying.

Or didn't know…

She swallowed hard. "Um, that's awesome," she managed to say. "And, uh, maybe this Mara person will let me go home? I mean, now that you have Caleb to help you find Emmy, you really don't need me, right?"

Rashida's smile faltered, though only for a moment. "Um, yeah, sure," she said, with a confidence that failed to reflect in her eyes. "If you have someplace you'd rather be…"

"It's not that," Scarlet said quickly, not wanting to hurt her feelings or raise her suspicions for that matter. "I mean, I think you guys are great. It's just, well, my mom. She's all alone right now, and she's not well. I'm the only one she has left."

"Right," Rashida replied slowly. "I understand. I suppose

if I had a mother, I'd want to be with her too." She sighed, staring past Scarlet at the blank wall beyond. Then she shook herself. "Anyway, just ask Mara when she gets here. I'm sure she'll be totally cool with it." She nodded her head a bit too vigorously. "Totally cool."

No way is Mara going to let you go.

Scarlet startled. What was that? That voice tripping across her brain. It wasn't Trevor's. It certainly wasn't Rashida's. Could it belong to Caleb? Was he not as passed out as he appeared?

You and I are the only ones who can lead them to the dragon.

Rashida looked at her strangely. "Are you okay, Scarlet? You look a little pale."

And once they get her back? There's no way they'll let you walk away. You'd know too much. You'd be a liability. They would have to tie up all loose ends, if you know what I mean.

"Scarlet? Earth to Scarlet..."

"I'm fine," she said quickly. "Just tired. When are the Dracken going to get here again?"

Rashida glanced at her watch. "Probably in a half hour or so. Do you want me to have someone relieve you for a while? You've been here all day."

Don't leave me, Scarlet. Don't you dare.

"No, I'm good," she stammered, forcing herself not to look over at Caleb. "I mean, I'll hang out here until they arrive at least. I don't want to miss meeting them. They sound really...cool."

Yeah, cool as cucumbers laced with arsenic.

"That they are," Trevor pronounced. "Now, how about we round up the littler ones and make sure they're packed up and ready to go? We don't want the Dracken to think we ran a loose ship while they've been away."

"What about him?" Rashida asked, pointing to Caleb.

"I think our girl Scarlet can handle one tied-up, sick Netherhead," Trevor replied. "Can't you, Scarlet?"

"Yeah, I can watch him," Scarlet agreed, her heart pounding in her chest. "You go get ready. I'll be fine."

Rashida gave her a strange look, almost suspicious, and Scarlet wondered if she'd gone too far with her willingness to help. But eventually the girl just shook her head and followed Trevor out the door. Scarlet stood in place, waiting to hear the lock click behind her before turning back to Caleb. His eyes were open and he was looking right at her. When he caught her gaze, his mouth quirked into a self-satisfied grin.

"Nice work," he said, his voice sounding a little raspy, as if he were a long-time smoker. "I'd shake your hand, but I find myself a bit tied up at the moment." He lifted his arms, his wrists straining against his bindings. "Perhaps you could help me with that?"

"Caleb!" she started to cry, then put her hand over her mouth to silence herself. She looked him up and down. "You're awake," she whispered. "Are you okay?"

"To be honest, I've had better days, but I imagine I'll pull through," he replied with a weak smile. "If you'd be so kind as to help me make my escape, that is. Unless…" He trailed off for a moment, looking down at his wrists again. "You've joined forces with the enemy? 'Cause that would be awkward."

"No," she cried. "I mean, I haven't joined anyone's forces. The only reason I was helping them was because they said Emmy needed me. But now…"

She looked around, her mind racing for a plan. Her eyes settled on the open window at the far side of the room. But they were on the second floor. Even if she were able to untie him, would he have the strength to climb down the side of the house and be away before any of these Dracken people showed up?

"Right. The Dracken," he interjected suddenly, evidently overhearing her thoughts. Seriously, these people and their psychic abilities were really starting to freak her out. His playful demeanor faded, replaced by stark fear that chilled her to the bone. "Fleck. I can't believe they're actually on their way. I swear, if I didn't have bad luck, I'd have no luck at all."

She turned back to him. It was time for some answers. "Caleb, what's going on here? They told me all these things. Like that you helped Trinity steal Emmy from them in the first place. And that they're just trying to get her back to the people who can help her." Her voice cracked, all her reserves crumbling. "I don't know what to believe. I don't know who to trust. All I want to do is what's right for Emmy, and yet all I seem to be able to do is put her in more danger."

Caleb sighed, giving her a sympathetic look. "I'm sorry, Scarlet," he said, sounding truly contrite. "None of this is your fight. You never should have been involved in the first place, and I'm sorry they dragged you back in. But I promise you, the Dracken are no good. And we had a very good reason to break her out."

"Which was…?"

He swallowed hard then seemed to come to a decision. "Come here," he beckoned, holding out his hands. "And I'll show you."

She stared at him for a moment, not sure what he meant. He was tied up. How could he show her anything? But eventually she gave in, stepping forward and placing her hands in his. They were cold, sweaty, and—

She stifled a cry as a shock jolted through her. Caleb's nails burned into her palms, as if they were made of fire. For a split second, everything went black.

Then she could see again. And all she could see were dragons.

Dragons. Sick, mutated, baby dragons, stacked in cages from floor to ceiling on every possible wall. Some sported three eyes, others a fifth leg or a stump where their leg should be. Some had no legs at all, flapping their misshapen wings against the wire cages, looking at her with hollow, desperate eyes.

"Just like Sodom and Gomorrah, the world has become a filthy, corrupt place—far beyond the point of redemption."

Scarlet whirled around at the voice. A man, dressed in a fancy suit, stood by the door. He smiled at her—a smile that chilled her to the bone.

"And so we are left with no choice but to raze the Earth to the ground and then rise again, like a phoenix from the ashes. Except this time," he added, "it will be on the backs of dragons."

Scarlet broke from the trance, finding herself now inches away from Caleb, his eyes a kaleidoscope of colors, swirling madly. She fell back, breaking their connection, her own eyes filled with tears.

"What was that?" she whispered. "Was that…real?" Her mind flashed back to what she had just seen. Those poor, poor dragons. That horrible man. Suddenly everything started falling into a sick sort of place. No wonder Trinity had stolen poor Emmy away.

"The Potentials believe that man, Darius, is out to save

the world," Caleb informed her quietly. "Something I once believed myself. In fact, I gave up everything to follow him and his quest for salvation. But I had no idea what he really planned until Trinity came along."

He glanced up at her, all his arrogance gone, replaced by a desperate pleading. "If the Dracken get a hold of Emmy, they'll breed her to those sick, mutated dragons you just saw. They'll create a hybrid species of monsters that will go on to destroy the world."

"But that's so horrible," Scarlet cried. "So sick." She shook her head, trying to clear it. "Do the Potentials know? I mean, I know they lied to me about the vaccine, but they don't seem like monsters. Not like…like him."

"They don't know," Caleb replied. "Trinity tried to tell them; she wanted nothing more than to rescue them all. But they refused to believe her and they blocked her from their minds so she wasn't able to show them what I showed you." He shrugged. "You have to remember, the Dracken saved their lives, pulling them out of the gutters and giving them more than they could ever dream of. And now they're so blinded by their gratitude they can't see what's really going on right there in front of them. By the time they do, it'll probably be too late."

"Right." Scarlet thought of her mother. How she could never recognize the monsters she let through her front door. "I guess that makes sense."

"Now, not to rush you…" Caleb nodded to his bindings. "But we're running a bit behind schedule here."

"Oh. Right. Sorry." Mind made up, Scarlet started working on his right arm first. The rope was thick and drawn tight and she struggled to undo it. What she really needed were some scissors or, better yet, a knife. She looked around the room, desperately trying to find some tools to work with, but came up empty.

Suddenly she heard voices downstairs. A door, opening and closing. She looked up at Caleb. His face had drained of all color.

"Don't stop!" he hissed. "Come on, Scarlet. Keep trying."

She nodded, going back to her task. The rope had thankfully started to loosen just as she heard the footsteps on the stairs. "Pull your arm out," she instructed. "Now!"

He didn't need a second invitation. He yanked his hand through the loosened loop then turned to start working on the other side himself. But the rope was just as tight and the voices were getting closer.

"Get out," Caleb said suddenly, stopping to look up at her. "Go out the window. I can take it from here."

"Don't be stupid," she surprised herself by saying as she circled the bed to the other side. "It'll be quicker if I do it."

And it almost was. Ten more seconds and they both could have been climbing out the window to freedom. Instead, the door banged open behind her and a tall blond woman stepped through, flanked by two men in black suits and sunglasses and several of the Potentials, including Rashida herself. Scarlet froze, realizing she was totally busted.

"What are you doing?" Rashida cried, horrified, even though it was beyond obvious. "Are you trying to let him go?"

She made a threatening move toward Scarlet. But the blond woman held up a hand, stopping her in her tracks. Rashida scowled but obeyed.

Scarlet watched, frozen, as the woman took a step toward her. Her face was ageless. Her eyes glowed like Caleb's. Even more surprisingly, she didn't look a bit angry about the intended jailbreak.

"Is this her?" she asked calmly, her voice sounding like the tinkling of Christmas bells. "Is this the one who Emberlyn came to rescue?"

Rashida nodded, still looking annoyed. "Yeah, this is Scarlet. She can speak to the dragon too. I've heard her do it. They've got some sort of connection or something."

"Very nice," the woman said in an approving voice. "Now if you don't mind," she added, leveling her gaze on Rashida, "we'd like to speak to these two alone."

Rashida looked as if she did mind, very much indeed, but reluctantly obeyed, ushering her friends out the door and shutting it behind them. The woman waited for the door to click then turned to Scarlet, a slow smile spreading across her face. A smile that didn't quite meet her eyes.

"Hello, Scarlet," she said. "My name is Mara. And these two gentlemen are part of the organization called Homeland Security. Thank you for agreeing to meet with us. We've been working to rescue the poor dragon from her captors for some time now. And we greatly appreciate any help you might be able to give us in the matter."

Scarlet swallowed hard. Homeland Security? Like the guys who look for terrorists? The Dracken were working with them now? This did not seem good at all. Maybe she should have taken Caleb's suggestion to get out while she still had a chance.

But how could she have just left him behind?

Mara turned to Caleb. "My dear, dear boy," she cooed. "You've been quite the needle in the haystack, haven't you? But here you are. Looking..." She trailed off, pursing her bow-shaped lips together. "Well, I can't actually say you're looking well, Caleb. In fact, to be honest, I'm pretty sure I've seen ten-week-old corpses in better shape." She clucked her tongue pityingly. "Poor dear. You always were so hard on yourself."

Caleb scowled, squeezing his free hand into a fist. "Go to hell."

"And where, may I ask, is your little Fire Kissed friend?" Mara continued, ignoring him. "Has she abandoned you already? I suppose it only makes sense. Once she got what she needed, what reason would she have for hanging around someone like you?"

Caleb winced, as if her words struck too close to home. But he said nothing, only glared at the wall.

Mara's pleasant expression hardened. Her eyes grew cold. "Fine," she said in a clipped tone. "You want to cut to the chase? Then tell us where the dragon is."

"Never."

"Now, Caleb, be reasonable."

He turned to face her. "Do you think I'm that stupid?" he demanded, his eyes flashing fire. "It's bad enough you've got all these idiots fooled, now you're conning the government as well? What did you promise them in return for letting you out of jail? A pretty little dragon, tied up in a bow, ready to burn down the world?" He shook his head. "Trust me, I would never in a million years tell you—"

"Cerrillos Road," Mara interrupted, turning to one of the agents. "Fauna, New Mexico. Write that down."

Caleb staggered as if he'd been struck. He stared at Mara, all his arrogance vanished from his face, leaving only pure, unadulterated terror behind. Scarlet felt a cold chill trip down her backside.

"How did you…?" he trailed off, as if unable to continue.

"Please," Mara scoffed. "Did you really think you could hide Emmy's whereabouts from me? In your condition? My dear, your brain has practically atrophied from all the time you've been spending in the Nether. Your walls of resistance are like Swiss cheese. A child could have reached in and plucked the information out."

Caleb's face had drained of all color. "But…"

Mara tsked sadly. "I'm sorry, but you did this to yourself. We all warned you about the dangers of the Nether. But you refused to listen."

Caleb let out a soft moan, collapsing onto the bed and staring up at the ceiling, as if all the fight had been beaten out of him. Scarlet watched him with dismay. She didn't understand half of what had just happened. But the end result seemed clear.

And now Mara and the government knew where to find Emmy.

"My poor, poor boy," Mara said, her voice softening. "You suffer so much." She walked over to the bed, looking down on him with pitying eyes. "But don't worry. I can help take the pain away."

She reached into her pocket, pulling something from its depths. Something blue and sparkling. Scarlet's eyes widened. Was that a Nether gem?

"Here you go, my love," Mara said sweetly, holding out the

gem. "It's time to let go of the pain. To forget all of this. To go see your dragon."

She held it out to him. It glittered temptingly in her palm. Caleb sat up slowly, his dull eyes affixing to the gem. For a moment, Scarlet thought he would bat it away. Send it sprawling to the floor in one last display of strength and resistance. To prove to Mara he was stronger than she gave him credit for. That he wouldn't give up without a fight.

Instead he opened his hand.

"No!" Scarlet cried, trying to dive for it. But the agents were too quick, grabbing her by the arms and dragging her out of reach. "Don't do it, Caleb!" she cried. "You don't need it! It'll only make things worse!"

But even as she screamed, she knew in her heart it would do no good. After all, how many times had she said something similar to her brother? And had she ever once convinced him to change his mind?

Sure enough, Caleb only looked up at her with glassy eyes. "How could things get any worse?" he asked in a voice that sounded nothing like his own. He plucked the gem between his thumb and forefinger then slid it down his palm, closing his hand around it. "Good luck, Buttercup," he said. Then, closing his eyes, he fell back onto the bed.

"No!" Scarlet cried. "Caleb, no!"

But it was too late. He was already gone.

Mara's lips curled. "You, get him in the truck," she barked at one of the agents. "And take this one too," she added, motioning to Scarlet. "Bring them both back to headquarters and keep them locked up until I return." Then she turned to the other guy. "You and I will mobilize a team and get us to Fauna before they move the dragon again."

"No!" Scarlet cried, trying to fight her captors. But they were too strong. They started to drag her out of the room. "Please no!" But her words fell on deaf ears.

They brought her down the stairs and toward the military truck idling outside next to a luxurious BMW sedan. The Potentials all filed out behind them, surrounding the vehicle.

"Are we riding in the truck?" she heard one of them ask.

"How far is it to our new home?" chirped another eager voice.

"Will there be food to eat once we get there?"

"Will we all have our own beds?"

The fools, she thought wildly. These crazy fools still believed these people were here to help them.

"Silence!" Mara commanded, coming out the door. "We're taking Caleb and the girl. We don't have room for the rest of you. We'll...have to come back," she added after catching their faces. "Once we have the dragon. We'll come back for you all. And everything will be as it was." She smiled serenely, regaining her composure. "Stay strong, little ones," she added as she slid gracefully into the BMW. "The Dracken will repay your loyalty."

No they won't! Scarlet cried silently, directing all her thoughts to Rashida, pushing them as hard as she could. She didn't know if she could do the same trick Caleb had done back in the house, but she realized she had to try all the same.

Don't you see? They got what they wanted. They don't need you anymore. They're going to leave you here to die.

Suddenly she remembered what Caleb had told her. Trinity

couldn't save the Potentials because they'd blocked their minds against her. But Scarlet still had an open channel ready for broadcast.

She closed her eyes, gathering up the details from the vision Caleb had sent her. Of the poor, deformed dragons. Of Darius's promise to destroy the world. She wrapped it up in her mind as if crumbling a piece of paper, then lobbed it in Rashida's direction as hard as she could.

This is who the Dracken really are.

She opened her eyes. Rashida was staring straight at her, face pale, eyes large as saucers. For a moment she didn't move. Then she turned and ran back into the house, the door slamming shut behind her. Had she gotten Scarlet's message? Would she believe her now?

And in the end, would it do any good?

The agents closed up the truck, leaving Scarlet and the unconscious Caleb alone. A moment later, she heard the engine rev and the truck pulled away with them still trapped inside.

Chapter Thirty-Two

Hang on, Caleb. I'm on my way.

Connor raced down the road, trying not to slip on the fresh dusting of snow, as his mind worked overtime to reconnect with his brother's spark. Back at the hotel, he'd heard him—clear as if he were in the next room—his desperate voice begging Connor for help. But the voice had faded away as quickly as it had come, and by the time Connor had found his shoes and his coat, it was gone all together, leaving him only a vague idea of where his brother might be.

But it was still the best lead he'd had for the past two days.

Admittedly, there was a small part of Connor that had wanted to ignore his brother's cry. A part lodged in the deep recesses of his brain that prickled with dark thoughts he'd never admit aloud. The part that whispered that it was his brother's fault that Trinity had felt forced to strike out on her own. Forced Connor to renege on his promise to keep her and Emmy safe. If anything happened to her now, Connor would never be able to forgive his brother.

Or himself, for that matter, but that was a different story.

But at the end of the day, Caleb was his brother and he couldn't just sit around if there was a possibility he was in danger. And so he ran through the town, over a bridge, down a road, across a freeway, until he came to a large billboard, cracked and faded and partially hidden by undergrowth.

Bella Vista Estates, the billboard read. *Coming 2009.*

Connor grimaced. They'd come across quite a few of these places while on the run. Even hid out in a couple of them. "Master planned communities," Trinity's grandpa had called them. Prefabricated suburbia tied up with a red ribbon and gifted to rural communities that didn't want them and couldn't afford them even if they did. It would have been advertised as the perfect oasis, complete with sparkling swimming pools, fancy tennis courts, and maybe even its own exclusive elementary school so the new residents' children wouldn't have to slum it with any country folk.

But then the housing market's bubble had burst and investors had refused to go down with the ship, abandoning their half-built dream communities and leaving a graveyard of skeleton houses to haunt the land. By this point, he guessed most people would have forgotten Bella Vista Estates ever existed to begin with.

Which made it a perfect hideout.

Could Caleb have been hiding out here these last two days? Was that why he hadn't been able to find him during his earlier searches? Connor pressed on, gingerly avoiding potholes and rusted-out construction equipment littering the unpaved roads. Reaching out with his mind, he could discern no sign of his brother. But there were others here, he realized. Quite a few actually. Maybe they would at least know where he had gone.

He kept walking, eventually reaching what must have once

been designated as the neighborhood's activity center, complete with an empty concrete pool beside a pair of net-less tennis courts, both ornamented with colorful graffiti. Connor scanned the cul-de-sac, his eyes falling on the solitary finished house at the very center. The model home.

Unlike the rest of the community, the windows of the model flickered with light, and Connor thought he caught a few dark shadows moving about inside. Definitely occupied, he decided. But who was living here? And would they know where his brother might have gone?

There was only one way to find out. Stepping lightly, he crept to a window, peering inside. The place was packed with teenagers, just hanging out, looking listless and bored. A few appeared to be crying. Not exactly the party of the century by any stretch of the imagination. He scanned the group, but he didn't see his brother among them. Maybe he was in another room. Upstairs perhaps?

Connor debated just going to the front door and ringing the bell, but then reconsidered, remembering the fear he'd heard in his brother's call for help. Not to mention Connor didn't want to be recognized by any of these kids and reported to the authorities. He wasn't sure if he'd been on any TV reports concerning Emmy, but Caleb certainly had been after going AWOL from his military gig, and Connor didn't want to be mistaken for his twin.

He looked up to the second story, reachable by what appeared to be a semi-sturdy trellis. He headed over to it, carefully placing one foot and then the other into the rungs, then reaching up with his hands to pull himself higher. He wasn't afraid of heights like Trinity was, but sweat still beaded his forehead as he made the climb. From time to time, he glanced down to the ground, half-afraid someone would exit the house and find him there in this very vulnerable position.

You'd better appreciate this, you duffer, he thought to his brother as he struggled up another few rungs. *'Cause you certainly don't deserve it.*

Finally, after what felt like an eternity, he reached the house's second story. Clinging to the trellis for a moment, he attempted to steady his pulse before trying to peer through the window. Unfortunately, the window in question was covered on the inside by a curtain and he couldn't see through. Carefully he felt for the edge of the sill, wrapping a hand underneath it and pulling it up.

But before he could push back the curtain, cold metal pressed hard against his temple. "Stop right there," commanded a female voice from inside the room. "Or I'll jam this knife into your ear."

Startled, Connor lost his grip, his foot slipping on the slick wood. He fell backward, tumbling away from the semi-security of the trellis, the ground below rushing to meet him.

"Caleb? Oh my God, are you okay?"

Connor looked up, his vision blurred from his fall. A somewhat familiar-looking Asian girl with blue braids was hovering over him, a concerned expression on her face. He struggled to sit up, his ankle protesting at the sudden movement. Great, he must have jarred it in the fall. It had been weak ever since he'd broken it as a child, falling off the roof the day his father was killed. Back then, the injury almost kept him out of the Academy.

Now it left him helpless, vulnerable, exposed.

Three other teens had reached him now, looking down at him with the same worry in their eyes. "Are you okay, mate?" a boy asked. "What are you doing back here anyway?"

"Did the Dracken send you?" added another girl. "Are you here to take us home?"

Connor shook his head, confused. What were they talking about? And how did they know about the Dracken? He squinted up at them, his mind racing. Then suddenly his eyes widened in recognition. "You're the Potentials," he realized aloud. The ones the Dracken had been training to become Dragon Guardians before he and Trinity had intervened. What were they doing out here in the middle of nowhere like this?

"That's not Caleb, you morons. That's the Dragon Hunter, his brother."

Connor craned his neck to see behind the crowd. A black-haired girl stood in the second-story window, looking down on the scene, her arms crossed over her chest. Even from here he could see the glint of the knife still in her hand.

The other kids shrank back a bit, giving him space. Connor used this to his advantage, finally forcing himself to his feet, wincing a little as he put pressure on his ankle.

"Where's my brother?" he demanded, looking up at the girl in the window. It was the one they called Rashida, he remembered. The one who had tried to kill Trinity and ordered the others to kill him. His hand reached for his weapon, ready to draw if need be, though he was admittedly rather outnumbered.

"Did the Dracken take Caleb?" he asked the rest of the kids when Rashida didn't answer.

"They were supposed to take all of us," piped up one of the younger children. She had purple and red hair and cheeks covered in a mixture of glitter and freckles. She couldn't have been more than twelve years old. "That's what Rashida said. That they would come and take us all back to the mall. And that they'd feed us and give us our old clothes back." She sniffled. "We haven't eaten much of anything in days."

"Go inside, Noa," Rashida commanded, coming through the front door, still holding the knife in her hand. She approached Connor, giving him a steely glare. "Look, your brother isn't here, okay? So get lost."

Connor ignored her, surveying the rest of the kids. Back at Dracken Headquarters, they had seemed like monsters, hungry for blood. They'd ruthlessly attacked him—a few had come close to killing him.

But now, standing in this suburban graveyard, in the light of the fading sun, they looked different somehow—smaller, less threatening. Lost, scared, alone.

They were supposed to take all of us, the girl—Noa—had claimed. Had they all been left behind instead? Abandoned by the very people who had brought them together in the first place?

He wondered how they'd even survived this long without the Dracken protection they'd originally relied on. They were only kids, after all, and foreigners at that. Probably didn't even have valid passports. They'd have no money—and no way to legally get any either. Of course they were all gifted—maybe they were using their gifts to convince people to give them what they needed. Though that, he realized, would be a brutal way to live. And they wouldn't be able to sustain enough spark to keep it going long term—at least not without serious repercussions to their health.

He struggled with a stirring of pity. They might have been in bad straits, he reminded himself, but they were still the enemy. "So, what?" he said, turning back to Rashida. "You kidnapped my brother and handed him over to the Dracken?"

"Kidnapped?" Rashida repeated incredulously. "Please. I saved that worthless Netherhead's life. He was out cold in an alley and about to be turned in to the police. We handed him over to the Dracken—as you put it—so they could help him deal with his...problem." She leveled her eyes on him. "Since obviously no one else gave a damn about what happened to him."

Connor stared at her, at first unable to speak as she effortlessly volleyed the blame back into his court. Was that really what had happened? Had Caleb been that close to being caught? He should have never let him walk out that motel door to begin with. Or he should have at least gone after him once he didn't return right away. But no, he'd been selfish, wanting to spend time with Trinity. Essentially abandoning his own twin to make out with a girl.

Not exactly the stuff heroes were made of.

"Where did the Dracken take him?" he demanded. "And..." He regarded the lot of them suspiciously. "Why did they leave you behind?"

"They didn't," Rashida declared quickly. Too quickly, and Connor caught her eyes darting to the other members of the group with a nervousness that belied her words. She was putting on a strong face for the rest of them, he realized, but deep down she knew a different truth. "They just didn't have enough...room for all of us in the truck. So they took Caleb and Scarlet and are coming back for the rest of us later." She made a showy gesture of looking at her wrist, even though she wasn't wearing a watch. "In fact, we expect them back at any moment now. So I suggest you take off, if you know what's good for you."

Connor's heart panged, despite himself, at the fierceness flashing across her face, a desperate attempt to mask her blatant fear. She had obviously been acting as the group's leader. The one who had somehow scraped things together to keep them all going these past few months. Most likely by promising them it would only be a temporary situation. That the Dracken would return. That they would take them back into the fold and everything would be like it once was.

At one point, she may have even believed that herself. But she didn't anymore. That was clear.

Which meant maybe she'd finally be open to hearing another side to their story.

"Can I talk to you?" he asked Rashida in as gentle a voice as he could muster. "Alone?"

Rashida looked startled. Then worried. Then, at last, resigned. "Sure, I guess," she replied before turning to the others. "Why don't you guys go inside and start packing up?" she suggested. "So you'll be ready when the Dracken come back."

"I don't think that's a good idea," hedged the blond boy. He glared warily at Connor.

"Please," Rashida scoffed. "I can take care of myself." She held up her knife.

The boy still looked suspicious. Connor sighed and reached to his side to pull out his gun. He handed it, hilt side forward, to Rashida, praying his instincts were right about her. She accepted it wordlessly then turned to the boy and raised an eyebrow.

The boy shrugged, as if to say, "Your funeral," then started ushering the other kids inside. Rashida watched them go, waiting for the last one to enter the house and close the door behind him. Then she turned to Connor. She gestured for him to follow her and they fell into step, walking side by side, until they reached the empty swimming pool. Rashida plopped herself down, hanging her legs off the side. Connor joined her.

"You know I could just kill you, right?" she asked, not looking at him. "I mean, if I wanted to."

"If you wanted to, sure," he said mildly. "But I don't think you do."

"And why wouldn't I?"

He turned to give her a steely look. "Because I'm the only one who can help you now and you know it."

She squirmed, obviously uncomfortable. "As I said before, the Dracken are on their way and once they get here—"

"The Dracken aren't coming," Connor interrupted. "I know it and I think you know it too. They got what they wanted from you. And they're not coming back." He paused then added, "Ever."

She didn't answer, staring down into the bottom of the pool. Someone had written "Hope Floats" in scrawling red paint and it seemed to stare up at them mockingly.

"It's funny," she said after a long pause, in a voice scarcely above a whisper, "growing up I used to see places like these in books and magazines. I mean, real ones. Finished ones with sparkling pools and laughing children. I used to think they must be from another planet. Surely there was no way something this beautiful could exist in the same world I lived in each and every day."

"You grew up in India, right?" he asked, wanting to keep her talking.

She nodded. "I was orphaned when I was young and there was no one to take me in. I used to wander the streets by day, begging strangers for money, then sleep under piles of garbage at night. It was safer, you know, under the garbage, than being out in the open. Less chance of getting robbed or attacked. But it came with its own hazards. I was always petrified the pile of garbage would shift in the night and bury me alive." She stared down into the pool and shuddered.

Connor thought back to his own childhood, the days before his father had been killed. They'd roamed the Surface Lands, sleeping in burnt-out corpses of buildings, always searching for the next dragon. Never enough food, never enough uncontaminated water. And always living in fear of the next dragon attack.

But in the end, they had each other. He had his brother. This girl before him, this strong, willful girl, had had no one.

"You got to understand," Rashida added. "Where I come from, there is no American dream. You can't hope to escape the life you were born into." She paused then added, "Except somehow I actually did."

"The Dracken," Connor concluded.

She nodded. "It was a Monday. I was hanging out in this Internet café. My boyfriend was a gold farmer for that *Fields of Fantasy* video game, and his boss had promised him a bonus if he and his guild could score this particular epic sword from one of the big dungeons. It was enough money to get an apartment for at least a month so he was really trying hard. Since they couldn't stop for breaks, I'd bring him curry from time to time to help keep him going.

"Anyway, it wasn't going well. He hadn't found the sword, and we were completely out of cash. Then this white guy came into the café. He was obviously rich, wearing a three-piece suit. And he asked if I would join him for dinner." She snorted. "I thought he wanted something else, you know? What they usually want. But I said yes anyway. At that point, I pretty much would have sold my soul for a bowl of rice." She grimaced.

"Instead he brought you back here," Connor concluded. "And asked you to help him save the world."

She glanced over at him, a regretful look on her face. "You gotta understand, Connor. For the first time in my life, I had clean clothes, real food, safe shelter. We even got to go to school—something I never thought I'd get to do." She stared down into the pool, a bitter smile playing at the corners of her lips. "It may sound cliché, but it really was a dream come true. I should have known that eventually I'd have to wake up."

Connor's heart wrenched at the pain he recognized on her face. He reached over, putting a hand on her shoulder in a vain attempt to comfort her.

"It's funny," Rashida continued, her voice now taking on an acid tone. "When I was finally able to contact Mara and she said she was coming today, I was as excited as the rest of them. I thought this was it. We were going to be rescued. I knew things probably wouldn't be as good as they'd been at the mall—at least for a while. But we'd all be together again.

The Dracken would have a plan. The kids could go back to relying on them instead of me." She sighed deeply, kicking her legs against the cement. "Boy, was I an idiot."

"What happened?" Connor asked gently, though he thought he had a pretty good idea. "Why didn't they take you?"

"Mara's working with the government now," she replied bitterly. "Maybe it was part of a deal to get her out of a prison sentence—I don't know. Doesn't matter, I guess. Point is, their plans have obviously changed and they don't need us anymore. They don't need any of us."

She paused and Connor saw her swallow hard. "The kids all think they're coming back. But I know the truth. The dream is over. They're done with us. And from now on, we're truly on our own."

"I'm sorry," Connor said.

Rashida squeezed her hands into fists, fury radiating from her lean frame. "How could they do this?" she blurted out. "Take us from our countries, give us hope for the future, then just dump us as if we were nothing more than the piles of garbage I used to sleep under?" She pounded her fists against the side of the pool. "It's like…if I never knew how good things could be…If I never had any hope to begin with…"

She trailed off, as if too devastated to continue. Connor said nothing. He knew all too well how hard it was to face the truth sometimes—even if it was staring you straight in the face. But in the end, everyone had to come to their own conclusions. Rashida had to want to help him. On her own terms. Or it wouldn't work.

"When Scarlet was leaving," she said slowly, staring down at her trembling hands, "she pushed me these pictures. I don't know where or how she got them, but I could tell they were real. They were of these dragons…."

Connor met her eyes. "Let me guess: deformed baby dragons? Locked in cages?"

She stared at him. "How did you…?" Then she shook her head. "Yeah, of course you'd know. You guys knew all along. Trinity tried to tell us. But we refused to listen…" She broke off, closing her eyes for a moment before continuing. "We've all been such fools. So blinded by all the stuff they did for us, we never thought to question what they were planning to do to the rest of the world."

"Well, maybe it's time to start," Connor said gently. "It's not too late, you know."

She gave him a sharp look. "What do you mean?" she asked.

"You came here to save the world, right?" he said, piercing her with his gaze. "Well, how about we start by saving my brother?"

Chapter Thirty-Three

"Come on, Caleb, wake up!" Scarlet begged, poking him for what felt like the thousandth time. The back of the truck was hot, and the air tasted stale with the pungent odor of rotten bananas assaulting her nose. They'd been driving for at least an hour, and the motion of the vehicle combined with roads that had seen better days had her *this close* to puking her guts out.

"Please!" she tried again, attempting to pry his eyes open with her fingers. "You have to wake up."

Of course, even if he did, she wasn't sure how much good it would do, at least in terms of making an escape. The truck's back door was locked from the outside, and even if it weren't, jumping from a fast-moving vehicle would only get them hurt or killed. Maybe Caleb would have some kind of miraculous plan on how to break free, though what it could be, she had no idea.

Still, at least if he were conscious, she wouldn't feel so alone. She'd have a fellow prisoner. A partner in crime. Someone who could give her more information about what the hell was going on and, more importantly, whether there was anything they could do about it.

Part of her wanted to shake him. To slap him across the face and scream at him for giving up on her like he had. For retreating to the Nether and leaving her to face the monsters alone. Just like her brother had done to her two years before.

But no. It wasn't totally his fault. Not really. She didn't know exactly how this whole Nether thing worked, but she knew enough to recognize the look in his eyes when he saw that gem flash from Mara's hand. He was sick, just like Mac had been sick. And it was his sickness that had made him make that selfish choice to take the easy way out. To leave her behind.

She looked down at him, her heart aching. If only she could reach him. To let him know it didn't have to be like this. That it wasn't too late. But once again she was stuck, utterly helpless, while faced with the suffering of those she cared about.

Caleb shuddered violently and she grabbed him to keep him from falling over. Wrapping her arms around him, she hugged his shivering frame close to hers.

"Come on, Bad Seed, stay with me," she whispered. "It's going to be okay." Though of course she had no assurance that this was true—that anything would be okay ever again. For all she knew, this journey could be their last. Still, she reached out, putting her hand around his and squeezing it tightly, hoping she could offer some small comfort at least.

Instead, she found herself falling into blackness.

✦ ✦ ✦

A moment later Scarlet opened her eyes, her jaw dropping in disbelief. Gone was the truck. The stench of rotten bananas, the stale air.

Gone was, well, everything, in fact.

In its place was a white void, stretching out as far as the eye could see. Like a blank canvas or the training room that Morpheus had taken Neo to in the beginning of the first *Matrix* film.

She gasped. "What the...?"

At first she thought she must be dreaming. That the truck had lurched. That she'd hit her head. Passed out cold. But all she remembered was comforting Caleb, wrapping her hand around his.

The hand that had been holding the Nether gem.

She started, her heart pounding in her chest as the implications hit her hard and fast. Had she somehow managed to hijack his ride? Arrived at the dragon dream world Rashida and Trevor had spoken of back at the house? It seemed impossible. But what other explanation could there be? She bit her lower lip, panic rising at an alarming rate.

Was she actually in the Nether now? And if so, would she be able to find Caleb?

She looked around, hoping to catch sight of him, but came up empty. He wasn't anywhere nearby. Actually, there didn't appear to be *anything* nearby. Just blankness—total blankness. Worry clawed at her gut as she wondered what she was supposed to do now.

"Hello?" she cried out. "Anyone there? Caleb? Can you hear me?"

At first there was no response. So she repeated her cry, a little more desperate this time, her voice quaking with fear.

But still there was nothing. Only silence, emptiness, a vacuum that threatened to swallow her whole.

Then suddenly, she heard it. A strange thundering sound coming from high above. She looked up, her jaw dropping.

"No way..."

It was a dragon—no, make that two dragons—swooping down at her, coming in for a landing, their massive wings beating the air into submission. She gasped, shocked by their sheer size and blinding brilliance. And here she thought little Emmy was impressive. These beasts had to be the size of small houses.

The first dragon landed a few feet in front of her, dark pink with long, translucent claws, violet wings, and eyes just as purple. The second—which touched down a moment later—was black as night, with hints of gold flashing under its scales.

They observed her for a moment with piercing eyes. Then, to Scarlet's surprise, the pink one dropped its front paw and dipped its purple wing so that the tip brushed against the ground. The wing rippled once, then folded in upon itself to create a sort of leathery staircase leading up to the dragon's back. Scarlet stared at it then up at the dragon, incredulous.

"You want me to...?" She nodded at the wing, almost afraid to say it. "Get on your back?" It seemed the obvious conclusion to come to, but she wanted to make sure before she just started climbing.

We will take you to the one you seek.

The female voice whispered across her consciousness, much like Emmy's had back in the real world. Did all their species have some sort of mental telepathy? she wondered.

In any case, she certainly wasn't going to look a gift dragon in the mouth.

Somehow she managed to pull herself together then started the climb, using her hands and feet to scale the dragon's wing. When she reached the top, she straddled the creature's back then examined its neck, searching for handholds. Finally she gave up, throwing her arms around its neck, her fingers latching on to two scales on either side.

The dragons seemed to nod at one another then stretched out their wings, giving one after the other a tentative flap, cracking the air like a pair of twin whips. Before Scarlet could even say, "Holy wingspan, Batman," her pink dragon leapt off the ground.

They were off.

They shot upward, faster than even that roller coaster she'd ridden at the State Fair a few years back, and Scarlet found herself squealing in a mixture of delight and excitement as the wind blasted her face. Her stomach roiled, but in a good way, and as they quickly gained altitude, she wondered if she should be freaking out. Any rational person would be, she supposed, but at the same time it just felt so powerful, so free, flying through the air like this. How could she waste the moment by being afraid?

The dragons crested some ways up, settling into a horizontal flight pattern. Scarlet looked down at the all-encompassing whiteness below, exhilaration swimming through her as she imagined what it would be like to have a whole world beneath them—forests, fields, and oceans spreading out into infinity.

And then, to her surprise, suddenly they were there. The same forests, fields, and oceans she'd imagined, magically rolling out before her eyes, exactly how she'd pictured them in her head.

She stared down at it all, marveling. Was that how things

worked here? Why everything seemed so blank when she'd first arrived? Because she hadn't yet filled it with her own imagination? No wonder Caleb liked it here. An entire world of possibilities, dancing at your fingertips; a world where you pulled all the strings. A world where you could banish all the monsters and live among mighty dragons.

But it was also a world of illusion, she reminded herself, sobering. A temporary escape no different than her and Mac's little hideout or, later, Mac's big habit. You couldn't run from the real world forever. At least not without leaving the ones you loved behind.

She turned her attention back to her winged guides. "Thank you," she said sincerely. "I don't know what I would have done if you hadn't come along."

The black dragon regarded her with golden eyes. *You have the blood of the dragon swimming through your veins,* he said sagely. *You would be amazed at what you can do.*

The blood of the dragon? Scarlet swallowed hard. Did he mean Emmy's blood? Could he tell, somehow, she had Emmy's blood inside of her?

"I'm Scarlet, by the way," she told them. "And I really appreciate your help."

The pink one turned her head for a moment. *I am Zoe,* she said. *And this is my twin brother, Zavier.* She paused then added, *And we are always pleased to help a friend of our mother's.*

Scarlet did a double-take. "Wait, what? What do you…?" she cried. Then her eyes widened. "You don't mean…Emmy's your mother?"

Emmy had seemed so young. And she had said she was the last dragon. How could she have children of her own?

Well, not yet, the black dragon—Zavier—corrected. *Which is why we're still here.*

All dragons yet to be born as well as those who have already died exist here, added Zoe. *In the Nether.*

This was getting crazier and crazier. "So when are you supposed to be born then?" she asked, struggling to understand all of this.

Zavier shrugged. *A few months? A year? Perhaps we will never be born. The future is not certain. Especially not for the world's last dragon.*

We can only wait, Zoe added. *And hope.*

The entire race of dragons has pinned its hopes on our mother, Zavier added. *She cannot fail.*

Scarlet shook her head. As if she wasn't already all consumed with the idea of saving Emmy, now the fates of two more dragons—no, make that an entire race of dragons—depended on her survival. She looked from one majestic creature to the other, determination rising within her. She had to make this work somehow. She had to get to Caleb and figure out a way to make this all okay. Whether he liked it or not.

The journey took what felt like maybe ten minutes, but it could have easily been ten hours. Or maybe no time at all—she wasn't even certain time existed here, at least not in the way she knew it. But at last, a tall glass structure rose up before them, like a crystal ball on top of a long, clear stem. A building manifested from someone else's imagination, not her own.

Was this where she'd find him?

The dragons began their descent, touching down on a glass landing pad that looked too fragile to hold their weight but somehow did. Once they were settled, Zoe gently lowered her wing and Scarlet slid down, making a rather graceful landing, if she did say so herself.

She looked around. "Is that where I'll find Caleb?" she asked.

"Depends on what you want from him."

She whirled around, her eyes falling to none other than the boy himself, slouching against the doorway to the glass house. He was gaunt, worn, shadowed, wearing tight, black leather pants and a collared shirt he'd left half unbuttoned. His hair was tousled and his eyes were rimmed with red.

"Caleb!" she cried with relief. "Thank God."

She turned back to her dragon, looking up into her purple eyes. "Thank you," she whispered. "And don't worry. I'm going to do everything I can to save your mother. Trust me, I know how important mothers can be."

Zoe seemed to smile at this, dipping her wing in a salute. Then she rose into the air, following her brother into the sky. Soon they were only two dark shadows burning against an orange sun. Scarlet watched them go for a minute, feeling a little wistful, wondering if she'd ever get to meet them again. Maybe in the real world, she decided, if everything managed to turn out okay.

Then she remembered Caleb. She turned back, realizing he was staring at her, an annoyed expression on his face.

"What do you think you're doing here?" he asked curtly, his body stiff and his arms folded across his chest.

She nodded slowly, recognizing the stance all too well. He was in full bad-twin mode now. Ready to lash out at her to shield himself from whatever it was he didn't want her to see. Just like Mac back in the day.

But she knew better now. And Caleb wasn't getting off that easy.

And so she said nothing, just strolled casually into the house, purposely invading his fantasy space. Inside was a circular room encased entirely in glass. It appeared to have once been very beautiful. A mansion with luxurious appointments. But it had clearly fallen into ruin. The crimson drapes were moth eaten. The couch was saggy and tinged with mold. The wooden furniture was scarred and broken.

Just like a certain boy she knew.

She sat down on the couch anyway, ignoring the swampy smell that filled her nose. She closed her eyes, thinking hard about the most beautiful flowers she'd ever seen—a bouquet of red roses from an old Technicolor film. Sure enough, a moment later that very bouquet appeared on the coffee table in front of her, nestled in a crystal vase. She grinned. She had to admit, she kind of liked the way things worked here.

"Just make yourself at home, why don't you?" Caleb said sarcastically, observing her handiwork with disapproving eyes.

"Thank you. I absolutely will."

She looked around, her eyes falling upon a sweeping staircase in the center of the room with several broken stairs. Using her mind, she set about fixing them one by one by one, restoring the beautiful marble to its finest, sealing up any cracks. When she had finished, they gleamed. Then she turned to the windows and started smoothing out the warped glass panes.

"Enough already!" Caleb cried. He threw himself in front of the window she was working on, as if his body could block her repair. "Stop fixing things! This is my house. My—"

"You know, this place could be really amazing," she said calmly. "If someone cared enough about it to put in the work." She moved on to the curtains, sewing up each moth hole.

"Well, no one does, okay?" Caleb retorted. He stalked over to the newly repaired drapes and grabbed them, purposely ripping them in two. "So cut it out."

She stopped. She folded her hands in her lap and stared down at the roses.

"Is that why you come here?" she asked quietly. "Because you think no one cares?"

His pale face flushed bright red. He dropped the drapes. "Why are *you* here?" he growled. "Why can't you just leave me to my misery like everyone else?"

She rolled her eyes. Here he went again. "God, you remind me so much of Mac," she couldn't help but mutter.

Caleb frowned. "Who's Mac?" he demanded, as if he didn't really want to know. "Your boyfriend?"

"My brother," she corrected quietly. "He was just like you."

"Super hot with a biting wit?"

She shook her head. "A drug addict."

"What?" he cried, losing his cool. "I'm not—"

Scarlet held up her hand. "Don't even bother," she interrupted. "Trust me, I've heard it all before. You're not addicted, you only do it for fun, you can quit anytime, blah, blah, blah."

"But it's—"

"No. It's not true," she bit back, her voice rising. "You know it's not, so don't waste your time trying to lie to me. I saw you passed out in the alleyway. I saw you go through detox symptoms for the last two days. And I saw that hungry look in your eyes when Mara pulled the gem from her pocket."

"Now hold on," Caleb interrupted. "That all may be true. Except for the Mara thing."

Scarlet raised a skeptical eyebrow. He blushed.

"Okay, so I wanted it. Of course I flecking wanted it. But I wouldn't have taken it, I swear. Except that I realized it was my one last chance to save them."

"Excuse me?"

His mouth twisted. "Look, I know what they think of me, okay? I know that's why they offered me the gem in the first place. Put poor little bad twin out of his misery so he'll come along quietly." He scowled, and the lights in the room flickered, reflecting his mood. "But I figured maybe for once in my life, my pathetic reputation might work in my favor. I could palm the gem, then leave a message for my brother through the Nether somehow—like we used to when we were kids. I could let him know that the Dracken had their location and were on their way. Then at least he'd be able to get Trinity and Emmy to safety." He sighed, looking a little sad. "He's good at that kind of thing, don't you know? Protect and serve and be a goddamned hero. I should have just let him have the job from the start."

Scarlet bit her lower lip, feeling a little ashamed. Here she'd thought he'd taken the easy way out. But had she been wrong? Had he really been making one last-ditch effort to help them? Sacrificing himself to save his friends?

"So that's good, then," she said, trying to sort through what he was saying. "Connor will protect Trinity and Emmy? And maybe they'll come rescue us as well?"

Caleb looked at her sharply. "What do you mean, *us*?" he asked. "Did they take you too?" Guilt flashed across his face. "Man, I told you, you should have left when you had the chance."

She shrugged. "Yeah, well, it's too late now," she said. "We're both in the back of some kind of military truck, headed to some government facility or whatever. But it's okay," she added. "If your brother can just save Emmy, I'll be—"

"He can't," Caleb interrupted, in a strangled voice.

"What?"

His face darkened. Outside thunderclouds cracked across the sky. "I couldn't do it, okay?" he blurted out. "I tried, but I couldn't make it work. I don't have any spark left."

"Spark?" She shook her head, confused. "What do you mean?"

"I mean you were right about me," he retorted. "They were all right about me. I'm nothing more than a burned-out Netherhead who willingly went and wasted his gift. I couldn't steel my mind against Mara's probe then, and I can't get a message to my brother to warn him that she's on her way now. Hell, I don't even know when I'll be able to release myself from this god-awful place—even if I wanted to." He stared down at his feet, his hands squeezed into fists. "It's like I'm trapped here. Just like Trinity's mother was. And there's nothing I can do about it."

Scarlet's heart wrenched at the agony she saw flash across his face. It reminded her of another night. Another boy, trapped in another prison—also of his own making. He'd been cruel too. Calling her names, pushing her away, telling her to leave him alone. But those angry jabs hadn't been weapons; they'd been cries for help.

"Oh, Caleb," she whispered, placing a tentative hand on his shoulder.

He shrugged it off angrily. "Don't feel sorry for me," he growled. "I deserve everything I get. I was selfish, weak, stupid. I deserve to be left here to rot."

"No," she said firmly. "You don't. And you're not selfish or weak or stupid either. You're sick. Just like my brother was sick. And you need to admit that. Admit you need help."

"Of course I need help!" Caleb cried, turning away from her, his whole body shaking. "But who the hell is going to help me? I've pushed away everyone who tried to care about me away. Trinity, my brother, even my own dragon." His voice broke. "There's no one left."

"Actually there is," she said, placing a hand on his arm again, gently turning him around. She lifted her eyes to meet his own. "Me."

For a moment he said nothing, just squeezed his eyes shut, as if unable to contain the anguish he was feeling inside. Then he opened them again. "Why would you help me?" he rasped. "You barely even know me."

She was quiet for a moment. "I don't know. I guess I kind of feel like I do. Maybe it's because of all the craziness we've been through in the last week. Or maybe it's because of my brother."

"What happened to your brother?" he asked hesitantly, not sounding as if he was sure he wanted to know. She didn't blame him. After all, she didn't really want to say. But she didn't have a choice now.

"He died," she said slowly. "Two years ago—of an overdose or maybe a bad batch of meth. Who knows? It doesn't matter, does it? Just that he died. He died and left me to face the monster on my own." She could hear the trace of bitterness at the edge of her voice. The one that always came when she spoke of her brother.

"The monster." Caleb looked up at her, his eyes widening. "You mean your mom's boyfriend, don't you?" he added, a growing realization reflected on his face.

She turned away, unable to meet his piercing gaze. She didn't know how he knew that. More mind tricks, she supposed. At this point, what did it matter?

"Did he hurt you?" he demanded. "He did, didn't he?"

"Mostly he hurt my mother," she corrected, suddenly feeling very tired and very old. "I only got it when I tried to break things up between them." She paused, realizing she was making excuses for him, just like her mom always did. Caleb needed to know the truth, no matter how ugly it was. She squared her jaw and met his eyes. "Yes. He hurt me. For years he's hurt me."

Caleb swore under his breath, his hands squeezing into fists. Outside, lightning slashed across the sky, followed by a roar of thunder. "That bastard," he growled. "How could he do that to someone like you? You're so small. So sweet." He looked up, his face a mask of frustration and anger. "God, if I were your brother, I would have killed him the first time he laid a finger on you."

"Yeah, well, years of getting the crap kicked out of you kind of dissuades you from that kind of bravado," she told him. "Especially when your own mother knows it's going on but refuses to do anything about it." She shrugged. "Mac felt like he couldn't escape. So he chose a different way out."

Promise me, Scarlet. Promise me you'll look after Mom…

"But that's so…cowardly," Caleb cried, looking indignant. "He just gave up? Left you to face the monster on your own?"

"Yup." She let the word hang in the air then gave him a pointed look.

He sighed, obviously getting her meaning. He scrubbed his face with his hands. "God, Scarlet, you must think I'm the biggest loser ever."

She shook her head. "No," she said simply. "I think you're scared. And I think you're sick. Just like Mac was. But unlike Mac, I think there's still some part of you that cares. Some part that doesn't want to give up. That still wants to do what he can to make this right."

For a moment, Caleb said nothing. Only stared at her with eyes so intense she shivered, feeling naked under his gaze. Her knees buckled and her stomach flip-flopped madly. Had she made a mistake sharing all of this with him? Did he now think she was a fool, powerless to escape her family's demons? She'd wanted to show him that there was hope. But had she only mirrored her own hopelessness instead? Suddenly she couldn't bear the idea that he would think her pathetic, weak.

"Caleb…" she started.

He reached out, tracing her cheek with a gentle finger, brushing away a tear she hadn't realized she'd let fall. Her breath hitched as his gaze locked onto her, his expression transforming before her eyes. Not a look of disgust or pity, she realized with a shock. But of childlike wonder. As if she'd just revealed herself to be some kind of goddess or angel, come to take him home.

She peered at him with serious eyes. "There are still

monsters out there, Caleb. And I plan to take them on, no matter what. But I'd really love to have you by my side. Will you stand with me, Caleb? Will you help me fight the monsters?"

His answer came as a kiss. Tentative at first, his mouth whispering across her own, as if asking permission, then with more force when she didn't pull away. His lips were warm. Soft. His kiss impossibly tender. And as his hands reached into her hair, a shiver passed through her, her whole body breaking out into goose bumps, her heart hammering in her ears.

"Oh, Scarlet," he murmured against the hollow of her throat. "I'm so sorry, Scarlet."

"There's nothing to be sorry for," she assured him, her voice a breathless whisper. "Just tell me you want to keep fighting."

"I want to," he rasped. "God, I want to."

She smiled, feeling his earnestness like a warm blanket wrapping around her. Maybe they could still make this work. She leaned forward, giving him one more soft kiss—then pulled away. When she did, she saw color in his cheeks. A bright red against his otherwise translucent skin. As if she'd literally kissed the life back into him.

Then she looked around the room and started to laugh.

"What?" Caleb asked, glancing over at her, puzzled. Then he followed her gaze, his jaw dropping in disbelief. The glass palace in the sky—the one that had been in such grand disrepair when she'd first arrived—was now gleaming, shiny, looking brand new.

Caleb blushed. "Well, that's a bit embarrassing," he stammered.

"I think you mean a bit awesome," she proclaimed, rising from the couch and dancing across the room. "Oh, Caleb, it's gorgeous."

"It is, isn't it?" he said softly. And it took her a moment to realize he wasn't looking at the house. She felt her own cheeks flush. It was all she could do not to jump on top of him and start kissing him all over again. But there were more important things to discuss first. Like saving-the-world important.

"So let me get this straight," she said, sitting down beside him, folding her hands in her lap to avoid touching him again and losing control. "You're trapped here in the Nether and can't get word to your brother. But somehow we need to get him a message to let him and Trinity know that the Dracken are on their way."

Caleb's happy expression faded. "Right. But there's no way—"

"No way for you," she interrupted. "What about me?"

"You never shared a bond with my brother. He won't hear you if you call."

"If I call from here," she corrected. "But what about the real world? He has a cell phone right?" She paused, considering. "Of course I'm still trapped in that stupid truck…"

Caleb stared at her, a look of excitement dawning on his face. "There might be a way for you to escape," he said in a low voice. "I mean, I don't know for sure. It depends on how Emmy's blood has bonded with your own. But if you could pull it off, I'm pretty sure you'd be able to get out of the truck at least. And then you could call my brother the old-fashioned way."

"Yeah?" she asked, hope surging through her. "I'll do it. Whatever it is. Just tell me and I'll do it."

He took her hands in his, looking at her with worried eyes. "Are you sure?" he asked. "It won't be easy. And it'll probably be dangerous. After all, the Dracken that have us prisoner? They can be real monsters."

A slow smile spread across her face. "Well, it just so happens that monsters are my specialty," she proclaimed. "So why don't you go ahead and tell me what I need to do?"

PART 5:

CREVICE

Chapter Thirty-Four

Strata-A—Year 189 Post-Scorch

Connor stepped into the sterile hospital room, his eyes falling upon his mother lying in her bed. She looked frailer than ever, the veins in her skin like purple snakes winding around her body. She was hooked up to monitors, which beeped and whirled with information on her vitals that he couldn't interpret, and a ventilator to help her breathe. When she saw him, she smiled weakly.

"My Dragon Hunter," she proclaimed. "You came."

"As soon as I could," he said earnestly, knowing it hadn't been soon enough. They'd been out on the Surface Lands when he'd first gotten the message on his transcriber that she'd been admitted after collapsing in the market. The cancer had spread to her lungs, the doctors had told him. They weren't sure how long she had left.

He'd begged his commanding officer to give him leave to go. But they were too far out, he was told. They couldn't spare a vehicle to take him back to the closest surface elevator, and walking back was suicide. So he'd been forced to stay until they'd found and slayed the ruby dragon that had been plaguing the glass gardens by the western block. A tough old geezer that refused to leave his lair—even with the lure of the hunters' songs. And so they had laid siege until the dragon finally got too hungry to hunker down and flew out, giving them a clean shot. As the days had ticked by, Connor's worries had grown. Would his mother even be alive when he returned?

"I'm sorry it took so long," he said, sitting down in the chair beside her bed. "We were out on assignment."

He told her the details, assuming she'd be excited to hear them as usual. But when he saw the look on her face, he stopped midstory.

"What?" he asked, puzzled.

She glanced toward the door. "Can you close that?" she asked.

He rushed to do her bidding. When he had returned, she smiled at him. "My cancer is gone."

"Wait, what?" he blurted out. Of all the things he'd expected her to say, this was certainly not one of them. "What do you mean, gone?"

"Lower your voice," she hissed. "They'll find out soon enough, and it has to seem natural. Or they'll arrest your brother."

Connor raked a hand through his hair, even more confused. "What are you talking about, Mom?" Was she starting to suffer delusions as well?

"Two days ago, Caleb came," she told him, a smile creeping to her lips. "He injected dragon's blood into my IV."

"He did *what?*" Connor almost roared. Then he remembered himself. "Oh God, Mom, I'm so sorry. If I had been here…"

His mother waved him off. "You're not listening," she admonished him. "Your brother saved my life. I was so weak

I could barely sit up in bed. Now I feel like I could dance around the room. Run a marathon. Slay my own dragon."

Connor felt like he was going to throw up. There had always been rumors that dragon's blood had healing properties. But no one had ever synthesized it properly. And the rats and other animals the scientists had experimented on had all died after a few days. He felt tears well in his eyes. What had his brother been thinking?

"Connor, don't cry. This is a good thing. Your brother met up with these people—the Order of the Dracken—you know, from the Sky Houses. They gave him a job. They gave him a dragon. And they gave him the blood to heal me." She smiled up at him, a guileless smile that broke his heart. "The doctors won't understand, of course. They'll probably call it a miracle. But I'll always know. It was because of my son. My Caleb."

Connor felt as if the lump in his throat would strangle him. He wanted to shake his mother, tell her she didn't know what she was talking about. That the blood would not heal her—that she would be dead in a week like all the others. But how could he? How could he steal away the first sparkle in her eyes he'd seen for months—maybe years?

All this time he'd slaved away, doing what he could to keep her in food and medicine and shelter. Draining, dirty work that made him want to curl up in a ball at the end of the day and sob like a baby. For months, for years, he'd done it without complaint—all for her. And now his brother had waltzed in and poisoned her with what he told her was a cure. And in a week she would die, Caleb's praises still fresh on her lips.

"Mom…" He started then he stopped, realizing that he'd been so angry at the blood transfusion news, he'd missed the other thing she'd said. "Did you just say Caleb has a *dragon?*" he said. "Like a real, live dragon?"

"Oh yes," his mother agreed. "Her name is Trinity—like that girl—the founder of the original Dracken. He showed me a video of her on his reader. She's beautiful, Connor. A descendant of the great Emberlyn herself." A smile played at the corners of her lips. "I've never seen your brother so happy—so alive. And after tomorrow, their bond will be complete. They'll be together forever." She locked her eyes on him. "But don't tell anyone," she added, as if remembering. "Of course it's extremely illegal to own a dragon. If someone were to find out…"

"Oh I won't tell anyone," Connor managed to grind out, forcing himself to his feet. "Trust me. I won't tell a soul." He started toward the door, his heart hammering in his ears as rage and worry fought for dominance.

"Where are you going?" his mother cried after him, sounding concerned. "You just got here—are you really going to leave?"

"I'll be back," he promised her. "But first I've got to go find Caleb. I've got to…thank him…for all he's done." He paused then added, "And, of course, I'd like to meet his dragon."

Chapter Thirty-Five

"Okay, Emmy, are you ready to do this?"

The night was warm and dry and dark, with a waning moon casting only minimal illumination down on the New Mexico subdivision. And while Trinity had managed to procure a flashlight from the garage, she was too afraid of getting caught to turn it on.

I'm ready, Fire Kissed, Emmy assured her, tossing her head with confidence. Trinity bit her lower lip. At least someone was.

"Okay. Let me know if I'm hurting you," she told the dragon as she lifted one leg to straddle Emmy's back. The dragon had grown some since the football stadium and now had just enough room between her wings and her neck for Trinity to straddle between. It wasn't exactly the most comfortable of positions, but it felt secure enough for short term. At least, that's what she told herself.

Are you ready? Emmy asked.

Trinity glanced back at the dark house, wondering what the Dracken kids would think when they woke up and found her gone. They'd been so great to her, rescuing her and taking her in, trying to shake the authorities from her trail. She felt bad just taking off in the middle of the night like this. But she had no choice. The note had said to come alone.

"Ready as I'll ever be," she assured the dragon as she squeezed her neck. "Let's do this!"

She could feel Emmy's head nod, followed by a small breeze at her bare ankles as the dragon began to flap her wings. A moment later they were off the ground, rising into the air. Trin bit down on her tongue to avoid screaming in a mixture of terror and delight as her fear of heights warred with her trust of Emmy.

Higher and higher they went, passing the rooftops and then the power lines, until there was nothing in front of them but dark, empty sky. There had been no wind on the ground, but now she could feel the currents of air caressing her face. Burying her head in Emmy's soft scales, she inhaled the dragon's musky scent, trying to concentrate on her rather than the reality of what they were doing.

Someday maybe we'll be able to do this every day, she told the dragon.

Would you really want to if we could? Emmy teased. *You're shaking like a leaf.*

Trinity blushed. *Yeah, well, maybe every* other *day...*

She could feel the dragon's chuckle rise up her throat. Emmy turned her head to look at her then nuzzled her cheek with her snout.

It's going to be okay, Fire Kissed. I know it will.

"I hope you're right," Trinity whispered, more to herself than to the dragon. "Remember this could still be a trap. When we get there, I need you to keep your ears open and all your senses tuned. If anything seems strange or wrong—even if you're not sure why—let me know."

You know I would never let them hurt you.

"I'm more afraid of them hurting you," she admitted.

Do I have to remind you yet again of my fire-breathing superpower?

Trinity laughed, squeezing Emmy's neck. "Okay, okay, Smaugie. Let's do this."

With Emmy's wing power, it didn't take long for them to reach the Wal-Mart. The store was dark and even the RVs that were parked there this morning were gone. In fact, there was not a single car in the parking lot, which made Trinity a little uneasy. If her father was waiting to meet her here, wouldn't he have a vehicle?

"Maybe he's running late," she told herself. But her heart beat a little faster all the same.

On her instruction, Emmy dropped down to the ground, landing with a grace that made Trinity proud. She dismounted then checked the dragon over. "You okay?" she asked. "I didn't hurt you, did I?"

Emmy snorted and shook her head, as if offended by the question. Trinity laughed and reached out to scratch her nose. "Thanks Ems," she said. "That was a great ride."

But as she leaned down to kiss the dragon on the snout, she heard a noise behind her. Someone clearing his throat. She whirled around, half expecting to see that the cops had been lying in wait. Instead, she saw…

"Dad?" she whispered.

He was older, obviously, than he'd looked in the vision she'd gotten from the Ouroboros. His once over-gelled hair was now a wild mess, sticking out in all directions. He was thin too—almost scrawny—and not much taller than Trin. He wore thick, black-rimmed glasses that appeared to be held together by a My Little Pony Band-Aid and his shirt illustrated the periodic table of bacon.

But it was his eyes behind those glasses that gave her a real start. Even under the parking lot lights, she recognized them. The same eyes she'd seen a million times before—every time she stood in front of a mirror.

"Hello, baby girl," he said quietly, his voice cracking at the edges. He looked like he wanted to both laugh and cry at the same time. "You came. You finally came."

For a moment they both just stood there, taking one another in. Trinity opened up her mind, trying to listen for anything suspicious. But all she felt was an overwhelming love radiating from the man who had helped bring her into the world. Love, affection, longing, and regret. But mostly just pure, radiant love.

He's okay, Emmy concurred. *He wants to help.*

It was all Trinity needed to hear. She threw herself into his arms, burying her face in his chest. He wrapped his own arms around her, squeezing her tight.

"Oh, Trinity," he whispered. "You don't know how long I've waited for this day. I was afraid it would never come."

"I thought you were dead," she admitted, feeling the tears cascade down her cheeks as she inhaled his warm, earthy scent. Her father's scent. "If I had known…"

He pulled away from the hug, a stern look on his face. "You couldn't know. That was the whole point. The time line is very fragile. It cannot be disturbed more than necessary or we risk catastrophic results." He gave her a rueful smile. "Now come," he said. "It's not safe out here. We must go under."

"Under?" she asked a little doubtfully.

Her father didn't answer. Just reached down to what appeared to be solid pavement. Then, to Trinity's surprise, he lifted it, revealing a dark hole in the ground.

"What…how…?" She stared at the ladder leading down into the abyss, her heart beating a mile a minute.

"Our lab," Dad explained. "We built it sixteen years ago, when there was no development on this side of town. Five years ago they approved the Wal-Mart being built on the property. We couldn't move at that point. There was too much fragile equipment and no way to transport it. Not to mention I had given you this address to meet me at. So we let them pave it over and then we added a little trapdoor."

Trinity shook her head, hardly able to take it all in. "So you don't work at Wal-Mart?" she asked.

"I do actually," he said. "Both Virgil and I do. We figured it was the best way to keep a look out for you and let you know where we were without rousing suspicion. Also, it enabled us to hack into the store's surveillance cameras so we could watch for you when off duty." He shrugged. "Truthfully, we expected you around three months ago. Virgil was worried something went wrong and that you didn't get the Ouroboros." He smiled sadly. "But I learned long ago never to underestimate your mother."

The love and affection that shone from his eyes made Trinity's heart ache. All her life she'd wondered about her father. Who he was, what he was like, how things would have been different had he been around. Now, with this one look, all the puzzle pieces finally slid into place and she saw the life she'd been meant to live unfold before her. A life with no foster care, no broken promises, no lies. A life with two parents who loved her—and each other—and would do anything to keep her safe.

Which was exactly what they had done.

"Dad," she said, her voice barely a whisper. "About Mom…"

His expression tightened. He shook his head vigorously. And Trinity realized he knew. Somehow, deep down, he already knew.

"There will be time for talk later," he said, gesturing to the stairs. "Right now, it's time to meet Virgil."

Chapter Thirty-Six

The ladder creaked under Trinity's weight, and for a moment she was worried it would collapse out from under her. But she pressed on and managed to make it to the bottom floor, the hum of a generator soundtracking her steps. When she reached solid ground, she looked up, watching Emmy glide gracefully down to join her. Her father came last, shutting the trap door behind him and locking it securely. For a moment, everything was completely black and Trinity couldn't see the hand in front of her face. But just as panic began to rise in her throat, her father flicked a switch and the room was bathed in light.

"Welcome to the lab," he said, meeting her at the bottom. "Sixteen years in the making. All leading up to this moment."

She looked around, trying to take it all in. The space was long and narrow, lined with all sorts of unidentifiable equipment stacked from floor to ceiling—large metallic bins, control panels with flashing lights, a few beakers bubbling on a Bunsen burner. She didn't know where to begin to look.

"Was this…a bus?" she asked suddenly, noticing the glass windows lining the room, looking out onto solid dirt. "Did you bury a bus?"

"Four buses, actually," her father explained. "And one RV. Old rundown ones we bought from a junkyard. I think the men we hired to bury them thought we were building a meth lab." He laughed. "If only they knew the truth."

Trinity walked the narrow aisle, observing all the equipment, her heart fluttering in her chest. They'd obviously been hard at work at something. But what? What did all this stuff mean for Emmy?

"Hey, Virgil!" her dad cried. "They're here." He turned to Trinity. "We have sleeping quarters off of the main laboratory in the RV in case we're here all night. A full kitchen, satellite TV, everything we need to hunker down long-term if need be. Virgil doesn't like to leave the place unguarded, even for a moment. Much of the stuff in here is irreplaceable."

Before Trinity could reply, a balding man, who appeared to be in his late sixties, popped his head out of the rear doors. The guy from Wal-Mart, she realized with a start. When his eyes fell on Trinity, a huge grin spread across his face. He stepped into the bus, heading over to her with eager blue eyes. Like Connor, Caleb, and the rest of the time-traveling Dracken, his eyes seemed to have an unearthly glow.

But the man—Virgil—did not stop when he came to her. Instead, he pushed by her and went straight to Emmy. She watched as he reached out, stroking the dragon's snout. "Amazing," he said in a reverential whisper. "Simply amazing. I can't believe she's really here." He looked up at Trinity. "Thank you for bringing her to me. I'm sorry you didn't get the message earlier as you were supposed to. If all went to plan, she never would have hatched here. But you've obviously taken good care of her. She's large for her age and looks healthy too. That's what's important."

Trinity frowned. *Never should have hatched*...No, he said she never should have hatched *here*. But she hadn't hatched here. She'd hatched miles from here...Another state entirely.

She closed her eyes for a moment, opening her mind again to listen to what Virgil wasn't saying. But all she could get was an overwhelming sensation of relief radiating from him. As well as a natural affection and respect for Emmy. He didn't want to hurt the dragon. In fact, if anything he was giving off a protective vibe as he scratched her behind her ear.

She decided it was time to get to the point. "So, uh, what is all this?" she asked, waving a hand around the room. "What's it all for? And how is it going to help Emmy?"

"All in good time, my dear," Virgil assured her, giving Emmy one last pat then rising to full height and turning to face her. "But first I think a little background is in order. I'm guessing you have a lot of questions."

"That's the understatement of the century."

"Come," he beckoned. "We'll go into the RV and have a little snack. And I will explain everything."

Trinity wasn't hungry in the least, but she followed Virgil anyway, her father and Emmy taking up the rear. They walked through two more of the buses, the first lined with more equipment, the second serving as a storeroom for supplies. At last they reached the RV, which was still set up as it would have been aboveground—a kitchen and dining room area in the main room and a bedroom in the back.

She sat down at the dining table, still feeling more than a little freaked out. She watched as Virgil reached into the refrigerator and pulled out a bowl of fruit and set it down in front of her while her father rummaged through the cabinets for a moment, emerging with a box of Oreos.

"It's been both a blessing and a curse to have a Wal-Mart right above us," he said with a grimace, reaching into the bag and pulling out two cookies, popping them into his mouth.

"Uh, yeah," Trinity said, staring down at the food, not sure what to say. The whole thing was so surreal it was making her head spin. She watched as Virgil went back into the fridge and pulled out a large rack of ribs, setting it on the ground before Emmy.

"Have at it, girl," he said with a smile.

The dragon didn't need a second invitation and set about attacking the raw meat with gusto. Trinity smiled. The guy obviously knew the way to a dragon's heart.

Virgil slid into the booth, placing his elbows on the table, head in his palms. He stared at Trinity for a moment then shook his head and turned to her father. "She's beautiful," he said. "You have a beautiful daughter."

"A beautifully impatient daughter, I should think," her father said with a small laugh, giving her a knowing look. "So how about you get talking, old man? Tell her what she needs to know. After all, she's waited too long already." He winked at Trin, and she couldn't help a small smile, still hardly able to believe her long-lost father was actually sitting in front of her.

"Okay, okay," Virgil said, waving him off with mock grumpiness. "Kids today." He huffed, turning back to Trinity. "Well, I'm glad you're sitting down," he said. "Because what I'm about to tell you is going to rock your little world."

"Let me guess. You're from the future," Trinity said,

meeting his eyes with her own. "And you came back in time to stop the dragon apocalypse."

Virgil raised his bushy eyebrows. He glanced over at her father and then back at her. "How would you know that?" he demanded.

"Trust me, everyone's doing it these days," she replied wryly. "Now get to the part where you have a master plan to save Emmy."

"She's definitely your daughter," Virgil grunted at her father. "Okay, okay, smart girl. Since you seem to know it all, I suppose you also know that I was once a member of an organization called the Dracken. They enlisted me to help with a plan to send them all back in time to the Reckoning, so they could steal the world's last dragon egg out from under the government and help with the hatching. The idea was simple: if we could raise dragons the right way, we could use them for the greater good. They could help save our world."

"Right," Trinity said. "But that wasn't their true plan."

"But that wasn't their…" Virgil sighed. "Right, right. But just so you know, I didn't know about this so-called true plan until a few days before we were meant to leave. And when I did find out Darius's true intentions, I wanted no part of it. For them to go back and purposely set about destroying innocent lives, all in some misguided religious campaign… well, let's just say that wasn't my idea of saving the world." He shook his head. "So I went in and destroyed all of my equipment, hoping it might keep them from making the trip. But after I did all that, I realized it still wasn't enough. And that's when I decided to come up with my own plan."

Trinity nodded eagerly. "Which was…?"

"You gotta understand, I love dragons. I had my own, once upon a time, a gorgeous yellow diamond named Solaris. She was killed in a fight with one of the hybrids." He shook his head. "Worst day of my life, let me tell you. There's nothing more awful in the world than losing one's dragon…"

Trinity's mind involuntarily flashed to Caleb and Fred, and her heart ached a little. Then she shook her head. She needed to stay focused here.

"In any case," Virgil was saying, "after seeing what the Dracken had planned, I came to the conclusion that there could be no safe way to bring dragons back into the world after all. Sure, they had gifts that could save mankind. But the risk was too great. There were too many people, like the Dracken or the government, out to exploit them for their own gain. And even if I stopped the Dracken and the government, who's to say there wasn't some third group out there, ready to take their place and start the apocalypse all over again— whether on purpose or by accident?"

He frowned. "But at the same time, I couldn't let the Council just sweep in and destroy Emmy in her egg. After all," he added, glancing affectionately at the dragon, "she's the innocent party here."

Trinity let out a breath of relief. She hadn't realized, up until that moment, how afraid she actually was that this master plan could involve Emmy being put down like a rabid dog.

"So what are you going to do instead?" she asked, her voice trembling. "What can we do about Emmy? How can we keep her safe?"

Virgil paused and she found herself tensing, knowing somehow that this was it. That they had reached the moment of truth. That what he said next would change everything forever. That nothing would ever be the same again.

Virgil pursed his lower lips. "We're going to send her back in time."

Wait, *what*?

Trinity stared at him, at first certain she must have heard him wrong. Of all the things she'd imagined him saying since she had found the Ouroboros to begin with, this was certainly not one of them.

"What do you mean, send her back in time?" she managed to croak. Was he for real? She rose to her feet, her stomach clenching. She glanced over at Emmy, who was still busy crunching on the ribs. Looking over at the RV's rear door, she wondered if she and the dragon could make a run for it. It seemed crazy to even try. But the guy was old…and Emmy wasn't exactly defenseless.

"Hang on!" Virgil scolded, catching the look on her face. "Before you start to freak out on me, don't you think you should at least hear me out? I've waited sixteen years for you to show up. All I'm asking is for five minutes of your time."

Trinity hedged. "Fine. Start talking."

Virgil nodded vigorously, wiping his brow with a napkin. Then he swallowed down a strawberry and cleared his throat. "This is not some haphazard plan. You see, I've been studying dragon origins for most of my adult life. Interviewing them in the Nether, charting family trees. And through this, I have been able to pinpoint the exact period of time when dragons were on top of the food chain. Sending Emmy back there now will enable her to live out the rest of her life in perfect freedom and among her own kind."

Trinity frowned. That did sound good. But still…

"I want you to look at her," Virgil added in a slow voice. "I mean really look at her. Does she look like she belongs here? Can you think of any scenario where she'd easily fit into our world and be accepted by the masses without having her life threatened?"

Trinity bit her lower lip, her heart beating fast and furious in her chest. She thought of the football stadium. Of the angry mob. "Well, no. Not easily…" *That was supposed to be your job,* she thought wildly. *That's why we came here. So you would tell me how to do that.*

"No. Because she doesn't belong here," Virgil stated flatly. "And she's little more than a prisoner in our world. Unable to hunt, unable to fly, unable to mate. In our present time, she can't do anything that dragons are supposed to do. Do you agree?"

Trinity looked at Emmy, wanting to say she disagreed. That none of what he was saying rang with even the tiniest tinge of truth. But, of course, none of it was stuff she hadn't thought herself a million times before. The only difference was he had a way to make it better.

She'd wanted a plan to save Emmy. Now, one had dropped into her lap.

But still…

"She'll have her family back," Virgil continued. "She'll have her life back as she was meant to lead it. As long as she remains here, she'll be hunted, trapped, tormented. She'll be forced to live out an existence of fear or agony or maybe both." He paused then gave her a sympathetic look. "I can see how much you care about her. I know you don't want her in any more pain. Now you have a chance to make things good for her. To let her finally fly free. Isn't that what you wanted from the start?"

Trin stared at him dully. It was a question she didn't want to answer. That she couldn't answer. At least not without sounding incredibly selfish. Of course she wanted Emmy to be happy. She wanted it more than anything else in the world. And yes, there was no arguing that Emmy wasn't happy here. And things would only get worse, with the dragon growing bigger and the military closing in. She couldn't feed Emmy. She couldn't hide Emmy. She couldn't guarantee her safety.

Except now she could.

"Can I have…a moment?" she asked the two men, trying desperately to hold back the floodgate of tears. "I want to talk to Emmy. In the end, it's really her decision, right?"

Virgil and her father exchanged sympathetic glances then rose to their feet. "Take all the time you need," her father said. He reached out and placed a comforting hand on her shoulder. "We'll be in the next room."

They turned and headed out of the RV, closing the door behind them and leaving Trinity alone with her dragon. Emmy had stopped eating and was looking up at her with concern on her face. She realized she must have missed most of the conversation while she was chomping down on her dinner.

I don't understand, she said in a confused voice. *I thought you said he would help us? So why are you crying?*

For a moment, Trinity couldn't speak. She just stared at the dragon as her heart seemed to smash into a thousand pieces. It was all she could do not to run screaming from the RV. To grab Emmy and never let her go.

But that wouldn't be right.

That wouldn't be right for Emmy.

"I'm crying because I'm happy," she assured the dragon. "And, yes, he has a plan to help us. He knows of this place—this special place." She bit her lower lip. Emmy was smart, but she wasn't sure she could grasp the intricacies of the whole time-travel aspect of the plan. And she didn't want to complicate things further. "A place where no one will try to hurt you," she clarified at last. "A place where you can fly around all day long and hunt anything you want to eat." She paused then added, "And there will be others just like you for you to hang out with."

Emmy's eyes widened. *Other dragons? Like me?*

Trinity felt the tears slipping from her eyes now. "Yes," she managed to croak. "Lots of other dragons to make friends with and play with. You'll never be lonely again."

That sounds wonderful! Emmy cried, her eyes dancing with excitement. *When can we go?* She started hopping around eagerly, puffs of smoke escaping her nose. *I want to go now! I want to see the other dragons! I want to talk to them—there's so much I don't know about being a dragon. I bet they can tell me so many things!* She turned back to Trinity. *What are we waiting for? Let's go to this special place.*

"Emmy…" Trinity sucked in a breath. "That's the thing. *You'd* be going. Not me."

Emmy stopped short. She looked up at Trinity with horrified eyes. *What do you mean?*

"I mean…this is a place for dragons. Not people. I'd have to stay behind."

What? No! She could see the panic rising in Emmy at an

alarming rate. Her nostrils flaring, her scales bristling, her eyes rolling. She shook her head vehemently. *No, I won't go without you. You're my Fire Kissed. We're bonded. We're destined. There's no way I'm going to leave you behind.*

"Emmy, listen to me," she said firmly. "I don't want you to leave me either. In fact, it's the last thing I would ever want in the world. But don't you see? This is your opportunity. A chance for you to live the big, fat, beautiful dragon life you deserve to live. I can't give that to you if you stay here. All I can offer is more danger. More suffering. Possibly even death."

She shook her head, the tears flowing freely now. "I made a promise to protect you, Ems. To keep you safe. Now it's time for me to make good on that promise."

The sobs rose to her throat, preventing any more words. She closed her eyes, pressing her forehead against the dragon's, unable to look at her, unable to face the unhappiness she knew she'd find written on Emmy's face.

It was too much. It was too sad. It was too—

But I promised to protect you too. The dragon protested in a plaintive voice. *How can I protect you if you send me away?*

Trinity winced. The question was so simple and yet so damn complicated—all at the same time. But suddenly she realized what she had to say.

The only thing she could say.

"I won't…need protection anymore," she explained slowly. "Once you're gone, I'll no longer be in danger. My dad and I can get an apartment. I can go back to high school. Apply for college. Get a job. Live a normal life." She forced a smile to her lips. It was nearly impossible to hold. "Don't you see,

Emmy? This isn't just about you and your happiness. Once you're gone from here, I'll get to fly free too."

It was the worst lie she'd ever told, and pulling the words from her throat was nothing more than sheer torture. But what else could she say? If Emmy knew the truth, she'd never agree to go. And she had to go. It was, as Virgil said, the only possible solution.

You'll be free? Emmy questioned, looking her straight in the eye, as if she didn't quite believe her. *You swear you'll be free? That no one will want to hurt you anymore?*

"Yes," Trinity affirmed. "No one will want to hurt me anymore."

Then... The dragon drew in a breath and ruffled her wings. *Then I will go.*

Chapter Thirty-Seven

S carlet opened her eyes. Paradise was gone. The glass palace in the sky was gone. All the dragons of the Nether were gone. She was back in the rear of the bumpy, smelly truck with Caleb still unconscious by her side. She looked down at him, her heart squeezing. He looked so helpless lying there. So pale, so weak. Almost as if he were already dead. But she knew deep inside there was still a spark of life. And she had to hold on to that.

She reached out and brushed a lock of hair from his face then, on instinct, leaned forward to kiss him softly on his forehead.

"I won't let you down," she whispered. "I promise. I'll get to them in time."

A sudden nausea gripped her and she leaned to the side, puking her guts out as far away from Caleb as she could manage on short notice. She stared down at the vomit, her head pounding and her fingers trembling. Her whole body was flushed and sweaty and she felt an almost overwhelming weakness—as if she'd come down with the flu. The Nether hangover, she realized, just as Caleb had warned her about. She shook her head, a little amazed. If it felt this crappy to come down from one single trip, what must it be like for an addict like himself? No wonder the last time he'd been out for days.

"We'll get you help," she whispered, even though she knew he couldn't hear her. "Once we get out of this mess, we're going to get you the help you need."

But first things first. Drawing in a breath, she focused on the plan they'd made, trying to remember all that Caleb had taught her. Would she really be able to do this? Had Emmy's blood really given her the power to play with people's minds? She thought back to how the Potentials had done it to her. Sinking their fingers into her consciousness and changing her thought patterns. Could she really do the same if she tried? Now that she was back in reality, the whole thing seemed impossible. Crazy, even.

You have the blood of a dragon swimming through your veins, Zoe and Zavier had told her. *You would be amazed at what you can do.*

Squaring her shoulders and crossing her arms over her chest, Scarlet closed her eyes, reaching out, trying to connect with the minds of the two men driving the truck. At first she felt nothing—just a big, black void, stretching out as far as her mind could see. But she forced herself to press forward, widening the search, as Caleb had taught her, until finally the two consciousnesses danced in front of her like shiny balls of light.

She gnawed at her lower lip. Here went nothing.

He's sick. Stop the truck. You have to help him.

She opened her eyes, listening, feeling for a change in movement coming from the vehicle. But the truck kept barreling on down the road with no signs of slowing down. She exhaled. *No big deal,* she told herself. *Caleb said it might take a few tries.* Then she readied herself for push number two.

You'd better stop and check on him. If he dies, you'll be in big trouble with Mara. You know you don't want to mess with her.

She thought of Mara as she pushed. Of her cold, dark eyes. Of her knowing sneer. She thought she was so great. So superior to poor Caleb who was lying before her, sick and shivering. Scarlet hoped she would be around when Mara realized her plans had been thwarted. That Caleb—through Scarlet—had beaten her at her own game.

But first she needed the damn truck to stop moving.

You have to stop. You have to stop the truck NOW.

Her stomach lurched and it felt as if there were knives stabbing at her brain. But still she pushed with all her might, concentrating hard on the hope she'd seen on Caleb's face. She had to do this. She couldn't let him down.

Stop the truck! Stop the truck! Stop the—

The vehicle jerked hard and she was thrown against the wall, slamming into the metal side and crashing to the floor. Tears sprang to her eyes and she bit down on her lip to keep from screaming as the pain reverberated through her entire body. It hurt so bad that it took her a moment to realize what had happened.

The truck had stopped. She heard two doors outside, opening then slamming shut. Footsteps, accompanied by two voices, coming closer. She bit her lower lip, her whole body gripped with fear.

The blood of the dragon. Emmy's blood.

She heard a click of a lock and the rear door began to slide upward, the sudden outside light blinding her for a moment.

When she could see again, she found the Homeland Security agent and another guy standing at the exit, peering into the truck with matching annoyed expressions on their faces.

"What's wrong with him?" the agent asked.

"He's sick," she told them quickly. She pointed to the puddle of vomit. "He threw up all over himself and almost choked on it. Then he started having this…I don't know… seizure or whatever. Like he was OD'ing or something."

The men exchanged looks. The agent sighed then gestured for his partner to follow him into the truck to check on Caleb.

"Stay there," he warned Scarlet, waving a gun in her direction. She nodded meekly.

"Just help him," she begged. "He's…my boyfriend. I don't want anything to happen to him."

The two men exchanged amused looks at this and the guy with the gun stuck it back in its holster at his side. She hid a small smile. Good. Let them think she was some silly girly girl who wouldn't leave her guy behind in some crazy effort to escape.

Head still pounding, she readied for another push. Probably the last she had in her. Caleb had talked about depleting your spark, and now she understood firsthand what he'd meant. She felt like she could easily sleep for a week. But first she needed to bring this home. She squeezed her eyes shut. Here went nothing.

Oh my God! He's convulsing! Help him! Now!

The men dove toward Caleb, who in reality wasn't moving a muscle. One grabbed him by the head, the other held down his already-limp arms, using all his strength. It would have been funny, actually, if so much hadn't been riding on the whole thing working.

"Keep him still!"

"Don't let him swallow his tongue!"

As they busied themselves with their "patient," Scarlet made her move, grabbing the gun out of the guy's holster, then winding it up and slamming it as hard as she could against his jaw, just like she'd seen in the movies.

SLAM!

He didn't even cry out. Just slumped over, a shocked expression frozen on his face as he was knocked out cold. She stared at him for a moment, pretty surprised herself. Caleb had told her the guy's mind would be weakened from her manipulation, making him easier to render unconscious, but she'd still thought she'd have to hit him at least twice.

"What the hell?"

The agent dropped Caleb's head. It hit the ground with a loud thump. He scrambled to his feet, reaching for his own gun.

"Don't even think about it," Scarlet growled, training her weapon at his chest.

He froze, his eyes lifting to her and her gun, as if assessing them both. "Do you even know how to use that thing?" he asked at last.

"I'm from Texas," she spit out. It was sort of an answer anyway. "Now drop your gun and drag your buddy here out of the truck."

He sighed but obeyed without her even having to push him this time. Which was a good thing, since she was pretty sure her spark was all gone at this point. Grabbing his partner under the arms, he slowly dragged his unconscious body to the truck's edge. She joined him, kicking the body with her foot. A moment later he went tumbling onto the desert floor. The man jumped down after him.

"Now toss me the keys."

The man looked up. "You're going to be in big trouble, little girl," he told her. "Attacking government agents is a pretty serious offense."

"So, what, I should just kill you then? So you won't tell on me?" she asked sweetly, tightening her grip on the gun.

He swore under his breath but reached into his pocket, throwing the keys up onto the truck bed. She scooped them up in one hand, then turned back to him. "Walk a hundred steps into the desert," she told him. "When you see me pull away, you can come back for your little friend here."

The agent scowled, stepping off the road, counting under his breath. She watched him for a moment then dropped to her knees to check on Caleb. Thankfully, he still seemed okay. Still locked in the Nether but breathing normally. She wished she could move him to the front cab of the truck, but he would be too heavy for her to drag. Better to keep him here for now.

"It worked, Bad Seed," she whispered. "And now the misfit toys are going to save the day."

She rose to her feet and hopped out of the truck, pulling the door shut behind her. Then she leaned over to the unconscious man and pulled his cell phone from his pocket.

"Blood of the dragon," she whispered to herself then headed to the driver's seat.

Chapter Thirty-Eight

That night Trinity tossed and turned in the back bedroom of the underground RV, unable to sleep. And who could blame her, really? These were the last hours she would have with her dragon before losing Emmy forever. How could she close her eyes and let them slip away?

When she'd gone back to Virgil and her father, armed with Emmy's decision, they'd explained some of what would have to happen before the time travel could take place. Because Emmy would be living out her entire life and dying millions of years before Trinity was born, Virgil would have to perform an de-bonding beforehand, so their life forces would no longer entwine. At first Trinity had balked at this—she remembered the de-bonding she'd almost been forced to go through back at the Dracken headquarters.

But Virgil had assured her this was different. That was an involuntary de-bonding—two minds ripped apart that wanted to stay together. Emmy had the power to voluntarily release her most of the way on her own. The machine would just work to neutralize the last traces of their connection—such as the blood Emmy had given Trinity when she'd been shot. It would not hurt Emmy, he promised. And it would not kill her. Sure, she might be a little weak for a few days, maybe some flulike symptoms, but in the end, she would be back to her old self.

Her old dragonless self.

She looked over at the sleeping dragon beside her, and her chest tightened as thoughts of the impending loss settled like a dead weight in her stomach. She found herself trying desperately to memorize everything about her. Every scale, every tooth, every claw. Every part of her that, after tomorrow, she'd never see again. She was so sweet. So beautiful. So…Emmy. How could she just say good-bye?

"You're getting so big," she whispered. "Soon you'll be as big as a house." She swallowed hard. "I wish I could see you like that. You'll be so amazing."

The tears came again, splashing down her face. Silently, she rose, so as not to wake her, and headed into the adjoining kitchen. There, she found her father, sitting at the table, picking at the remains of some takeout Chinese. Complete with empty packets of duck sauce strewn about, she noticed. He looked up as she closed the door behind her.

"Hey," he said. "Couldn't sleep, huh?"

She shook her head, sitting down across from him. It was so strange to have him here. The father she never knew. And yet, somehow, he didn't feel like a stranger. Maybe it was because she'd seen him in the vision with her mother. The love that had reflected in his eyes. He had been important to her mother. And that made him important to Trinity too.

"I'm sorry, baby," her father said, reaching across the table to place a hand over her own. "If all had gone to plan, we would have transported her back months ago. Before she ever had a chance to hatch from her shell. She would have never known the difference." He paused, searching her face with his worried eyes. "And neither would you."

Trinity felt the tears slip down her cheeks as her heart squeezed in her chest. Back then, before Emmy was born, she would have been ecstatic to have such a simple solution. A way to keep the dragon alive and still save the world. But now…

She thought of Emmy. Her sweet, beautiful, wonderful Emmy. How could she just let her go?

"I remember that night I left you and your mother," her father continued. "I can't even tell you what that felt like—to walk through that door and know I could never return. That I'd miss your first steps, your first words, your first smile. Your first ballet recital."

"I…never took ballet," Trin managed to choke out. The most ridiculously inconsequential statement to make at a time like this but she'd lost all ability to speak rationally at this point, her mind was so consumed with pain.

Her father smiled gently. "The point is I didn't want to miss any of it, just as I'm sure you want to experience every moment with Emmy. But I had to let you go—even if it literally tore my heart in two. Because I cared about you guys that much." He paused then added, "I know you care for Emmy very much the same way."

"Yeah," Trinity agreed. "I do. And I want what's best for her. And if that means letting her go, well, that's what I'm going to have to do."

Chapter Thirty-Nine

I s this the place? Are you sure?"

Connor peered out the bus window as Trevor turned into a sprawling parking lot of a giant store called Wal-Mart. He glanced over at Rashida, who was studying the GPS coordinates on her phone. She looked up. "Yeah, this is definitely it, where Scarlet said that she'd be." She squinted at the store. "I don't get it though. I mean why would Trinity come to a place like this with a dragon?"

"Because her father told her to," Connor said with a sigh, watching all the people outside pushing carts and loading up the trunks of their cars. If only she'd never broken the music box and found the pendant. She would still be with him, under his protection. Instead of out there, somewhere, on her own—with the Dracken and government hunting her down like a dog.

They'd all been more than a little surprised to get Scarlet's frantic call the night before. Even more so when she told them what she knew. Here he'd been trying to rally the Potentials to help save his brother, only to learn it was Trin who was in actual danger.

After that, they'd mobilized immediately. Driven all night.

Now that they'd all shared the vision of the mutated dragons and the Dracken's true mission, everyone wanted to help. So they all filed onto the stolen bus and headed straight to Fauna.

Connor pursed his lips, scanning the parking lot. He knew it could very well be a trap. That the Dracken could have forced Scarlet to make the call to lure him into their sights and take him down once and for all. Even Scarlet's story—that the Dracken had forced her to give up Emmy's location—seemed to ring untrue. But at the end of the day, it was a risk they all agreed they had to take. They couldn't just leave Trinity to face the military herself. And they certainly couldn't risk Emmy falling into government hands.

As Trevor parked the bus at the back of the parking lot, Rashida turned to the other kids. "Okay," she barked. "Listen up." She threw Aiko a couple of walkie-talkies they'd picked up at a sporting goods store a few towns over and clipped another to her belt. "Team blue, you circle the store's perimeter. Take note of all the available exits and call them in." She turned to one of the other girls, handing over two more walkies. "You case the parking lot. If you see any suspicious vehicles, let us know."

"How will we know they're suspicious?" Trevor asked.

"Out-of-state license plates," Connor interjected. "And anything remotely military looking."

"Remember, Mara is working with the government now," Rashida said. "She'll probably bring an army with her. Or at least some kind of black ops team. But at the same time, they'll probably want to keep things on the down low. To not scare away the public."

She turned to Connor. "You and I will check things out

on the inside. Perhaps your connection with Trinity will help us narrow down her whereabouts." She cleared her throat, her eyes roving over the busload of kids. "If any of you spot her, alert the rest of us immediately and bring her back here."

"What if she won't come with us?" Aiko piped in. "I mean, we did sort of try to kill her last time we saw her. She's not likely to just go along quietly now."

Rashida grimaced. "Good point." She looked questioningly at Connor.

"Tell her you're on Team Dragon now," Connor said. "She'll understand."

Everyone nodded and it was time to go. At Rashida's command, they spilled out of the bus and split up into their teams. Connor exited last, scanning the parking lot, his hand involuntarily traveling to the waistband of his jeans, where he had stashed his gun.

"You're worried," Rashida observed.

He shrugged. "I'm always worried," he admitted. Then he smiled at her. "But it's nice to have backup. I'm impressed with how you rallied the troops like you did. You could be a good soldier, you know?"

She groaned. "No, thank you. And anyway, it's the least we can do. Trust me, everyone here wants to help Emmy just as much as you do. I mean, maybe the Dracken don't really want to save the dragons. But we still do. And we're ready to do whatever it takes to make that happen."

He held up a hand. "Let's not get ahead of ourselves," he said. "First we need to find her."

And Trinity too, he added silently, his heart pounding in his chest. He didn't want to think about what would happen to her if the Dracken found her here.

They walked up to the glass doors, which silently slid open before them, granting them entrance. As they stepped inside, a woman in a blue smock welcomed them to the store. Connor looked around, giving a low whistle. He'd never seen anything like this place. So large and packed floor to ceiling with useful items. If only they'd had just one of these stores back home. These common goods would have meant a lifetime of difference for his people.

"Do you feel her?" Rashida asked. "Do you think she's here somewhere?"

He closed his eyes, reaching out. For a moment he thought he felt something, but it was gone as soon as it came. He opened his eyes, frustrated. "I don't know," he said, scanning the store again. "This place is so huge and there's so much stuff everywhere. I'm not getting a good read."

"You don't think the Dracken and the government already showed up, do you?" Rashida asked worriedly. "I mean, they did have a head start."

"It's possible," he admitted. "They could be observing the store from afar, waiting for a sign of Trinity and the dragon. Obviously they wouldn't want to make their presence known until they were sure they had her in their sights." He glanced up at the ceiling above him and shivered a little. "For all we know, the Dracken are watching us right now."

"We certainly are."

Connor whirled around, heart in his throat. But instead of seeing what he expected—Mara or maybe one of her Dracken friends—his eyes fell upon a tall, lanky, Asian teen with blond hair, his skinny arms crossed over his chest. He was flanked by two other kids around the same age, both with brown hair and black-rimmed glasses.

"Luke, it's him!" cried the brown-haired girl. "One of the twins!"

Her friend—Luke—nodded vigorously. "You're right," he agreed. "I remember him from the museum surveillance tapes they put on TV."

Connor glanced over at Rashida, his hand hovering over his gun again. He didn't know whether to deny it or demand these kids tell him what was going on. Who were they? And how did they know about the Dracken?

"Where's Trinity?" the other boy demanded, taking a threatening step toward Connor. "What did you do to her?"

He knows Trinity too? Connor's heart was now beating a mile a minute. "Who are you?" he asked. "And how do you know about Trinity?"

"We're her protectors," Luke shot back, not missing a beat. He puffed out his chest. "The Order of the Dracken."

Connor stared at him, speechless. What? What did he just say?

"Uh, no. I don't think so," Rashida broke in with a snort. "Trust me, I know the Dracken. They're, like, old and well dressed and from the future and stuff. Pretty much the opposite of you tools." She smirked and turned to him. "Right, Connor?"

But Connor couldn't speak. In fact, he couldn't even move, the fear inside threatening to throttle him.

Rashida's eyes narrowed. "Connor? Are you okay?"

He wanted desperately to tell her he was. To toss the whole

thing off as some kind of freaky coincidence. But his soldier training wouldn't let him. The puzzle pieces were all there, fitting together far too perfectly for his comfort.

The Order of the Dracken. The new order. Here. Standing in front of him.

Had the time line they'd worked so hard to bend now snapped back into its original, horrifying place?

He had half a mind to reach for his gun. To shoot the three of them point blank, forcing fate to stand down. But how could he do that? These were just innocent kids. They hadn't done anything wrong…yet.

Still, the Dracken. The very first Dracken, back on the time line. He felt like he was going to throw up.

"Listen," he said. "We can handle this ourselves. Maybe you should go home and—"

Suddenly a female voice broke out over the store's loud-speaker. "Attention Wal-Mart shoppers," she said calmly. "We're experiencing a malfunction with our sprinkler system and will be forced to close the store early today. Please put aside your purchases and file out of the store in an orderly fashion. We apologize for the inconvenience."

No sooner did the announcement finish than Rashida's walkie-talkie crackled to life. "They're here," the voice—Trevor's by the sound of it—said urgently. "A bunch of unmarked trucks. They're circling the store and dropping a group of men off at each exit."

"And I see Mara. She's at the front of the store," someone else reported in next. "They're stopping everyone as they walk out and asking for IDs."

Connor swallowed hard. He didn't know whether to be

horrified that they were actually here or relieved that they obviously hadn't found Trinity yet.

"Ask him if they're armed," he hissed at Rashida. He could feel the questioning stares of the new Dracken kids on him, but he didn't have time to explain.

Rashida asked and a moment later Trevor's voice returned. "I don't know," he said. "They're dressed in plain clothes. But they have that military look to them. Buzz cuts and biceps, you know."

Rashida and Connor exchanged glances. "They probably don't want to cause a panic," she said. "Or alert the media. Emmy's so famous now, they can't just capture her and then hide her away to experiment on. The public would demand answers."

"Right…" Connor paced the aisle. "They want to steal her away, right out from under everyone's noses. Without them even knowing." He closed his eyes, searching for Trinity again.

Wherever you are, he tried to send. *Hunker down. Do not make a move until I tell you to.*

"So what are we going to do?" Rashida asked, her face pale. "How are we going to get out of the store without them seeing us?"

Connor rubbed his chin. "I'm not sure," he mused. "If only there was a way to create a diversion. To distract them so we could slip out."

"We could get on the loudspeaker. Tell people there's a bomb threat or something." Rashida suggested. "If they're all panicking, trying to get out of the store at once…"

"Not a bad idea," Connor agreed. "Though a riot like that could end with innocent casualties. People getting trampled, squished against glass…"

"If we don't, then *we'll* be the casualties," Rashida reminded him wryly.

"What if *we* alerted the media?" Luke piped up.

Connor and Rashida turned to look at him. Connor had almost forgotten they were still there. "What do you mean?" he asked warily.

"I don't know. I'm just thinking, nothing screws up a sting operation like a bunch of rabid reporters on the scene. If we get them all here, surely they would cause enough chaos to allow us to slip through."

"But how arc you going to get them to come?" Connor asked. "We'd need all of them at once, not just a random reporter or two. By the time you called them all and told them the story…"

"Oh, I don't need to call anyone," the brown-haired boy interrupted. "I just have to harness the power of the interwebs." He held up his phone and snapped a photo of a surprised Connor. Then he started pushing at the screen. A moment later he looked up and grinned. "One order of lamestream media, coming right up."

Chapter Forty

"Okay, if you just sit here, I'm going to place this cap onto your head and we'll begin."

"You sure this isn't going to hurt?" Trinity asked, looking with wary eyes at the blue cap threaded with red wires he held in his hands.

Virgil gave her an apologetic look. "I said it wasn't going to kill you," he clarified. "You may feel some...discomfort... during the actual procedure."

"It's going to hurt like hell, sweetheart," her dad interjected. "But you'll get through it." He walked over to the television set at the opposite end of the former bus. "Here, I'll put on the TV, so you can have something to distract you while the procedure takes place."

Trinity nodded, gritting her teeth. Truth be told, she didn't really care too much about the physical pain. It would be nothing, she knew, compared to the mental anguish she'd suffer after Virgil flicked the switch—the moment when she and Emmy's bond would be shattered and her dragon would become a stranger. No more hearing Emmy's voice whispering across her mind. No more feeling the dragon's love and affection wrapping around her like a hug. A lifetime of suffocating emptiness seemed to roll out before her.

I'm going to miss you so much, she told the dragon.

Emmy looked up at her with her big, liquid eyes. *But you'll have him back,* she said in an earnest voice. *So you will not be alone.*

Trinity cocked her head, puzzled. *Uh, what?*

You know, Emmy pierced her with her gaze. *The Hunter. You told me you didn't have time for happily ever afters with me around. But now you will. Now you can find him and be with him, and it'll be just like the movies.*

Trinity's heart flooded. As if things could be that simple. As if life were just like a film. But still, she loved that the dragon believed it. That she had created her own little happily ever after for her Fire Kissed. So she could leave without guilt or worry.

And here I didn't think you liked him all that much, she couldn't help but tease.

Emmy gave her a stern gaze. *You like him,* she said simply. *And he will keep you safe. I like that.*

Trinity swallowed past the lump in her throat. *Thank you, Emmy.* It was all she could say.

The dragon nodded then took a deliberate step toward her. She bowed her head low, exposing her long, scaly neck with some ceremony. At first, Trinity had no idea what Emmy was trying to do. Then she realized.

"No." She shook her head. "I couldn't. You love your necklace."

Emmy looked up at her. *I love you more.*

Oh God.

A raw, primitive grief overwhelmed Trinity and it was all she could do not to crumble to pieces. Instead, she forced herself to reach out, lifting the golden chain from the dragon's neck with trembling fingers. As she slipped it over her own head, the jewel settled against her throat, warm and heavy.

"Oh, Emmy," she cried, unable to hold back the floodgates of tears a moment longer. She grabbed the dragon, clinging to her with all she had left, which admittedly wasn't very much at all. Together their minds reached out, desperate to share a lifetime of memories in the few seconds they had left.

She'd already lost so many people in her life. Her mother, her grandpa, Connor, Caleb. Now she was about to lose her dragon too. Her sweet baby dragon. And she wasn't sure she'd be able to handle it.

No. She shook her head. She couldn't think like that. This was not about losing Emmy. This was about Emmy gaining new life. And that, at the end of the day, was all that mattered.

Emmy would be happy.

Emmy would be safe.

Emmy would be free.

"Sweetheart," her father interrupted in a gentle voice. "It's time."

She looked up at him in horror. She wanted to say no— that it was too soon, that she wasn't nearly ready, that she needed far, far, far more moments with her dragon before she said good-bye. But she knew all that would only prolong the inevitable. Better to rip off the Band-Aid than keep torturing herself and Emmy with an extended farewell. And so she somehow managed to force her hands from the dragon's neck.

She had to be brave here, she told herself. If Emmy heard her have second thoughts, she might change her mind and refuse to go. And she couldn't let the dragon sacrifice her own happiness for her.

It's for the best. It's for the best. It's for the—

Emmy met her eyes. *Thank you, Fire Kissed. It was an honor and privilege to be your dragon.*

Trinity's breath caught. Her heart lurched and panic slammed through her. She started to rise from her seat. *Oh God. No, Emmy. I can't—*

Virgil flipped the switch.

A bolt of lightning slammed through her, knocking her back into the chair. She let out a scream. Her hands gripped her thighs and it took all her effort not to pass out, her brain feeling as if it was being burned from the inside out. Emmy's essence being torn away for good.

Emmy. Oh Emmy!

The whole process felt like hours but might have lasted only a few seconds—she wasn't sure. In any case, eventually the pain subsided and her vision cleared as Virgil reached over to pull the cap off her head.

"It is done," he said quietly.

It was done. Never had one sentence held so much weight. It was done. It was over. Finito. The bond broken. The connection between her and her dragon severed forever.

"Oh, Emmy." She choked back a sob, meeting the creature's eyes with her own. For a moment, they just looked at one another. Just looked and looked and looked, as if their lives depended on it. Then, slowly, Emmy turned away.

Trinity's heart broke. Completely and utterly broke. Desperate, she forced her eyes to rise to the television set her dad had turned on before the procedure. To focus on something inconsequential—meaningless—as her whole world crumbled all around her.

Unfortunately, what she saw there was not meaningless or inconsequential at all.

"What the…?"

She leapt to her feet, running to the TV to get a better look. She felt Emmy come up behind her, but she couldn't tear her eyes from the screen.

"Turn it up!" she cried to her father. "The volume. Turn it up, now!"

Her father did, the reporter's voice filling the school bus. "According to the free Emmy dot com website, this teenager, rumored to be one of the dragon thieves, has been spotted at the Fauna Wal-Mart on Cerrillos Road." The screen flashed with Connor's photo, apparently taken from a camera phone, inside the store.

"Is that the Dragon Hunter you were with?" her father asked worriedly. "Did he come here to find you?"

The video cut from Connor's photo to an aerial shot of the parking lot above them, now filled with a caravan of unmarked trucks. To Trin's horror, the store appeared to be surrounded. Then the camera cut to a live shot on the ground, the reporter standing just outside the store. Behind her, people appeared to be evacuating one by one, with plainclothes men interviewing each and every one of them before letting them on their way.

"Authorities won't comment on the operation," the reporter was saying. "But it appears a manhunt is underway. Reports say the dragon could even be inside the store."

"Oh, Connor," Trinity cried. "Why couldn't you have just stayed away?"

Worried, her father switched from the TV to the surveillance cameras in the Wal-Mart itself. Trin watched as he flicked from camera to camera, searching the store for some sign of Connor.

"Wait!" she cried, pointing to the screen. "Go back!"

Her father obliged and the cameras swapped. Trinity swallowed hard as she recognized none other than Mara herself, backed by six men, storming through the store.

"Connor, get out of there," she whispered.

"I'm not sure he can," her father said solemnly. "They've got all the exits blocked. He's trapped." He rubbed his chin. "Virgil, maybe we should do something. If he were to be captured, he might have information on my daughter that—"

"No," Virgil broke in. "That's just what they want. They'll use him to flush her out of hiding. We can't fall into their trap. We have to get the dragon into the time machine. Now."

Trinity glanced over at Emmy, who was looking at her with worried eyes. She shook her head to clear it. Virgil was right. Once they got Emmy to safety, she could go try to help Connor herself, but not a moment before. That was what she'd promised. That the dragon would come first. And she couldn't go back on that promise now.

"Okay, Em," she said to the dragon. She gestured to the entrance of the large metal box that Virgil had rigged to take the dragon back in time. "Go ahead."

But Emmy didn't move. She just stood there, staring at the TV screen, whining worriedly. Trinity's pulse kicked up in alarm. She didn't need to hear the dragon's thoughts to know exactly what Emmy was thinking.

He will keep you safe. I like that.

But if Connor were captured...If he were killed...

"He'll be fine," she tried to assure Emmy. "You know how Connor is. He can take care of himself."

Emmy turned from the TV to the time machine. She pawed the ground anxiously with her foot. But she didn't take a step forward.

"No," Trinity said again, more firmly this time. "I know what you want to do and I love you for it. But you can't save him this time. You have to save yourself."

Emmy's eyes flashed fire. Steam shot from her nose.

Trinity grabbed the dragon by the head, forcing her to face her. "Emmy, Connor knows what he risked by coming here. If he were here now, he'd tell you the same thing. Believe me," she added, her voice cracking, "I don't want him to get hurt either. But I need to know you're safe first." Swallowing hard, she gestured toward the time machine again. "Go on," she begged. "Please. It's the only way."

But the dragon refused to move.

"You need to get her in there, now," Virgil broke in, sounding both angry and worried at the same time. "I can't keep the power grid up for much longer. We're going to blow a circuit and it'll take weeks—maybe months—to get up and running again. She has to go now."

Suddenly the dragon's eyes flew back to the TV. Trinity couldn't help but follow her gaze, her eyes widening as she now saw Connor himself—surrounded at gunpoint by a group of men. He was holding up his hands. His expression was full of fear.

Oh no. Oh, Connor.

Emmy turned from the TV. Then she started to flap her wings.

"Emmy, no!" Trinity cried, realizing what the dragon planned to do.

"Oh no you don't!" Virgil leapt forward, throwing a make-shift lasso over the dragon's neck. "I'm not going to let you go and risk the fate of the entire world—just to save one guy who isn't even supposed to be here to begin with."

He yanked the lasso hard, sending Emmy sprawling back toward him. The dragon's eyes bulged from her head and she bared her teeth at the scientist, a hissing sound winding up her throat.

"Virgil, stop!" Trinity protested. "Just give her a moment to think it all through. She'll do the right thing. I know she will. Don't try to force her to go."

But Virgil ignored her, turning to her father. "Help me!" he demanded. "Get her into the box! Now!"

But Trinity's father stood as if frozen in place. He looked from his daughter to the dragon then to Virgil. "Trinity's right," he said at last. "She has to make her own decision. I'm not going to force her."

Virgil scowled. "This is ridiculous," he cried. He lunged at Emmy, grabbing her, tossing her in the direction of the machine. "Get in there, you stupid beast! No one wants you to stay! The world doesn't want your kind! You can only cause devastation and ruin!"

Trinity gasped as Emmy dug in her heels. Then she whipped around, her eyes flashing fire as she stared Virgil down. It was a look Trinity knew all too well.

"Virgil, watch out!" she cried.

But it was too late. The flames shot from Emmy's mouth, hitting Virgil square in the chest. The scientist screamed, stumbling back into his equipment, the fire tearing through his clothes and hair. A moment later, the control panel burst into flames, sparking and spitting as a warning siren began to wail.

"We need to get out of here!" Trin heard her father cry. "The whole place is going to blow!"

Trinity looked around for Emmy, but the dragon was already gone. Up the ladder, burning a dragon-shaped hole through the trapdoor.

"Oh, Emmy…"

Lungs choked with smoke, she forced herself to wrap her hands around the rungs, pulling herself up one by one by one, her father hot at her heels. They had barely made it to the surface when the ground shook with an explosion, shooting them across the parking lot. Trinity hit the pavement hard and spun into darkness.

Chapter Forty-One

Emmy tore through the parking lot as fast as her wings could take her, her eyes locked on to the large building in front of her. The store, Trinity had called it. The place where the Hunter was trapped.

She glanced behind her, feeling a twinge of regret. She hadn't wanted to hurt the old man. And she certainly hadn't wanted to destroy the machine that would take her to the special place with all the dragons. But she had no choice. The boy Trinity loved was in trouble. She couldn't let him die.

Trinity had sacrificed her entire life—her entire happiness—to help Emmy.

Now it was Emmy's turn to do the same.

She flew at the store, crashing headfirst into panes of glass so clear she hadn't seen them until it was too late. The windows exploded around her and her ears caught the following screams of terror.

Let them be scared, she decided. *Let them see the true power of a dragon.*

She soared through the store, skimming the tops of the shelves, knocking over whatever impeded her path in her attempt to reach Connor. All around she could see flashes of light going off, shocked people holding up small electronic devices in her direction. But Emmy ignored them all. They didn't matter to Trinity. He did.

Finally she found him, at the very back of the store, surrounded by men, a gun pressed to his temple just as she'd seen on the screen. When he spotted Emmy, his eyes widened. He tried to shake his head no, to tell her to turn around and leave the store. *Stupid boy*, Emmy thought. *Always trying to be the hero.*

But it was her turn now.

She dive-bombed the men, claws out, teeth bared, spearing the one with the gun right in his stomach. He screamed in pain, dropping to his knees instantly, his guts spilling out onto the floor as his gun skittered across the ground. Emmy turned and went after the weapon, locking it in her talons, then tossing it to the Hunter. He caught it, a surprised smile ghosting his face. He didn't want to approve of her actions, but he couldn't help it a little.

That will teach you to doubt a dragon.

The other men were backing away now, their faces filled with fear. Emmy roared as loud as she could, driving the point home, the power she was suddenly wielding as tasty as a steak bone dripping with blood. If they walked away now, she wouldn't kill them. But if they even thought to fight...

Emberlyn...Emberlyn...

My darling Emberlyn...

It's time to go home.

Emmy scrunched up her face, confused and distracted by a sudden sound that seemed to echo through the store. It was a song, she realized after a moment. Some kind of sad, slow song, sung by the most heartbreakingly sweet voice she'd ever heard.

Where was it coming from? Who was singing it? And why?

Against her better judgment, she turned toward the song, everything inside her suddenly yearning to find its singer, though she had no idea why. Out of the corner of her eye, she thought she saw the Hunter gesturing wildly in her direction, trying to call her back, but try as she might, she couldn't seem to focus on him—only the haunting melody rising louder and louder in the air.

And then, there she was. A breathtakingly beautiful woman, with long blond hair and glowing eyes, standing before her, still singing the song. Emmy lowered herself down, bowing her head in worship, her whole body trembling to the tune.

Please, don't stop singing, she found herself begging.

The woman smiled. But it was not a beautiful smile like the beautiful song. It was a cold smile. A twisted smile. And a moment later, Emmy felt something hard and sharp snap over her jaws.

The cold metal of a trap.

Chapter Forty-Two

"Trinity! Wake up, sweetie, wake up!"

"Five more minutes, Grandpa," Trinity moaned, trying to shrug off the rough hands shaking her awake.

"We don't have five more seconds. Get up. Now."

She opened her eyes. Her father was staring down at her. His face was covered in ash and his hair was half-singed from his head. Her jaw dropped, everything coming back to her in a flash of horror.

Connor! Emmy!

Somehow she managed to scramble to her feet, her bruised ribs twanging in protest. "Where's Emmy?" she cried.

Her father gestured toward the front of the store. "She went that way."

She nodded grimly. "Okay. Let's go."

But to her surprise, her father just shook his head. Trin opened her mouth to ask him what was wrong but then saw for herself. His left leg was blackened, charred nearly to the bone. There was no way he could move now.

Or maybe ever again.

It was all she could do not to throw up. All the work he'd done…all the years he'd sacrificed…and this was to be his reward? "God, I'm sorry," she said lamely, not knowing what else to say. "Oh, Daddy, I'm so sorry."

He waved her off. "Go find your dragon, sweetie. Go save the world."

After giving him one last tortured look, Trinity ran down the parking lot, barely able to breathe as panic wound up inside of her at a frightening rate. The place was a madhouse now—screaming people, police, fire trucks, the media.

And somewhere out there, the Dracken.

"People, I need you to stay calm!" a man's voice broke out over a bullhorn. "You need to get in your cars and go home. There's nothing to see here."

But there was plenty to see and everyone knew it. As Trinity raced toward the front of the store, a policeman stepped into her path. "Sorry, miss," he said. "You can't go inside."

"You don't understand," she cried. "I can help!" Her eyes fell to the broken window and her heart sank. Something inside of her, something very small indeed, had been holding out hope that maybe the dragon had decided to flee the scene instead of making a rescue attempt.

She should have known better.

"Wait, who are you?" The man's eyes narrowed. "You look—"

"There you are!" Suddenly Luke was in front of her, grabbing at her arm. "Come on, Sis. We have to go. Now!"

Trinity allowed herself to be dragged away from the police officer. The man watched her go, squinting at her hard, then reached for his walkie-talkie, speaking in a low voice she couldn't hear. Crap. He'd recognized her, she was sure of it. He'd be alerting the others to be on the lookout for her now. But what could she do? She ran after Luke, skirting the thick of the chaos, then around to the side of the store.

"Connor!" she cried as her eyes fell upon a familiar figure pacing the parking lot.

"Trinity!"

They ran to one another, throwing their arms around each other in a desperate embrace. "Oh, Connor," she cried again, unable to help herself.

She could feel his whole body trembling as he clung to her, his face buried in her curls. "She saved me," he told her in a tortured voice. "They were about to kill me and she swooped in and saved my life."

Trinity didn't have to ask who. "Where is she now?"

He gave her a tormented look. "They have her. Mara was able to lure her away from me using a Hunter's song." He winced. "She actually got Emmy to walk straight into a trap. I'm guessing they're going to try to bring her around to one of these side exits and take her away with as few witnesses as possible."

Trinity's heart wrenched. "We've got to save her!" she cried. She turned to the store, her mind whirling for a possible plan. But what plan could there be? They had the numbers. They had the guns. They already had her dragon.

Connor shook his head. "I'm sorry, Trin. There's no way…"

"But we can't just let them take her away!" she protested, horrified. "If they do, I won't be able to find her. We're not bonded anymore. If they take her away now, she'll disappear forever."

His eyes locked on hers, his expression grave. "I'm sorry, Trinity, but there's only one thing left to do."

For a moment, she didn't understand—she couldn't understand. Except somehow she did. She knew exactly what he was suggesting.

Sacrifice one to save the world.

"No," she said in a hoarse whisper. "You can't. She saved your life."

"Do you think I don't know that?" he demanded. "Do you think this is how I wanted it to be? But what choice do I have? You yourself said there's no more bond between you. That means they can give her to someone else. Someone who has *their* best interests at heart, not Emmy's. They'll abuse her, clone her, use her for their own gain…"

Destroy the world.

Suddenly the side door to the Wal-Mart burst open. A group of men poured out, dragging a dragon-sized cage, Emmy thrashing behind the bars. Mara was barking orders to each of the men, thankfully not looking in Connor and Trinity's direction.

Trinity let out a horrified cry. Connor grabbed her, pulling her down behind a car so as not to be seen. Then he squeezed her so tightly she was half-afraid he'd break her bones. Not that, at the moment, she would have cared.

"I'm an ace shot, Trinity. I know where to shoot so she won't feel any pain. It'll be over in an instant."

Trinity stared at him, her whole body numb. She had no idea how she was even upright at this point. Everything inside of her told her Connor was right. It was the only thing they could do now. For Emmy. And for the rest of the world.

She drew in a breath. Her heart squeezed. She opened her mouth to speak, hating herself for the words that would move past her lips. Emmy's pendant seemed to burn at her throat as if it were made of fire.

Oh, Emmy. I'm so sorry. I'm so, so sorry.

But the dragon couldn't hear her now. She'd never know the bullet was coming. Or why it had to come. Trinity could only hope she died instantly. That she didn't realize she'd been shot. Didn't realize Trinity had been the one to give the command. Emmy had sacrificed her own happiness to try to save the boy Trinity loved. And now he was about to put a bullet in her.

Oh, Emmy…

She squeezed her eyes shut. Then she opened them again, losing herself in Connor's large blue ones. "Trinity?" he choked out. "Trinity tell me to do it. I won't do it unless you tell me to. It has to be you."

She peeked over the hood of the car. Across the parking lot, the men were almost ready to load Emmy into one of the trucks. It was now or never.

"Okay," she managed to spit out. "Okay, you can—"

"Connor! Trinity!"

A military truck screeched to a halt in front of them. Trinity's mouth dropped open as she realized it was none other than Scarlet herself at the wheel. As she watched, the girl popped open the door, half jumping, half falling out of the large vehicle.

"What's happening?" she cried as she ran toward them. "Where's Emmy? Are we too late? Did they get her?"

Connor nodded grimly, reaching for his gun. "But don't worry. We're going to—"

"Wait!" Trinity interrupted, looking at Scarlet, a strange

feeling of hope rising within her. "Scarlet, go to that truck over there! Go to Mara and tell her you're the one bonded with Emmy. That you're her Fire Kissed now. Tell them that you'll go with them. You'll do whatever they want. That you can't leave the dragon behind. Tell them..." She swallowed past the huge lump in her throat. "Tell them that you are destined."

Scarlet stared at her for a moment then at the truck, looking utterly confused. Trinity closed her eyes and pushed her as hard as she could.

If you love Emmy, do not ask questions. Just go now. Or Connor will have to kill her.

Scarlet's eyes widened. Trinity could almost see the war going on in her head as she grappled with what to do. Then, without another word, she took off, tearing down the parking lot toward the truck and the soldiers. Connor watched her go, a look of dismay on his face. Then he turned back to Trinity.

"What have you done?" he whispered.

She met his eyes with her own. "What I had to do."

His face twisted. "Don't you get it?" he cried, sounding distraught. "If Scarlet bonds with Emmy, you're never going to get her back. That'll be it."

"Yes," she agreed sadly. "I'll never get her back. But she'll be alive."

Her voice broke. Her knees trembled. Emmy. She'd lost Emmy.

But Emmy would not be lost. And that's all that mattered in the end.

"And what about the Dracken?" Connor demanded, still looking angry and frustrated. "You do realize you just sent the girl into the hands of the Dracken, right? Not to mention the government. What's to say they'll even believe her? Or take her back to their headquarters?"

"Because they need her," Trin said quietly, watching the girl cross the parking lot with determined steps. "At least for now. Until they find a replacement." She shrugged. "And that will give us some time to come up with a plan to break her out. When I went inside Scarlet's head, I opened up a back door to her mind. Just like you did to me once upon a time. Wherever they take her and Emmy, we'll be able to track them down and break them out."

Connor's eyes narrowed. "Break them out?" he asked in a slow voice. "From the secret government lab? And let me guess. You're going to ask your new friends the Dracken to help you out. Is that what you're saying to me?"

A shiver tripped down Trinity's spine as she realized what he was getting at—what had sent the flicker of fear across his pale face. "Connor..." she started to say.

But a loud banging interrupted the rest of her words. Trinity squinted at the truck that Scarlet had pulled up in. Was someone still inside?

Connor motioned his head to the back of the truck while pulling the gun from his waistband. Slowly she wrapped her hands around the back handle, sliding it upward as Connor raised his weapon.

"Don't shoot!"

Trinity let out a strangled cry as her eyes fell upon Caleb, on his knees inside the truck, his hands out in front of him in surrender. He was ghostly pale and sick and shaking and in horrible, horrible shape.

But he was here. He was alive.

"Caleb," Trinity cried, the tears streaming down her cheeks. "Oh my God, Caleb!"

He squinted at her then at his brother. For a moment, his cracked, bruised lips seemed to move, as if he were trying to force words out that refused to come.

"What is it?" Trinity asked, the emotions swirling inside of her, too fast and furious to catalog. "Can I help you? Do you need something? Water? Food? Anything?"

"Scarlet," he rasped. "Where's Scarlet?"

Then he collapsed onto the truck bed.

PART 6:

SHATTER

Chapter Forty-Three

The Surface Lands—Year 189 Post-Scorch

O h yeah, baby! That's how it's done!"

Caleb gave out a loud whoop as the wind thundered across his ears and then blasted him full in the face as he and his dragon, Trinity, tore across the burnt-out ruins of the Surface Lands. She dove low, skimming the top of the world, then pointed her nose to the sky, wildly chasing the sun. At Caleb's command, she even performed a few barrel rolls, and his stomach lurched in a mixture of excitement and pure, radiant joy with each and every one. But it wasn't just the adrenaline rush that had him grinning like a loon. It was the freedom.

For the first time in his life, he was free.

Finally, they landed on the side of a cliff, a narrow ledge leading to a shallow cave. Caleb gathered firewood into a pile then looked up at his dragon. "Would you do the honors?" he asked with a grin.

Trinity bounced her head in affirmation and he laughed. For such a majestic creature, she certainly had a silly side. Just like her namesake, Trinity Foxx, was supposed to have had back in the old days with her own dragon Emmy. Caleb watched as his Trinity pulled back her mighty head and let loose her flames, torching the wood and creating a fire that would make any scout proud.

"Nice one," he praised, reaching into his pack and pulling out the leg of lamb he'd brought with him. Carefully, he set it down into the fire and soon it was bubbling with heat. Trinity let out an excited whine and shook her head, splashing Caleb with a gob of drool.

"Ew, keep it in your mouth, girl," he scolded playfully. "The food will be ready soon enough."

After dinner, the two of them curled up by the fire as they'd been doing every night that month, Caleb working to clean the grime out of the dragon's scales. It was a daily job—and not an easy one—but he found the process soothing all the same. And Trinity seemed to love it too, always purring and grunting the whole time he worked.

"This is all we need, right, girl?" Caleb asked with a happy sigh. "You, me, some undercooked meat—and the rest of the world can go to hell." He looked out over the vista, trying to remember a time when he'd been so happy. He couldn't.

Everything was right with the universe now. His lifetime of failure was behind him. He was a member of the most powerful group on the planet, the Dracken, and they had entrusted him—the one everyone always said was no good—with his very own dragon. And what a dragon she was! One look at her shining teal scales and sparkling eyes and suddenly Caleb found himself wanting to be a better person. The best person in the world—just to prove himself worthy of this magnificent gift that Darius had bestowed upon him.

And after tomorrow, they would be together forever. The bonding between them would be complete and their lives would be intertwined. After tomorrow, Caleb would never have to be alone, ever again. He'd live his life with someone who loved him and cared for him—who would gladly die for him if need be—always by his side.

It was the ultimate dream come true. And he had to keep pinching himself to believe it was really his life. The no good, forgotten, bad seed Caleb. The one everyone had written off. He would be a dragon guardian forever.

Even better, because of him, his mother would live. Three days ago, Trinity had offered him a priceless gift—the healing blood from her one soft scale. The blood that would cure his mother of her cancer. At first he'd been scared—he'd heard stories of people trying to use dragon blood for healing, only to have it kill them instead. But Darius had explained this blood was special and secret and in limited supply. And if given willingly by a dragon, rather than harvested against their will, it could do almost anything.

The dragon nudged his hand, a warm blast of air tickling his fingers. He laughed and gave her a hug. "You're just sweetening me up for a second course, aren't you?" he teased. "You know I have that other bone in my bag."

But before he could serve his dragon her dessert, he heard a scraping noise behind him. Puzzled, he turned to find none other than his twin himself climbing up the side of the cliff. When Connor reached the top, he held out his hand. One of those bouncers the Council had invented flew up, settling in his palm.

Caleb scrambled to his feet. What was he doing here? He

motioned for Trinity to back into the cave, where she wouldn't be out in the open, exposed. Had Connor come alone? Or had he come here with his dragon-hunting team?

"What the hell are you doing here?" he demanded, hating how shaky his voice sounded. He crossed his arms over his chest, scowling, as he stepped in front of the cave's mouth.

Connor didn't answer. He looked past Caleb, into the cave. "So it's true," he said in a resigned voice. "God, I was hoping you were lying to her."

Caleb shot an involuntary glance at Trinity, who was pawing the ground nervously, eyeing the stranger.

Who is that? she asked. *He looks like you.*

He's no one, Caleb told her. *Just let me get rid of him, okay?*

He turned back to his brother.

"Connor, go home," he snarled with as much bravado as he could muster. "Once again, this doesn't concern you."

"How can it not concern me?" Connor demanded, not stepping down. "My brother is cavorting with monsters."

"She's not a monster!" Caleb protested, losing his cool despite himself. But still! He wasn't about to let anyone talk crap about his dragon. "Look at her. She's beautiful. Majestic. Powerful. Wild."

And she chose me, he added silently. *Out of everyone on the earth, she chose me.*

Connor's face twisted with anguish. "Are you even listening to yourself?" he asked. "We're talking about a dragon. The same creature that killed our own father." He gritted his teeth. "Look, I know it's not your fault. Dragons can be very persuasive. They can put humans under a spell. You don't really want to be with this thing. You just think you do because it's screwed with your head."

"No!" Caleb protested, shaking his head vehemently. "That's not true! That's just what the Council says to keep people from discovering the truth about dragons. Trinity is loyal and brave and completely devoted to me. She's more like a sibling than you ever were."

Connor's face paled. "Caleb, you don't mean that," he protested.

"I certainly do. Now get the hell out of here before I have her blast you to kingdom come."

He waited, praying his brother would just leave. He didn't want to have to kill him, after all.

But of course, this was Connor. And Connor never stood down. "I'm sorry, Caleb. But you leave me with no choice," his twin said resignedly. And then he opened his mouth...

...and started to sing.

"No!" Caleb cried. He ran to his brother, trying to cover his mouth with his hands. But Connor was too strong, shoving him backward, sending him sprawling. Caleb hit the ground hard and rolled off the cliff. Only his fingers, clutching a hanging root, kept him from plummeting to his death.

"No. Trinity! Don't listen to him!" he cried as he strained to pull himself back on the ledge, his whole body breaking out into sweat. "Blast him with your fire!"

But the dragon seemed not to hear him. She was stepping out from the protection of the cave, her eyes glazed and her tongue lolling from her mouth.

"No!" Caleb begged as his feet kicked uselessly against dirt sides. "Please, Connor, don't do this! She's all I have in the world."

Connor turned, leveling his gaze on Caleb. "Then you don't have anything at all," he said.

And then, with one quick movement, almost too fast to follow, he reached for his gun-blade, plunging it into the dragon's soft scale, like a hot knife through butter.

Trinity screamed. And Caleb screamed with her. He flailed and almost fell. But it was his brother who ran to him. Grabbing him by the hand and yanking him back onto the ledge. It took him a moment to regain his senses. Then he ran to his dragon.

"No. Please, Trinity, no," he cried, his voice choked with tears.

The dragon looked up at him with watery eyes, filled with pain. She stretched out her neck, then licked him on the face, her rough tongue scraping his skin.

I'm sorry, she said.

Then her muscles failed and she fell to the ground with a loud crash, one last heartbreaking, shuddering sigh assaulting Caleb's ears. Then she lay still.

"I'm sorry," Connor said. "But it had to be done. You'll thank me one day."

Caleb looked up at him. He opened his mouth, trying to speak. But the words wouldn't come. In fact, at that moment, he wasn't sure they'd ever come again.

And he wasn't sure if he cared if they did.

Chapter Forty-Four

"Trinity…no, please. Connor, don't… Please don't!"

Trinity sighed as Caleb screamed again, his face twisted in anguish, then watched as he fell back into unconsciousness. She dabbed his sweaty forehead with a cold, wet cloth, studying him closely to make sure he didn't go into another seizure. All night he'd been seizing and vomiting and she hadn't been able to get much fluid into him to replenish the electrolytes he'd lost. His skin looked almost shriveled now, as if he were a man at the end of his life, instead of the beginning.

"How's he doing?"

Trinity looked up to see Connor, hovering in the doorway. Tall, strong, stone faced. These days, a stranger would never believe the two of them were identical twins.

"I don't know," she confessed, her heart aching as her eyes roved over his shivering body. "No better, no worse, I guess. I keep hoping he'll wake up so I can get some Gatorade into him."

"He'd probably just throw it up anyway," Connor said with a heavy sigh. "I'm sorry, Trin, but we need to be realistic here. That last trip he took to the Nether? That was one trip too many. I've seen it before, back home. It's that one last trip…"

Trinity stared down at Caleb, tears welling in her eyes. "I should have never left him behind." She looked up at Connor. "Either of you."

Connor shook his head vigorously. "No," he said. "You did what you had to do. To keep the promise you made to Emmy." He gave her a rueful smile. "That stubborn little dragon," he said fondly. "I still can't believe she went and did that. Sacrificing her one chance at happiness to save my life. Seriously, the whole thing—it just goes against everything I know about dragons."

"Maybe you don't know as much as you think," Trinity replied, giving him a wry look.

"Yeah, I'm beginning to realize that." He looked down at his brother mournfully. "If only I'd listened to him from the start. He tried to tell me what dragons were really like. But at the time, I was so locked up in my own hate and fear…" He looked up at Trinity, his eyes filled with anguish

"I almost killed you, you know," he added flatly.

"What?" Trinity stared at him, confused. "When?"

"When you were in the Nether, trying to find your mother. I was this close to killing you in an effort to end it all," he said, his voice thick with regret. "But Caleb talked me out of it. He told me there could be a better way." He sighed. "For all my grand plans and soldiering, at the end of the day, I'm pretty sure he's the smarter twin." His mouth twisted. "If he wakes up, that'll be the first thing I tell him."

"*When* he wakes up," Trinity corrected, determined to stay positive as she looked down at Caleb's pale and sweaty face, her heart aching. "Poor Caleb," she whispered, reaching down to trace his cheek with a finger. "I hope you're at least getting some good dragon time in."

She could feel Connor's stern gaze. "We're going to get Emmy back, Trin."

"Yeah, I know," she said flatly. "And once we do, maybe she and Scarlet can give you that lesson on dragon 101."

She didn't try to hide the bitterness in her voice. She knew she'd done the right thing. The only thing to save Emmy's life. But that didn't mean she didn't still feel incredibly sad about it all. Whatever Scarlet was facing now, she was facing it with Emmy by her side—an honor and a privilege Trinity would never have again.

Connor reached out, squeezing her hands in his own. "Don't talk like that," he scolded. "Emmy will still love you when she returns. Just because the two of you are no longer bonded doesn't mean—"

"Stop." She pulled her hands away, holding them out in front of her, the lump in her throat making it difficult to breathe. "I don't want to talk about that right now. I'll deal with whatever it is once she's back safe. That's all that matters now."

Connor nodded. "Yeah," he said. "Actually that's what I came to talk to you about." He shuffled from foot to foot, looking nervous.

"What?" she asked, her heart fluttering in her chest as she recognized his unease. "Don't you think we have a good plan? Everyone else seemed on board with it." They'd had a team meeting earlier that afternoon, going over the details. The Potentials, her father (who had not only survived the ordeal but was recovering nicely from his leg injury), and the new Dracken kids.

"Yes…no…" He wrung his hands together, sputtering. "I

don't know. I mean, it seems solid enough. The soldier in me says it'll probably work."

"But?"

He drew in a breath. "It's just…too close for comfort, I guess. I mean, Emmy locked away in some secret government lab. You joining forces with a group that calls themselves the Dracken to break her out…"

"But it's not the same Dracken," she reminded him. "I didn't form the group like the first time around. They found me. And Emmy wasn't even captured yet when they did. Also there was no Scarlet the first time around. And it was years later."

Connor met her eyes. "I'm not arguing that the ripples are different. But what if they build to the same tidal wave?"

His words sent a chill of fear tripping down her backside. Truthfully it wasn't anything she hadn't thought about herself a thousand times. But at the same time…

"We can't do this without them," she said flatly. "They have the hacker skills we need to infiltrate the facility, disable the security system, all the rest of the things we talked about."

"We could come up with another plan. Another way—"

"No." She shook her head. "I may not be the Fire Kissed anymore, but my priorities have not changed. And when it comes to rescuing Emmy, I don't have the luxury to turn down help. We'll deal with the larger implications later, once she and Scarlet are safe."

Connor raked a hand through his hair. "Did anyone ever tell you how stubborn you are?"

"Maybe once or twice." She gave him a rueful grin. "So what do you say, Connor? If you don't want to join us, I'll understand. I'd never force you to go against what you believe. All I ask is you don't try to stop us."

For a moment he said nothing, and her heart squeezed at the torment she recognized on his face. He looked so lost, so scared—a little boy playing soldier. It took everything inside her not to throw herself into his arms to try to comfort him now, to tell him everything would be okay. Even if she had no idea if it were true.

"Of course I won't stop you," he said at last. "Hell, when have I ever been able to stop you at anything? And yes, I'll do whatever you need me to do. After all, I'm still part of Team Dragon, right?"

A slow smile spread across her face. She rose to her feet, wrapping her arms around him, burying her face in his chest. She could feel his long exhale as he allowed himself to melt into her embrace. He may not be okay with the plan. But he was okay with her. And that was all that mattered for now.

"We can do this," she whispered as they held one another tight. "You'll see."

"Oh, I know we can do it," Connor replied in a voice so low she could barely hear it. "I'm only afraid of what will happen once we do."

Epilogue

The monster was back.

Somehow Scarlet could always tell. As if she had a sixth sense, warning her when she was near. A hint of antiseptic, tickling her nostrils, the sound of stilettos echoing through her ears. An uneasiness prickling at the back of her neck as her pulse throbbed in her throat—her consciousness gearing up for the inevitable fight or flight that was sure to come.

Should she face her this time? Or was it better to run?

But this time, there was nowhere to run.

The door creaked open and the monster stepped inside, flanked by two of her regular guards. Though on the surface she looked more like an angel than a devil, with long, beautiful blond hair and serene glowing eyes, Scarlet had learned all too well of the ugly beast that lay just beneath the surface.

"How are you feeling?" the monster asked, stepping toward her and giving her a careful once-over.

When she first arrived, Scarlet probably would have retorted something smart-assed back to her. But now she was just too weak. They'd taken blood—so much blood—over the last few days that she could barely stand anymore.

She'd been here six days, by her count, though it was

becoming harder and harder to keep track. She was passing out so frequently now, and there were no windows in her cell to offer up any clues. Only the routine they went through each day gave her some sense of the passage of time. They'd show up, all smiles, escorting her down to Emmy's pen and ushering her inside, locking the door behind her. Then they'd leave them alone, retreating behind their obviously one-sided mirrors to observe from a distance.

At first Scarlet enjoyed this part of the day. As much as she could enjoy anything in this horrible place. She got to spend time with Emmy. Got to curl up with the dragon and not feel so alone. And at first Emmy would speak to her, telling her how her day had gone and what she'd had to eat. In turn, Scarlet would describe the rescue that would be coming, using her own imagination to fill in the details. Trinity had promised she'd come for them, Scarlet would assure Emmy silently. It was only a matter of time.

But as the days passed, Emmy had started to change, right before Scarlet's eyes. First she became more restless, more anxious. Then she became more reluctant to talk. On the fourth day she had stopped talking altogether, and when Scarlet entered her cage on day five, the dragon grew wild and frightened, backing into the corner, regarding the girl with wide, distrustful eyes, pillars of smoke puffing from her nose.

It was a look Scarlet knew all too well. A look she'd seen a thousand times on her mother's face. And suddenly she realized exactly what must be happening to the dragon at the hands of the monsters when she wasn't in the room. And the helplessness that washed over her nearly took her breath away.

Trinity had sent her here to protect Emmy. But what could

she do? Once again, the monsters had taken the one she loved and she was powerless to stop them.

And if the promised rescue didn't come soon....

"Please hurry, Trinity," Scarlet whispered. "I don't know how much longer she has left."

Acknowledgments

It's always scary when your acquiring editor leaves the publishing house mid-series, but in the case of *Shattered*, I had no reason to fear. Aubrey Poole and Jillian Bergsma stepped in like the literary superwomen they are and helped me sculpt the book into what it is today. There is no denying their brilliance. Not to mention the brilliance of Derry Wilkens, publicist extraordinaire, who worked tirelessly all year long to bring about world dragon domination! I can't tell you how awesome it is to know she has my back. In fact, the entire Sourcebooks team has been totally Team Dragon since the very beginning, championing the series to booksellers, librarians, and, of course, readers themselves. I heart them all madly.

I also want to thank my agent, Kristin Nelson, for her unwavering support and ability to talk me down off a ledge when things don't go exactly to plan. I wish every author could have an agent like her on their team.

And, of course, I want to thank my wonderful husband Jacob who, with each book, has become more and more a collaborator and partner. I know whenever I'm stuck on a plot point I can turn to him, and when my ideas get too crazy, he reins me in. *Shattered* would not exist as it is without his ideas and feedback.

And a writer has to have her author buds. Diana Peterfreund, Simone Elkeles, Ally Carter, Alesia Holliday, Cindy Holby, Serena Robar, Victoria Scott, Cory Putman Oakes, PJ Hoover, Jo Whittemore, the Austin RWA and SCBWI crowd, and so many more that I don't have space to name. And I can't forget my awesome hairdresser Iana Wi at Hearts and Robots—the genius behind my dragon hair!

And lastly to all the wonderful librarians and booksellers and bloggers that I met during promotional events over the year and later on tour. Your enthusiasm means everything to me and I applaud all the amazing work you do to put books in kids' hands. You guys are the true superheroes of the written word.

About the Author

Mari Mancusi always wanted a dragon as a pet. Unfortunately the fire insurance premiums proved a bit too large and her house a bit too small—so she chose to write about them instead. Today she works as an award-winning young adult author and freelance television producer, for which she has won two Emmys.

When not writing about fanciful creatures of myth and legend, Mari enjoys goth clubbing, cosplay, snowboarding, watching cheesy (and scary) horror movies, and her favorite guilty pleasure—playing video games. A graduate of Boston University, she lives in Austin, Texas, with her husband Jacob, daughter Avalon, and their dog Mesquite.